Vulcan

and the

Golden Teachings

Diana Yvonne Walter

David,

May this book bring
you joy, love +
self-awareness.

Diana Walter

Dedicated

to

Greta, Ruby, Rhea, Bodhi and Tess

IN GRATITUDE ✠

This book was written after a personal kundalini opening in 1989. During a full eclipse of the sun on my birthday, I had a vision of the whole story in detail. While working, I often felt transported by the stream of consciousness that I was channeling and joyous at the breathtaking synchronicities that kept occurring. I printed off a few copies of the book and put it away. After a recent experience with *Deeksha*, a blessing given by *AmmaBhagavan*, I felt inspired to bring this time capsule out into the world. After multiple edits/revisions, I humbly submit this, asking your forgiveness for any errors I've missed.

I gratefully acknowledge the many authors that I have listed in the back as references. Vulcan's story is fictional, however is set within many known facts. It was fun playing with scientific concepts to build a story. However, I admit ignorance about whether any of my ideas are possible. I would love it if Vulcan, really *was* discovered soon, along with an unlimited source of energy.

I gratefully acknowledge the support of my husband and best friend, who over the past twenty nine years has stuck by me, through thick and thin. Also thanks to my parents, brothers and sisters for their talent and service to mankind.

My counseling, astrology and yoga clients have served as a source of inspiration since I began my practice in 1982. Their passion for transformation and growth has fueled my work.

Special thanks go to my brave readers Kathleen Crowley and Suzanne Young for expertise and advice. Also, I'm grateful to lifetime friends, Kristi Denton and Lucinda Abbe for their encouragement and support.

May *Vulcan and the Golden Teachings* bless you as you connect to the divine within on your path to higher consciousness and Awakening.

CONTENTS ✠

In Gratitude

Chapters

CHAPTER 1

✠

Mythology of vulcan

The rhythmic whirring of the spaceship's electronics and the measured clicking of the computerized console were hypnotizing Stella. In the dimly lit atmosphere of the flight room, it was difficult to keep from drifting to sleep as the cadence wore a deep groove down into her subconscious.

Dr. Stella Miren was taking a break from her laboratory slides. She got a glass of water, sitting back in her chair with a sigh. Her mind stayed in overdrive, as she noted the regular beep from their video satellite. Repetitive sounds must awaken a primitive cellular memory of safety, she postulated silently. Animals find comfort in the beating of their mother's heart.

A long ago memory washed through her. She could hear grandmother's antique clock, the ticking like a drug in the warm stuffy room. The faint odor of mothballs and cedar reinforced her feelings of frustrated boredom. She was lying still for her nap, but vibrating inside with the need to run, muscles quivering with barely controlled energy.

"Stella Maris, stop wiggling," her harried mother had scolded.

Yes, it's primitive cellular memory, Stella concluded rather smugly, blinking repeatedly to keep her eyes from drifting shut.

She sighed again, wishing for the smell of sweet grass. Then, slipped back to become the unruly child, running at top speed while her brother chased gleefully behind. She would spin in blissful circles, arms open to the sun, until, she fell down giddy and satisfied, floating with the clouds that reformed in the endless sky.

This is really the pits, she thought. I've been trying to keep from 'wiggling' most of my life. I'm too young for this lack of motion. What could be more restrictive than careening through the endless black hole of deep space in an undersized, outdated spaceship.

Stella shifted her focus to the only other crewmember, Dr. Dagon Andrew, the scientist and Air force officer that had been paired with her for the journey. She had secretly nicknamed him, Dr. Dragon, when he was in a bad mood. Stella furtively observed Dagon's steady hands across the room as he adjusted the indicator dials that monitored their in-flight coordinates and approach to mission target, the planet Vulcan. His face looked like granite, completely oblivious to her restlessness.

What could he be seeing in those readings that they hadn't observed countless other times in the last 119 days since launching from Beta III? she thought.

Colleagues knew her as a nerdy, preoccupied scholar. They were always trying to get her to let go and have more fun. Yet, Stella seemed 'loose' in comparison to Dagon. His courteous professionalism and 'business as usual' attitude made six months in space together torture. Controlling her temper and tongue was fraying her edges. Yet, she couldn't help but admire his unbroken focus and concentration. Every act was ordered, every movement planned out when he was working on a task.

Dagon had assumed full command of the ship from the beginning of their long journey. Stella's position as co-commander was only a figurehead, with no real duties other then conducting biology experiments and taking turns keeping watch while Dagon slept.

Rightly so, she thought. To be truthful, Stella wouldn't have wanted his job. Captain Andrew had stepped up quickly to his title as 'Dr. Dragon' after their first flight simulation together when she had gotten sick from weightlessness. NASA operated by the book. She found it hard to follow procedure. After a particularly embarrassing incident, where she had crashed the ship in a mock flight maneuver, she had been demoted.

Besides, Dagon was always organized and seemed to have experience bossing people around. She wondered if their roles had been reversed, if he would have been as willing to follow *her* orders. That is, if she could have found them under her chaotic mess of books and papers.

They had been working closely together for two years and had spent the last three months totally alone with each other. The entire time, Stella had been open to deepening a friendship, while Dagon had been remote and distant. It was driving her crazy.

This is ridiculous, Stella thought, sneaking a glance in the mirror behind the microscope. I'm trying to win his attention. We're as different as night and day. I'm as irritated by him as I am attracted. She grimaced at the image of a space regulation baggy tan uniform with hair caught in a tight ponytail and plastic cap. She pulled off the cap with disgust. He seemed oblivious to her as a woman anyway. She wished she could say the same.

Dagon was tall, rangy man with long, muscled arms and capable hands. He looked Greek with olive skin, dark hair and unusual gray eyes. Every movement seemed efficient and determined when there was physical work to be done. During training she had seen him running outside at dawn. She knew he lifted weights religiously. Boot camp, while a nightmare for her, had seemed like a walk-in-the-park for him. Let's face it, Dagon was attractive, which made conditions on board even more challenging for Stella. Just then, he looked up and caught her gaze, quizzing her with deep gray eyes that looked coldly right through her. He noticed something that made him narrow his eyes, thoughtfully.

Dagon's enigmatic, like a Russian spy, Stella thought. Wow, I like his hair. With a little nervous jolt, she noticed how his normally trim hair had grown over the back of his shirt collar during their last three months in space.

He's still watching me, she thought. With a reflexive jerk, she put her hand protectively over her computer screen, hiding the journal entry.

Her wayward mind began playing an entertaining game, creating a little internal drama perfect for the screenplay of a movie. They wanted her research on Vulcan. She was chained to a wall, but she had a plan to call the guard, then with one swift karate kick, knock him out and get the key. She imagined herself racing up a flight of stairs onto the roof of the jail. "I'm free!" she would laugh spinning in circles. Coming back to earth with a jolt, Stella noticed Dagon squint his eyes again at her from across the room.

Perhaps, I need to listen to some sensory stimulation tapes, she diagnosed and treated herself. Recent space research had shown that astronauts suffered greatly from loss of normal earth sights, sounds, and touch. The latest research showed that pairing a male and female in space helped with SDCT, Sensory Deprivation Confinement Trauma.

Of course, that was assuming the male actually *interacted* with the female, thought Stella.

The possibility for SDCT had been her weakness in the psychological testing for her admittance to the space program. She had scored high as a Psychic/Sensitive. Stella had inherited the gift from her mother. This ability to live in an expanded world got her in trouble when she needed to focus on details and formulations. But it brought her success with all abstract concepts in math and science, such as energy, time and unification theories.

Fortunately, she had completed an extraordinary research project for her master's thesis, discovering a way to map the energy within plant species as electrical impulses. Her research had proven that their electrical fields responded to their environment with intelligence. This breakthrough had brought her thesis to the attention of the space program. Psychological testing aside, it had landed her this mission.

Stella's mother, Lilith, used bioenergetics to measure energy fields in humans to see their responses to various allergens, viruses, fungus and genetic weaknesses. Using a scanner, the body was introduced to the electrical frequency of thousands of substances, then, diagnosed and treated, both homeopathically and with prescribed medications. Bioenergetics was a well-respected profession that had grown in the past 15 years. Now, in 2032, even small hospitals invested in a bio-scanner as standard equipment.

Influenced by her mother, Stella had expanded her view to see energy fields within all life, making this an area of specialty. This had radically changed her philosophical and religious views, bringing up the question, 'What is Self?'

All life shared the same energy field. How, then, had humans separated themselves through ego? This lens of 'self as separate,' seemed to be the root of human greed and attachment. It was the origin of fear and suffering as mankind fought to defend 'self,' to the exclusion of all other life.

Researching electrical energy in plants and animals, Stella had quickly learned she was revisiting an ancient science. The Hindus had called it prana or kundalini. She called it Aura Kinetic Saturation, AKS. Secretly, she had chosen those letters from the ancient Hindu mantra, Aim Klim Suara that was used by goddess devotees in Kashmir to raise the energy of kundalini within the chakras. Her research in AKS had been very successful. Her name was now associated with the phenomena, called The Miren Effect.

AKS research proved plants communicated negative and positive preferences to complex stimuli on a moment-by-moment basis. This could be measured in the electrical flow of energy through their stems. Stimuli included many things such as subtle variations of temperature, barometric pressure, time of day, music and even their human caretaker. Paying attention to plant communication resulted in phenomenal harvest increases in hydroponic greenhouses. Stella had found an easy way to measure plant response. The research had been franchised by a large food producing chain named Gainbee. Her published papers had reached a wide audience. NASA had interviewed her to be on the space team because of her meticulous, carefully documented studies.

With an inward sigh, Stella stretched slender, expressive shoulders, shrugged off depression, and freed messy red curls from their rubber band. She clipped on earphones to listen to a favorite tape of earth noises. The sounds of the ocean, crickets, frogs in a marsh and a meadowlark were relaxing. Then, switching back and forth between that and women's folk rock, she began imagining a way to superimpose the guitar over the nature sounds. Libido stepped in, turning up internal heat with a base rhythm that set hips swaying. Simultaneously, her trained scientific mind noticed the pointed almost painful energy just above the root chakra, muladhara. Sexual energy was also electrical energy or kundalini. If identified it could rise to the third eye to become bliss and expanded awareness.

She felt a little orgasmic jolt, knocking over her water. Geez, I'm a basket case. Flushing with embarrassment, she mopped up the mess, sliding farther back into her chair.

Another image floated into her awareness as she relaxed. It was of a blue-black hilltop, the moon just peaking over the rock monolith. She could feel the sharp bite of cold as the wind moaned in the pine trees beyond the ridge. The sharp, pungent smell of rabbit brush hung in the air. There was a stirring in the grass as a fox slipped away to safety. Then, silent footsteps navigated rocks strewn in the path, as her companion brought another load of wood. She was sitting cross-legged in front of the fire calling on the goddess, chanting the sacred sounds to raise the snake energy coiled at the base of her spine. The resulting samadhi brought connection to the wind, fire, the pulse of the stars, the herbs and the man in front of her. Journeying inward felt safe with him guarding the fire, protecting them both.

With an inward wrench, she jerked herself back to the present, feeling the tweed fabric of the cushioned chair beneath her hands. The contrast between enjoying the smell and sounds of the earth and the sterile plastic and metal world of the spaceship was shocking.

Wow, what just happened? A familiar, inner shaking started. Meditating and fasting were her normal routes to astral travel, not daydreaming while listened to SDCT tapes. She chuckled. The space training program had not included Astral Travel 101.

Get it together, *now*, an inner voice scolded.

This opportunity for space travel was the culmination of a lifetime of inner preparation, education, and a little help from fate. Outside, pinpoints of light hung in deafening silence, an ever-expanding eternal vortex of oppressive noiselessness. Inside, claustrophobia set an insidious trap. The mission at hand was to free herself.

Usually meditating did the trick. Stella would imagine that her thoughts and emotions were only leaves floating down a stream. She calmly observed them bobbing up and down, or swirling around in little eddies and whirlpools. She was the tall, ancient wise woman watching from the bank of the stream.

Looking over at Dagon working with quiet concentration, she wished for his control. Then, she thought of the mess on her desk. Under the tilting pile was her precious journal, a secret notebook containing personal theories and research about Vulcan.

No, that's not true! I don't want control at all! Passion tempted Stella to throw away all convention, upsetting Dagon's carefully planned evening. She wondered if his hair would stand on end if he understood that, on her side of the room, the snake goddess, Kundalini, was rising.

Captain Dagon Andrew stretched his arms in an attempt to release the steel band at the back of his neck, recognizing exhaustion. I could sleep for a week, he thought, longing for an old couch, a hotdog and a Denver Bronco game. He chastised himself internally; I'll do some push-ups when it's my turn to rest. This tiredness is ridiculous. I haven't done anything strenuous at all. Determination made him re-focus on the console's flight graphs.

The EMF, or Electro Magnetic Frequency, reader was steadily rising as it picked up radiation being emitted from Vulcan. Since they were still a week away from their target, it seemed improbable that the electromagnetic frequencies should be this high.

Research had shown that radio towers produce high EMF readings, making human's respond with unusual feelings of body pressure, faintness and other mental phenomena. EVP or electronic voice phenomena occurred. These were sounds that could be picked up with a digital recorder. High EMF readings sometimes accompanied flashes of light that could be photographed in the infrared spectrum. Dagon was sure that he had heard an odd whispering last night as he was going to sleep. It had been a voice saying, '*remember,*' in a low drawn-out whisper. He had turned on the EVP equipment too late to record it. Vulcan was known for it's high radio frequency. They might be picking up some kind of anomaly. Should he warn Stella?

Recalculating the series of numbers again, he made a decision. Yes, this must be communicated back to Base Command after he and Stella had discussed it.

Observing her face as she took her scheduled break, Dagon noticed she had her eyes closed as she listened to a tape with an ecstatic expression. His guard went down as he took in her pale complexion and unruly, auburn hair. She exuded energy in every movement, crackling like static electricity. Now, she looked harmless, like a sleeping kitten. Feline grace stirred him while an inner voice warned him.

We're like oil and water, he thought, as he shut off his Link, clearing his desk. Fraternizing with crewmembers is strictly forbidden, he admonished himself sternly, as he organized his worktop according to a color-coded file system. Then, tucking his shirt in, he amended the thought. Forbidden at least by *my* code of ethics. She's bright, quick, competitive and always ready to use her wit as a weapon. In short, she's trouble. How could they have put me on a spaceship with someone so young? She's thirty years old for god's sake and I'm 41. How did she even get into the space program at that age. Obviously she's mentally gifted, but my Dad was too and he could barely tie his own shoes. Dagon reached up, clicking shut the top closure of his tan unisex space tunic. Definitely a NO! He was aware that his collar felt too tight.

Dagon had noticed that Stella's normally snappy bravado had been degenerating into what he now thought of as one of her 'dark moods.' Trouble with a capitol T as in Temptation. Dagon squared his Link on his desk, unconsciously straightening a corner of Stella's desk too. He was determined to maintain a healthy distance, at least until this mission was over. His control gave in to silent irritation. Damn, she broke another headset. Strike one. We won't have one left when this is over.

An hour later it was time for their shift change. Stella had slept through her alarm. She looked tiny, curled up in a chair that also tilted back for sleeping. Like a pearl in a seashell, the curved plastic sides folded around her while she clutched her chest in an effort to keep warm.

Dagon nudged her shoulder watching as she surfaced slowly out of a light sleep, opening her eyes dazedly. Unguarded passion was quickly extinguished by mutual agreement.

Live cams in their main living quarters were regularly viewed by a staff of medical doctors and psychologists, sometimes even being broadcast, with their cooperation, to public news satellites. It made good advertising copy for Interspace Research. The billing said, *One man, One woman, Facing the Universe Together.* They had been chosen for the mission, not just for their qualifications, but also for star quality. Beta III wanted an 'attractive young couple' to help them promote and fund the mission. A computer had matched them using complex relational data, including their DNA codes.

Base command expected them to become sexual partners. Dagon refused this invasion of his privacy. Being in a fish bowl made him even more determined to avoid personal contact. Fortunately, video connection with Base had been getting patchy as they got closer to Vulcan. After months of being on guard, Dagon felt like he could begin to relax.

Tiredness had been stealing over him all day. He needed to sleep. It showed in his lack of resistance to Stella's considerable force field. He jerked his arm back as if burnt. Wariness stole over her intelligent features, effectively raising walls of respectability between them. Everything went a little flatter as the cold set in again.

"Stella, before you go on your shift, we need to have a conference." Dagon adopted a matter of fact tone.

"Fine, give me a moment to wake up." She pushed her hair away from her eyes.

A short time later they sat facing each other, charts and graphs showing in front of them on the wide screen in the flight room.

BOB, their artificial intelligence Base Operator B robot, was speaking in a modulated tenor male voice with a slight European accent. "The oscillations of the radiation patterns are rising, possibly due to approach to Vulcan's synchron belt. Probability of accuracy 92%. Our radio signal to Base Command is now at 40.34 percent of capacity. My studies of the infrared wavelengths show the possibility of light and energy anomalies shipboard as we come into position. Electromagnetic Frequency readings have fluctuated between 3 and 8. EVP data is being examined starting at 08 hundred, space day 201112." BOB abruptly stopped reviewing data after saying, "waiting for instructions." The lights on the front plate of the metal robot blinked once, then dimmed, leaving one small blinking green light, as an indicator that he was still listening to questions.

"BOB," Stella asked. "Are you comfortable with your findings?"

Dagon frowned. Deductive reasoning with BOB was discouraged. However Stella insisted on playing games with the robot, treating it like a human. She found BOB's answers illuminating and sometimes humorous. BOB turned his mechanical head toward Stella, nodding slowly from side to side.

"No, I'm not comfortable. We have no contingency plan for this anomaly. Contact with an entity from Vulcan is highly irregular."

Dagon scoffed, "BOB is just accessing data that refers to EMF equipment in its use for paranormal research. Just because we're getting high readings doesn't mean we're making 'contact with an entity.' I'm only bringing this up to warn of possible EMF side effects like…"

Stella interrupted him, "Wow!"

Making a silent motion to catch Dagon's attention, she drew a finger across her throat, pointing to the video feed with Base Command. Dagon flipped the switch off with a frown, thinking, Strike two!

Stella noticed his face. "Hey, I'm sick of not being able to have a private conversation. We can turn it back on later." Stella flipped her hair back impatiently. "I have something to ask you. Did you do any research on the mythology or ancient cosmology of the god, 'Vulcan,' before we embarked on this mission?"

"What has that to do with the EMF problem?"

Stella put her hands on her hips, her stance defensive.

"Nothing! Because your findings aren't a problem. We're discovering an unchartered planet for god's sake. Discovering! That means you won't know what to expect!"

Dagon was surprised by her burst of temper. Her eyes were flashing fire and her hair looked electrified. He backed off, moderating his voice to low and calm.

"You wanted to say something?"

"Yes, to tell you what ancient cultures on earth thought about Vulcan. Stories and myths passed from generation to generation, give insight." Stella gathered her courage when he sighed. "Hey, it's entertainment if nothing else!"

Dagon's chair creaked as he settled back, putting his feet up.

Stella stood for her oration, swallowing nervously.

"The Greeks and Romans had different names for Vulcan. To the Romans he was Vulcan, but to the Greeks he was Hephaestus. He was a popular figure in their mythology. This story combines both versions."

Dagon's penetrating focus caused Stella to lose her place for a second. *Geez, he's like a laser, scorching me,* Stella thought as she gathered herself together again. Stella was a natural storyteller. She decided on the spot to dramatize the plot.

"Vulcan's beginning was remarkable, but tragic. A shrunken limb deformed him at birth making him undesirable to his perfect parents, the immortal Hera and Zeus. They threw the baby down to earth to get him out of their sight."[1]

"Vulcan was a Thunder and Fire God who was immortal. Fortunately, after falling all day from heaven, he landed in the ocean and was adopted by Oceanids who taught him how to become a skilled craftsman and artist."

"Oceanids? Okay what in the hell is an Oceanid?" Dagon sputtered.

Stella laughed, "Actually, I'm not sure. I'd have to do a little bit of research on that. Hey, you remember mermaids don't you."

"Living with the Oceanids, turned out to be a great boon for Vulcan and in the end for the earth. Fire, meant he had the gift of creation. He became such a talented artist, he was later known as the Master Architect or Smith that created everything of a solid nature on earth."

"So," Dagon ventured. "It's a cosmology of the creation of the earth."

"Yes," Stella voice rose with excitement, "Vulcan is a powerful creator god!"

Dagon was looking reflective.

"Almost every culture had a fire god or volcano god similar to Vulcan," Stella continued. "Order meets the ocean of chaos and births the world as we know it."

"The Egyptian counterpart to Vulcan is a Ptah, a builder, architect and craftsman whose wife was Sekhmet, goddess of destruction and chaos. The female counterpart of vulcanization was always the immense paint pot of unformed energy. In India it's Shakti/Shiva. The feminine, Shakti, is the great cosmic river. Shiva, the masculine, was the bank of the river that gave it order. Almost every culture had a male and female consort working in opposition, playing these two roles. Vulcan had our sun and earth. They were the yin and yang that enabled all life to exist."

14

Dagon was looking a bit dazed. "So," he said, "Are you saying Vulcan is the, what did you call it, the 'consort' of earth?"

"Yes," Stella said excitedly, amazed that Dagon was following so carefully. "Vulcan is the masculine to the earth's feminine."

Instead of seeing the resistance that she expected, Stella could feel sexual energy building in the room.

Dagon seemed riveted not so much on what she was saying, but on watching her as she talked. It made her feel self-conscious.

"What, what are you looking at?" she stuttered.

"Nothing," he seemed to shake himself, "Nothing at all."

Stella continued on bravely. "Thirdly, supposedly, Vulcan could not only execute flawless workmanship, but he also had the amazing gift of imbuing his creations with intelligence and the ability to communicate. This is the part that relates to those high EMF reading you've been getting."

"Oh, come on now!" Dagon was looking exasperated.

"Just let me finish," said Stella. "Mythology says Vulcan created golden shoes that would transport the wearer simply by the power of thought. He fashioned golden chariots that could whirl through the air and chairs and tables, which could move themselves in and out of the celestial hall. And, if that wasn't enough, his crowning achievement was to impart intelligence to golden statues, allowing them to think and reason.[4] In ancient cultures, 'Words' spoken out loud were imbued with power for creation. God said, 'Let there be light,' and it happened."

Dagon scoffed, "You're talking about astral travel, telekinesis and magic?"

"Yes, well consider this. Vulcan is composed of super heavy metal that acts as a transmitting 'radio' station broadcasting from earth out into the universe beyond. This is how we located Vulcan in the first place. How are we to know that there isn't intelligence on this planet? These EMF and EVP readings might give us a clue about it as we approach Vulcan. Secondly, the synchron belt is the unknown element that might make *anything* possible."

Stella looked up, noticing that Dagon's attention was fixed on her Link, the personal computer that she had clutched to her chest.

"Is that whole thing full of this research?" Dagon queried.

"Well, I've had a lot of time to study this. World religions and mythology have always interested me."

Recklessly, she went on drawing her final conclusions.

"I think the mythology says we'll find volcanic activity on the planet. Volcanic activity figures prominently in all of the stories of Vulcan. He was identified with volcanoes in areas of the Aegean Sea. On Vulcan's Feast Day, they venerated him by throwing fish into a blazing fire to re-enact his connection to the water element as well as to fire.[3] Volcanic activity is a key evolutionary factor in the creation of new life forms. The great mountain of liquid fire comes down. Bam, we have a new island, a new valley," she gestured dramatically.

"Hey, I know!" Stella smiled. "I'll let BOB help me out."

"BOB, tell us how volcanoes and the creation of the earth are connected."

The robot immediately turned, upon hearing his name, gesturing in a human-like way as he gave his answer.

"Volcanoes are how the earth is built. Lava flows cause new landforms to rise. Simultaneously, ocean plates plunge. Super continents, like Pangaea, pass away. New ages arrive with new DNA, new chemical codes for life. It is the cycle of death and renewal that creates the rich soup that holds the chemical elements necessary for life."

"Wow, BOB, you are very poetic," Stella was impressed.

"Just information programmed in my memory banks. Would you like me to recite poetry for you?" BOB asked.

Stella laughed as she gave him permission to go into sleep mode, and then looked over at Dagon to see if he was having fun too.

Instead of being playful, Dagon was looking serious and skeptical. "You think there may be volcanic activity on the planet Vulcan? What is your reasoning for that hypothesis?"

Stella shrugged casually, "Just a hunch. The few partial photos that we've managed to capture show that possibility. It has been debated in scientific communities for the past 10 years. Volcanoes mean carbon, the most essential element for life. By the way, the presence of water means it's possible that bacteria have evolved that are releasing oxygen into the atmosphere. We could find life on Vulcan, just like the mythology suggests."

"My original point, however, is that mythology gives us a deeper truth about how the Universe is organized into opposites: order-chaos, generation-destruction, positive-negative and masculine-feminine. Thousands of years later, science proved what the myths were describing when they looked under a microscope. The myths came first, science second."

Dagon's intensity made Stella squirm. One-sided monologues seemed to be her specialty. Once a nerd, always a nerd, she thought self-consciously.

Dagon was tapping his foot impatiently.

Challenging words spilled out of her. "What about those EMF readings? Suppose we find intelligent extraterrestrial life, like the myths suggest? You must admit, Vulcan orbits close enough to its sun to be in the goldilocks zone, not to hot, not to cold."

Dagon frowned. "There's a big difference between mythology and reality. We must concern ourselves with the facts at hand."

"Right," Stella flushed. "And, the fact is that Vulcan is relatively close to its sun. The fact is that..." She broke off, trying to soften her vehemence and strident tone. Dagon was looking decidedly ruffled.

Stella continued in a more measured voice. "You know as well as I do, that the universe has always abounded in the chemistry necessary for life. We've been searching for extraterrestrial life through robot spacecraft on thousands of planets, satellites, comets and asteroids."

BOB seemed to wake up at hearing the word 'robot.'

"Affirmative. Using magnetometers, charged-particle detectors, imaging systems and photometric and spectrometric instruments, we have been transmitting observations back from flyby spacecraft. Robots were used to study the ancient riverbeds, lakes and oceans of Mars, reconstructing life on a warmer, water surface. Asteroids between Jupiter and Mars are covered with organic matter. The moon of Saturn, Titan, is rich in the organic products, which form amino acids that are the possible beginnings of life. Organic matter in our own solar system strongly suggests the possibility of intelligent life on other worlds."

"Thank you, BOB," Stella said, and then took over. "Look at the discovery of Kepler 2B in 2011, a planet with the balmy temperature of 70 degrees!"

Dagon condescendingly said, "So, how is it you are extrapolating this to Vulcan?"

Stella adopted a matter-of-fact tone, trying to diffuse the tense situation. But, there was pride in her voice. "That part is easy. Vulcan lies in the perfect zone for life to exist. Not considering this is like putting our head in the sand. The science and the mythology say this. I have published a number of papers on archetypal mythology of ancient world cultures. The mythology says not only will their be life on the planet, Vulcan, but, that Vulcan was responsible for creating life on earth. I'm curious to see if there is any truth in it."

"Ridiculous," Dagon interrupted. "You believe that myth and stories have some basis in fact? What? That they are some kind of extraterrestrial communications clueing mankind into things we haven't even discovered yet?"

"There is reason to believe that mythology does have a basis in fact, yes!" Stella said defensively, throwing up her hands. "How do you think humans have had revelations or moments of genius? They arrived after casting aside the restrictions of pedantic reasoning, by using expanded consciousness, dreams and symbols to envision other realities. This worked when we discovered gravity, when we began to understand atoms, when the Dogon tribes of Africa imagined dwarf stars and black holes and when the Mayans understood that all those dots in the heavens were suns just like our sun. Everything we have learned has come because we imagined something greater. In fact, it's possible that the world of words is so limited that it is only through symbol that we can access the right brain's ability to 'know' truths about the cosmos. Mythology has always carried both the archetypal stories of past history and the freedom for humans to use the more complex part of the cerebral cortex to imagine new possibilities."

Stella's voice had been rising in frustration. She threw up her hands. "This discussion seems to be getting us nowhere."

"Because I am not going along with it?" Dagon persisted stubbornly.

"No, because we're not really 'talking.' Talking requires listening and exchange. You have listened, but you haven't exchanged ideas with me," she said petulantly. Oh brother, our first real conversation, and we're already having an argument, she thought.

"Well, let me formulate my thoughts. I'll tell you them later," said Dagon straightening his cuff as he turned away and switched back on the video cameras. She could hear Base Command frantically asking what had happened to their video connection.

Stella felt a rush of heat course through her body, barely stopping herself from grabbing his shirttail as he walked away. She bristled inside, thinking, I run when he comes toward me yet want to tackle him when he walks away. What a mess. Wow, he's cute when he's angry. I think he liked it, arguing with me. This would be fun, if he weren't such a stick-in-the-mud.

She dismissed him, vexed with her errant need to storm the citadel of his reserved nature.

Her grandmother had once told her, "Stella, Stella. Be silent. You'll hear more if you stop talking."

Yet, her heart was pulsing in her throat as she tried to concentrate on work again.

Later, Stella opened the Satellite FLIP Center, initiating a networking video link with Base Command. Through bad reception and white noise, they relayed their Vulcan orbit rendezvous plans and informed Command of the measurements currently being received from the synchron belt. Calibrating rockets for entry into Vulcan's atmosphere was the main topic of discussion. Landing would be aborted if the surface of the planet appeared unstable for transport. Who knew what dangers they faced, since to date there were no good photos of Vulcan because it was usually obscured by the synchron belt.

Fortunately, this flight, December 2031, followed 70 years of experience and rehearsal in space travel. Many of the early risks for launching and landing had been minimized. If everything went as planned, they were hoping for a seven-day stay. Stella noticed they never got around to discussing EMF readings, possible volcanoes or BOB's theories.

Six hours later, when Dagon and Stella met to change shifts again it was business as usual. Conversation stalled, she concentrated on her backlog of lab work.

Her workstation sat like a small private country in a corner of their shared space. While Dagon kept his side neat as a pin, Stella's was chaos. Books and papers were piled in all the corners and a hodge-podge of lab supplies littered the only tabletop that she had. A chair on wheels could roll up to her desk, which was well lit from three separate light sources. After working in huge, sterile labs in large universities, Stella liked this little kingdom better.

One advantage was the view. From her desk she could watch Dagon come and go as he endlessly plotted, planned and mapped out their journey. They had developed a routine, while working or eating, that didn't require pesky conversation.

Dialogue had been a mistake, she thought. Sometimes, it's better to keep your mouth shut.

After supper, Dagon surprised Stella by asking her to join him for a few moments. They met in the only other private, video free room they had on the craft other then the bathroom and their sleeping quarters. This room was almost completely filled by a large conference table and some comfortable chairs.

Dagon walked into the room so quietly that Stella was startled. His face looked carved from marble, his expression shuttered and unreadable, as he pulled a chair up to the table.

Stella felt a little flutter of nerves. What was this about? It was a pleasant shock when he began to share personal feelings.

"I've been thinking about mythology. While I prefer to examine things through deductive, logical reasoning, I am willing to concede that there are mysteries I know nothing of."

His reflective tone and pensive face couldn't have prepared her for what he said next.

"That said, I must admit that as a kid I was fascinated with the Star Trek series. My favorite character was Spock, from the planet Vulcan," Dagon's mouth lifted in a barely discernable, half smile.

Stella tried to hold it in, but a giggle escape. She put her hand over her mouth. "Now you're teasing me!"

"Actually, I'm not, I'm serious. I'm thinking of this as a modern myth." Dagon smiled and Stella caught her breath. It was an exquisite smile that transformed his face, making his eyes crinkle with laugh lines and creating dimples on the sides of his mouth.

"Okay, say it," Dagon said.

"Say what?" Stella hoped her breathlessness wasn't showing her instant attraction to him. "Okay, okay, I was just imagining your ears with points," she blurted out.

She experienced momentary panic, thinking, Geez, just shut up or he'll freeze back into an ice-cube. Smiling warmly, she tried to encourage him to keep talking. Thinking, Maybe *you* can live like Spock, but *I'm* languishing here.

Reluctantly, Dagon began his story. "I remember a movie re-run I watched as a kid called *Star Trek III, The Search for Spock.* It was a classic where the Enterprise crew travels to the planet Vulcan."

Stella's attention was captured. Dark blue eyes glowed with animation. Dagon braced himself for playing *100 Questions*.

"Just let me get through this. The Enterprise crew had been involved in an experiment to create a new planet called 'Genesis,' a revolutionary formula that could create life from lifeless matter. The evil Klingons saw this as the secret to ultimate power, setting out to seize the secret formula."

Stella was fidgeting with excitement. "Wow! There it is! 'Genesis,' a creation story like the other ancient myths! What an inspired script!!"

Dagon ignored her. "There is a battle. Spock logically sacrifices his life to save the Enterprise crew. Vulcan mysticism says however that the soul is eternal as long as body and soul are re-fused. Spock 'melded his mind' with Bones, the doctor on the ship, so that Captain Kirk could take him back to Vulcan for the re-fusion of body and soul."

Dagon heard Stella gasp, but plodded steadily on.

"Kirk loses his own son in a battle with the Klingons as they begin the risky journey to Vulcan. Upon arrival a High Priestess performs the ritual. Spok is saved. In the end, it is knowing that Kirk is his beloved friend that brings him back from death."[5]

Dagon paused saying, "I saw this movie when I was eight, but I can remember the whole damn thing."

He looked up to find Stella sitting on her hands trying not to speak.

"Oh, go ahead," Dagon smiled. Thinking, *She's acting like she's been in solitary confinement.*

"I used to love the Star Trek series, too," Stella burst out enthusiastically."

"You did?"

"Yeah. I thought it was great how Spock tried to be so rational and intellectual all the time, but got regularly fouled by his emotions."

"What is so great about that?" Dagon asked, puzzled by her humor.

Stella just rolled her eyes and continued. "You've never tried to be totally rational, then gotten emotional, even though you didn't want to be?"

"Of course, but its not something to keep doing, especially when you have responsibilities."

Oh brother, Stella thought, then, bit back a reply, trying to keep her response more impersonal.

"I think it's a thing men go through all of the time. They try to stay rational, but emotions always break through. Women are usually comfortable with their emotions, but sometimes have difficulty expressing what they really mean in words since language is controlled by the left-brain. Females are often right brain dominant."

Dagon looked skeptical at her ramblings, so she decided to go for broke. She found herself pulling at the sides of her uniform, wishing it wasn't so baggy and unappealing, and then noticed him looking at her appraisingly.

At home she had friends who spoke the same language. But, she had long ago learned it didn't always pay to just start talking about esoteric philosophy. Deciding it was worth the risk, she jumped in.

"Remember how I told you that the mythological story of Vulcan is that he was god of fire, yet raised in the ocean. He was imperfect, remember, so he had to go through a journey to 'find' wholeness. I think the journey was to experience polarity and the balance between the male and female energies within life. Fortunately, the trip brought 'Genesis,' the creation of life from lifeless matter."

"From a Jungian point of view, Vulcan's fall from heaven to the ocean symbolized the connection of the masculine fiery world of heaven to the feminine, watery realm of earth. His disability had broken all of the taboos that required masculine perfection. His limp was a mutation in a flawless world. Yet, it was his lack of completeness that brought him to his feminine self, uniting both parts of himself for dynamic and creative action."

"It's critical that men accept that *everything* is flawed. Otherwise, they are filled with despair and anger every time they, or something around them, fails."

She peeked up, catching a look of surprise on Dagon's face. *Lighten up*, she scolded herself internally, but couldn't resist expounding further.

"I think the masculine gift is intellectualized, focused concentration and actualization. The feminine gift is diffuse awareness, or the ability for abstract conceptualization. The feminine searches for unity, the masculine categorizes and separates. Masculine makes rules, feminine flows. Feminine is earth and water, masculine is mind and fire. In the example of art, masculine understands color theory, while feminine is the physical matter that makes up the pigment. Masculine is the spirit of action to paint the picture, while feminine is the emotion and passion expressed.

"Interesting," said Dagon

"Vulcan was both. Nurtured and supported by the feminine, yet, catalyzed by his fiery, masculine, the creative force flowed, making him the world's greatest artist. Some of the greatest poets and artists have been men who were driven by their emotional and spiritual connections to the feminine. Think of Rumi, Picasso or Beethoven with their complex, emotional lives."

"I agree, it seems especially talented men usually have a well-developed feminine side," Dagon leaned back in his chair. His face was unreadable, but his eyes were still intensely focused, seeming to be almost black.

She quickly looked away, unaccountably finding herself blushing.

"Go ahead," Dagon seemed to read her mind. "Apply your ideas to my story about Spock."

"Okay," Stella felt oddly rebellious as she rushed on. "In your story, the bones and soul of Spock need to be refused by the High Priestess on Vulcan. Soul/masculine and body/feminine are joined by the electrical life force of the goddess, Kundalini. In India, they called this the Tripurna. Ida and Pingala meet in Sushumna, the conduit to the upper chakras, to awaken and re-fuse the Self. Body and soul meet through the work of the High Priestess, Shakti."

Stella shifted uncomfortably then started to move away. "I have a couple more things to finish in the lab before my shift is through."

"Wait," Dagon reached for her arm. His hand was so large it completely circled Stella's upper arm. They both froze at the contact. He held her arm for just a second too long before dropping it. "What is making you so nervous?"

His uncanny perception made Stella even more jumpy. Man, he was intense. Having his intelligence and will focused directly on you was like being incinerated. It was hard to even think clearly. She chose not to answer his question.

Dagon changed tactics, asking another succinct question. "What is the rest of your theory about the movie?"

She ventured forward again. "Your story about Spock is a good example of an attempt for evolutionary growth between Intellect/Male and Emotion/Female energies. At the point of death, Spock must trust his emotional love for his friends, believing it will bring him a 'fusion' to his immortal Self. Captain Kirk acts out the part of the emotional man. He's kind of like the biblical Jehovah because he sacrifices his own son, like Jesus was sacrificed, in the rescue mission for Spock."

Stella tried to keep the smugness she felt out of her tone. "It's clear to me, that, the Captain was demonstrating that, within each individual soul, the work of 'being in balance,' body with soul, means men must honor the feminine principle. It's only then that the world can change," Stella concluded.

"Those are interesting thoughts," Dagon interjected, refusing to rise to her bait.

A mischievous glint came into his eye. "Of course, without sperm and egg there would be no life at all. It takes female and male, *together,* to make the world."

Stella felt a deep dissatisfaction rising. "No thanks to men, if you ask me. The feminine has been persecuted for thousands of years because at the root of the masculine is a win or lose attitude that makes males compare and compete with the feminine, rather then embracing it. They even created a male god that was a trinity to replace the pre-existing, ancient three-fold goddess. Originally, the first solar gods were feminine.[6]

Dagon ignored her outburst, infuriating her even more. "Interesting, however, that Vulcan, the creator of the earth, is male. Didn't the Greeks and Romans give him a mate?"

"They did, Venus, but she didn't love him, probably, because he was flawed while the other gods were perfect," Stella answered thoughtfully.

"So, maybe the lack of acceptance that men suffer from lies in women. I really don't think women like men very much. They certainly think their gender is wiser."

"That's probably right. But, only because men see themselves as the holders of absolute truth," Stella interjected as she turned her chair toward Dagon, gesturing with her hands to make the point.

"Instead of dogma, the feminine sees truth as having gray areas and being more relative. Yes, there are women who buy into male dominated religions. However, deeply embedded in the feminine essence is the awareness of unity. Women see everything as equal, and equally true."

"Sure," Dagon countered, sarcastically. "Then, what about Venus? In your story, she should represent 'love,' yet, she judged Vulcan for his weakness. Women want a man to be successful, to make money. This need is in their biology too, to find a strong male to protect them during childbearing years. Women create part of the cage that men have to live in. And, women who preach right wing dogma are the worst offenders in terms of their rigid belief systems. Probably, because they've sold out on their own sex."

"You're right," Stella said, surprised by Dagon's reasoning. "Jungian therapy says we each are both masculine and feminine. However, women are primarily feminine and secondarily masculine. Women can have a strong negative masculine, being overly opinionated for instance. And, men can have a negative feminine, making them overly emotional. It is always worse to see that negative opposite in *either* sex."

This made Stella feel sad. Of course, what Dagon said was true. Women constantly judge men. They need men to do hard, physical work, but don't understand that it takes testosterone and anger, just to get the hard jobs done. Women are brutal toward a man who shows weakness. They are often as unforgiving when he shows strength because it seems too aggressive to her.

Stella realized she was enjoying their debate. So she rallied in defense of the feminine. "According to the movie, it took a woman, the high priestess of Vulcan, to unite body and soul. The High Priestess is the actual spiritual conduit, kundalini. This is the link for re-fusing the root, or body, with the crown, or heaven. It is the feminine in both men and women that helps us save ourselves."

Dagon looked thoughtful. "I agree and disagree. If Spock represents the Seeker on an evolutionary journey to integrate intellect and emotion, then the Captain and High Priestess are both examples of priests and priestesses."

"What do you mean?" Stella was fascinated with this thought.

"Captain Kirk is a man, but he commits himself to a highly emotional journey to rescue someone he loves. This is somewhat reminiscent of the story of Christ who dies for those he loves. The priestess is a woman, but she uses focused intellect to dispassionately cut through to the truth. It seems both men and women are stronger when they embrace their opposite. Spock becomes a whole person because of both of them."

"It's true," Stella admitted, amazed at where their discussion had led them.

"True, true and blue."

Stella looked up, startled.

"Blue?"

"Your eyes."

"My eyes are hazel," she sputtered.

"No, they are blue, with dark brown specks in them and an almost violet ring around the pupil."

"My eyes have always been hazel."

"Then, you have never really looked at your eyes," Dagon concluded firmly, turning away.

How dare he, Stella sputtered inside. A violet ring, that's just ridiculous.

Stella was sitting over her breakfast the next day, trying to ignore Dagon, when he sat down next to her. He began talking as if it were the most natural thing to do, his nonchalance immediately mowing down her resistance.

"Did you go take a good look at your eyes?" he teased her without cracking a smile, flipping off the video camera with a devil-may-care attitude that made even Stella nervous.

A hot blush started at the roots of her hair, tinting her cheeks pink.

"Of course, not." She would never admit it, but, she had actually spent five minutes staring in the small mirror in her sleeping compartment, something she rarely did. Tiny lines, little crows feet fanned away from the corners of her eyes and a few stray strands of gray were sprinkled throughout her curly hair. Instead of noticing the color of her eyes, she only saw their dismay.

I'm going to be thirty-one this year, she realized with shock. I'm successful, but starting to feel I've missed something. I'm healthy, but out of breath on the stairs to my apartment. Crap!

Stella tried to control her reaction. I don't want to go back to those years of dependence and innocent idealism. I'm finally me. I'm happy, she insisted. Yet, her face in the mirror was etched with her years of hard work. She had been seriously working all through middle school and her teens, getting her Doctorate early at age 23 and her research recognized by the time she was 28. Being gifted as a kid meant she didn't even *know* how to just have fun. Come on, live a little, she tried an internal pep talk. Let go. Be more trusting!

She blinked out of her reverie, realizing slowly that Dagon was talking.

"We need to start preparation for landing. I need you to be able to concentrate. Should I start again with my list?"

"I, really, don't appreciate being scolded and talked to like a child, Dagon. You can stand in my shoes right now, or, not. As you could see, before you sat down, I was eating breakfast and thinking, not ready to be 'at work.' Try being a little more sensitive to me, that would help these little meetings go better."

Dagon sat back, a bit shocked at her bluntness. He checked to make sure the video feed was off.

"Why do I have the clear impression that not only is your mind somewhere else, but it's wallowing around in self-pity while you use me to get even?" Dagon asked slowly and evenly.

The accuracy of Dagon's shrewd assessment stunned her, as well as stirred resentment that he would speak to her so personally.

Pretending to ignore his comment, she tried to keep her voice detached and analytical. "We both need to stop this. And, for god's sake, turn on the video camera again. If we don't, we're going to end up getting a directive from Base Command. I don't want them asking me questions. Also, I definitely don't want to have a fight with you in front of thousands of people."

"That's why I turned the video off. About this morning, you weren't listening to me. I'm trying to have a meeting. You weren't listening to me," Dagon said.

"Well, you weren't listening to me, either. If you had opened up yourself a bit more, you would have sensed that I wasn't in the mood to talk just then. Try to be more observant."

Dagon's voice rose with frustration, "It is my *job* to have the meeting! It is 9:00. It is the time we set for the meeting. We *agreed* to have the meeting at 9:00!"

"Well, those are just rules. They have no flow to them. They don't allow us to connect. They don't take into account that I might be tired, that you might be sick, that having the meeting then would be a complete waste of time!"

"Why am I the villain if I just want to have a meeting at the time that we both agreed to?" Dagon pointed out. "Okay, see *me*! See that I feel tired, worried and responsible for us landing on this damn planet safely! You weren't sensing me, *either*! You weren't being very observant!"

"Are you always this condescending?"

"Are you always so self-absorbed?"

Stella took a long, shaky breath. "No, I didn't used to be, sorry," her lip was trembling as she turned away to hide her confusion.

Dagon gently touched her hand, his voice softening. "I'm sorry too. You're right. I wasn't paying attention to you."

There was a little pause. Dagon was the first to breach it. "I've admired your spunk and courage for a long time."

"You have?" Stella raised surprised eyes. Her stomach somersaulted at Dagon's warm look.

"Well, didn't we both have to spin upside down in centrifugal gravity machines, eat only pills for days at a stretch, and get poked and prodded by doctors for weeks?"

The beginning of a grim smile transformed his rugged face. He looked softer, more vulnerable.

Stella, unconsciously, reverted back to familiar ground. "I'm sorry I over-reacted. I guess it just feels cold when you come at me with an agenda too early in the morning. I need a bit of wake up time, coffee and a friendly chat."

Dagon countered, "Yeah, well, I'm not trying to be unfriendly, I'm just trying to do my job. I have a scheduled communication with Base in a half-hour and need to run some reports for it. I think I got a bit blown out because you don't appreciate the pressure I'm under as we get closer to target."

Dagon still had his list in his hand, but he set it down for a moment to give her his full attention.

"I *do* appreciate you," Stella said. Then laughed, "If *I* was driving, we'd be lost somewhere in deep space."

The fight was like a dam breaking. Stella and Dagon looked at each other silently, both aware of the change. Energy crackled like electricity between them.

"We might have to give in to it," Dagon said quietly.

"Give in to what?" Stella flushed.

"You, know. It's inevitable." Dagon reached over Stella for the carafe of coffee on the table between them, accidently brushing her arm with his. His forearm felt warm and hard. "If it wasn't for those damned videos and Interspace's interference, I probably would have acted on this before now."

It was Stella's turn to feel a kind of shocked fear. In one fell swoop, Dagon, had crossed all of the barriers between them.

Stella noticed that he had moved his hand onto her arm as he spoke, definitely a possessive gesture. She self-consciously moved it away, but felt as if his warm fingertips were branded into her sensitive skin on the inside of her elbow. She felt a sudden urge to kiss him. Jumping up from her chair, she almost knocked it over trying to get away. They both looked a bit shell shocked at their awareness of each other.

It's like there's a magnet pulling us together. Are we being affected by the pull of Vulcan? Dagon wondered to himself, and then chastised himself for fanciful thoughts. Yet, another part of him wanted to consider the question more empirically. What about the EMF readings? It had been proven decades ago that humans responded to electromagnetics in the atmosphere and the pull of the moon and the position of the planets. This pull, toward Stella, felt particularly primitive, on his end. I want to drag her to my bed, then put a stamp, that says, "mine", on her. Like a bloody caveman. I'm starting to want her like a bloody caveman.

He shook himself, embarrassed by his ridiculous need to 'conquer.' I've *never* wanted to conquer a woman. Something's, definitely wrong. Switching on the video again, he offered Command an excuse. "We're working on trying to get better reception."

He turned away from the table, formulating mental lists, planning the tasks that needed to be accomplished during the next six-hour shift. Soon, he was able to subjugate his wayward thoughts, so that he was calm and peaceful again.

It's too bad we wasted months without any real conversation, Stella silently mused, as she kept her distance. But, right now, Dagon feels like a flame that could burn me up.

CHAPTER 2

✠

Fusion and alchemy

The next morning, Stella woke to a text message on her Link. "You left the navigation console off. This is strike three. Please be more careful." Clutching her Link to her chest, she pushed open the door to their meeting room and found Dagon carefully dictating facts and figures into his Link. He had graphs all around him on the conference table and a coffeepot and cups in the center of the table. The noise from her entrance interrupted his concentration, making him lose his place in the long row of numbers.

"What's this reminder about?" Irritation bubbled up that she tried to tone down. All of their days seemed to start this way. Even when they were doing a task together, he was constantly taking it out of her hands, commenting on, or questioning her actions. She realized that she looked like a witch, with her hair uncombed and her sleep clothes still on, but, geez, enough is enough!

"Just, what it says," Dagon said crossly, gathering his notes to start the calculation again.

"We talked about this yesterday. How about a nice 'good morning' sometimes and the offer of a cup of coffee?"

Dagon just looked irritated. "You're taking the note personally. It's dangerous to leave the console 'off.' It has to be 'on' at all times!"

"But, what's this, 'strike three,' bit. I don't think it's over-reacting to want a cooperative atmosphere instead of feeling like you're watching every move I make for mistakes. And, anyway, how do you know *you* didn't leave the controls off?"

Dagon just raised his eyebrows, shaking his head incredulously.

"It really isn't fair..."

"Stella, listen. You take, then break, my headset. You leave on the oven, overcook our meals and leave messes in the common areas. Toxic chemicals unsealed on your table? Really! Wouldn't you feel *better* if you were more organized?"

Stella could feel steam starting to come out of her ears; she was so mad at his condescending tone. "Wouldn't *you* feel better if you removed yourself as judge and jury, and relaxed a bit? By the way, what were you doing looking on my table? Private property!" Hands on her hips, Stella stalked over to the conference table.

"It's *our* table, *our* ship. I am the Commander of it."

"Like hell you are, we're co-commanders. This is what I'm talking about. I may be a bit spacy, but that's because I'm always thinking of new ideas, concepts and working on my scientific research. Life floats. How else do you get the creative juices flowing?" Stella paced back and forth as she blew her hair out of her eyes.

"Well, god help me if you destroy everything around you being creative." Dagon pulled his notes closer so they wouldn't get pulled off the table by her shirttail, as she swept past.

"What a gross exaggeration from someone who is being way too rigid." The coffeepot was just out of reach as she leaned forward for a cup. Her breast touched his arm. They froze. Heat seemed to rise from her lower belly, as she looked down at him dazed.

"This isn't fair." Her impulsive honesty embarrassed her. "How can we not like each other and have this happen."

The thin caftan was showing more then she knew. Picking up a plait of wild hair, Dagon pulled her closer. Stella closed her eyes and gulped, noticing the flush under Dagon's well-pressed collar. She pried Dagon's hand away from her hair, making certain to keep her eyes averted. *Serves you right*, she thought, when she saw his discomfort. Dagon noticed the room felt empty when she stalked out.

The rest of the day went by quietly, with each of them lost in their own thoughts. Working efficiently, Stella made an effort to get everything done from Dagon's list.

Apprehension grew about their long-awaited encounter with Vulcan, as well as the encounter that could probably not be avoided between each other.

By that afternoon, Stella had finished most of the tasks that Dagon had given her the day before. She decided to take a break in her sleep quarters. Rubbing tired eyes while scrolling through the research notes on her computer Link, she let her computer read to her. The computer voice was a lovely modulated female voice that had been nicknamed SonyaSX by its developers. SX's careful inflection and pronunciation often made Stella giggle. Stella lay back on her bed, putting her arms under her head. If the subject matter hadn't been so technical, she would have felt like she was having a conversation with a friend.

"Hello, Stella. You would like to read the file titled Vulcan1015?

"Yes, thank you, Sonya. You may begin." Stella spoke into her earpiece.

"Paragraph 1: Note 221: The statistics of the planet estimate a diameter twice the size of earth. Question? Could this planet be composed of gas rather then solid mass? See file 1022 for more details. File shows a 79% probability that the planet is a solid mass, with the possibility of water and ice on its surface. Need more data as we approach."

"Vulcan is just outside of the solar system, orbiting a sun very similar to the earth's sun. The annual orbit creates marked summer and winter seasons. Vulcan sits in the center of a spinning belt called the synchron belt that creates its own gravity field. It is postulated that the tremendous pull of the synchron belt keeps our sun and solar system stabilized. This is a new theory postulated in the last decade called the Strong Solar System Theory. See File Strong Theory2210 for proofs. To enter the Synchron belt as it rotates by will require perfect timing. There will be one chance to achieve this. If this opportunity is missed, the mission will have to be aborted."

"Other notes to consider: Vulcan has two small moons. Footnote: they are twin moons named Appolex and Dhyana. Question mark. Flag this to study their relationship to the mythology of the brother and sister gods, Apollo and Diana. Revolves on axis once every 36 hours, with an 18-hour day and an 18-hour night."

There was a pause as if Sonya was confused. Then, the computer said in a questioning voice, "Stella, the note ends with xxooxxooxxoo? This traditionally means hugs and kisses."

Stella giggled and rolled over on her bed. She remembered when she had made that note. Merlin, her black and white cat was staying with a friend while she was gone. Wow, had she really put kisses and hugs on a note to Joshua? He would have loved that.

Stella got up, making her way, like a sleepwalker, to the ship kitchen where she began fixing herself a cup of hot chocolate. The warm drink provided the comfort and ease she was seeking. The kitchen was streamlined, compacting everything into a five by ten space with one cabinet top and an island that doubled as a table. The stove was next to a revolving cabinet that stored food and ingredients for meals. When you asked for an ingredient it dropped down behind the glass door. Of course, like the ship, cold fusion powered it all.

Stella stirred her chocolate. Then, with one hand precariously balancing her cup, she flipped through her index. Odd, she thought. "Open File Vulcan Fusion2320," she directed her Link. SonyaSX began to read to her as she ambled back to her sleep quarters, barely missing hitting her shin on the table or knocking over the sensitive equipment she had balanced on the edge of her lab table.

Sonya read, "Vulcan was formally discovered by astronomers on December 8, 2016. Space exploration accelerated during this year with the discovery of cold fusion."

Stella felt excitement rising and directed SonyaSX, "Begin search on all files regarding fusion and Vulcan." Then, she lay back again with her hot chocolate to listen as SonyaSX found what she was looking for right away.

"Astrologers and psychics had long been predicting the discovery of this planet, that they had already named 'Vulcan.' True to the prophetic forecasts, Vulcan was pinpointed by a group of astronomical physicists almost simultaneous with an incredible scientific breakthrough, the discovery of an endless source of energy." The computer went on, linking Vulcan to other mythological stories of endless energy.

Stella turned off her notebook, thinking of her own life in relationship to Vulcan's sighting.

She had been born at the millennium, sixteen years before Vulcan's detection, a child of economic, social and spiritual reform. She was a young idealist when the world had hung in the balance because of global warming, food and water shortages. The economic collapse of 2013 transformed public consciousness, marking resurgence in alternative power sources.

Bioenergetics, as a method to diagnose and treat illness, had come to the forefront of healing when Stella was eighteen. Her mother, a leader in the area of energy fields, had led a following of dedicated believers who had benefited from her skill as a seer and healer. Love, akin to worship, drove Stella to mirror her.

At thirteen, Stella was a precocious teenager, obsessed with her science fair projects on the forces behind matter and antimatter, as well as her biology research isolating and identifying plant antigens. Biology came in first. Winning the International Science Fair a year later resulted in a scholarship to a scientific university as she tested out of her junior and senior years. A doctorate and research followed. Eventually this won her a place in the space program.

Stella kicked at the covers, looking at her little bedroom. It was a shrine to her rebellious spirit, with a neon poster of MasterX in drag on the wall with some of his rap scrawled across the poster. "Live Big, Kings and Queens of the Universe."

Boundaries exploded when you had parents that encouraged reckless mental freedom. The military environment of NASA clamped down on that freedom. It had been difficult to rein rebellion in. Personal expression was limited to two square feet of space above her bunk and locker. But, hey, thank god for that! She always had her tattoo to look at when she turned around in her tiny shower. Stella smiled about her secret piece of body art, continuing her reverie.

Travel in space was a dream from age fourteen on. Reading, world religion and philosophy, was a hobby fanatically pursued as quantum physics and holograms became her experience of God. While investigative work in biology forged her entrance into the space program's aeronautical division, much of her personal research had been scientific experiments, conducted around metaphysical themes.

Fortunately, biological research in space was at the leading edge in her profession. She had been given a rare chance to prove herself. The mission was to supervise a series of lab experiments on electric energy within both animals and plants, testing the biological diversity of Vulcan. Now, as they moved closer to their destination, she felt a crawling fear that Vulcan would be a lifeless hunk of rock, suspended in space, caught in an endless, unchanging orbit around its sun.

To empty her mind, she turned on her video feed of their main living space, luxuriating in a study of Dagon's face. He was lying back in a chair, his hands folded in his lap, eyes closed, giving the appearance of deep concentration. Ruminating over his job, she thought. Fittingly, so. Absolute precision and a miracle would be needed to pilot a ship through the synchron belt. However, irritation rose again about their fight over breakfast. Why am *I* upset when *he* looks so relaxed? she fumed.

Wow, talk about a lifeless hunk of rock! How dare he accuse me. Of course, I left the console 'off.' Oops, 'on'? Still, he didn't need to spend so much time noticing, she thought. The rat!

She grabbed her computer and rooted around restlessly, finding a cartoon of a male and female rat, plugged into electrodes while looking at each other as they held hands. The humor lay in the frazzled looking scientist pictured behind them.   The computer dinged as her text went through. He must be sleeping, she thought, because he didn't notice.

Recently, there had been a resurgence of research on the difference between the male and female brain. Fights between her mother and father had led to a sit down talk with her mother.

"We're just different," her mom had said. "Your dad listens with 28% of the left hemisphere of his brain. He doesn't hear what I'm saying unless he is looking at me. You and I, Stella, we hear everything. Volume control is *our* problem."

"Listen, don't you hear it?" she gestured around the room. "That plant needs watered. The vase wants to be moved over an inch. Your brother is having a bad dream and your dad is hungry. We can hear *all* of it."

I listened. She was right.   It was all there in stereo sonic surround sound. Even more, I could hear voices inside of my head explaining things to me about the world.   Grandma's voice gave instruction from the grave. Birds chirped and sang in choreographed conversation and strangers walking down the street sometimes threw stray thoughts my way.

It was scarier, however, to think that *all* Dagon might hear was that a dial needed to be kept turned 'on.'

It makes me not like him. It makes him *seem* judgmental. It makes me *appear* ditsy when I am actually trying to absorb *everything*, she thought.

Stella rolled over, deciding to get up. Thinking about it wasn't helping, and sleep eluded her. She ambled into the flight room.

Did she dare broach the subject of the mythology of Vulcan with Dagon again? Stella wondered. Their recent conversation had only scratched the surface of a deep subject.

She remembered her college days: animated, late-night discussions about the state of the world and god, coffee shops, the grassy common areas, loitering in the lobbies. They had been a nerdy group, always, brainstorming, synthesizing and challenging each other.

Dagon couldn't be totally immune to this. He might have conventional ideas, but he had seemed to truly enjoy their talk earlier.

Stella walked from her sleeping quarters to their main living area, sitting back on the cushions of the couch, as she studied him.

Is he sleeping? she wondered.

Sinking into the current moment, she emptied her mind. In a theta wave state, the artificial sounds were amplified, the feeling of her skin more exquisite, her awareness of Dagon more intense.

I wonder if it's possible to send a message to someone in his or her sleep, she thought.

Concentrating hard enough might do the trick. Dagon stirred and groaned. Stella shifted her energy away from him quickly. It seemed unfair to direct psychic energy toward him when he was so vulnerable.

Now, I'm really in trouble, she silently teased herself. Soon, I'm going to start babbling, bumbling, burning bras, oops. So much for an empty mind.

Just at that moment, Dagon shifted, opening one eye, and caught her giggling before she could cover up her thoughts.

He held a hand over his eyes. "I didn't intend to sleep on the job. Now, I seem to be having my first migraine headache. I'm seeing blurry waves."

"Oops, I might have done that to you," she admitted sheepishly.

"What, given me a headache?"

"I was focusing on sending you a thought in your sleep. It must have disturbed your brain wave patterns."

Dagon smiled at her innocent belief in the ability to manipulate energy patterns with thought. Of course, she would believe in something so crazy. A small smile hovered around his lips at her discomfort. He remembered her storming out of the room that morning, leaving every nerve on high alert.

"Sorry," Stella seemed humbled. "My mother taught me never to send energy to someone without their permission."

"And, your mother?"

"She was a Seer, but, also a recognized physician. My father worked for Genocantron Corporation on DNA and genetic research. They were as different as night and day, but perfectly paired in other ways."

Dagon smiled slightly. "And, what were you trying to communicate to me? Have you been observing anything interesting while I was sleeping?" he asked her evenly.

Stella blushed with embarrassment, trying to stop the slow spread of color under her freckled, pale skin.

"Hmm, I was thinking of our earlier conversation about Vulcan."

"Which part, the male uniting with the female or the female uniting with the male?" he drawled softly. "I think the operative word was 're-fusion' of the body and soul."

44

"You certainly have an outsized ego if you think..." she dropped off sputtering.

"Forget I said anything, Stella, you're right," he looked contrite and a bit upset with himself. "I'm not sure what's getting into me."

Recanting his flirtation so quickly? she thought, pulse hammering. What's up with that?

"I *was* thinking about Vulcan. Would you like to hear my thoughts or not?" Stella persisted.

"Sure, we've got nothing but, time on our hands," Dagon replied.

"Oddly, I was thinking about, not, 're-fusion,' but, 'fusion.' I had just been reading about it in my notes."

Dagon nodded to show he was listening.

"I'm sure you have heard that, in popular lore, the planet Vulcan is linked with fusion, because it was discovered at the same time as cold fusion," Stella said.

"Yes, we all grew up on that," Dagon said, sitting up, reaching for his water and rubbing a hand over his bristled chin. He wasn't thrilled to be talking just yet, as he still had a headache. But, talking beat silence, which was starting to drive them both crazy.

"What you probably didn't know, is that Vulcan was linked with a discovery of an endless energy long before fusion was discovered." Stella threw out her information like a gauntlet.

"Hmm," Dagon was looking her up and down.

"Are you sure you're up for this?" Stella teased, her face lighting up as her eyes sparkled, flirtatiously.

Dagon's eyes darkened. Oops, thought Stella. I might have woken the sleeping tiger.

Tremulously, she ignored the change of atmosphere in the room.

"Well, okay then," she said with false brightness, backing off from Dagon's intense sexual energy. She dug out her computer, reading out loud:

"The ancient Egyptian god and goddess pair were named Ptah and Sekhmet. Sekhmet was the daughter of Ra, the sun. She was a destructive force that rose from the chaos of the universe and had thousands of names including: 'The Flaming One,' and 'She Who was Before the Gods Were.' Sun goddesses and gods had the job of re-fusing a soul as it traveled from death, back to life again. Mayans worshiped the sun for this reason. They sensed a source of endless energy. They had also noticed that periods of catastrophe, like in 2012, correlated with sunspot cycles, giving rise to draught, hurricanes, earthquakes, flooding and fires. Carbon dating of trees rings show that climate change corresponds with the rise and fall of all the great civilizations in earth's history. It is recorded deep in our subconscious that the sun, our fusion dynamo, is the key to life…. or death."

"Wait a minute, Stella," Dagon looked alarmed. "You really believe climate change caused the upheaval in 2012?"

Stella looked up from her computer, answering succinctly. "Yes, but, my point is more that this archetypal message about the power of the sun is deeply embedded in our DNA."

"Secret societies in the Dark Ages, alchemists and a religious sect of the 12th century called the Rosicrucians, believed Vulcan was 'the celestial sun.'[7] They postulated that the secret to unlimited power must lie in the sun, creating alchemical models for ways to tap into that strength. Most of their drawings included a meeting of the sun and moon, the male and female." Stella spoke with the confidence of someone who had spent many years studying her subject.

"Centuries later, scientists learned that the sun was powered by fusion. This began the search for a virtually unlimited supply of energy on earth. The discovery, just outside our solar system, of Vulcan showed us that galactic polarization stabilizes our sun, keeping it from burning itself out. Vulcan is the celestial sun."

Dagon was stretching and eyeing the empty coffee pot longingly, "I've always been fascinated with fusion," he mumbled.

"You have," Stella cried enthusiastically, "Me too!" Stella went over, beginning to empty a coffee packet in the processor, not noticing Dagon wince when half of it seemed to end up on the cabinet.

"Hot chocolate for a snack?" He commented on the mess on the cabinet top from earlier. Stella froze as she felt her temper start to rise. The heat turned into lust, unexpectedly.

Dagon was pulling off his nylon tunic, reaching for a sweatshirt that she had never seen him wear before.

Denver Broncos? *Hey, wait*, that's *my* team, she thought. A muscled chest, tight abs and a six-pack made her mouth fall open. Then she remembered. Oh, yeah, body building. He trained with weights.

Dagon didn't seem to notice her interest as he focused on carefully snapping the closures of his tunic, and then folding it.

Heat rose all the way from Stella's lower belly to her cheeks. Turning away seemed like the best choice. It was either that or be seen looking as red as a beet.

"Stella, I thought you wanted to talk?" Dagon was saying as he pulled the sweatshirt down over his head. "It amazed me as a young adult to realize how long it took us to find cold fusion. It seems unbelievable now that we used fossil fuel, wood and coal when there was enough energy to run the world in a cup of water. And, the archaic years of nuclear reactors! Unbelievable! Heating hydrogen to tens of billions of degrees within magnetic coils to split atoms. We're lucky we didn't blow ourselves up!"

"Well, we practically did." Stella sat down with a "hrumpff," putting her chin in her hands, still feeling the sexual heat. "They couldn't reproduce in a laboratory what was natural for the sun. It was too big for them."

She reached over to BOB where he had been quietly parked in a corner by the table and smiled. "What do you think BOB? Have you been listening?"

The robot lifted his mechanical arms gesturing in a human-like way. "Master Andrew and Mistress, of course, yes, I've been following your dialogue since you began this discourse. Regarding fusion, in our universe, it is immense gravitational attraction that pulls matter together, condensing it until the temperatures rise high enough to bounce hydrogen molecules off each other causing nuclear fusion reactions. Molecules naturally repel each other unless forced together or attracted to each other."[8]

"See," Stella giggled at BOB's succinct recital. "It takes immense gravity to force molecules together. Puny man couldn't create the necessary attractive power." She caught Dagon's eye, flushing again. She could smell the coffee brewing, so she got up, rooting around for another cup while leaving a pile of plastic cups on the counter. "Here it is, she exclaimed excitedly, "My 'Life is Good' cup! I couldn't find it!" She clutched the cup to her chest looking ecstatic.

Dagon shook his head. "It was behind the door in the conference room yesterday, on the floor." Stella felt an easy kinship with Dagon as she poured a cup for him too, even wishing he had a special cup like she did.

"Do you remember the cold fusion experiments?" she asked, handing him a cup of coffee.

"Yeah, I was 24 years old when they first tried a test tube electrochemical process for fusion. It didn't work, but they were on the right track. I had just begun serving in the Air force then, so I didn't get much chance to follow it all."

BOB wanted to speak and Stella gave him the okay. In the meantime she thought about what Dagon had said. There is so much that I don't know about him, she ruminated.

BOB recited with precision, "The experiment involved passing an electrical current through a solution of super heavy hydrogen molecules. The action of the current pushed the molecules into hydrogen absorbing metal rods called electrodes. The goal was to condense the molecules within the metal, forcing a joining or fusing of them. The result would be the creation of helium and the release of incredible heat and energy."[9]

Stella laughed at the ridiculousness of having a three-way conversation that included their robot, saying, "Vulcan was not only linked to the sun, he was also the volcano god, representing the heated core within our own earth." She looked at BOB, giving him permission to speak again.

BOB lifted his hand in a gesture as he spoke, turning his head to look at both of them. He seemed remarkably life-like, as he had been programmed even to smile at appropriate times. "If I remember correctly from my data bank, Utah scientist, Steven Jones began his cold fusion research from his desire to explore a theory that it could be fusion which kept the furnaces within the core of the earth heated. This idea was spawned by the discovery of helium, a byproduct of fusion, in geysers or hot springs in Yellowstone."[10]

"Hmmm," Stella said considering that imagery as she took a big gulp of her still hot coffee.

"This has been interesting," Dagon said. "Why don't we talk about it more later, when I fix us something to eat." It's your turn to man the flight room while I take a short break. Dagon took off for his bedroom to lie down. Stella made her way over to the chair that Dagon usually sat in.

In front of her was a viewing port that could be open or closed. They usually kept it closed, viewing space through cameras mounted around the outside of the ship.   The chair was a sleek black leather chair with wheels that could lock into the floor during landings. It felt too big for her. She sat forward on the edge of the seat so her feet could reach the ground. They had made this seat for a giant, she thought.

It always made her a little nervous to look at the complex bank of dials, indicator switches and gauges on the flight panel. While they were on automatic pilot, she wasn't expected to direct the operation of the ship. However, she worried about having to do this in the event of computer system failure.

With trepidation, she toggled between programs to go through their checklist: fuel, distance traveled, speed, atmospheric conditions on board ship, food supplies, position in space, other space bodies nearby, the International space map and video feed around the ship as well as through the view port.

I don't know why they ever passed me on this in training, she thought. I keep thinking I'll hit some button that will initiate hyperspace or eject us right out of our seats into space. Stella laughed at the comical image she was creating in her head.

 It was entertaining for a while, but Stella quickly got bored. Putting her feet up on the desk, she wished she could play with her

Link again. All that talk about fusion had given her some ideas. The two hours dragged by. It was with great relief that she greeted Dagon, who checked the automatic pilot, putting the system on alert that they were breaking for supper.

Stella had already made some notes that she wanted to run by Dagon.

"What interests me especially about the cold fusion experiments," said Stella, "Is how it relates to alchemy of metals. This leads us to more Vulcan imagery."

Dagon was standing with his hands on his hips reading the menu of possible menu choices.

"Here, let me read you some stuff out of my computer, again," Stella began searching for the file. "Oh drat," she muttered. "It's in my other computer notebook. I think you'll find it enlightening being a chemist yourself."

"Okay, but, I'm starting to get hungry. I'll cook while you read." Dagon ambled over to their tiny kitchenette and began pulling out packets of dried foods, grimacing at their unappetizing appearance.

"You would think they would have figured out a better way to feed us by now," he muttered to himself as he began hydrating the first package of noodles, carefully reading the directions as he lined up the ingredients in an orderly fashion around him.

Stella was throwing things around in her locker. She emerged clutching her office notebook computer. Turning it on, she pulled up the file.

"*Fusion. Electricity... Metals ...* here it is"

Putting on her reading glasses, she cleared her throat.

"Vulcan was a master of metalworking. Besides, being a smith, he was also an alchemist and magician." She looked up, smiling. "Probably, the first mad scientist. Magical shields, telekinetic objects, talking statues were nothing to him. This guy was Dr. Frankenstein."

"So, I did some research on metallurgy, smiths, and alchemy, finding out some rather interesting things."

"Here, BOB, come here," she said.

Dagon looked at her askance as she playfully put her arm around the robot's shoulder.

"First, the etymology of 'metallurgy.'

BOB recited, "Metallurgy is the science of working with metals. Metals are the class of elementary substances such as gold, silver and copper, which are crystalline when solid and possibly conductive. Metals yield positively charged ions and are generally viewed as formative material."

"Now, 'Meta'"

BOB's lights flashed. He turned his head, gesturing expressively and said, "The word 'meta' in chemistry means 'pertaining to or occupying two positions.' Used in the word 'metabiosis' it means the dependence of two parallel organisms. A 'metacenter' is the intersection between two vertical lines. 'Metabolism' is the process whereby material substances are produced, destroyed and energy made available."[11]

"You see," said Stella excitedly, "from one material comes another creation."

Dagon had raised one eyebrow, watching her childlike enthusiasm and animated expression. "You're talking too fast, and you really shouldn't be teasing our robot," he quipped.

"Well, you get the idea!" Stella asked, practically stamping her foot.

"Simply put, metallurgy, or working with metals, is connected in our language history with producing energy by working with two opposite poles, the poles of order and chaos, construction and destruction. Appropriate then that fusion was possible through a negative and positive, i.e. masculine and feminine, current meeting in a metal heated to extremely high temperatures. It wasn't until they discovered a way to titanize platinum that we discovered the secret. Platinum is the only metal in existence balanced and complete in its molecular structure, making it naturally conductive without overheating. The Alchemists had the right idea earlier. They were just mistaken in thinking the metal needed would be gold."

"As a metalworker, Vulcan was the master of the 'meta' world of opposites. As a smith, he used metallurgy, the science of working or heating metals, to keep certain properties while discarding others. He forged solid matter within the fire, keeping the pure elements and discarding the dross. Thus, he created magical, new creations."

Dagon was taking down bowls for their soup and setting the table while Stella paced back and forth.

"This *looks* like dross," he muttered looking down at his soup.

The document file for her term paper in college was easy to find. She checked the grade. "B plus!" she muttered out loud. "I didn't deserve that!" Then, looked up to see that Dagon was still listening, a wooden spoon in each hand with an apron on.

My god, she giggled thinking, *Where did he find an apron?*

Water hissed as Dagon began hydrating the vegetables. "Go for it!" he playfully called out, like he was cheering the Broncos. "I'm listening while I chop."

Stella giggled, "This paper is about past cultures and the importance of smithcraft through history." She waved the paper playfully in front of him.

"Smithcraft affected all activities of pre-modern society in peace and in war." Stella paced back and forth reading from her document with frenetic zeal. "Many cultures had smith gods. The Irish and Celts carried on the worship of Vulcan through the smith gods, Goibhnbiu and Gofannon."

"What?" Dagon asked.

"I can't pronounce them again. Just trust me, they were smith gods."

"That my dear," said Dagon, "Is the reason for the B plus."

Stella ignored him. "The Smith was a person of consequence in Celtic society, carrying an aura of supernatural competence or magical ability. An eighth century hymn invokes god's aid 'against the spells of Smiths because the Smith was believed to know certain charms and spells and had the power of healing through natural and supernatural means."[12]

"Hmmm", Dagon said adding spices to their soup as he mixed the vegetables and noodles together.

"As the magical metalworker, Vulcan was the first mythological and allegorical representation of The Great Alchemist. Alchemists claim to be able to transmute base metals into gold, the substance from which Vulcan crafted his greatest and most glorious works of art."

"The practice of alchemy is one of the oldest sciences known to the world, extending to prehistory times. Alchemy was considered divinely revealed to man and was the father of modern day chemistry. Alchemy sought to look behind the veil to the mysteries beyond, not only to perform experiments with matter, but, also, to answer the question, what is life. What is intelligence? What is force? Ultimately its goal was to create matter from spirit."[13]

"The father of chemistry you say?" Dagon was taking his first bite of food. He pushed Stella's bowl toward her. "Eat before this gets cold." Stella sat down, but didn't seem to notice her food.

"Yes. If you think about it, you're an alchemist too." Stella was flushed with excitement. You are not only a chemist, you made this meal following a formula. She picked up a big spoon, slurping broth with a sigh of contentment.

Dagon watched her expressive face as they both slipped into a comfortable silence. Her antics reminded him of his little sister. She was a big mouth too. Hey, all of his brothers and sisters were too smart for their own good. He wished he had recorded some of the conversations they had had around the dinner table when his dad had been alive, looking like a reincarnation of Einstein with messy hair and his shirt buttoned crookedly. Unexpectedly, his thoughts drifted back to a poignant memory from his childhood, the day he had first become fascinated with science.

It was Christmas Eve. All day long he had been anxiously awaiting the opening of the overflowing presents under the tree. For a week he had been sneaking out late at night to turn on the lights of the tall fir, their glow creating a magical circle in the darkened room. It had been decorated in harsh daylight, four other brothers and sisters scuffling to put up the ornaments amid a flurry of chaos and confusion. It was only in the deepest part of night that the tree took on its full presence, a silent shrine in the quiet room with snow gently drifting down outside. His soul seemed to crave deep stillness and the promise of discovery. That Christmas had been a turning point for him. He had unwrapped a portable handheld microscope and spent the first night examining every piece of hair, lint, plant, and bug that he could find, trying to keep it away from the other kids.

His parents had laughed, pleased with his inquisitiveness since his dad was always ready with a complicated answer to a simple question. But, his serious nature had concerned them. "Go ride your bike," They'd say. However, Dagon preferred to be alone. Dirt roads between the fields of sorghum and alfalfa outside of their small hometown went deep into the fields where you could only smell pungent sun-warmed earth. Lying down on the warm ditch banks, he watched ants crawl around in the weeds, observing their sandy anthills and wondering why they had this inborn ability to organize themselves. It seemed that he had always wanted to know why things worked the way they did and who made it that way.

Becoming a chemist had been natural for him. Yet, somewhere along the way, through the years of memorizing countless formulae, throughout the repetitive experiments and paperwork, his sense of wonder had dampened. As a child, he had been more curious; now, what was he?

His mind drifted back to the present. He slowly became aware that Stella had left the table and was pacing back and forth. Her bowl was empty and had been pushed aside on the table while his still sat full of food.

"*Adam, Achernar, Alchemy...* Great! Here it is," she scrolled through her index. "You'll absolutely love this!" she exclaimed effusively, straddling the chair backward, her hair pulled back in a pony tail, the red curls springing out with a life of their own, her face shiny and pink with excitement.

Dagon looked up from his introspection, enjoying the sparkle in her eyes. Thinking, Why, she's like a little fairy, with her hair sticking out every which way, her tunic tied carelessly with... what, is that a rope, and her glasses falling off the end of her nose. She's like a noisy fairy.

"Chaldeans, Egyptians, and Phoenicians all implicitly believed in the multiplication of metals as well as other great principles. And, in the 1500's this process was described in terms of solutions, filtration, evaporation and distillation," Stella said. "Ancient alchemical documents read like a modern day chemistry book."[14]

"The difference was profound, however. Alchemists believed that the scientist himself could connect to universal power and create through a meeting of matter and spirit. The Alchemists supreme secret was that the scientist needed spiritual initiation so that he could be the conduit to enable the formulae to work."

As Dagon absorbed the content of her words, he felt jolted out of his daydreaming. Alarm ran through him. "Okay, now this is getting really far fetched," interrupted Dagon.

"Which part? You have background as a chemist. You know that you affect your experiments, don't you? A scientist is no different from a magician. The true magician knows that he is a channel for energy which he transfers to his laboratory."

"Think about it," Stella continued, "In the modern day world, we have only recently learned that all experimentation produces subjective results because of the subatomic link between the experimenter and the experiment. Communication occurs between interlinking particles in a network that defies objective boundaries. Even our world may simply be a hologram created by our own thoughts," [15] Stella challenged Dagon.

"Alchemists knew this long ago. Their formulae required that they, as the scientists, use the power of their minds and their connection to universal energies to transmute matter. The highest magic was to transform themselves, to become the enlightened, magical *real* self that was illuminated." She went on quickly before Dagon could interrupt her thoughts.

"Masters of the mind belonged to secret sects. It is believed that some of these great masters lived in the Himalayans and had special powers, not only to control their body temperature, and heart rate, but, also, to stop aging. In fact, there is a strong tradition that suggests some lived hundreds of years through the consumption of special elixirs or through awakened consciousness. Their alchemical formulae included knowledge of immortality and the secrets to endless energy."[16]

Dagon weighed the resistance within him. He was aware of a strong desire to be alone, to think about what she was saying privately. Stop talking! he thought.

He almost said it out loud, but thought better of it. In an attempt to change the subject, Dagon looked down at his bowl of gray food, commenting wryly, "Well, I wish I had a magical potion instead of this slop."

Stella smiled mischievously. "Take heart. While answering that request would be an example of low magic, i.e. using spirit for mundane personal requests, maybe you can close your eyes and 'imagine' that it looks delicious. Or, we can say this 15th century prayer over it." She reached for her journal turning to a page that had been flagged.

"Close your eyes," she said dramatically.

"Are you kidding, Stella, forget it." Dagon squirmed uncomfortably.

"Come on," she pleaded. "Didn't you ever pretend as a kid, didn't you believe in God?"

"Sure I did, but..." Dagon saw her disappointment. "Okay," he relented, "But I feel ridiculous."

"Okay, now just close your eyes and put your hand over your plate. Believe that you have the power within you to change matter at its most subtle level, even this plate of food. Repeat after me," she began to intone.

> In great measure it ascends from the earth up to heaven and descends again, newborn, on the earth, the superior is increased in power as we infuse it with light. With this thought, we wilt be able to overcome all things and to transmute all that is fine, refining the subtil Oxygen into its own fiery Nature, overcoming solid things, to find them in a more perfect state. In this manner, the world was created. Here is the perfect Seed fit for multiplication. [17]

She finished almost reverently.

"Now, with your eyes closed, taste your food again," she suggested.

Caught up in the novelty of the moment, Dagon picked up his spoon, tasting his food. A smile spread over his features transforming them.

"It tastes great," he said incredulously. "It must be because I feel different. I'm imagining it as better, somehow."

"Right," said Stella excitedly. "It not only tastes different now, it actually *is* different because *you* are different!"

"Saying that prayer was quite a rush, wasn't it?" she said with child-like radiance. My mother taught it to me."

Dagon felt his barriers dropping, interest replacing skepticism.

He ventured carefully to respond to Stella. "I see now how the mythological god, Vulcan, was linked to the creation of endless energy through his association with smiths, metallurgy and alchemy."

"Do you also see why all the work of scientists today could be called alchemy?" continued Stella excitedly. "That Utah scientist,

Smith, that BOB told us about was doing experiments with cold fusion by mixing iron, palladium, calcium, sodium, lithium, gold, titanium and a host of other things to try to recreate the elements found in a typical volcanic hot spring. His laboratory must have looked like a witch doctors, full of vials and mysterious potions."[18]

"Those guys were so close to a discovery and didn't know it," said Dagon, shaking his head.

Stella's voice shook with the intensity of her conviction. "Yes, they were taking base metals and searching for precious radiant light and energy. But, the radiance remained shrouded and the mystery veiled, because unlike the true alchemist, they didn't honor the most basic principle behind energy."

"What do you mean?"

"They didn't understand the unified field."

Stella studied Dagon's serious face, slowly becoming aware of her racing heartbeat. She noticed that she was leaning towards him, almost within touching distance. The next time she spoke her voice was huskier.

"The discovery of fusion was actually 're-fusion.' It required the blending of the positive and negative currents, the weakening of atomic resistance."

Stella gazed at Dagon's solid, strong strength, remembering all the times she had depended on him during their training and now in space. She let Dagon's quiet presence and penetrating intellect soothe her.

Dagon seemed oblivious to this psychic link. My god, he thought, questions careening around his mind. Is this what Stella thinks about all the time? Dagon felt buzzed by the thrill of the chase. Vulcan's story was like a search for lost treasure. On top of that, after a lifetime of anticipation, they were only days away from sighting the planet. The possibilities were endless.

He looked across at Stella. Her face was peaceful. One moment she was a firecracker that couldn't stop pacing, talking or moving her hands. The next moment she was this serene, daydreaming innocent. Would he ever understand her, much less Vulcan?

Stella saw him studying her and a gentle smile lit her face, joy shining out of her dark blue eyes.

"I have another beautiful quote in my journal, let me read it to you. It's an anonymous prayer that is over 600 years old." She opened her journal while Dagon gazed transfixed at her face.

Transformed, a light shining from within her, soft hair curling like a silky curtain over one shoulder, she began to recite:

> 0 hallowed Unity, sink me into limitless eternal fire, Transmute me so that rising, I may be changed into a pure spiritual body of rainbow colors like unto the transparent, crystal-like, paradisiacal gold, that my own nature may be purified like the elements before me in these glasses and bottles. Diffuse me in the water of life, so that with the aid of this fire, I may also attain unto immortality and glory.[19]

His world was spinning, not only because of her words, but also, because of her simple, devoted manner.

"It's beautiful," he responded solemnly, "Why is it in your journal?"

"Let's just say I've prayed it often." Their eyes caught and held.

"*Remember*" He heard it again, a drawn out whisper near his right ear along with a strong cold draft and a feeling of a presence. It was a male voice that made the hair on his arms stand on end.

"Stella, did you hear anything just now?"

"What? No."

"It was like a whisper, right beside my ear. It seemed to be saying, 'Remember.' "

"How odd," Stella said. "Do you think it was an EVP? Did it sound almost digital?"

"Actually, yes! That is what I thought yesterday. This is the second time that I've heard it."

"Wow," said Stella. "Could we possibly have a ghost on board?"

Dagon was looking alarmed. "I think you're going too far with *that*, but, it *is* odd." However she had hit on something just beneath the surface of his awareness. The 'voice' sounded like his father who had died when he was twelve years old. Shaking off an impending feeling of loss and sadness, Dagon turned away, making his way back to their navigational console. Brooding, he gazed disconsolately at the dials in front of him. Dagon was beginning to resonate with Stella's fascination to discover the secrets of Vulcan. Traveling to Vulcan, walking on the soil of this mysterious planet was a quest, a burning obsession to know the truth that lay beneath the surface of life. His desire had been buried for fifteen years as he struggled to meet the stringent requirements of the space program. But, his other self, his deeper self, seemed to be surfacing again, a self he didn't trust.

He was remembering how his father had sacrificed the family livelihood to follow his passion for crazy inventions that had never made it out of the cellar to be manufactured. A poor farmer and a tortured genius, his father had spent every extra cent they had as well as all his free time sequestered away or daydreaming at the kitchen table with a wild, unkempt look about him. Once Dagon had stolen into the basement and found complex diagrams plastered on the walls. How had his father come up ideas like this? His dad was a self-educated man, a farmer in Iowa. Or was he? Dagon, as the oldest sibling, had early memories of a long ride in a huge gray car with people wearing suits. They had spent time in a house where he wasn't allowed outdoors. His mother had said it was dangerous. His father was a terrible farmer. It just didn't seem natural to him. Who was his father, really?

Permanently etched in his mind, was the image of his mother and sisters bent working in the field on that hot dusty day when his father had put on his sweat-stained hat and drove away without packing a bag. They found his body weeks later in a ravine, the old truck totaled, a bottle of whiskey beside him on the seat. More men in gray suits, wearing dark glasses, had visited them the next day for the funeral. His mother had been depressed for years afterwards.

Dagon's mother had died four days before they had left Mars for this mission. His Mom's death was something he hadn't shared with Stella. He had even refused to talk about it with the Base Command psychologist. He didn't think he could stand hearing a psychologist's patent consolation. He felt so guilty at not being able to help her when she had been sick, that he hadn't yet been able to read the letter his mother had sent to him the day before she died. Guilt and grief lay next to excitement and joy. He was barely holding on. Carefully controlled thinking was all that protected him from a tsunami of emotion. It didn't help that Stella was breaking down his walls, while a 'ghostly voice' was insisting that he 'remember.'

CHAPTER 3

✠

Eclipses, the sun and astrology

The next twenty-four hour period was difficult for Dagon. New thoughts and buried memories surfaced without his permission. Sleep was difficult and grief made his body tense.

Concerned, Stella began to prepare regular meals to help out. This was beyond the call of duty, since she usually ate on a bizarre schedule and didn't like to cook. She had never been trapped together in close quarters with anyone for an extended period of time. She found herself aware of everything that Dagon seemed to be feeling. If he was distant, she felt tearful. If he was whistling under his breath, she felt irritated. If he was grouchy, she was determined to be cheerful. It was like a seesaw of opposites, everything connected between them. Besides, both of them were feeling the strain of over three months in space. Landing on Vulcan would be the culmination of a lifetime of work and the danger was high. It was important they keep rested and on track with their mission.

She pondered again the twist of fate that had brought them to this junction. Pandora's box was open. Now, neither wanted to close it. Sexual tension grew steadily. They had crossed a line with each other and were unsatisfied with business as usual.

Dagon sat quietly drinking his juice, contemplating the unappetizing breakfast Stella had made him. He drew a hand across his brow, still shaken by the vivid dream he had had during his six-hour nightshift. He had lain awake for hours afterwards, wasting the, short, but, precious, time he had to sleep, yet not willing to take a sleep aid.

In his dream, he had walked down stone steps into the bowels of the earth. Ancient sandals with worn leather ties clad his bare feet.

Scorching hot sand of the Saharan desert stretched out endlessly. Transported to the top of a huge plateau, he could see rocky outcrops overlooking a panoramic scene of subtle colors and undulating shapes. His heart was beating quickly in his chest, his mouth was dry and a cramp was gripping his stomach. Panic! The sun, an orange disc above him, was beating down unmercifully, yet he could just see the beginning of a solar eclipse. In his hand lay a shiny, wet bee, the nymph just hatched and vulnerable. If only he could cover the bee with the strong black body of a beetle lumbering towards him. However, in a flash, it changed into a golden scarab with luminescent wings, flying away.

Suddenly, he was transported to a stone tower with a winding staircase. He ran up the stairs noticing through a small narrow window a twin moon. A call for god escaped his lips, "Lotto," he prayed fearing it was too late to stop the catastrophe. At the top of the tower was an odd laboratory. Before him a priestess in full Egyptian royal garb was intoning a blessing, her hair a thick, dark fall around kohl-lined eyes. The repeating cadence of her voice echoed off stone walls. She held a vial, etched with the same golden scarab. Next to her was an old man with a beard. "Stella," he called out. "Is that you? Stella?" Her dark eyes beckoned mysterious and sad. The old man looked directly into his eyes. He was shocked to see it was his father.

Tossing and turning, Dagon called out in his sleep, a guttural cry of anguish. His own cry awakened him.

It took hours before he could sleep again, for his mind struggled to remember some other language. What had been the words the priestess had intoned? He had remembered dreams before, but they hadn't seemed as profoundly vivid, symbolic or real.

Fighting off fatigue, Dagon gave up on breakfast. He opened up his personal computer. The first thing that he noticed was that he had a text from Stella, a cartoon of two rats in a lab holding hands.

Ha, he thought, laboratory humor. This was probably appropriate in their case. He couldn't imagine even *having* that dream had it not been for Stella talking non-stop about gods, goddesses and alchemy.

Dagon decided to approach his dream with his usual logical sensibility.

First, he wrote down the dream, trying to understand what it might mean in Jungian symbolism. Walking down the stairs had been like going deep into the subconscious. He recognized someone with more imagination would have said, down into past lives.

It might be time to get some help from BOB's data banks, he thought. BOB, of course, relayed all of his data very unemotionally. But, the result still left Dagon feeling dazed.

Symbolically a bee meant royalty. It appeared that in Egypt there was fear that the Pharaoh would die during an eclipse. The psychologist in him recognized that he might be dreaming about the loss of his mother and not being able to protect her. But somehow, the 'eclipse' felt more real then symbolic.

Next, he programmed BOB to see what 'Lotto' meant. The answer came back 'Lotus or God.' How could that be possible? he thought, This had to be some crazy reference to the lottery. On top of that, a scarab was a symbol of immortality or Ra the sun god to the Egyptians. Oddly, Vulcan actually had twin moons.

Dagon started searching through his own research files. It was now an established fact that Vulcan served the earth by balancing and stabilizing our sun, much like electrons did with the proton and neutron in the nucleus of an atom. A small group of doomsayers had begun expressing concern about what would happen if Vulcan was destroyed, eclipsed or occulted. How would that affect the sun and life on earth?

Somehow was he mixing all of these stories with Stella's talk about alchemy? The dream had seemed to be beckoning him, asking him to do something. And, why was his father there?

Stella had discussed how ancient mythology connected Vulcan to the sun. He picked up his research, finding it interesting to note that fairly modern day astronomers had mistakenly done the same thing.

It was a false trail, but, still a trail. An astronomer thought he had discovered Vulcan in 1846. This well-known astronomer, named Dr. Leverrier, was the director of the Paris Observatory and one of the world's leading astronomers. When comparing the predicted orbit of Mercury with the planet's actual orbit, he found a discrepancy that led him to believe that there was a planet even closer to the sun than Mercury. He and Dr. Lescarbault named it Vulcan the Overlord.

At the predicted transit times, astronomers all over the world waited in vain for Vulcan to return. Astronomers discounted Leverrier and Lescarbault's observations by explaining that

Mercury's orbit fluctuations were simply an expression of its elliptical orbit around the sun.[20]

Vulcan was not to be seen nor heard of again until the year 2016 when its discovery rocked the scientific community.

In the year 2014 and 2015 radio signals were picked up from a planet nearby in space. In 2016 another occultation of Neptune was sighted, which was positively identified as a planet. What Leverrier could not have known was that Vulcan was orbiting around a nearby sun out of the elliptical plane, but crossing paths with the outer planets, then periodically moving closer to the earth and our sun.

The discovery of a planetary orbit, 90 degrees square to our solar systems elliptic plane caused a flurry of new research, giving rise to the theory of galactic polarization. The question was asked, how did this affect our sun and its position within the galaxy. In 2022 it was discovered that this might have something to do with extreme temperature variations over millions of years on earth, accounting for ice ages, the extinction of dinosaurs and the reversal of polarization between the north and south pole of the earth with its resultant weather changes.

It was theorized that Vulcan's relation to the sun was similar to an electron's relationship to the nucleus of an atom. The electron serves to bond the atom's nucleus, also acting as a handle to connect it to other atoms. Because Vulcan was composed mainly of heavy metals including iron, magnetite, gold and radium, it also naturally functioned as a strong conductor and generator of radiation.

Dagon took a break, going back to the kitchen. He never skipped meals normally. Being a bachelor, he had fallen into very predictable patterns.

However, now he was so excited about thinking through his Vulcan research again, he just grabbed a piece of toast and coffee then moved into the conference room taking his holographic pad and BOB.

"BOB," he began, "tell me more about radiation."

"Radiation is energy propagated through space like rays of light. These rays are all electromagnetic in character; the states of electric and magnetic intensity being perpendicular to the original source ray. Propagated through space at the velocity of light, each ray is independent, differing in wave length or frequency, having the ability to move simultaneously in different directions."

Dagon mused to himself. Vulcan then worked as a huge electromagnetic radio source pulled in by the sun's gravity field. Radio waves are simply traveling electrons. After pinpointing the exact location of Vulcan in 2016, it was possible to pick up signals from Vulcan on radio transmission equipment.

The possibility that Vulcan held the key to contacting or communicating with other planets in other solar systems had been bandied around by scientists for years.

The belt that spun around Vulcan was named the synchron belt. It acted like a Hoover, vacuuming up space debris, meteorites and gas. Vulcan sat like a jewel in the center. Actual photographs of Vulcan were rare because the synchron belt blocked it from view. Vulcan had a 448-day orbit around its own sun, creating a marked cold and warm seasons on the face of the planet, yet within the temperature zone for life.

Dagon got out his holographic pad.

"Vulcan and the sun, Vulcan and the sun." The words continued to burn a groove into Dagon's weary mind. There was something to understand here. Dagon closed his eyes, imagining the powerful pull of the sun. Both the earth and Vulcan resonated to the pull of this giant electromagnetic source. Massive x-class super flares caused fluctuations of solar wind, which, in turn, affected the geomagnetic field of earth, affecting protein and water molecules. It's all interconnected, he thought.

He turned on voice control on his pad. "Show me our solar system." Hovering in front of him was a three dimensional holographic model of the planets in their current orbital position in space around the sun.

"Add Vulcan." A spinning object marking Vulcan's path through the solar system.

"Add Vulcan's sun." A glowing orange disk appeared outside the boundary of earth's solar system.

"Show our spaceship in its current position." A blue flashing light pinned their position.

Dagon studied the model for a while considering. Galactic or cosmic radio waves from the black hole at the center of the Milky Way Galaxy effect earth's solar system, he thought.

"Place our solar system inside of the Milky Way Galaxy."

The three-dimensional model suddenly expanded so that it was as large as the room he was in. Dagon could see how the Solar System connected to the Galaxy. He imagined the earth rotating through the precession of the equinoxes until it lined up with the galactic center on the winter solstice in 2012. This 26,000-year cycle had produced catastrophic earth changes.

Shining like jewels in the darken room, the planets spun in their orbit around him. Dagon felt humbled. Interconnection had its flaws, he thought. If you pulled one string would it all unravel? An eclipse or occultation of Vulcan might be that one string. Was that what his dream had been trying to tell him?

Planetary alignments weakened the mantle of the earth causing earthquakes such as the record 9-point earthquakes that had shifted the earth off her axis from 2011-2013.   What would happen if Vulcan eclipsed?

Dagon turned off the holographic pad, flipping on the room lights.

Dream flashes came back, the tower, laboratory, alchemy, an eclipse and his father.

"BOB, list effects of eclipses," Dagon requested.

"Current research has proven that during an eclipse the earth's geomagnetic zone is significantly disturbed. The surface tension of water becomes more elastic. Humans, being composed of 80% water are affected.[20] Moreover, it now proven that humans respond behaviorally to the electromagnetic pull of the sun, the planets and the galaxy.[21] A modern branch of scientific astrology had been growing to plot out these vibratory radiations and how they affect inanimate and animate life forms on earth. There is a strong scientific contingency that disagrees with these findings. The two camps have been presenting papers in opposition for the last decade.

Dagon put his hand over his eyes, tired and ready for a break. Read-outs from the console in the flight room were calling. With a heavy heart, he dragged himself back on task. What's wrong with me, he thought. I must be thinking about my dad. How could he kill himself like that?   He thought he heard a voice whispering, "*I didn't.*"

Meanwhile, Stella hummed happily over her specimens, saying brightly, "I'm giving them a little burst energy. They need a happy face."

Dagon checked his watch.   Hours had gone by with him obsessing over his notes. This was ridiculous. Some things just didn't have answers. If all of science hadn't figured it out yet, he sure wasn't going to get the answer here in deep space.

Dagon settled back down to work in the flight room as Stella began whistling a Broadway show tune. Unbeknownst to him, a more mysterious force was at work. Information began to type itself into his computer as a text for him to see when he opened his computer back up.

> Vulcan is a source of radiation and radium. Therefore it has the ability to spontaneously and continually emit rays capable of passing through bodies opaque to ordinary light. An intensification of Vulcan energy therefore reconstitutes and liberates electrons from solid matter, causing the phenomena of fluorescence or phosphorescence and creation of new matter. It acts as a celestial source to encode the terrestrial. Ask Stella.
>
> Vulcan's perpendicular relation to the sun functions to hold together the solar system. It also serves as a conductor of radar waves to similar planets from other solar systems and galaxies.
>
> Vulcan is a metallic conductor of positive/negative currents. An eclipse, if aligned with other planets constitutes, therefore, a total shutdown of electromagnetic energy to earth, bringing global and galactic catastrophe.

Whoever or whatever had typed in the information left it as a ticking bomb for Dagon to unwrap the next time he opened his Link.

Dagon enjoyed a few days of normalcy. Stella kept busy in her lab. The world was looking rosy. But, Dagon couldn't get the dream out of his mind, and he was stubborn by nature. Once he got on a topic, it usually obsessed him. Obsession had been a problem when he was a child, a problem in school, and a problem when he was serving in the Air force in Special Services. And, as far as he was concerned, it was a problem now.

Dagon pictured the golden light of the sun, the sun god, Re or Ra, always seeing the golden scarab on that flask in the laboratory of his dream.

To the ancients, the sun must have seemed an immortal force to be reckoned with. It was the center point that acted as reflector, radiator and catalyzer of all life. At some point in history, Vulcan had become synonymous with the harnessing of the principle of sun energy, fusion and 'golden power.' The ancient scholars had not known about the galactic polarization principle, and the sun's relation to Vulcan in space. However, the mythological stories demonstrated an intuitive knowledge of these concepts, none-the-less. This is what was mind bending. How could mythology so closely mirror reality? Why did ancient stories resonate with deep truth? Stella seemed to think it was because the archetypes existed first in Divine Mind.

Pleasure transformed Stella's face as she spoke cheerfully to her lab specimens. She could tell him more, explain the missing pieces. Was she the priestess of his dreams? Yes, he recognized her stance by the way she was inclining her head as she concentrated on her work. Fanciful thinking or not, Dagon approached her, seeking the information he needed.

"Stella," he interrupted her, "I've been thinking a lot about our discussion over the past few days."

She smiled, lighting up her already expressive face. "You have?" She seemed so pleased it made him feel a bit foolish for being so unavailable in the past few days.

Stella rushed on, "I thought I'd blown it, like I usually do. You know, saying too much too fast.   And, no one wants to be evangelized. I felt a bit foolish after I shared those prayers with you, without you asking me too. Religion is so personal. I'm not at all mainstream.   According to my mom, I haven't been since birth." Stella laughed again as she pulled her white coat off, taking the plastic cover off her hair.

Dagon held his hand in a fist so he wouldn't reach out and touch her hair. The red was so bright it looked alive. He found himself blurting out, "Do you dye your hair?"

"You've been in space with me for three months, you know I don't!" A look of sheer irritation passed over Stella's face as she said, "Now, that *really is* personal. I have friends who are 70 who look like they are 25 after getting youth enhancers. I've never wanted to do it, not, that I'm against it if they want to get new organs, muscles, skin, and younger faces."

Dagon immediately back-peddled holding up his hand, "Whoa, sorry, go ahead, share some of your personal religious beliefs, I don't care if they're not mainstream."

Looking mollified, Stella put a stopper on the vial she was holding, carefully placing it in its stand as she removed her gloves. A stray hair fell down over her face as she bent over the table. Dagon couldn't help himself. He reached down, holding it in the light for a moment and then tucked it over her ear, surprised by the blush that spread across her neck from this small intimacy.

"Okay," Stella adopted a matter of fact tone, stepping back to put distance between them. "Tea first, then I'll tell you everything I know from the research that I've completed."

After they were settled down comfortably around the table she began.   Soon, her voice changed as she took on the voice of a lecturer. Dagon could imagine her giving this talk to an audience. It reminded him of the way that his dad had gotten into subjects at the dinner table. In fact she was sounding very much like his dad now. Dagon watched and listened, wondering how Stella retained all of the information that she seemed to know as if second hand.

"As you know, we have discovered that Vulcan is synonymous with the power of the sun because it acts as the sun's electromagnetic 'skin' so to speak, its outer boundary. The sun through a process of fusion sends light out in luminous sheets to all of the planets within our solar system. Yet, Vulcan has a unique function, to bond together our solar system and connect it to other galaxies."

"Scholars from ancient times started with large concepts, extrapolating down to truths and laws of natures. For instance, the Greeks and Romans understood instantaneous creation, but hadn't yet identified particles and anti-particles within the unified field. Sun to them was a microcosm of the sustaining and unlimited power of a much larger source that existed in the greater universe. In an uncanny way, they hit on truths that we have just now discovered. Only recently for instance has science recognized that the Milky Way Galaxy exists in a group of local galaxies that include the Andromeda Galaxy. These galaxies collide, communicate and interact within a universal, unified field."

She looked up, noticing that Dagon was listening carefully, so, she went on.

"Ancient teaching in India saw this field as shining, non-duality with millions of myriad parts flowing together in a dance of complexity, and unimaginable genius and light. They knew that language couldn't begin to describe what they called ananda or bliss. Adepts used body postures, sound, images, color, light and electrical impulses through the spine to achieve a shift of perception so they could see this great mystery through the higher center of the brain. Using drugs like soma, the Aryans saw a mind blowing cosmic oneness, or unity underlying all of life."

"Worship of the sun was automatic because of its steadfastness and immutability. Albert Pike says that even as the temples honoring the sun, the houses of Brahma, Osiris, Adonis, Apollo, and Christ, crumbled, eroded by the centuries of wind and rain, the sun continued to shine on their forgotten ruins."

"The rebirth and awakening of the sun through the seasons was the source of most of the festivals and religious ceremonies of man. Many of the Christos, or death and resurrection gods, enacted the birth and death of the sun at the winter solstice and spring equinox."[22]

"But, the Mayans went further. They prophesied a possible death of the sun. The sacred Aztec calendar, called the eagle bowl, pictured a sun in the center that was represented by the horned toad, the 'little sun dragon.' Horned toads live where the sun beating on the arid landscape produces ground heat that is unbearable to humans. Unfortunately, horny toads were vulnerable to mankind. Solar energy panels in the Mohave Desert decimated their population in 2017 by destroying the anthills that were their main source of food."[23]

"The Hopi referred to the dragon or horned toad clan as they prophesied great destruction that would rock the world to and fro. The Hopi described a time at the end of the world when a mist would surround heavenly bodies and another ice age would begin."

"The sacred Aztec calendar was used for more then 2,000 years and is linked to the Mayan prophecies. Mayans like the Egyptians worshipped the sun and even sacrificed thousands of humans to it on their altars. In their prophecies, they say that at the 5th age ending in

December 2012, mankind would realize their spiritual destiny. In the 6th age, we would realize that God is Ourselves. And, in the 7th age, we would be so spiritual, we would be telepathic. Interesting, huh."[24]

"And, Ra?" Dagon asked, remembering his dream.

Stella's eyes took on a far away look. "I guess to answer that I would have to talk about Atlantis."

"You do believe in the civilization of Atlantis, don't you?" She looked over at Dagon, surprised to see doubt.

"I'm actually not getting off topic, you'll just have to bear with me for a moment. Beneath the ocean near the Bimini Islands archeologists found the remains of a great civilization. Plato and his compatriots, called this civilization Atlantis. These people escaped the meteoric destruction of their island chain by going by boat to the Yucatan. This resulted in the Mayan system of astronomy and mathematics. They also crossed the ocean to Europe ending up in the cradle of civilization, Africa, Egypt and the Indus Valley. Both the Mayans and Egyptians had pyramids and they were both worshippers of the sun because the Atlantians were. This civilization of people had a very advanced priest and priestess cult that worshiped what they called the sun behind the sun. This was later synonymous with Isis to the Egyptians. Atlantians knew that points of light in the sky were actually suns like our own. Their religion included astronomy, galactic calculations and advanced mathematics."

"The Egyptian's had a pantheon of lion god's to symbolize the sun. Sekhmet, Bast, Ra and Nut were a few of these. Another of their sun symbols was the scarab, which represented immortality and rebirth. Ra was often pictured as a circular disk with wings because they believed he was the sun, drawn across the sky by a chariot of winged white horses. In fact, gold and white horses are other sun symbols in many cultures as they are linked to the idea of resurrection. To the Egyptians you died passing through the terror of death, back onto the light of Ra, the sun."[25]

"Other sun symbols have included the revolving wheel, the disk, the circle with central point, a swastika, and animals like the eagle, phoenix and Chinese dragon."

"Here is an even more interesting idea. Remember how we talked about how the gods of pagan antiquity came in male/female pairs. Well, that wasn't always the case in regards to the sun. Here they sometimes made the god hermaphrodite, or both sexes in the same divine being. The sun had male generative energy as well as feminine fertility. So, it was symbolized as a circle, that being the feminine or universe, and the point in the center of it, representing the masculine. The Hindus call the midpoint in a circle the bindu, the male spark of life within the feminine cosmic womb. This is the same symbol that I use for the sun in astrology." [26]

"Hmm," said Dagon, "Let me think about all this. We'll talk a bit later after you take your rest break."

"Great," said Stella, "I'm feeling a bit drained." She went into sleeping quarter and lay down, head pounding. What in the world was going on. Something weird seemed to be happening to her. Just now, when she had been talking to Dagon, it had felt like she was being spurred on by some other super intellect. Everything that she had ever read was at her fingertips. She was drawing it together with lightening speed. Perhaps, there was something to the theory that high electro magnetic frequency created odd mental effects. She felt her mind was amped up and she couldn't turn it off. If she hadn't known better she would think she was getting a little help from some other entity.

Later at lunch Stella noticed that Dagon liked to concentrate on only one thing at a time. He read the instructions carefully for the oriental salad they were having. He carefully dehydrated each vegetable separately for the recommended time. By the time they sat down to eat, Stella was feeling impatient and hungry. Dagon precisely spooned the mix onto their plates, one spoonful at a time. By then, Stella had just about lost it. She managed to bite her tongue, but, found herself feeling the same impatience as she watched him eat. He ate one bite at a time, moving things around on his plate, so that they would be in the order that he wanted them. Also, he saved the best for last. It wasn't until he had taken that last, perfectly compact bite that he was ready to focus on her again.

Stella was flabbergasted. That would take me over the edge, she reflected silently.

Dagon seemed aware that he was being studied, but, was not willing to give it any attention. When he had poured himself some tea, he looked at her expectantly. "Okay, now, I'm ready." He seemed to be grimacing rather then smiling.

"Ready for what?" Stella had completely lost track after watching him eat.

Dagon's mind was like a steel trap. He went right back to the last thing he had heard Stella say before lunch. "You use astrology? Since when did you start using astrology?" Dagon asked.

"Well, I'm kind of an amateur astrologer," Stella said.

"You believe in astrology?" Dagon was looking skeptical now.

"Of course. I've done my own chart as well as the charts of others and found astrology to be oddly accurate. I've been following current research and have even completed some of my own studies.

You have to admit they have found strong correlations in astrological research regarding personality traits, sickness and career choices."

Dagon's gray eyes looked like lasers as he directed his attention solely to her.

Needing to diffuse the tension, Stella adopted a nonchalant approach as she talked. "Astrology is ancient stuff, thousands of years of symbolism and predictions, mostly used to tell us about our own self. The sun's sign describes how energy, will and ability for creative action will play out. I guess you could say, how we will manifest our life and be powerful."

"When you calculate a chart you look at relationships between planets called aspects that are favorable or unfavorable. It is very geometric. The circle is divided into angles, which have meanings. For example three planets 120-degree from each other would form a triangle inside the circle, called trines. This is considered positive resting energy and often indicates gifts or abilities."

"With the discovery of the planet Vulcan, astrological theory had to account for a planet that would transit every planet in the native's chart at 90 or 180 degrees activating or catalyzing action through the creation of 'square' or 'polarized' aspects."

"The sun in astrology is synonymous with a quality of 'beingness' that is unique to each individual. Radiant, unlimited power form dynamism, both externally and internally, so that actions can manifest form. Vulcan amplifies that movement and action. This forces resolution of conflict and requires balance of lost and energy supplied."

Dagon was looking pensive and unreadable.

"Have you ever had your astrology chart done?" Stella continued. Stella stretched, rubbing the back of her neck as she leaned back in the chair.

"I'd love a neck rub," she hinted.

Dagon felt his pulse speed up. Oh, brother. Just how much control did she think he had! Irritation touched them both.

"Well, have you had your chart done or not?" Stella snapped.

Dagon couldn't help but smile at her frustration.

"No." Dagon rubbed his own neck, thinking, I could use a neck rub too.

"Oh, well," Stella sighed, "You're a Scorpio with Pluto on your Ascendant. That means your deep, intense, secretive and apparently stubborn. Some would also say you're also magnetic, psychological and sexual. You're a water sign. I'm a double Aries with Mars and Uranus conjunct my Ascendant. Take it from me, with all that fire, I understand Ra. It hasn't been easy being a natural born rebel and getting along with Base Command. My code name is even Eris, after Discordia, the sister planet of Mars. What's your code name?"

Dagon lifted his eyebrows and crossed his arms, the secretive part of himself refusing to tell her by ignoring the question all together. "You really believe in astrology?"

"Yes," Stella replied, crossing her arms, mimicking him. "But, it's one of those things you have to spend time with. Until you've worked with your own chart, you can't see the synchronicity. I'm constantly amazed, so, I've become a believer like many other great thinkers in history," Stella said with a little flip of her hair.

Dagon tried not to smile at her obvious defensiveness.

Stella went, on ignoring Dagon's skepticism. "Traditionally, astrology holds that physical matter is either in a steady state, a changing state, or initiating movement between one form or the other. As a fixed sign, Scorpio, you would want to hold things in, especially emotionally. As a cardinal sign, I would want to initiate new movement through spirit, to inspire with enthusiasm."

Stella was looking pensive. "Long time ago, I calculated the astrology chart for the planet Vulcan using as its birthdate the hour and day it was discovered. The amazing thing about the chart was that Mars, Uranus and a bunch of other planets were on the Ascendant in Aries, exactly opposite the sun in Scorpio. In fact, everything in the chart lined up in opposition, fire on one side and water on the other. I think it's uncanny that our personal suns sit on this axis. It's like we're playing out the Vulcan chart just by being in close proximity to each other."

Stella stood up, stunned by what she had just said out loud, embarrassed she was talking about them as if they had a 'relationship.' She looked ready to flee but grabbed a cloth instead to clean off the table. "Sorry, I guess it's a habit of mine to boldly go where angels would fear to tread."

Unruffled concentration was all she got in reply. Dagon's steady focus proved to be her undoing. She couldn't help blurting out the rest of her unruly thoughts to him as she began to clear off their lunch mess from the table.

"Do you know what my name means? Stella means 'star fire.' It was also my great grandmother's name. My last name, Miren, means 'sea white, sea fair.' It's Irish for a mermaid who was transformed into a human." Stella reached past him grabbing his bowl and putting both of theirs in their sink. She turned her back as she began washing them but kept talking. "Stella Maris was a name for the Virgin Mary and meant Star of the Sea."

As she turned toward him, some suds fell onto the floor. Dagon almost stood up to get a rag but sat back in his chair instead with a smile. She looked so animated, he felt captured.

"But your name is *really* unusual!" Stella lifted the bowl up to her chest squeezing it in excitement. "Dagon was a Phoenician god of agriculture and the earth. He was also a mythological Fish god that lived in the watery realms of the ocean. Gideon, your middle name means 'mighty warrior' and Andrew your last name means 'warrior man.' Isn't that cool!" Stella turned back to the sink.

"What do you think is 'cool' about it?" Dagon smiled openly at her back.

"Our names both connect us to the ocean. Mine is the name of a goddess and yours is the name of a god." Stella could feel herself starting to turn red, so she kept her back turned away.

Dagon stood up, however, and took the dish from her beginning to dry it. "How did you find out my middle name and my birth time? When did you run my chart? Nobody knows that information unless they have been doing research on me."

Stella stepped aside, running into the corner of the cabinet as she tried to put more space between them.

Dagon just shifted, taking the other bowl out of her hand so that they were shoulder to shoulder again. Stella stepped back and began washing the silverware, keeping her face averted so that Dagon couldn't see her embarrassment.

Dagon said, "Those astrologers you talk about, could not have known that the sun is simply an enormous furnace of plasma fusing million of tons of protons into helium nuclei every second and releasing the energy of ten billion hydrogen bombs in the process. The sun is pouring out its radiant energy at a steady, constant rate, consuming its own mass. She is running out of energy even as we speak, and some day will burn out completely."[27]

Stella sat down her dishrag and turned to face him. She found herself saying in a cross voice, "Surely you haven't reduced the death of the sun to the death of energy."

She put her right hand, suds and all, on her heart, a familiar gesture of affection. Then she raised her other hand in the ancient symbol of the crux ansata, the Egyptian Ankh, raised palm, three fingers up, forming a V between the third and fourth finger, also the symbol of Vulcan.

"Remember this from Star Trek? It's the ancient symbol for the Egyptian Ankh, transformation. From life to death, passing through Ra to Nutt, the goddess holds all the stars in her belly. Riding on the goddess's 'boat of a million years,' we wait for that moment when we can be reborn again. Ra, or the sun, was one half of the equation, the other was death, itself. It is in death that we are transformed."

"Transformed?" Dagon asked startled as he bent over to put the bowels in the lower cabinet. "How? Into what?"

"Remember!" Stella looked irritated, crossing her arms over her chest again.

That word again! Dagon thought as he stopped and straightened to look at Stella astonished.

Stella rocked back and forth. "You were different then, you were more trusting. Things were simpler. But, then you were just a little boy." Her voice took on a soft, wistful quality.

Dagon looked at her suspiciously.

"Back when?"

Stella seemed to snap out of it. "I don't know, what did I say?"

"You don't know what you said?" Dagon's voice was rising now in alarm.

Quickly getting control of his emotions, he focused his attention back to Stella, who seemed to have recovered her composure.

Stella leaned back against the cabinet and assured him, "Every power source has to enter back into the darkness through dissemination and eventual decay. Yet, energy is never lost. The sun will come back again in another form." She put her hands on her hips, "You know what the Hindu Vedas contain. Remember!"

Dagon shuddered, she was right, he *did* know this. He knew what the Hindu Vedas contained, but he didn't recount ever having read it or heard it spoken of before. How could he know this?

Dagon recited out loud with incredulity, "They contain ancient texts that describe just such a burning out of the sun, even describing what will happen to other planets in our solar system when this occurs. They knew that the death of the sun would only be a new beginning. As the sun begins to expand then shrink, in its last stages of life it will melt the frozen oceans of Jupiter's moons forming inhabitable environments on other planets."[28]

Dagon broke off in confusion and sat back down at the table, putting his hand over his eyes.

She stepped over to him. "Are you okay, a headache again?"

"No, it's just…" But then he put his head in his hands looking stunned. "First, how could the Hindus have had information about this thousands of years before mankind even understood what the sun was composed of or that Jupiter had an ocean or moons? Secondly, how is it that I can remember these Veda texts when I've never read them before?" Dagon queried.

"This has been a weird afternoon for me too." Stella continued cleaning, putting the last of the food ingredients away. "I feel like some other force is inside of me, martialling everything in my memory bank. It's like being 'quickened.' "

Dagon thought about it for a moment. "This could be the high EMF readings we've been getting. It is stimulating our thinking process, causing some weird kind of thought transfer. You knew what the Veda's said and transferred it to me."

"Wow, I don't know. But, as of right now, I'm putting a stop to it. It is winding me up too tight."

Stella was leaning over Dagon grabbing the salt shaker as she said this. He glanced up, becoming aware of how close her breasts where to his face. Light was reflecting off her pendant as it dangled in front of his eyes. Reaching out, he touched the pendant gently, requiring her to stay close to him as he held the chain.

"What is it?"

"A blue-green tourmaline, tourmaline is electrical."

"It's so cool to the touch," he said.

"Yes, it is isn't it," she replied, looking away self-consciously, fighting the desire to snatch the pendant from his hands.

"So, you're a fiery person?"

Stella gripped the salt shaker, not catching the mischievous smile that he was trying to suppress.

"Temper, Temper. You told me I would need to learn about Mars and fire from you. I'm just asking, that's all."

"Well, I certainly have no desire to play word games with you." Stella pulled the pendant from his grasp and stepped away turning her back on him.

"You didn't answer my question," Dagon said.

Stella whirled around still holding the shaker, "Because it wasn't worth a response. Oh, brother."

86

"Stella, believe it or not, I'm serious about this. What do you think fuels you?"

"Energy that is balanced between the polarities within my own body, energy that connects my root chakra to my crown chakra, what in India they call Kundalini."

"Isn't that sexual energy?"

"Not in the way you're thinking of sex. But, yes, it's the prana that is in everything. Everything living is 'sexual.'"

Dagon stood up and stepped in front of Stella prying her fingers off the shaker, reaching around her to set it on the counter behind him. He took a step back and leaned back against the table. "I'm not the kind of guy who throws around sexual innuendos. It's all these bizarre flashes of déjà vu, odd dreams, and strange thoughts." He was talking almost to himself, but then he straightened, stepped forward and turned down her collar mischievously. "I guess we are going to have to do some experimental research between us to try to get to the bottom of all this mystery. I've always loved a good mystery."

"Dagon!" Stella gasped.

He gauged her reaction to his teasing.

"It's not like we don't know each other, like we haven't spent almost every waking moment for the last two years together."

Stella considered the temptation. Oh, crap, she thought. Base Command had been grooming them for this. They wanted a couple in space. It burned her up to think about it. But, she had been wanting this to happen for years.

Other men had courted her over the last few years. The last had given up after seeing she spent every waking moment with another man. However, sparks flew every time she and Dagon interacted. It was like a raging wound that was bigger than both of them, that left her raw each time they had a conversation.

"No," she shook her head regretfully, "Not a good idea. The mission needs our focus right now."

"What is the mission?" Dagon murmured. He took one of her hands.

With the cabinet behind her she couldn't step away. Dagon was so tall that she felt dwarfed by him.

"The fact that we are now within five days of sighting and landing on the planet Vulcan," Stella said averting her eyes.

"And, our other mission?" Dagon reached for her other hand, so that she had to look up at him.

Inner heat began to rise, scorching the breath out of her. Her heart was hammering and she felt faint.

"I'm trying to kiss you and you're refusing to acknowledge the most important principle of Vulcan."

"What?" Stella stammered breathlessly.

Dagon cupped the back of Stella's head making a little circle with his thumb behind her ear as he drew her closer. She could feel every cell in her body vibrating until she had to close her eyes.

"Sex. It's a male/female thing, this balance of energy you're talking about," His voice changed and deepened taking on a soothing quality.

Fear suddenly came over her. "Stop it," Stella pulled away.

Dagon looked genuinely surprised, dropping his hands and stepping away. "You don't feel the attraction?"

"Yes, of course, I do, but attraction and seduction can fool you. We've spent two whole years together in the space program. This is the first time we've actually had a meaningful conversation." Stella said with hurt. Dagon stepped away retreating into his silent, inscrutable self.

Stella realized she was making a mistake in turning him away, but her stomach clenched with fear. Confusion took over. She settled for the emotion of anger. "Anyway, You don't even like me."

"What?" Dagon looked surprised, his dark gray eyes assessing.

"Do you like me?" she asked boldly.

"I have always liked you, from the first time that we met. I suppose you don't remember the first time we met, do you?"

Stella frantically searched her memory. "Actually, I don't."

"It was in the parking lot; you stole my parking place."

"I, what?" her voice rose indignantly. "I've never stolen a parking place in my life."

Dagon's eyebrows went up. "And, I suppose you've never told a lie either. September 20, 8:00 a.m., the space lab."

Stella searched her mind; with a rush it all came back.

It had been one of those Indian Summer days. The air was so sharp and clear in the morning that you could see your breath. She had been driving quickly, running through a yellow light trying to make it to her 8:00 appointment with Professor Schneider at the space lab. That day was to begin the first phase of her flight training for the Vulcan mission, and she didn't want to be late.

"Oh, shoot," she swore under her breath, "The parking lot's full. I'll have to walk for blocks if I can't find a space here," she fussed, managing to carefully check her lipstick in the mirror and gather papers together with a free hand while driving slowly around the lot.

Her eyes lit up. *A spot*, her mind registered gleefully.

Quickly calculating, she decided her Mini would just barely fit in the narrow slot.

Gulping down coffee and competently swinging the wheel a sharp right, she squeezed into the space. She had slipped off shoes, changed them within seconds of parking, clutched her bag and checked her hair one last time.

"Oh, shit, there was someone waiting for this spot," she realized with a glance at the dark blue motorcycle. The driver, a man, didn't swear or flip her off as most city dwellers would. Instead, he simply looked at her steadily. He was wearing blues, and a tie, a uniform showing rank at NASA. Dark sunglasses made him seem mysterious. Stella just stood there not quite knowing what to do. However, he seemed resolved and with a little wave and a check at his watch he drove by, still holding her gaze. In fact, she remembered now, they had both found it hard to look away.

She shrugged, mouthing the word, "Sorry," as she got gracefully out of the car, straightened her pencil thin skirt and walked away with a snappy, quick stride.

A wave of momentary guilt passed over her. Maybe I should have let him have the spot, she thought. Too late now. Damn, it's five after. I'm already late.

Ten minutes after her meeting with Schneider had started, Dagon knocked discretely, letting himself quietly in the room.

"Sorry to be late," he nodded to the small group pleasantly, without a word or glance toward her to indicate that she was responsible for his lateness. His cool politeness and guarded manner had immediately put her off.

She had been chagrined to find out that the man she'd insulted was to be her partner in space.

Dagon had never once mentioned by word or deed that he was upset. Within days of the incident, she had forgotten about it.

Evidently, however, he hadn't forgotten because it was coming up almost two years later.

"When I saw you maneuvering your car with one hand, while managing to have breakfast, get dressed and prepare papers with the other, I developed immediate respect for your multiple talents," Dagon teased.

Stella flushed. "I always figured you hadn't noticed anything about me. You seemed so distant and removed while we were in training."

The embarrassing thing was that she hadn't been beyond *trying* to get his attention. He had seemed immovable and remote most of the time. The training had required the courage to conquer every fear she'd had since childhood. As a result, Stella had put up strong protective guards so she wouldn't seem as vulnerable as she felt most of the time.

"Of course, I was. But, I don't believe in mixing work and play."

"Well, what are you suggesting now? Isn't this work?"

"No, this is three months, soon to be six, in space. It's hard to be on the job all the time."

Stella turned away and walked over to her workstation and her lab specimens, actively ignoring Dagon until he came over and stood quietly behind of her. There was a long pregnant pause as she waited for him to speak.

He put a warm comforting hand on her back. "Forget it, okay? I don't want you to feel uncomfortable. I'm fine with just being friends. We can talk more about it later if you want." Stella just nodded and went back to work.

CHAPTER 4

✠

The ray theory, and fate

The rest of the day went by slowly. A certain tension remained unresolved between them, but they had agreed to a truce. At suppertime, Stella chose to cook again, but she couldn't seem to get into a rhythm of it. The potatoes had already burned and the cabinet and tabletop was a disordered wreck. As a final straw, a glass of water spilled into the main course. She blew her hair out of her eyes, giving up in frustration.

Dagon's deadpan face didn't even register surprise at seeing the mess in front of him. He just started to calmly pick things up, fixing them both a bowl of cereal. Sitting at the table, he studied her carefully.

"You look like you're about to explode."

"You don't have to mention it."

"Eat, it'll make you feel better."

"If I need a parent, I'll ask you."

Dagon held his temper, but took his bowl of cereal out of the kitchen to go eat somewhere else.

After a few moments more of brooding, Stella began to feel contrite. Normally good-natured, her own fickle emotions were making her feel guilty. She followed Dagon into their small sitting room and sat down. Dagon didn't look up or comment. Finally, she cleared her throat. "Sorry, I've been such a grouch."

Dagon said very evenly, "Okay," and kept eating. That was that.

A little later they both got a chance to sit on the couch together. Stella was playing a computer game when Dagon picked up his Link.

"Did you send me a text message?"

"You mean the cartoon?" Stella smiled ready to share some humor.

But, Dagon wasn't laughing. In fact, he looked rather spooked and pale.

Stella tried to peek and couldn't help noticing that his computer files looked extremely organized. She saw most of the file names started with the word Vulcan.

Dagon covered what he was reading with his hand.

Stella couldn't stand secrecy. She wasn't the type to be quiet or hold on to a grudge for long. "What are you studying?" she blurted.

Dagon was the one looking moody *now*.

Stella started feeling impatient as she watched Dagon shut down his computer.

He just shrugged, "It's personal."

For a while they ignored each other. Stella couldn't stand the restrained silence.

Dagon, however, was thinking about the text message. How could he have possibly received a message here in space if Stella didn't send it? Had he accidently gotten it from BOB or had it blipped in from one of his files? While he knew that was improbable, he preferred that possibility to any other.   The text had mentioned the 'celestial sun,' then said "Ask Stella."

Dagon debated for a while, and then decided to ask the question. "I'm thinking about something you said earlier. What is this idea of a 'celestial sun' that the Rosicrucians believed in?"

Stella, still miffed, gave him a quick version then looked back down at her book. "The basic idea is that the sun's original source is the consciousness of god."

"Stella?" Dagon forced her to look at him. "I really do want to hear this, so please, talk."

Reluctantly Stella began again, but was soon warmed up to her normally mercurial speed. "Remember in the 1990's when scientists were bent on trying to discover the origins of the universe? They tried dating all the stars, measuring their apparent movement outward from a central source. Every few years, they would realize that their theories were wrong, that the methods used for dating the ages of the stars and galaxies had been faulty. Mapping a path within 'time' to identify the beginning and possible ending of the universe was their goal. Well, the ancients had it all figured out a long time ago."

Stella shifted uncomfortably again rubbing the back of her neck.

"Sit down in front of me on the floor," Dagon's voice was firm. "I can't stand to see you rubbing your neck when mine hurts like hell too."

Pleasure and heat flowed through her as large warm hands made circular motions, lifting her hair, to lengthen her neck. She leaned back against his legs, groaned and closed her eyes, noticing a little pause before Dagon started again.   Don't stop, please, her inner voice pled. She barely stopped herself from saying it out loud.

Her head dropped farther forward. She moaned again. Dagon stopped suddenly and gave her a friendly pat on her shoulder. "That's enough," he said, looking away from the flushed pleasure and innocent open look in her eyes.

"Wow, that was great. You could do my shoulder if you want. You want me to do you?" Stella got back up and settled on her corner of the couch again.

Dagon voice was firm, "No, that's enough for me."

Stella missed the pained look of control on his face. With contagious enthusiasm she began to expound on the 'celestial sun' again. "You see, to fully understand the universe, you must examine the Ray Theory and see how the creation of life occurs within the mantle of 'Time.'" Aware of Dagon's puzzled expression, she continued on ardently. "Time cycles are simply a sequence of solarized release of energy that interacts with matter to create specific events. For instance, the earth interacts with the sun through days, weeks, and years. The result was the birth of civilization, the evolution of earth."

"Ho, there! Wait a minute. This isn't sounding scientific." Dagon was looking frustrated.

"Switch to a holographic model and it all starts to make sense. Most of science has been limited, as I said before, through reductionist thinking. The Ray Theory was more of a philosophical concept of the Rosicrucians, but, it fits perfectly when viewed as a holographic model today."

Dagon gazed at her perceptively, taking in the flush of her skin and the brightness in her eyes. Formulating thoughts as she spoke, her inventive, inquisitive nature was breathtaking to him. He gestured for her to continue.

"The Vulcan Time Ray is associated with a specific time cycle linked to the transits of Vulcan with our solar system. Have you ever heard of the Ray Theory?"

"Do you mean the current theory that each planet emits a specific ray or radiation of electromagnetic energy based on its composition?"

"Yeah, that vindicates astrology, but, there is more to it than that. Viewed holographically, practically everything in our universe could be a material manifestation of a ray sent from Cosmic Source. The underlying mystery is to find the central source from which all rays are emitted. Unveiling the vertex of the universe would be to enter the mind of the creator."

"The Rosicrucians held that each planet had a ray. They described Vulcan as 'the celestial sun that creates everything of solid nature within the terrestrial world.'[29] They saw 'celestial' as 'coming from heaven,' while terrestrial meant 'born of earth and matter.' They described something called the 'sacred marriage.' Celestial and terrestrial would meet and like male and female these two principles would not only birth all life, but, also, create Zion or heaven on earth. Terrestrial gained its perceived meaning from celestial source. Celestial source found expression in the terrestrial."

"A simple way to say this would be that god would be part of what she/he created. Also, the created would be part of god. Celestial source experiences perception through the manipulation of matter."

"To illustrate this, Dagon, as you read the words on a piece of paper you are actually simply gazing at ink dots on a page. The viewing, reading and understanding all happens as a reflection of your internal process of perception. You've learned over a long period of time how to recognize a letter, register its sound, and connect a meaning or concept to it. You painstakingly learned how to generate sentences, form paragraphs, and then finally share them with others. In this example, the writing is terrestrial matter and you are celestial source. It is your light ray, your radiation of energy, that gives life or meaning to what would otherwise be simple splotches of plant extract on the dried and flattened bark of trees. The fact that other celestial sources formed agreements defining certain orders of reality for the purpose of shared communication makes it possible for me to relay these thoughts to you. But, without the ink, and the paper you would lack the medium for manipulating creative exchange. In this case, it is the connection between your consciousness and matter that acts as the celestial and terrestrial force. You are the celestial or solarized force that creates form."

"Conversely, without the page and the simple splotches of ink you could not have written words. The paper participates in the creation."

"The point is that the principle of terrestrial vs. celestial applies to all radiating waves of energy. All energy, both animate and inanimate, is at times both celestial and terrestrial, energy and matter. This is the key to understanding Vulcan, because Vulcan is a myth about both, a celestial god who fell to earth and became everything created on earth. The whole system is networked, interdependent, and interconnected with one change affecting the whole, as well as with everyone changing roles and faces."

Dagon blinked hard. He imagined he could see the dark hair and brown kohl lined eyes of the priestess of his dreams, her eyes on fire as she stated her convictions with eloquence and power.

"It is through the meeting of masculine and feminine, the earth and heaven, the celestial and terrestrial, thought and emotion, particle and antiparticle, that life, and the meaning in life, finds a pathway for creation."

Dagon couldn't help throwing in. "But, we don't have 'two.' We have only 'one' in the story of Vulcan. One god. Where is his goddess? It doesn't seem right, since in mythology part of the whole problem is that he was married to Venus and she left him to run off with Mars."

"You're right," Stella replied. "Some believe that Vulcan's consort is the earth. True, the earth was originally made up of a huge primordial ocean. Vulcan was fire and the earth was water. But in a perfect world, his mate would have been the feminine Goddess, Venus, who rose from the ocean on a half-shell. This is part of the problem on earth and the reason we haven't been able to be our true God Self, to manifest creation the way that we are capable of. The true male and true female are not united yet."

Dagon continued, making another point. "Also, If you are talking about time cycles programmed by another intelligence, then I feel uncomfortable. Are you saying that when you read a person's astrology chart that their life has been programmed to the movement of the planets or the transit of the moon, that everything that happens to us is in some way fated by celestial source?" queried Dagon.

"I'm saying *we* are celestial source. Life dances to the tune of karma that we have chosen. God's grace keeps the dance going until we see we are *leading* the dance. Without that grace, we would simply disappear, ceasing to exist at all."

"Fate is self-created. The future is visible because we are the source of it. Our life is a movie script being created by the ego until we realize the truth that we are celestial source, the source of the light that is behind the projector. It is this knowledge that liberates mankind from suffering and death. Awakening to the fact that god is in ourselves is called enlightenment. Sure some fate is karma coming from past lives. We've sent an arrow out from a bow. The motion can't be stopped until the karma is completed. However, it is still us who originally shot the arrow. God set it up that way, by making us co-creators, by putting her/himself inside of us."

Stella thought back on how she had first found out about her fate.

When she was fifteen she found an ad in the local paper for astrology readings, surprised when it led her to a polished middle-class neighborhood.

Selena had invited her into a sunny room with a wood floor and light rugs that were strewn around comfortable, overstuffed furniture. Switching on a recorder, she began the reading with very little preamble.

"You have chosen an interesting life. You have decided to be an explorer." Selena had said. You must face your fears, to help bring change in human consciousness. I see you traveling in your future." She looked at Stella's bright eyes, "Space? Yes. There will also be long spiritual journeys, perhaps journeys to other states of consciousness, as well as to places yet undiscovered. I would love it if you contacted me again in 14 years, because most of the outer planets will be transiting your Ascendant with Uranus opposite it. It will be a frightening, yet exciting, time for you. My guess is that you are going to be doing big things then, very big things. You will also be in the public eye, bringing ancient teachings into public awareness."

In retrospect, Stella realized that it was uncanny how the astrologer had hit the nail on the head. How was this possible? Even at fifteen as she had walked away, down that well-clipped sidewalk, with the smell of fresh grass and the bitter sweetness of daffodils wafting in the air, she had been struck by the rightness of it all.

Blinking, Stella snapped out of her reverie, focusing again on Dagon.

"I understand your concerns, Dagon, and I've fought against predetermination, myself. But, contrary to our linear perspective of reality, time is fluid and changing. Ebbing and flowing like the moon or the ocean, it bends in and out, circling back on itself, bringing infinity into the current moment. That is why we can see our future coming."

"Call me old-fashioned if you want, but, I believe in an intelligent 'source' that underlies all of life. Every moment viewed closely enough has the pattern of the creator in it. To us it feels like synchronicity or 'fate.'

Dagon had been watching Stella with fascination. Now, he jumped up from his chair and began pacing back and forth across the room with her while absent-mindedly rubbing his forehead.

"Since we are sharing our philosophical beliefs, I will share mine. I don't really disagree with you; I just think there's more to it."

Stella looked up expectantly, a warm glow filling her. She had never had a conversation with anyone like this before. We are dancing with choreographed words, she thought. It's about time!

Dagon was aware of the heady excitement that he used to feel in the past when he formulated information for a hypothesis, or when he read a new theory in physics. He remembered the smell of chalk in a musty classroom, acrid solutions, the periodic clicking of a monitoring machine, and empty paper cups with coffee rings overflowing from the wastepaper basket. He had always enjoyed research and deep thinking, but he had often been frustrated by the limitations present in scientific or mathematical equations. The philosophy behind the ideas, and their spiritual impact, had been off bounds by unspoken agreement between him and his colleagues at the university. Dagon had longed for a companion to share his ideas with. Now, it looked like he was getting the opportunity.

Church for him had been time spent alone in the cornfields. He had pondered the difference between him and the ant he was watching. How was it that he was conscious of the ant, but the ant, living totally in the moment, was not conscious of him other than as a shadow above him?

Dagon poured himself some tea and began pacing again.

"I believe that 'Self' is the essence, core or heart of what it means to be a human. By this I don't mean ego, mind or emotions. Instead, I mean the part of the self that is connected to Source. To avoid confusion we could call it the 'Higher Self.' "

"Higher self is synonymous with Source. Source is the essential element in higher self, whether in life or death. This first came to me with the death of my father, who instead of being actually 'dead' began to constantly be in my mind. This kept reoccurring for a few months. I would think as a kid, 'Dad, is that *you* or is that *me* thinking it is you.' Then, in high school, I noticed a theory in physics about 'base energy.' According to physics, my father's higher self could be described as 'base energy,' the purest essence of a substance, which cannot be destroyed, which can only be metamorphosed after its distillation into another equal form. In chemistry, to distill something to its most elemental form is to determine its spirit or essence. This essence is, in turn, the underlying motivator of all new forms of action and reproduction. Higher self is then the 'animating' or essential component in 'being alive.' "

Dagon continued, "It's possible that animals have this higher self too. Certainly dolphins, whales, horses, dogs, cats, monkeys, pigs, birds have all proven they are intelligent sentient beings."

Stella couldn't help widening the net. "Well, since sentient means being capable of sensation, perception and consciousness, as a biologist, I would say that all species learn, grow and evolve towards self awareness. For example the red crossbill is a bird that has developed a scissor-like bill to extract conifer seeds from cones; but the tree retaliated by growing bigger cones that are harder to open. My research on plants emitting electrical impulses shows they experience discomfort when disturbed. In India, they believe even insects are reborn, constantly evolving toward the Higher Self."

Stella continued with a question. "But, are we an essence separate from god? Or is god us? Remember the Mayan prophecy? In the sixth age, mankind should learn that 'God is Ourselves.' "

"The question seems mute to me," Dagon said. "If Higher Self is made up of God, we are one and the same. Perhaps, God also has consciousness and personality," Dagon ruminated. "Then, we might be one of God's dreams."

Stella laughed out loud at the idea. "Yeah, a nightmare." Sobering she said with a stab of longing, "Perhaps, God needs us as much as we need him or her."

Dagon took the ball into his court. "Or it's possible the creation and the creator have always been equal partners. You are God. I am a part of you. You are a part of god. God is a part of you. That would mean that there has never been separation from base energy, except in our mind, which has freedom to believe and create whatever we want. The more, however, we stay connected to that Source, the more quickly we live out 'fate,' which is actually the path that would most quickly further our evolution."

Stella's eyes were wide as she followed Dagon's thought process. "Of course," she smiled excitedly, "that accounts for our ability to have choice. Source is the initiating essence, the original seed for what may be created within the mantle of time. The ray is time itself, timing for something to happen as well as the realization of the creative impulse in matter at the appropriate moment. But, we have absolute freedom to create any future we can imagine. We can beam out celestial rays with our thoughts to make instantaneous changes in our physical environment. This gift for creation can be used to radically alter the world that we live in."

Stella continued excitedly, "Should enough people choose to create a world without pain, this world would appear in an instant. Creation does not have to follow the same evolutionary rules of slow karma and Darwinian evolution."

Stella surfaced from their conversation dazed and enchanted, but, then her eyes filled with tears.

"What is it? What are you thinking about?" Dagon noticed her expression as he sat back down on the couch.

"About the destruction that we encounter on earth. I read a story once that touched me deeply about a manta ray."

Dagon felt sympathy for her depression. "Here come back over here and I'll massage the top of your shoulders, too."

Stella gratefully slid down onto the floor again and immediately groaned with pleasure as he began pressing down on the tight muscles on the top of her shoulder and running his thumbs up either side of the top of her spine.

"Unbutton your top button," Dagon said, Then he pulled her shirt down off her shoulders modestly so he could put warm hands on skin. "Now, tell me your story."

Stella groaned with pleasure. "A group of underwater photographers encountered a manta ray that was quite large, 20 feet wide. The gigantic, graceful creature was moving very slowly. A closer look revealed that it had pieces of rope from a fisherman's net trailing from deep slashes and painful wounds. The net was holding it in place so it couldn't swim away. One of the women in the diving crew drifted on top of the manta, carefully pulling the ropes from the manta ray, pushing the torn flesh back together in a brave and loving gesture. Instead of fleeing when it was free of the ropes, the ray carried the amazed woman on its back until she ran out of air. For three days the manta ray gave rides to any interested divers until it finally disappeared into the dark ocean floor. This ray was demonstrating a rare and splendid gesture of goodwill to thank these humans for rescuing it. The sad part is that humans were responsible for the injury in the first place."[30]

Dagon hit a particularly sore part of her shoulder and Stella put her head down, and groaned involuntarily, her eyes glazing over with bliss. Dagon said, "So you feel we are like this manta in bondage to 'power,' or to ropes of our own making."

"Yeah," Stella said, "We are just soul rays instead of manta rays."

Dagon was finished massaging but pulled Stella back against his knees where she sat companionably. "I can see why you're sad," he said. Then continued, "We have to decide if we want nets slashing and dragging us down. We haven't yet freed ourselves from a dominance-submission mentality. We believe that the only way to protect our lives is to control others."

"Right," Stella agreed, "We need liberation as desperately as that manta ray did."

Dagon touched her hair, stroking it softly.

Stella closed her eyes with pleasure, then crossing her legs in lotus posture, she stretched forward. "I once wrote a poem inspired by the many ways that the word ray could be used. Would you like to hear it?" Stella asked.

"Sure," said Dagon. Stella was unaware that behind here Dagon's eyes were dark with passion he was controlling with an iron fist.

Stella moved to the couch reaching for her Link. Dagon closed his eyes, trying not to notice that she hadn't buttoned her shirt back up. She read out loud her poem.

RAYS
Are you a thin, straight beam of light?
Gleaming and ready for manifestation,
Radiating from luminous Soul.
Great rolling waves
With streams of particles
That will become thoughts

Are you the extended arms
of a starfish,
A ray flower bursting into beauty?

Are you grabbing some rays?
As you relax in the sun?
Lying in a moon beam as it
Sends long blue fingers
From a soft lunar crater.

Are you the ray of a crown
spiked and elegant?
With circlet honoring a saintly face?
Or are you exploding
with lethal rays?
Sparks, whirring noises
until you stop
and, start believing again.

A silence descended between them, filled with quiet solace. Dagon reached over putting his arm around Stella's shoulder again in a warm, comforting gesture of acknowledgment.

Stella seemed a bit dazed, she was so relaxed from her backrub and stretching. "How could we be chosen out of thousands to make this trip together? How could we be the first to ever see Vulcan? I try to get my mind around it, but I'm amazed at the series of things that had to happen to get us both here. I think it must be fate. There are other forces at work here."

Dagon decided it was time to seal their partnership with gentle kiss as he pulled her toward him. Stella automatically resisted.

"Resistance fertilizes response," Dagon murmured against her lips.

"What do you mean by that?" Stella asked though it was difficult to keep from grabbing him to deepen the kiss.

"It's the deeper meaning of the Hebrew word for '*lover.*' "[30]

His kiss was gently exploratory while Stella reined in passion she could barely control. The heady feeling made her feel disoriented and dizzy. Fighting the tide, she leaned away. Dagon, pulled back and keeping his arm around her sat back against the cushions. After a moment she put her head against his chest, resting in a comfortable hug while they both calmed down.

"I would still rather we thought about it a bit more before we rush things," Stella said nervously, her voice muffled against his shoulder. Dagon studied her, seeming to see into her effortlessly. "You're right, you need more time. However, I don't think this little question is resolved yet. Do you?"

CHAPTER 5

✠

Sexuality

The next day Dagon looked up from his work and caught Stella looking quickly away, a sheen of tears in her eyes.

"What's the matter?" he said, moving to stand by her to quietly listen.

"Oh, nothing," Stella said making a valiant attempt to cover up her emotional state with a wry smile. "I must have allergies."

"Allergies?" Dagon raised his eyebrows. "In space? Your nose is getting longer. Come on what's really the matter?"

A small smile started to twitch at the corner of Stella's mouth, her heavy feeling of misery lifting. "There is wonderful book called *Women Who Run with the Wolves*. The author says if you meet a man who asks, 'What's wrong,' when you're crying and when you prevaricate saying 'Nothing,' counters with, 'No really, tell me, what's wrong.' Then, marry that man. Because he may be one of the few men who really wants to 'know' you. Expressing feelings is important for women, but we often try to save men from our feelings."

Dagon began looking rather proud of himself.

Stella reflected. "I guess though, it isn't always helpful to talk about things. Sometimes it seems to make me feel worse. The mind runs away like a train without a brake, fueled by my emotions."

"Releasing *deep* emotions is probably necessary," Dagon replied. His own grief weighed on him like a heavy stone. At some point he would have to talk, maybe cry. He didn't know how to do it and wasn't keen on finding out.

"So, what's *really wrong*?" He and Stella both smiled at his reference back to her book.

"It's nothing, I guess," Stella said.

Dagon gazed down at the same the blue/green stone glittering on her finger that he had noticed on her pendant. He reached out to touch it, but Stella stepped back quickly, avoiding the intimate contact.

"Those are interesting stones," Dagon said, raising an eyebrow at her skittishness.

"The ring is an antique. It's made from glass faceted from the ashes left when the volcano Mount St. Helens erupted. My folks grew up near there. After success on my first science project my grandmother, who is a well known Seer, made a ceremony of giving me a ring. I always thought it was magical. Later, it became my Vulcan talisman. I only have a few pieces of jewelry that I wear all of the time, this and my pendant."

"I thought somebody might have given you the ring. Steady boyfriend? Partner?" Dagon asked casually steering the conversation back to her upset feelings.

Stella began to fidget uncomfortably.

"I would rather not talk about it. Relationships are rather personal, don't you think?"

Dagon grimaced, speaking with irony, "I thought things were getting rather personal between us."

Stella flushed. "Oh, really? Yes, well, they have. But, you actually don't know me very well. Also, I practically know nothing about you."

She wasn't quite sure why she felt so self-protective. Well, duh, he had never shared anything personal, she reminded herself.

"Aren't you involved with someone?" she answered his original question with a question.

"Some friends with benefits. Too busy. All of my energy and time has been directed toward getting on this ship. I stay in touch with family and have a few close buddies in Washington, but I'm married to work 70 hours a week."

"So, I answered your question, are you going to answer mine?" Dagon realized he was hedging on all the important stuff and he could tell Stella was sensing this.

Stella was still thinking about the 'friends with benefits' part with irritation. Who was he sleeping with? "Oh, all right," Stella said, "I had a disastrous marriage and divorce when I was 18 and a few other significant relationships that didn't work out. Other then that, I have a great group of close friends, terrific parents, a close brother and a happy life."

"Hmmm, marriage?" Dagon asked.

"I was only 18. Just old enough to make the choice without my parent's permission. I met a computer geek and began an online romance. We decided to meet in Las Vegas. Regret made me sick moments after the ceremony. The honeymoon was even worse. But, I felt too guilty to annul it. Running home to your parents after marrying a 44 year old man doesn't engender much trust from them. Instead, I ran away to school. Rodney wrote bitter cynical emails blaming me. We didn't get divorced for two years, while I hid in my dorm room at school. Dating pretty much sucks with other guys when you're married. Besides, we saw each other a few times, each time turning out to be another lesson on abuse. Then, there was my master's thesis, a short moment of fame and this."

"But, I have a seventeen-year-old cat named Merlin." Stella laughed, "I would say he is my longest relationship. For the past three years, I've become really more comfortable with my women friends."

"Not the cat?" Dagon said with irony. He was definitely more comfortable with cats and dogs then with most women he met, Dagon thought.

"You wouldn't know unless you were a woman," shrugged Stella. Then, her eyes twinkled mischievously, "We can talk freely, and it's like meeting soul to soul. With men everything is just different. Frankly, I'm tired of compromising myself all of the time to get along with them."

She looked up to gauge Dagon's reaction. "Anything wrong with that?" she said.

Dagon shook his head, "Of course not, I can relate. But you never answered my question."

Stella looked startled.

"I'm just saying you haven't told me why you were crying," Dagon said. "Fine, I don't really need to know."

"Oh sorry, I forgot you were a Scorpio, they're all psychologists."

"No, just a keen observer," Dagon smiled lazily, silent for an uncomfortable moment.

She looked away, stalling for time while she busied herself making a cup of coffee, wishing he would go away.

Dagon gazed over at her, sensing her need for solitude. It didn't take long for him to shift his attention to his work. "I'll just finish these graphs," he said, already starting to focus on the work of the day. In passing, he reached out, squeezing her hand. "But, I'll be back."

Sitting down with her steaming cup, Stella felt her misery coming back. Her chin sunk down into her hands.

She remembered all of the feeling of restlessness and rebellion she had suppressed as a teenager as she dove headlong into science projects and research. Getting recognition for her work at such a young age, and skipping her Junior and Senior year to go right into college, meant she had missed out on sports, teenage play, and young romance. She had never really let herself have fun. That was probably why she had ended up married to a sexually violent older man when she was only eighteen.

Even later, after she had started venturing out into the world, seeking out relationships with young men her own age, she had felt lost. She was brainy, offbeat and inquisitive. The men she met seemed overwhelmed by her desire to talk about her wild ideas. Sex was expected from the outset. Yet, how could you be intimate and barely know someone? Since she hadn't experimented when she was younger, and her only sexual experiences had been with an abusive partner, she felt scared as well. Now, she was 30 with a few satisfying affairs that were more fleeting then memorable and a deep loneliness that told her she was missing out on marriage, children and love.

In her late twenties she had begun a practice of meditation. She practiced yoga, did pranayama or breath work to raise chi, as well as had a spiritual practice of devotion. All of this helped with some phobias that she had begun having since childhood.

She had begun steadily dating a couple of different men, each that she had spent over a year with. Something about the relationships had felt incomplete. She was searching for a deeper commitment with someone who matched her. Then, she had met Dagon and found herself putting all her focus on something that was probably impossible, a soul mate. Perhaps it was better not to desire it at all. Ideals of human love always let you down, creating expectations and pressure. But, it also didn't seem right to settle for less then what was possible.

She remembered the first day she had met Dr. Andrew, the thirty-nine old, chemist and Air force Captain who was to complete the space-training program with her. She had felt intense recognition, his tall, rangy body, dark hair and gray eyes somehow familiar.

When he had been introduced as Dr. Dagon Andrew her heart jumped into her throat. Dagon... Dagon that name, it had to be a coincidence. She thought back on the last visit she'd had with a psychic. The woman had laughed saying, "I know it's a cliché about meeting a tall, dark and handsome stranger, but, this time it's the truth. You are going to meet him soon. He has an odd name, an old one that starts with a D. Hmmm, is it Darren? No, it's Dag something."

The psychic had shaken her head, her gold hoops swinging and grinned a big toothy smile. "Wow, you've known him for lifetimes, multiple lifetimes!"

Stella's excitement had died little by little over the two years of training. The more time they spent together, the more withdrawn and isolated she felt. His detached professionalism, and cold, rational approach to everything had shut down her emotions completely.

Now, it was as if a huge dam had broken between them. She could see it in the intense way that Dagon had been gazing at her since yesterday, almost as if he knew their being together was inevitable.

She felt the magnetic pull that was heating up between them sexually and her own panic, as she fought to push her desire and vulnerability back down. I will not lose my ability to be myself around a man again, she thought to herself lifting her shoulders with resolve. Never! Yet, it was still there, this nameless anxiety, afraid of some weakness in her self, of becoming too needy, of being rejected, of not being able to hold his attraction, of her own frustrated passion. Connection weakened her, the tension imploding every extra moment that she was stuck with him on this ship. An old feeling of claustrophobia kept coming back until she just wanted to escape.

What a basket case I am, Stella thought to herself, disgusted. I'm sure he wouldn't have wanted to hear the truth. Put simply. 'What's really the matter' is I've had a crush on him for years while he's been rejecting me without even knowing he was doing it. She set down her coffee cup with a bang, just as Dagon strode purposefully into the room.

"I see your mood has improved," he teased her.

"Stop it!"

"Stop what?"

"Just leave me alone, I will not be handled by you."

A little flush of red was all that showed he was angry. "I'm not sure what you mean by 'handled.' All I did was comment on your mood."

"Well, I don't need anyone to comment on my mood. I know how I feel and am figuring it out myself without your comments or judgment."

"I'm not sure where this got confused, but, I was just trying to tease you out of being angry. Maybe you're right, it is kind of like trying to 'handle' something I'm uncomfortable with."

Stella relented immediately. "I didn't actually expect an apology. I'm sorry too, and impressed that you've agreed not to try to *fix* me."

"I would never even attempt that, Stella ... too dangerous," he pretended to consider.

A giggle escaped her as she fought to keep a straight face.

"The very thought of it has me shaking."

"Okay, you can stop now," Stella relaxed.

Dagon smiled at her, then seeing her cup, began to fill a cup of coffee for himself. Dagon switched off the video, but as he did realized they were out of the range of Base Command's video feed. All of their conversations had been private for the past few days.

"We were talking about sex earlier," he said bluntly, without preamble, as he sat down heavily at the small table.

"I don't remember talking about sex," Stella said.

"Of course, we were. I'm a Scorpio, they don't want to talk about anything else."

"Tch, Tch ... there you go getting dangerous," Stella said, "Okay, Okay, we'll talk about sex."

"Great," Dagon was all business now. "On the other hand. We ought to both be sorting through our gear right now."

"You started this," Stella teased, "Now, I *want* to talk and you can't back out." Stella sat thinking for a minute. Then she began to speak, her voice rising with conviction as she warmed up to the topic.

"I believe sexuality is a primary human need. I mean look, it has become the central focus, either consciously or unconsciously in human life. Romantic separation or union fills the marketplace and permeates our songs, books, art and recreation. Humans are always searching for ways to fill their natural sexual cravings."

Dagon thought about it. "Compelling attraction, dramatic separations, TV soap operas, fantasy and fiction. No question about it, sex rules."

"Yeah, well sexual urges that have become sublimated result in perverts like my ex or religious fundamentalists that sleep with children. Incest is rampant in repressed societies."

"True," agreed Dagon, "But, there is always marriage. This is where things are supposed to get great," he tested her reaction. Dagon found himself wondering what her ex-husband had done to her that could have frightened her so much about sexuality. Someday he would ask her to tell him the story. But not now.

"Maybe," Stella agreed. "But, does it really happen for most people? Many of my married friends are miserable. Most people settle for food, alcohol or TV."

Stella thought for a minute. "On May Eve, the Beltane, a May pole was erected as a phallic symbol in the Middle Ages in Europe. This symbolized the coming fertility of the green month, the month of May. During that night marital rights were set aside, so you could sleep with anyone you wanted too."

"Hmmm, a night of free sex," mused Dagon.

"Yeah, to me it just sounds like a bunch of frustrated married people looking for some freedom. Not, that I don't like the idea of a pagan ritual where sex finally gets to be good rather then evil.

Obviously the goddess was in charge of things. But, I can't imagine sharing my husband with another woman. Children from the union of the horned god, Pan, and the triple goddess became priests or priestesses."

She stopped speaking, surprised at her excitement and the intimate subject of their conversation. She was talking to him like she would to a female friend. This is easy, she thought. Saying things out loud makes it clearer to me.

"It sounds as if you have had some unhappy experiences with sex," Dagon observed, getting right to the heart of it.

"Yes, I guess I have," Stella sat back not wanting to get into it.

Dagon didn't pursue it. But thought about his own sexuality. "Hey, but sex is still a good thing, right? You haven't killed the rabbit have you?"

Stella laughed. "Don't you think love can exist between two people without sex?"

"Sure, I love my mother and sister. But, I want to have *sex* with my partner. Sexual drive is great, it feels good, and it's necessary. And, while I can get it from a friend, I'd rather get it from a partner. What do they call it again? Sensory Deprivation Confinement Trauma, SDCT. On Mars, we called it Sexual Deprivation Celibate Trauma," Dagon laughed.

"Do you feel that both men and women suffer equally from this sexual deprivation you're talking about?" Stella asked.

"What do you think?" countered Dagon.

Stella thought about her biology research. "Personally, I think the female suffers more," Stella offered. "I mean, think about it, every month when a woman ovulates her body prepares her for union. Biologically the female body constantly seeks to attract the male. Her sexual drive gets more intense the older she gets. On the other hand, the masculine drive for sexuality grows from the thrill of pursuit. Men are most sexually active when they are young. It appears a lot of the thrill goes out of the experience when they have 'caught' their partner. Men often need to direct their sexual energy toward the challenges of the world and report being tired after sex with a woman. Also, men sometimes amass sexual partners as a notch on their belt more for ego and power then for sex itself."

"Well, I don't know about other men, but that just doesn't fit for me. I like sex. I always want more of it. I'm not trying to get a notch on my belt. I seem to like it more the older that I get and I'd like a partner who wants the same thing."

Stella blushed. "Hmmm, I guess I'd like to be that free. I'd like sex to make me feel more fired up and energized, more creative, more tantric. I'd like it to feel natural, to be connected to the earth instead of all the taboos."

"Well, I want intimacy, humor and pleasure," Dagon said. "But, I must say, sex is pretty intense for me." Dagon eyes were watchful.

Stella felt her pulse go up, knowing Dagon was reading the excitement in her body. A flush of anger went through her thinking of Dagon having sex with other women.

"I don't share, ever," Stella said firmly. "Monogamy, or nothing!"

Dagon looked fierce. "Neither do I. Never!"

"You are beautiful," Dagon said quietly. He was aware of a heat in his body that felt so intense it was almost unbearable. "I'm feeling very attracted to you right now," he leaned forward in his chair, rubbing her lower lip. "It's too bad one of us has to be on duty at all times. I'm afraid our job is going to make things a little difficult for us," Dagon said evenly.

Stella found herself torn again.

"I didn't talk to you about all of this to start a sexual relationship with you, Dagon. Seriously, it doesn't seem like the right time for this. We both need to concentrate on this mission."

"Well, I was enjoying our conversation. And, as much as I hate to say it, I agree with you. We only have four more days left before landing and a lot of preparation. We'll have plenty of time to spend together when we've set up a base camp on the planet. Just be warned, Stella. I don't see this as not happening between us. It's inevitable. You're not resisting, you're just nervous. And, believe me, I'm scared too. Relationships hurt. Someday, I'll tell you my story too. But, right now I just don't have the same courage that you seem to have."

Stella felt her heart warm up. She reached out and touched his sleeve. Now, that he had agreed to some distance, she didn't want it anymore.

Stella sat back hard in her chair. "To be honest, I was enjoying this exploration too," she admitted. "Let's agree to keep talking, but, no touching for now."

"I don't like rules like that. Let's just agree to let things take their natural course and not rush anything," Dagon countered. "It isn't that I don't enjoy talking. It's that I hate to limit things."

"You really are stubbornly persistent," Stella threw up her hands in a mock gesture of distress. "Well, it's my turn to monitor the flight computers, I'll wake you if anything unusual happens."

"Fine," Dagon agreed, his manner becoming all business as he recorded changes from his last shift in the flight log. The room grew quiet again as each of them concentrated on the task at hand.

This is going to be a long journey from this point forward, Stella thought to herself. Maybe longer then I have ever taken before.

CHAPTER 6

✠

Separation and healing duality

The intimacy of Dagon and Stella's discussion about sexuality had consequences that neither expected. The rest of the evening they studiously avoided each other. Amplified attraction wound them up like a bow strung too tight. Uncomfortable silence stretched as they continued work, changed shifts, and took turns doing chores.

Dagon was first to cross the barrier.

"Stella, what are you doing?" he asked, standing beside her workstation. A pile of books balanced precariously on the edge of her desk. He slid them closer to center.

"I'm observing the response of these amoebae to being in space." She concentrated again, bending over to look through goggles that were telescopic lenses, her back to him.

"Well, what have you found?" Dagon interrupted, not willing to be put off.

"Apparently, there is no 'fear conditioning' here. They are dividing and multiplying at a normal rate. A higher form of animal, even a fruit fly, fish, rat or rabbit, would probably be experiencing some excitement or fear. These guys are missing a brain, so they can't store the emotion in a neural pathway."[31]

"I'm also checking for physiological responses to inertia." Stella's scientific recital and clipped professional tone discouraged further response from Dagon.

She looked longingly at the organisms on her slides, thinking, At least *you* have no worries about tomorrow. You don't know you're in space, hurtling along at thousands of miles an hour heading for a possible crash landing. Turning towards work, she tried to stave off creeping feelings of claustrophobia.

The discovery of new methods for powering ships within the field of inertia had opened up high-speed travel. Fusion meant larger, faster ships in the space program.

The Golden Eagle, however, compared to the rest of the fleet, was small and dated. Close conditions oppressed, hemming her in. Without any feeling of speed, sound or movement, it was like being buried alive.

Stella restlessly pulled off her gloves and began to pace in front of the small work area, part of a large open space that included a flight room, couch and compact kitchen. The conference room and sleeping quarters were separated with doors.

"We need a bigger laboratory," Stella muttered, yanking a container out of the storage cabinet.

"Well, we won't get a new one," Dagon replied irritably.

"We'll never get requisitioned up, even if they *do* finally finish building the Beta III Station. This is driving me crazy." She blew bangs impatiently off her forehead.

"What do you want to do, stop and get off?" Dagon asked with mock gravity.

"*Excuse me!*" she huffed, jerking at the chair stuck between them.

"We *need* a bigger laboratory," Stella repeated, tugging a large container out of the over packed storage cabinet.

"*Well, we won't get one,*" Dagon's slowed his voice in exaggeration.

Stella restrained an unreasonable impulse to punch him in the arm, and forced herself to shift into a favorite memory to induce relaxation.

She was walking around behind her mountain cabin checking out the scraggly columbine plants grown from seed in an odd assortment of containers on her partially glassed-in back porch. A sweater clutched close was her only barrier against the chilly morning breeze. The mountain peaks wore white caps turning a spring green in the sloping valleys. Patches of snow lay in the shade under the pines and around the frozen edges of potholed roads.

It was the smell that relaxed her, the smell of wet leaf mold, a mustiness welcome after a sterile winter. It was the sound that calmed her, the roar of icy water rushing down the Snake River Canyon.

"Have you ever been fishing?" she asked Dagon, absently giving herself up to the easy flow of her thoughts.

"Fishing?" Dagon frowned, Stella's erratic thoughts surprising him. "You mean slime around the edge of a pond, smelly bait, warm beer, sitting in a boat while the mosquitoes have *you* for supper?"

"Actually, I was thinking about fly-fishing on a day after the winter run-off is over, a day when the air is so dry and clear it seems to magnify the mountains. A day when the trees and sagebrush stand out so sharply it almost hurts your eyes to keep looking," Stella said wistfully.

"My memories are more of mugginess and the sound of a million insects," Dagon said.

121

Stella pulled goggles down to her nose and looked over them assessing. "Have you ever caught anything?" Stella persisted.

Dagon sighed, "One, at a place called Catfish Corner."

"The lake was stocked to overflowing. Their motto was, *If you can't catch fish here, then shame on you.*"

Stella chuckled. "And, how did you cook this bottom dwelling beast?"

"For a small fee someone else would clean your fish and put it on ice or fry it up. I just let it go."

"Good," she pushed her goggles up on her head. "I don't have the heart to eat the poor things anymore either. At the time I was in Los Angeles, investigating chemical regents in plants, animals, and humans. We proved that a fresh leaf could emit pulsations similar to the human response of fatigue, excitation, or depression. I have to admit; it was *not* a good time for me to kill a fish or worm. That part already made me feel rather sick. After starting work on electrical energy in plants, I couldn't harm *any* living thing without guilt."

"Well, that's better then thinking we are supposed to be the Great White Hunter, that mankind is supposed to have dominion over animals," Dagon shifted angrily. "Until recently, heroism, love, dignity, and communication were considered only *human* attributes."

Stella registered Dagon's rigid stance, arms crossed over his chest, looking glumly down at his feet.

Suddenly, she softened. "You know, I couldn't *be around* someone who didn't believe this about animals. Thank you."

Dagon felt a flush spread through him of satisfaction. He was making progress.

Dagon walked back over to the flight desk, forcing himself to concentrate on the computer printouts. Measurements showed the rapidly increasing gravitational pull of Vulcan. Incongruent readings sprinkled the report producing odd variables. This was one of the possibilities he had hoped to avoid. Vulcan sat within a spinning belt that pulled gases, meteorites and space debris into it. Spinning faster then the speed of light, the synchron belt was creating a magnetic pull that was starting to affect their spaceship. Coordinates were oscillating, and his numbers changed rapidly, throwing off intricate calculations. They were fast approaching target rendezvous. Now read-outs looked dicey.

"I am seeing the effects of the strong radiation pull of Vulcan on our computers and sensitive electronic equipment. This is nerve-wracking. Perhaps, we are to be the sacrificial lambs of NASA, sent to find out what happens if you mess around with galactic polarization," he said sarcastically.

Stella gasped.

"Dagon, what's wrong with you? I've never heard you talk like this."

"Sorry, but, I feel a bit tense and strung out today. I can tell that you do too."

"Well, my theory is that since the polarization principle is evident in all life forms, we'll just learn more about this planet, not, be destroyed by it," she countered.

Dagon sheepishly caught her eye with a lopsided grin. "Sorry, tell me more about *your* theory, I like it better then mine." Dagon rolled his chair closer to her workstation, sliding down in it. He stuck his feet out.

Stella's tense jaw muscle began to relax as she began talking about one of her favorite subjects, biology.

"Polarization? Hmm, well okay. Cell's multiply by separating along an equilateral axis in male/female pairs and then splitting.[32] DNA strands are composed of a double helix of paired, bonded genes. The basis of the genetic code is formed by plus and minus threads of DNA organized in a polar structure created by the union of male and female germ cells. Can you beat that?" [33]

Dagon sat forward thinking, A game, great! "Sure, on the quantum level, the positron, a positively charged particle, orbits the negatively charge electron."

"Particles have electromagnetic charges." [34]

Stella's glum disposition was beginning to brighten as she tried to think of another example to 'up' his."

"The human body," she yelled it like she was playing charades and had just gotten an answer. Dagon felt a jolt of attraction that buzzed through him. Stella continued enthusiastically, "The human body is electromagnetic, it is a gravitational field surrounded by highly charged electrical energy that is both positive and negative. We do not attain power, we simply *are* power."

Her voice trailed off as she looked up to find Dagon out of his chair, standing in front of her. He rolled her, chair and all, into his body. Stella could feel the immense heat and size of him. Trapped in the chair she could only look up.

"We have to end this build up. It's frying me. We're both pacing like lions in a cage." He looked closer. Stella's skin had taken on a pale sheen and her hands were trembling. He could see that she was having trouble breathing. He pushed the chair back, squatting down to look in her face.

"It's okay, just a bit dizzy, need to breath…can't breathe." She tried to cover up her discomfort, but, even to her own ears, her voice sounded brittle and overly bright.

Her attention shifted self-consciously to her trembling hands. Pulling away quickly, she rolled her chair over to the laboratory station and began fiddling with the vials in their holders.

Dagon realized he'd seen this behavior before. In safety drills Stella had been required to go without oxygen for a few moments while connecting an emergency oxygen mask to his suit. Before the maneuver, she was reticent and shy, while he made an effort to stay detached and professional. The requirement to hold each other, chest-to-chest, in the weightless chamber had proved to be the undoing of both of them. He, to his chagrin, found her nearness arousing. She seemed to find the forced closeness too uncomfortable to bear. Fear escalated when the oxygen was cut off. She had panicked, requiring Dagon to rescue both of them. Afterwards, he decided the best approach was to ignore what had happened, letting her work it out on her own. Stella had a way of masking vulnerability with bravado, needing the fragile shell. On a repeat of the maneuver, she pulled through with flying colors.

An uncomfortable tension stretched in the silence. Stella avoided Dagon's eye as she feigned interest in the slides and vials.

Finally, Dagon broke the ice. "Stella, I think we need to talk," he said as he approached her workstation.

Stella looked up, startled. He could see the panic in her eyes. It disturbed him.

"What's the matter? You have been avoiding me ever since our discussion yesterday. Are you angry at me for some reason?" Dagon asked quietly.

Her face flushed, body trembling with the intensity of her feelings, Stella said, "Just call it a 'conditioned fear response.' I need safer ground. Emotional entanglement means trouble, even talking like this makes me feel vulnerable. I can feel my body starting to freak out. You have to back off."

"Well, what are you afraid of?" Dagon persisted.

"You're doing it now. You're pursuing me and you don't want to take 'no,' for an answer." Stella's voice had an edge to it.

"Well, it's not my intention to hound you. Personally, I feel uncomfortable with this silence between us. We are very aware of each other, or at least I certainly am of you." Dagon reached to grip Stella's hand, but she deftly slipped out of reach. "Talk about galactic polarization, can't you feel electricity between us? I am not ashamed of being attracted to you, but when you respond with fear I feel at a loss. I really don't know what to do. It makes me feel guilty, somehow. Although, I don't think I have done anything that I need to feel guilty about," Dagon said quietly.

Stella sighed, a look of exhaustion and resignation stealing over her face. She turned her chair towards him, slipping her lab coat off.

"I suppose it is unfair to you. Perhaps, you should know that I, well I," she stuttered, "have had panic attacks before and had to conquer some phobias to be here in space." She forced the words out quickly and distastefully, and then seemed relieved by her confession as she continued to tell her story.

"I've had anxiety for as long as I can remember, coming over me when I least expect it."

"Want to talk about it?" Dagon asked, "Sometimes that helps." He pulled his chair up, sitting down.

"Okay," Stella sighed again speaking with a tremulous voice.

"The fear started when I was a child. I have always had claustrophobia, but it got worse for a while after my ill-fated marriage. Sometimes I'd get anxious if I had to ride a plane or sit in a dentist chair or sit in a middle row at a concert. Believe me, I've come a long way in order to take this trip in such confined quarters."

"Now, with you moving in more intimately, I feel confused again. I'm just not sure if I have my own will when I'm in a

126

relationship or if I'll give it away like I've done before. It takes a lot of trust because I secretly fear I'm going to be annihilated anyway. Believe me, I've been working on it and praying about it for a long time. My best cure has been to empty my mind and stay in the moment. When we are together I think I also have to remember that it is excitement building between us not fear. They kind of feel the same to me." Even, as she talked she had calmed down. "Thanks, Dagon this seems to be helping me. I almost never have full blown panic attacks any more."

Dagon nodded his head listening quietly.

"The other problem for me is being distrustful of men." Stella sat quietly for a moment gathering her thoughts.

"There is something else we haven't talked about. Remember how we talked about Vulcan's missing wife? Well, Vulcan had a bitter hatred of his mother and his wife, for good cause. He was rejected and abandoned by his mother. His wife ridiculed him and was unfaithful. Vulcan made himself a laughing stock by pointing out her unfaithfulness to all the other gods in Olympus in a rather violent way. She finally left him. Vulcan had been granted marriage to Venus, the goddess who represents love, beauty and the feminine, but, was unable to hold her love. She seemed to hate him."[35]

Dagon began to look decidedly uncomfortable with the course of the conversation.

"In other words, it's also a story of the war between the sexes. The way that male/female energies *don't* mesh, the energy in the polarization that pushes them apart because of their differences. It is a story of pain, rage, violence and separation. I've always been very sensitive to this antagonism."

Stella continued, "Are you sure you really want to hear this?"

Dagon nodded carefully pulled his chair a little closer, wondering what was coming.

"Look, I'll start at the beginning, I mean the very literal beginning," she said with emphasis.

"My mother's name was Lilith so I learned *her* story early on. Lilith was the first wife of Adam before Eve. God threw her out of heaven for refusing to lie beneath Adam when making love. She wanted to be on top." Stella smiled at Dagon's amazed expression. "Lilith became an oversexed demon who stole semen from men walking alone in the dark. Amulets protected women in childbirth from her in many Jewish households. I personally think since Eve was eventually going to get a bum rap for tempting Adam with an apple, it's a good thing Lilith didn't stick around the garden."

She saw Dagon chuckle as he listened with full attention.

"For a while I studied creation myths, trying to understand and explain away this seeming hatred of women in the Bible. Since Stella Maris is another name for the Virgin Mary, I was angry to find her a docile, feminine, perfect goddess who had given birth without even having sex. Catholics made her Queen of Heaven, but her power was veiled."

Dagon nodded. "I've speculated about that too. Religion hasn't caught up with societal norms. In the space program men and women are treated with absolute equality."

Stella lifted her eyebrows like she didn't believe him, going on. "When I was doing my research, I got pretty sick of all of the men in my life: my department head was egotistical, my buddy, selfish, my employer, narrow minded and my research partner, power hungry. Like a game of 'king of the mountain,' they were playing, 'I win, and you lose.' Compromise wasn't considered winning. I went into traditional psychotherapy to work it out."

"I ended up talking about my bizarre marriage to a dominating and perverted man when I was only 18. He locked me in a hotel room once and tied me up. I escaped when a maid let herself into the room. I didn't call the police, even though I had been raped and tortured, because I felt too humiliated and ashamed. My parents still don't know the whole story. But, even telling all the details to a therapist didn't make the panic go away."

Dagon sat forward with a tight look of rage on his face. Stella noticed that his hand was closed in a fist. It comforted her that Dagon wanted to defend her.

Meanwhile, Dagon was thinking he wanted to kill the guy for hurting her and noticed it was mixed with anger that Stella had married someone like that as a teenager. The jealousy surprised him and he sat back and made himself get it under control.

"My psychic advisor suggested I try past life regression to figure out why I was so prone to panic attacks. I was finally ready."

"By the time I went in for the regression, I was so altered, I practically slipped into a self-induced trance during the interview. It was easy; I just closed my eyes intending to go into the past. Suddenly, I found myself spinning backwards, like watching a movie being run in reverse."

"I remembered in excruciating detail being brought before a tribunal, accused of witchcraft, tied up in a bag and drowned. Some day if you want, I'll tell you the story in detail."

"Past lives?" Dagon paled a bit.

"Yes," Stella choked out, "A miserable, past life."

Stella swallowed convulsively, tears welling up. "This lifetime I have spent time trying to understand how such a travesty could happen to me or the millions of women burned at the stake, persecuted, bartered like slaves, or sold for marriage alliances. I have also had to deal with panic, claustrophobia and distrust."

Dagon rolled his chair forward and squeezed Stella's hand sympathetically. She sighed, enjoying the warm comfort. "Also, I'm sad, really sad, for all those men that committed travesties against their mothers, daughters and wives in the 'name of god.' They lost their souls in the process."

Stella looked up to judge Dagon's interest,

"I thought going back to the beginning creation stories would help me reconcile this. Do you want me to go on?"

"Sure," Dagon said.

Stella flushed with pleasure.

"First, I looked at Genesis and the Bible. The biblical Genesis story of the creation of Adam and Eve, on a surface examination, appears a decidedly sexist account of the fall of mankind from heavenly grace. Eve is pictured as a flaw in the heavenly purpose, an unexpected mistake. She leads Adam to his death by following the Serpent's advice and picking the fruit of the tree of knowledge of good and evil."

Dagon sat forward, listening carefully.

"But, perhaps this simply reveals dualistic philosophy embedded deep within Hebrew culture. It allegorically portrays a long held belief in the fallibility of the feminine principal or the evil inherent within physical matter. It reflects the philosophic belief of the Hebrews that mankind was originally spirit and lost power by descending into the dense, limited world of matter. His fall from spirit to dense matter is synonymous with partaking of knowledge of good and evil. This dualistic philosophy describes the masculine principle associated with heaven and the goal of enlightenment. The feminine principle, or the earth, is associated with evil."

"Hmmm," Dagon said. "So, the feminine was, as the Old Testament says, 'unclean' from that time forward."

"Yeah, either that or subverted into the third Godhead, the Holy Spirit."

Stella went on, "It amazed me to read a similar story of shame, and sin in the mythology of Vulcan. You see Vulcan catches the god, Mars, and goddess, Venus, in an illicit sexual tryst. Here, let me read you something." Stella got up and went to her locker to pull out her Link. She cleared her throat and began reading from *Ovid's Metamorphoses*:

> The sun's loves we will relate. This god was first, 'tis said to see the shame of Mars and Venus; this god sees all things first. Shocked at the sight, he revealed her sin to the goddess' husband, Vulcan, Juno's son, and where it was committed. Then, Vulcan's mind reeled and the work upon which he was engaged fell from his hands. Straightway he fashioned a net of fine links of bronze, so thin that they would escape detection of the eye. Not the finest threads of wood would surpass that work; no not the web which the spider lets down from the ceiling beam. He made the web in such a way that it would yield to the slightest touch, the least movement, and then he spread it deftly over the couch. Now when the goddess and her paramour had come thither, by the husband's art and by the net so cunningly prepared they were both caught and held fast in each other's arms. Straightway Vulcan, the Lemnian, opened wide the ivory doors and let in the other gods. There lay the two in chains disgracefully, and someone of the merry gods prayed that he might be so disgraced. The gods laughed, and for a long time this story was the talk of heaven.[36]

Stella caught Dagon's eye. "It's an incredible story, isn't it? In a nutshell, Venus rejects Vulcan, the imperfect male. His rage makes him a cunning agent for revenge. Fashioning an invisible network or grid, he binds Venus and Mars together permanently in a web of shame. What blows me away is the symbolism. Venus represents here the whole female race, Mars is the whole male race!"

"It almost sounds like a soap opera the way it reads, especially ending with the phrase 'they were the talk of heaven,'" Dagon chuckled.

Stella laughed. "True, a lot of the stories of the Olympian gods and goddesses are like that, dramas."

Stella picked up her Link off her workstation desk and read:

> The Pythagoreans saw Mars as the body, which sustains lifeblood, and Venus as the soul, which seizes love in its corporeal envelope, and Vulcan as the demiurge that links body and soul. [37]

Dagon looked confused.

Stella broke it down for him. "The Pythagoreans were Greek philosophers who believed in the transmigration of souls. They were trying to understand how to link Mars and Venus and imagined Vulcan would be the Demiurge or creator god that could do this."

"The joining of the male and female energies should be a story of blissful union not grief. Like Adam and Eve, Mars and Venus are locked into a shameful path. Vulcan acts in a dominating and cruel fashion to punish them both. He abuses because he was abused and rejected by his own parents. Zeus and Hera's inability to love unconditionally resulted in duality, good/evil, light and dark."

"It is not surprising that the biblical story of Adam and Eve has had an incredible resonance, influencing mankind through history. Likewise, the story of Vulcan surprising Mars and Venus in their sinful betrayal has inspired many paintings, tapestries, and sculptures over the centuries, perhaps because of the dramatic tension of the plot, the pull of retribution, humor and outrage. Like you say, just like a modern day soap opera."

Dagon was looking discouraged. "We have been talking almost non-stop about *fusion* being the story of Vulcan. It's hard to switch focus and see it as a story of separation and heart break."

"Yet, it is." Stella said. "I wish that weren't the case."

They both sat quietly together, thinking.

Dagon said, "Well it's both. Opposites attract and opposites repel. Here, let's move over to the couch." Stella got up from her chair and sat down on the comfortable cushions with a sigh. Dagon sat down close to Stella and she realized she didn't feel uncomfortable or nervous anymore. The fear was gone. Instead, she noticed it felt companionable and safe. Stella leaned her head back against the big cushions and tucked feet up under her.

She said, "In ancient Egypt the god/goddess ruled equally. Ptah wasn't competitive or aggressive; he was a builder and architect. Sekhmet wasn't evil darkness; she was the dark womb of the universe that gave birth to all life. They were considered to be different, but, each equally okay."

"Hmmm," Dagon commented. "I think androgyny and equality is the accepted norm in our society now, but, you're right, a deep underlying tension still exists."

"There is an amazing pen and ink drawing by *Parmigianino* from 1503 that conveys Venus and Mars linked in the swirl of the net. It is in Washington at the museum.[38] You'll have to see it in person some day." She pulled her Link out of her lab jacket pocket and searched for the photo for Dagon to see. She leaned into Dagon companionably so they could both look at the picture together. "I've never noticed this before," she said, "The caption under it reads,

'Mars aggressive masculinity pulls against Venus's rounded softness as a visible psychic force through the artists' eyes.' "[39]

Dagon laughed as he bumped shoulders with Stella. "Well she looks pretty attractive in that photo."

Stella hit Dagon's arm, teasingly.

"In most of paintings, Venus is drawn as nonchalant, Mars as amused, and all the other gods as making fun of Vulcan. Sadly, Vulcan is pictured alone with his grief, his craft, and his craftiness.

Here let me read this to you." Stella picked up her Link again.

Homer recounts in the Odyssey that Vulcan gives out a terrible cry, saying 'Aphrodite loves ruinous Aries because he is handsome and goes sound on his feet, while I am misshapen from birth, and for this I hold no other responsible, but, my own father and mother, and I wish they never had got me.'[40]

"Doesn't that break your heart? He needed unconditional love. Love could be the answer for everyone. Like that net that Vulcan cast over Venus and Mars, unseen webs of energy, finer than a spider's web, invisible to the naked eye connect men and women nonverbally, and ultimately telepathically. This net or web is what needs healing. We need love."

Dagon was looking a bit done in. "I can see that you're right. I have just felt that we are farther along then all this now. I mean this artwork is from the early 1500's. A lot has changed since then."

"Yes, I agree that it has, but a lot is still the same too," Stella said. "Mars and Venus had a daughter that they named Harmonia. Perhaps, the answer is that story too."

Dagon started to think out loud. "Well, personally I feel for Vulcan. You think women have gotten the bum rap. But, just think about it from a man's point of view." Dagon got up and dragged his chair over so he could put his feet up as he lay back on the cushions. "We compete because survival of the fittest says *losers* die. A wounded, crippled or weak male will lose his position and be rejected. For men you either win or lose. We didn't get a choice about this, we were just born with those hormones."

"Just watch any guy during a football game and you know what losing really means. Your team may have played great, even gotten into the super bowl, the score can be as close as one point, but the loser still walks off the field shamed."

Dagon thought for a moment. "I have some really clear memories of being 'initiated' so to speak into manhood. Once was in our cornfield. The tractor ran over the back legs of a rabbit, but it was still alive. My sisters just put closed their eyes, unable to look. But, my father gave me a shovel and told me to go over and kill it, to put it out of its misery. I had to be brave enough to do that because I knew it was the right thing. But, the shovel didn't kill it right away. I had to strike it repeatedly finally with a rock while it jerked and twitched. I felt sick and dreamed about it for a couple of days."

"I remember another time that my father asked me to take the back wheel off the tractor so we could take it to town for some air. My other younger brothers had already tried to get the lug nuts loose to no avail. They had slunk away ashamed. It was up to me to do it. I really had no choice. I was ten years old, the oldest. But, even my younger sister was stronger then me. I didn't know how to use tools or the right tool to use. I worked on it for hours. My finger and knuckles were bleeding. It got dark. I stayed in the barn, determined. I got it off. Nobody said thanks, or noticed. It was just expected of me."

"That's when I knew that as a boy I couldn't give up. If I did, I failed. Fighting got me out of a poor family in the heartlands to college, into the Air force, through a war and eventually into the space program at NASA. I did the hard thing. That was my job as a man. During the war I did what I had to do. I don't talk about it, because I can't change it and it's better not to whine."

Stella nodded listening sympathetically.

"What about your father?"

"Not a good story. Let's just say he wanted to have creative freedom. One day he just gave up and ended up dead in a ravine with a bottle of whiskey beside him."

"Oh, no!" Stella said catching Dagon's hand.

He pulled it away not seeming to want any emotional attention, then said rather gruffly, "That's just the way that it was."

"Yet," Dagon said, "If I'm remembering our other conversation correctly, you said there was a possible solution in the mythology of Vulcan. Vulcan is rejected as masculine because he was born crippled. Because of that, he ends up searching for his more feminine nature, the side of himself that is artistic and passionately creative. Liberated, he becomes one of the most powerful God's in the pantheon, the God of Fire and Thunder."

Stella nodded, "Yes, that's right." Stella was amazed that Dagon had remembered what she had said almost word for word. "However, the story ends unfinished. He still yearns for Venus and the battle between the sexes continues. He is yearning for love."

Dagon was feeling decidedly uncomfortable. He was remembering his own mother. It was a complicated relationship.

Dagon said, "It seems unfair to blame men for always 'dominating' in our patriarchal culture. In your account of 'biological roots' it is females who shun weaknesses. Sociologists have proven that women choose men based on evidence of testosterone: a square jaw, muscle mass, body hair, a deep voice.

Then, they rate attraction based on how successful that man is. Men are much less discriminating. They would be happy with almost any woman as long as she ovulates. This doesn't *allow* men to develop the more vulnerable side of their natures."

"You're right," Stella said. "Men need freedom as much as women. They need ceremony, spiritual union, to lose themselves in something bigger, and to give up constantly fighting."

Stella went on, "We need to search for a better way to distribute power. In Egyptian times, under the worship of Isis, men and women had equal powers. In the *Tablet of Bembine*, an ancient artifact depicting the worship of Isis, each panel alternatively shows a man serving a woman with a woman serving a man. In the center of the balanced distribution of power is the female goddess, Isis, residing over all." [41]

Stella and Dagon sat quietly for a while pondering the question.

Stella spoke up first. "I keep going back in my mind to that original genesis story of Adam and Eve. Perhaps, we could experience more equality for both men and women if there was a different interpretation of Genesis."

Dagon thought about it. "Base energy always includes matter and energy, the masculine and feminine. God created in his/her image by creating Adam and Eve as a pair."

"Also," Stella continued with some excitement, "The word Adam or 'Adm' signifies a species or race not an individual. It is symbolic of an androgynous being." [42]

"Besides," Stella added, "The serpent and the apple are both ancient symbols of immortality and wisdom within the religion of the goddess. Adam taking the apple symbolized partaking of wisdom. Humankind gained conscious reasoning power and free will."

"So", threw in Dagon, "God might have wanted co-creators, males and females with free will. In that case Eve was doing Adam a favor."

"Yeah," Stella said, laughing.

"Also," Stella continued, "Women are the wise old crones who aren't afraid of death. There are tons of fairy tales that seem to include an old witch and an apple. To the feminine, spirituality requires the union of the cycles of both life and death."

Dagon added, "Besides, Adam had the courage to take the apple."

They both sat there quietly for a moment again thinking.

Stella was the first to speak, "If we could go back to the stories *before* the Genesis story we would be better off," Stella said. "Ancient civilization venerated both the male and the female, the god and the goddess. The goddess was the earth, the natural, temporal and earthly cycles. The male god was the Lord of light who embodied all things transcendent and immortal. Heaven and earth were equal and both okay."

"Well, it does seem that the Bible has put a rather negative swing on it. The original pagan stories sound much more egalitarian and connected to natural cycles," Dagon said, and then continued.

"Yet, change is slowly happening within Christianity too. In most churches women can be priests or ministers now. The Catholic Church brought Mary back as Queen of Heaven in 2021, making her Co-Redemtrix with Christ, placing the goddess back in her proper place within the Eucharist."

"Yes, that was an amazing move on the part of the Marions in the church. Were you raised Catholic?"

"My mother was," Dagon said.

"My mother was a New-Ager," Stella swung her necklace in circles as she talked. "She thinks we change because of timing of events on earth. For example she remembers the death of Princess Diana of Wales and Mother Theresa in August of 1997. This was just when the church was first considering a papal decree to make Mary Co-Redemtrix with Christ. It's her theory that the collective consciousness of man was confronted with deep grief for the three aspects of the goddess: Diana, the princess, Mother Theresa, the crone and Mary, the mother. We were longing for our mother. Fortunately, even through the Dark Ages, the Hindus had a whole Pantheon of goddesses to keep the ancient dance of tantric bliss alive."

Dagon thought about his mother. Had she ever been free from her work ethic and guilt? He couldn't even imagine her dancing. Maybe that had been the problem between his parents. Had his father ever found his spiritual calling or truth, his own age of enlightenment? Yet, Stella seemed to have experienced a completely different life with her own parents. It was nice to think that this was possible.

Stella appeared to read his mind as she began looking up a quote she kept in her journal.

"In the late 1980's, a renewal to embrace the goddess washed over society. One lovely writer and speaker about the subject was a Jungian analyst, *Marion Woodman*. She observed in many analysands a similar archetypal dream surfacing. It was of the Black Madonna, a woman who called the dreamer back into truth with dispassionate clarity. Marion knew that for the world to be saved it was important for both men and women to love the Black Madonna, the goddess, again. Woodman says,"

Not until we recognize the Divine Immanence, the light of the goddess in matter, can we hope to establish a balance, a reconnection with our own deepest nature that can root us in a world of meaning and imagination. Perhaps, we will have to face the darkness, walk out on the moor, alone at nightfall, or dive to the bottom of the sea before the old ossified ego boundaries can be shattered to make room for the dance. [43]

Stella's eyes misted over as a single tear rolled down her cheek. She hastily brushed it away. "When my mother read this to me, she cried," Stella remembered. "We were sitting at the kitchen table at night after dad had gone to bed. She read it to me and cried."

"Well, it sounds like your mother had a lot of freedom in her life. She was crying for women like my mother, who didn't have that. Hey, it's nice to know that someone was," Dagon said.

"Dagon," Stella rubbed against his shoulder with hers affectionately. "I like this part of you, the part that wants all men and women to have liberty and equality, the part that is so soft hearted. The world has changed so much in the past thousand years, even since our mothers were children. We have a chance to do it differently now."

Eyes welling with tears, Stella went on. "Yet, I can't seem to release my fear long enough to feel playful, to find the rhythm of this 'dance.' I can't seem to find the balance in myself. It is as if this imbalance is deeply engrained in my own neural pathways."

She went on, "And, has it really changed on earth? The earth is experiencing our rage and frustration as we throw infantile tantrums, asking for her to provide all of our nurturance and support without our response as adults to give something back to her. She is Maya, the feminine, our mother, and we are still raping her. Actually, what really makes me sick is we are taking the same philosophy to the planet Vulcan. This is a mission to harvest the marketable resources of this planet. It is a mission driven by the monetary goals of a huge corporation and we're simply pawns in their game."

Stella looked up with curiosity into Dagon's serious face. "Tell me, why did you want to go to Vulcan?"

Dagon looked thoughtful for a moment, "When we first began to dream of travel to planets in our solar system," Dagon said, "I was just a kid with an amateur telescope. I was fascinated that scientists had been able to locate microbes called extremophiles that seemed to thrive in seemingly impossible conditions. I couldn't believe that they could live where there was no oxygen, at temperatures above boiling, and at pressures greater than 500 atmospheres. It seemed that, with only a few necessary ingredients, life met any challenge in order to live. When they found extremophiles in meteorites from Mars and saw hints of primitive life on that planet, space travel became a kind of obsession for me. I was lucky to be able to go to college on a scholarship. Since my goal was the space program, I had to serve in the Air force, but, I kept my eye on the ball and eventually made it."

"You sound like one of those extremophiles," Stella said.

"Maybe in a way," Dagon shrugged.

Dagon continued, "My father had a little model of our solar system that he kept in the basement. I remember he had stuck a little flag on the planet Mars. Maybe it was for him, but, when they landed the *Habitation Module,* I volunteered to spend a couple years on the red planet."

He shrugged expressively, "I guess that's why I'm here. Our discoveries can accelerate scientific knowledge, find new medical cures, and strengthen our earth's natural defenses. I suppose I thrive on building a future using these new resources. I want to help the earth survive, just like those extremophile's survived."

"Hmm," Stella said. "I didn't know you spent two years on Mars. That's quite a stint. How long did you serve in the Long War?"

"Only four years. I was in active service for three and a half of those years before I took a laser to my upper thigh and had to spend six months in recovery."

"You don't limp or anything?"

"No, luckily I had complete recovery. It put me in a desk job coordinating some of the operations."

Stella sat back in the chair. "There is so much that I don't know about you, tell me something else I don't know."

Dagon laughed. "I had a collection of model spaceships as a kid. Let's see in 1960 we started trying to contact Mars, in 1964 we had our first successful flyby, in 1975 the U.S. *Viking* had its first soft landing, in 1996 the first U.S. *KY Land Transporter* and robotics probes landed on Mars. When we colonized it in 2022, creating *Alpha I, II and III* as a base for other missions, I bought those models and gave the whole set my youngest sister's kid."

Stella giggled, so Dagon went on entertaining her.

"From 1960 to 1996 there were no less than 28 attempts to explore Mars in the space program."

"It sounds like your reciting football statistics," Stella laughed, "You really *were* obsessed."

"I hear that's another trait of Scorpios."

"Hah, I knew you'd been reading your horoscope. Everybody does!"

Dagon switched back to their old topic. "I really think in the last century relationships between men and women have begun to change radically. Space exploration has made us more androgynous. Look at us," he gazed down at his gray and blue uniform. "We're both dressed to de-emphasize our sex on the Mars colony. There are an equal numbers of men and women, manning the greenhouses, drilling for water and living in the hab modules. Every man and woman is equipped with tool kits, analysis gear, and the same silver suits. Hell, it's difficult to even tell a man from a woman."

"In space, we left behind the old roles. And, look," he paused to look deep into Stella's eyes, "We went to Mars, your mythological 'masculine' planet to do it."

"You're right," said Stella, "Mars was an experiment to test our power to build new communities." She sighed as Dagon leaned back on the couch cushions and settled her against his broad chest. She realized all her nervousness and fear was completely gone.

She smiled impishly, eyes lighting up. "But, look at this. You put your arm around me. I'm submitting."

"Well, it's physically more comfortable. I'm taller. That's part of our differences and I, for one, think it's a nice difference," Dagon said.

Stella looked up, feeling strangely lethargic as Dagon brought his lips close to hers.

There was a soft exchange of breath as he murmured against her lips, "Yes, nice." Stella groaned, grabbing his face for a deeper kiss. Teasing, he moved his lips to the column of her throat.

Stella felt as if her bones were melting, her whole body was burning up as he ran his hands up and down her spine, lifting her to pull her under him full length on the couch.

Dagon started to slide her top up, his hands spanning her ribs.

Stella was having a hard time breathing. She wrapped her legs around his, gasping out raggedly, "A condom, did you bring one?"

"What?" Dagon surfaced looking dazed, lifting himself up by his arms to look down at her.

"The pill? Right?"

"No, I ... Oh, shit!"

Dagon groaned and sat up, running his hands through his hair.

"I was pissed off at Base Command for trying to engineer some kind of romance between the two of us," Dagon said.

"Me too. We'll be in space together for three months!" Stella cried with frustration. "I can't believe this." Stella pulled her top down where the bare skin at her midriff was showing. "If we run into any problems it might take us even longer to get home," she wailed.

Dagon ground his teeth.

"Rhythm method?" Stella pushed her hair out of her eyes hopefully.

Dagon just groaned, looking at her with astonishment.

"Yeah, you're right, that's a no."

Dagon seemed reluctant to let her go, his feelings mirrored in his dark, intense gaze. Stella returned his possessive look with a smile.

Dagon pulled her back, holding her hand in his examining her palm. Rubbing little circles on her wrist, he kissed it.

Little electric currents set Stella's body on edge again.

Dagon smiled, "I think I might just enjoy this fore-play. And, we can do everything, but..."

Stella squirmed in her seat, hot and cold at the same time.

Just then they heard the signal coming from command. It was time for their evening report then they each had to take night shifts at the flight center.

Somehow the communication had freed them both. A new level of comfort made it easy for Stella to snuggle against Dagon, enjoying his large, warm body. They separated reluctantly, both aware of duties requiring their attention. Yet, Stella found every excuse to touch Dagon.

The next day when she was passing by him in the workstation they rubbed shoulders. Once he sat down behind his computer terminal and she couldn't resist standing behind his chair to run her fingers through his thick dark hair until he groaned, grasping her hands to kiss her palms and pull her into his body.

They said hello and goodbye with soft kisses that often deepened with passionate abandon. Stella felt bliss and an expanded sense of consciousness while they were kissing that surprised them both, and left her limp with relaxation.

"I think I just had a cosmic organism."

Dagon just laughed.

They worked together comfortably, looking up occasionally to smile at each other intimately, forging ahead to accomplish all of the preparations for landing on Vulcan in three days.

CHAPTER 7

✠

Zeitgeist of a planet

During the next day it was necessary to check and double-check all equipment and landing gear.

Stella went through her stock of plants, placing them in special vials that could be oxygenated in case they lost pressure during the landing. Ethno-botanical research rocked in the public media. A world leader protecting the rainforests was popular footage. What the public didn't know was that it was a lucrative business. Scientific harvesting for drugs was funding the investigation of thousands of species and had hit the jackpot with huge breakthroughs in HIV and Alzheimer cures. While 265,000 flowering species graced the earth, what other plant life was possible in the universe and on other planets? The chemical and medicinal value would be enormous should they discover a planet with living organisms.[44]

Upon entering the atmosphere of Vulcan, space probes would be sent out to take soil samples from strategic points on the surface of Vulcan. Mineral compounds and soil samples would be collected and the information relayed back to the National Science Foundation, which encouraged bio-prospecting for pharmaceutical and biotech companies. Unfortunately, even the space program was holding hands with big business interests.

The twenty-five Vulcan probes were thermos-sized, 2.6-pound robotics that could penetrate the surface to the end of a 20-inch cable leaving a wide collar staying at ground surface. They could also relay temperatures, had built-in cameras, spectrometers, and inflatable struts and antennas. Vulcan would be 'bugged' after the mission was completed.

Another kind of 'bugging' was the focus of the second phase of Stella's research. She was commissioned to experiment with insects and cellular amoebae. Bees communicated and were social within a hive. Sensory stimulation and sound affected these behaviors. The small hive and amoebae would be studied in an inflatable greenhouse where Vulcan soil was to be tested for agricultural productivity. Interspace research had a clear agenda. Pioneers colonizing space was the ultimate goal.

To sustain a human colony in space required oxygen. Even a small amount in the atmosphere would be an incredible boon to her work. This, however, was not expected. Both she and Dagon were prepared to live in space suits and to assemble oxygenated environments for the laboratory specimens during the projected seven day stay. A pressurized KY Land Transporter was on board for extended field trips away from camp. In an emergency, this Transporter was sealed to provide life support in case of malfunctions within their spacecraft.

Fortunately, the days of cumbersome space suits were over. New, lightweight, but reliable, gear allowed the body to move and breath comfortably in temperatures as low as 500 below zero. Each of them would carry an instrument package used to measure atmospheric and seismic conditions. This instrument package featured a camera to allow viewers on the Beta III to monitor their activities on Vulcan. Equipped with their geological tool kits and chemical analysis gear, they planned to explore Vulcan, search for fossils and perform detailed surveys of the Vulcan surface. Tomorrow, it would be Stella's job to check every inch of their space gear. Any flaws there might prove fatal.

Rigorous training had prepared them for this moment. It included months of in-flight simulation, equipment rehearsal and weightless chambers. Leaving the spaceship's artificial gravity environment would be somewhat of a shock, but they were prepared.

Dagon was an old pro at this, having lived on the Mars colony. Cyberspace expertise and an aeronautical background made him comfortable with the complex computer network that was the nervous system of their spacecraft. His background in the Air force was another plus, in case they needed defense. Dagon had spent years as a chemist in doctorate study and had another degree in physics. A Commander on Earth and Mars, this was his first mission as Captain of a spaceship.

Dagon photographed the faint elliptical object that had been detected on their screen the day before. A new galaxy not on their star map yet? A high level of excitement gripped him, making him more dexterous, quickening his movements.

Stella loved watching his concentration as he worked.

Mission control had purposely limited the crew to two people. NASA's motto for the last 5 years was "faster, better and cheaper." A small craft lowered the budget. This, however, required that both Stella and Dagon be competent in all aspects of flight procedure. Dagon was flight Captain. Stella was the mission research biologist. Stella piloted in an emergency. They both hoped that would never have to happen.

Space travel was new to Stella and it had been an especially long and difficult journey. Nameless anxiety grew next to bone deep exhaustion. Teamwork, however, flowed easily, providing some relief to the tension.

The FLIP communication system succeeded because of Stella's natural tenacity, intelligence and a bit of luck. It was her job to patch together the hodge-podge of strategically placed satellites stations back to Mars. Beta III wanted nightly reports and video feed during the day. Vulcan interference reeked havoc as they got closer to target because of the synchron belt and its high radio frequency. While it was impossible to send or receive video feed now, they still were expected to make verbal contact. This, along with her other duties, was keeping her busy.

Fortunately, their mission was not funded by the Strategic Defense Initiative, but by a worldwide organization called Interspace Research that funneled money into NASA. To the negative, however, the Interspace Research Company (IRC) expected not only publicity, but also, bio-prospecting and harvest rights of marketable goods from space. Regulatory controls enacted by the United Federation of Nations on Earth protected the environment of the solar system, but, had not yet been enacted for a planets like Vulcan, that were technically rogue. IRC intended to reap the rewards before this happened.

Stella hated the economic market, which seemed to push their mission, requiring public appearances as well as support of the already existent International Space Station, Beta III. This 2 billion dollar project would have drained NASA without the involvement of private enterprise. Yet, Stella struggled with the daily compromise necessary to maintain a corporate relationship. Corporate rites and rituals sucked the blood out of the NASA command team.

The 'dream team' of the original Alpha III station hung by a thread, only barely warranting Beta III because of their breakthroughs in super-conductivity in space. Beta III had worked hard to get approval for an outreach mission. Outside funding had clinched the deal, but the pressure was on.

Stella mused at the improbability that a planet as large as Vulcan had not been discovered until the last century. A perpendicular orbit pattern hid it from view from astronomers. The dwarf planet Pluto, millions of miles farther away had been discovered almost 75 years earlier. Hundreds of thousands of smaller asteroids between Saturn and Uranus had been named 60 years before Vulcan was found.

It seemed another example of the validity of 'zeitgeist,' or the spirit of the age. A planet does not reveal itself until its time, Stella mused silently. This would be a good topic for the speech she was scheduled to give for the International High School Science Fair, she thought. The speech was to be broadcast by live video feed from space on a large screen mounted in the coliseum after they announced the winner of the fair. They had chosen Stella as speaker because she had won the fair when she was only fourteen. Winning that award had been the beginning of a new life for her that had led to her space career.

Well, Stella thought, if I'm not dead by then, I have to give this speech next month, so I'd better get busy.

Stella began dictating the idea for the speech into her small hand held computer called a Link that she kept with her most of the time.

Chewing on the end of her stylus she spoke while the computer converted it into text. This model Link also read text deductively, asking questions and solving problems. Spoiled with her supercomputer at home, however, Stella didn't use the function much.

She'd limited the upload of games and entertainment on her Link to keep goofing off at a minimum. The problem was that space was boring. Non-stop boring. Silence, no motion, no sound, black space, and endless night, kind of boring. Drive a person crazy, kind of boring. Keeping on track with her Vulcan studies was the only relief she got. She could lose herself, following the trail of the great mystery of Vulcan. To that end, she had downloaded a library of books on Vulcan research and biology. If they needed a supercomputer they could use BOB for more complex thinking.

She hadn't been keeping track of the days. After three months in space, the days all seemed to run together. But, Stella was surprised to see that it was New Year's Day, January 1, 2033. Last year, she'd spent New Year's Eve with her cat in her Washington apartment, recuperating from an especially grueling workout in the gym. This New Years Eve had been spent with Dagon on the couch. She flushed just thinking of some of the things he had been doing to her last night.

Get busy, Stella thought to herself. The speech for the high school science students was calling. She dictated it easily, with almost no edits.

"I'm writing this on our 124th day in space, waiting for our first sighting of Vulcan. Today is New Years Day, a good day to synthesize what we have learned from the past as we decide how to go forward into the future. What an amazing possibility we are facing. Our knowledge and experience has broadened at the same time that new discoveries have become available to mankind. As humankind has looked farther and farther afield, new pathways within our solar system have opened up, new planets been discovered. It strikes me that these planets took on the zeitgeist of man's current state of evolution."

"Pluto was discovered at the same time that atomic fission brought the Plutonian bomb and understanding of the strong binding forces of stored energy around the nucleus of the atom. The discovery of Uranus corresponded with breakthroughs in electricity, electromagnetism, radio waves, and computerization. Neptune appeared with mankind's understanding of the bonding and interconnectedness of all matter and a deep philosophical acceptance of this great truth. Vulcan was the harbinger of an endless power source, the power within galactic polarization. What will mankind know when the Transplutonian planets beyond Pluto are visited?"

"It amazes that it is possible for me to send this video feed from our ship, directly into this award ceremony. Even the smallest cities now own huge telescopes that can see the headlights of a car from 3600 miles away. We are looking farther and farther into space, and further and further into our future. At the same time we plunge to the depths in our study of the microcosm. Will we be able to keep up with our insights, be able to broaden our philosophical horizons as quickly as we discover new worlds?"

"What will we know after this journey to Vulcan is complete?"

"I'm sure I will have become a different person. I'm a different person already. I've turned my own telescopes inward."

"The discovery of the moons of Saturn by the Voyager came at a time when scientists were also in deep exploration of quantum mechanics. The microscope was turned inward to the particles that make up all life. Now, we know that the microcosm is a reflection of our understanding of the macrocosm."

She stopped, chewing on the nub of her stylus, and then continued dictating quickly.

"In the early 1800's, our vision was bound by Saturn, by what we could see with the naked eye. Saturn represented industrialized society, mechanical energy within solidified form, iron wheels turning on metal cogs, assembled through effort and work into an ordered, disciplined system of parts, each part playing a regimented and defined part in making the whole machine work together. Saturn brought the interaction of parts with specific individualized functions."

"Yet, with the advent of the 1900's, a deterministic view of the world had been absorbed into the new world of quantum research. The first experiments with atoms showed that they did not move in set patterns, but, in random ones, which could only be understood in terms of probabilities, putting into question all Saturnian boundaries. The philosophy of randomness in a chaotic universe replaced the deterministic view that matter was a passive substance acted upon by outside forces. We were suddenly into a full-blown Uranian/Aquarian age."

"I was your age, fourteen, when I felt my first conviction that I would someday travel into space. My mother was there at the turn of the millennium ready for a radical shift of consciousness. Here it is three decades later. I wonder how much has been accomplished."

"The manifestation of visions and spiritual ideas, Neptune, is converting to high voltages of power, Uranus. All of this energy is being manifested in earthly ways, represented by Saturn, with the help of the transformational energy of Pluto. We are now resonating to vibrations faster then the speed of light. This is pushing our evolution forward at warp speed."

Stella stopped dictating for a moment. Here, she thought, I'll insert something about what we discover on Vulcan and congratulate the winning project. All I need now is a conclusion.

She thought for a moment then began dictating again.

"It makes me happy to know that when we are ready to take that next evolutionary step that you will be the generation to do it for us. I have been reading your letters and have seen video feed of the great science projects you authored this year. I'm proud of each and every one of you. Study hard. Try to understand the past and carry it with you into a better future. We'll be keeping you informed as we research the surprises that Vulcan has in store for us."

"In the meantime, Love and Peace to you all. Dagon and I want to say, *Have a Good Day from Space*."

She stopped, reading over what she had written. Good enough.

The little catchy phrase, 'Have a Good Day from Space' was how all public video feed from Beta III ended.

Well, thought Stella. I've done my part. Dagon will have to do the next public appearance, assuming we even make it back from Vulcan alive.

She glanced up from her computer journal to find Dagon gazing at her quizzically. He seemed to be listening. She found herself setting down her Link to walk over for a cheerful hug.

"Happy New Year, Dagon."

He looked surprised. Then, she sealed it with a kiss.

CHAPTER 8

✠

Healing light

As Stella put her recorder away she saw the lights come on for their satellite receiver. She pointed at it so that Dagon could see, and turned toward the receiver that was called FLIP, the Fast Light Interspace Phone, to begin a voice interaction.

"FLIP On," Stella gave the unit a voice command and a band of green lights flashed across the face of the box. A faint voice could be heard through high-pitched static.

"Beta III to The Golden Eagle, Beta III to Golden Eagle... Come in Eagle."

"FLIP switch 8"

FLIP followed the vocal instruction and switched on an automatic equalizer to adjust the weak transmission.

"Golden Eagle, here." Stella said.

"Happy New Year from the crew here on Beta III. What do you have to report today?" said the faint, gravely voice of Colonel Greene. A steady rate of transmission was difficult to maintain. Stella looked over at the box again, giving it another voice command. "FLIP over." The receiver on the outside of the ship began to rotate until it was facing the opposite direction. The signal seemed to be steadier, but was still patchy.

"There is a lot of static, Sir. I think our transmission is being interrupted by high frequency radio waves that we have been picking up for the last three days. We are working on it now. As you know, we have lost all video feed," Stella said as she set another button. "FLIP up," additional antennae extended along the outside of the ship.

"I can hear you, but, only marginally. We have our equipment set at its highest range. We have no visual of you. Only voice," Stella said.

"Understood. Now, what do you have to report?" questioned the older man's deep voice. officer

"Sir," Dagon stepped up next to Stella. "We are on course and waiting for sighting of Vulcan."

"Dagon," said the Colonel, "What have you noted from your telescopic photographs?"

"Sir, we have a faint sighting of Xyla24 so we know we are within range of Vulcan now. We have no optic as yet, but, all other readings indicate that we are in the right position for entry into the synchron belt in 81 hours, 36 minutes and 16 seconds."

"Good," said Colonel Greene, "I have the flight doctor here. Pleased report the status of your physical health."

Dagon went first. "Pulse and blood pressure-normal, no sickness, normal appetite and elimination, some difficulty sleeping."

The medic began to question Dagon about his sleep patterns and seemed satisfied when he learned Dagon had only had a few sleep cycles that had been interrupted by strong dreams. Sleep in space was difficult for most astronauts, but, Dagon, to date, had managed to avoid sleep aids.

"And, you, Stella," asked the doctor. "Are you sleeping?"

"Most of the time," Stella hedged.

"What about your general health?"

Stella looked away from Dagon as she spoke. "Pulse and blood pressure high, a low grade fever which is just dropping, some abdominal cramping, difficulty eating the last two meals, but, it is getting better," she replied.

"What is your current blood pressure and pulse?" asked the medic.

Stella placed her fingertips on the pad, switching on that application that read her vital statistics. She kept her body turned away from Dagon's so he couldn't see the results.

"185/133. Pulse, 84."

Why hadn't she told him she had been feeling sick? Dagon frowned, crossing his arms.

"That's high for you. What do you think is wrong?" The doctor asked, his voice faint, but clear, through the speakers.

"Probably, just excitement, I've found that some of the meals here disagree with me. I am starting a simpler diet."

"Please, follow the cleansing diet in the manual. I want to make sure you receive all the nutrients that you need," said the medic. "Also, monitor your blood pressure. If it stays up, start medication #233 at 50 milligrams with a relaxant for tension, then medication #54, 5 milligrams up to 10 maximum as needed. I want a blood pressure reading 3 times per day, and a daily report, if possible."

"Affirmative," Stella said as she looked away from Dagon, discomfited.

Colonel Greene's voice came back on. "Okay, what is the status on fuel and your checks on the condition of the ship?"

Dagon stepped forward and went into a long account of the computer readings and calculations, he had been monitoring.

Stella found herself drifting as they spoke of aero-logistics, whatever the hell that was. She was startled when she heard her name spoken again.

"Yes?" she sputtered.

"Stella, remember to take all breaks allotted, and sleep extra time in the next few days. An entry into Vulcan's gravity field will be hard on both of your bodies. I want you in good shape for it," concluded Colonel Greene.

"Yes, Sir."

"We send our best wishes for the New Year and for a successful and safe mission."

"Thank you, Sir."

"FLIP, out." Stella gave the vocal directive to their system to stop the communication.

"FLIP, off." The row of lights turned off, leaving them alone in space again.

As usual, the sign-off with Beta III made her giggle. Then, homesickness struck. Colonel Greene's voice was their only connection to the Mars outpost. They were millions of miles into space, hurtling through a black void. She pictured Dorothy with her red slippers. "There's no place like home. There's no place like home." She wanted to go back to Kansas, somewhere where her feet would be on solid ground. The days seemed to drag by as her fear and claustrophobia grew stronger. Anxiety was making her feel sick. Suddenly, she felt she just had to talk to a woman, any woman. She looked around desperately, seeing only Dagon.

Dagon's head was down, a fleeting sadness twisting his features. He came to stand by her, drawing himself up into a ramrod straight posture.

"Stella, please tell me when you feel sick," he said in a formal tone. "Your health is of concern to me, in the same way that mine is to you, for the successful accomplishment of this mission."

His sternness was a clear rebuke. Given the frailty of her emotional state, Stella had to bite her lip to keep from crying.

"You're right," she said evenly, turning away to swallow the lump in her throat.

She took a deep breath, hiding her emotions. "I'll keep you informed in the future."

The icy professionalism they used seemed to increase the discomfort between them rather then relieve it.

Dagon let out a long sigh. "I guess I'm disappointed that you didn't trust me enough to let me know you felt sick. Perhaps, I could have helped in some way," he said seriously.

"Sure you could," said Stella sarcastically. "I'm sorry," she apologized immediately. Continuing tremulously after a slight pause, Stella let the dam inside her break. "I'm tense, understandable considering this is my first time in deep space. I'm isolated, stuck," she gestured wildly, "*Flipped out*, and ready to *Flip* everyone *off*."

Dagon began to look alarmed. But, Stella was just warming up.

"There isn't cappuccino, shopping, a girlfriend or a walk. I'm PMSing while I eat crap food and walk around in a place the size of a tin can, without even a bar of chocolate, some new shoes, or a box of condoms! What do you expect? Can't I fall apart, even for a minute?" She watched for a sign of understanding from Dagon.

His face looked resigned saying regretfully, "Yes, we're both under a lot of pressure. It hasn't been my intent to create more by getting involved in a personal way with you. But, what has happened, has happened. If we don't follow some honest path of communication now, the pressure will only get worse."

The hairs on Stella's head stood on end. "What are you *talking about*? I'm not backing out of our relationship. I'm telling you how I *feel*. This is *me*, being *in* a relationship." She practically screeched as her voice rose. "What's with the resignation? Didn't you ever *want* to be with me?"

Dagon backed away from Stella as she walked forward aggressively. He put his hand up to stop her, "I have to admit I was somewhat apprehensive about spending six months alone with a woman in tight quarters, it just seemed like a great way to light a fire that could cause problems from the onset. And, I have had my own things to deal with," he concluded.

A look of such sadness and vulnerability crossed his face that Stella found herself wringing her hands in sympathy. Then, she remembered the first part of his sentence.

"So, what you're really saying is that you've been avoiding me this whole time. For let's see, 2 years and 120 days! And, I have to say that really stinks! You've hurt my feelings and been a jerk!" Stella ran her hand through her hair and began to back away, realizing she might have overdone it a bit.

She tried to lighten up. "So, tell me the truth. You haven't also been hiding a candy bar all this time have you?"

Dagon actually looked startled and Stella couldn't believe it.

"My god, you have."

"*Now*, I want it *now*," she said starting to laugh with glee.

Dagon started rooting around in his locker, coming out with a beat up chocolate bar, but held it behind his back.

"I'll give it to you, but only if you'll do one thing."

"What?" Stella was surprised by the seriousness of his face.

"We are here together by some twist of fate. We're within 80 hours of landing on Vulcan. I have been waiting to do this all of my life. And, somehow I feel like what happens between *us*, including all the great talks we've been having, is part of the journey. So, don't leave me out when you feel sick. I don't think I could handle the guilt."

Stella looked alarmed. "Guilt, what do you mean guilt? Why would you feel that? Because I said you were being jerk? I meant before. *And, you were!*"

Dagon looked away. He had never allowed himself to be so open before. Maybe it would've been better to have just comforted her, he thought to himself. This was new territory. How did you tell someone you'd felt guilty most of your life?

Stella could see that Dagon was really struggling, so she gave in. "Okay, let's do this together." Stella reached for Dagon's hand, gathering her courage. "I have been sick with anxiety. I'll show you how to help me get through this."

Dagon sat down quietly next to Stella, not really sure what to do. "Perhaps, we should just talk about it first," Dagon suggested.

"Okay," began Stella analytically. "I'm a biologist. I know that fear is a conditioned response that forms a neural pathway in the cortex of the brain. Simple smells or other sensory stimulation can turn it on, even when there is no apparent reason to be afraid."

"I have a phobia," she continued in an analytical vein, "A conditioned fear response about tight spaces. Sometimes all I have to do is think about it and the fear begins to take me over and I lose control. What's worse is that I seem to be afraid of being afraid. So, sometimes just the thought of fear sets me off. I didn't tell anyone about it because I didn't want to get booted from the program. You can't imagine the courage it took for me to do this mission."

Dagon looked thoughtful, "Well, if you're afraid of tight spaces, a relationship with me must be making things feel even more closed around you," he said with uncanny perception. "Also being so brainy has probably always taken away your freedom ever since you were a little kid."

"I've never thought about that, but, it's probably true," Stella looked up with amazement.

"It seems to me then, that it's important that you condition your body to a different response when you are in the midst of a situation that brings on the fear," he said, the scientist in him speaking.

"Sure," Stella scoffed, "Easier said than done."

Dagon caught her gaze, squeezing her hand in encouragement. "Don't worry. We all have fear sometimes. Me included. I read a poem once that I memorized from a book called Dune. It went:"

Fear is a little death
Fear is a killer that paralyzes
I will face my fear
I will watch it pass through me
I will turn and watch its path
Until only I remain[45]

"My commander in special services used to yell out, 'Down the rabbit hole' when we were getting ready to do something especially dangerous. I had a chance to think about it in the trenches. 'Fear' *is* the rabbit hole that Alice in Wonderland went down. At the bottom of the long fall was a room full of doors and a key. The correct door to choose is the one that goes *toward* fear instead of away from it. I got to the point that I'd charge forward, just to see what might be on the other side of the door. Hell, *every* experience has a new edge to it."

"Also, when I got tense on an op in the military, I'd use very specific techniques. For example, concentrating on a sound or smell until everything slowed down. Then, if I had to act quickly or make a snap decision, it was like I was seeing everything around me in slow motion. I'd see clearly what to do immediately. It saved my life and the life of others a few times. If that didn't work, I'd walk or sort out my pack to empty out my thoughts."

Stella was looking miserable. "The problem is that here, in this spacecraft, we're missing flowers, Caesar salad, a bathtub, artwork, all the things that draw *my* senses. Work? Our discussions and, eehmm, other things, have been highly stimulating, putting chores on the back burner. I suppose excitement and fear illicit the same physiological responses. It would probably help if we both made sure we had time *alone* to concentrate on work right now."

"You should start doing this right away," Dagon said, taking on the tone of Commander in Chief. "I'll draw up a list of duties for you that must be completed by say..."

Stella interrupted his recital, "Geez Dagon. Stop it! It isn't your job to figure this out and fix me. But, hey," she began to giggle, "Aye, Aye, Captain." she playfully saluted, then got up, moving around restlessly.

"I know what helps me, but, I haven't been doing it," Stella made her confession to Dagon. "For one thing, I need to meditate regularly. Constant chatter is how my wayward mind operates. For example, I'm just sitting at my workstation and my mind goes ballistic. Suddenly, we are landing on Vulcan, but, I'm jettisoned out of the craft or a meteor storm puts us at near zero visibility. My mind buzzes with life and death scenarios and a doom and gloom approach to life. Gratitude helps and meditation helps."

"My favorite meditation technique is to notice your breath as you exhale, especially noticing the place of 'no breath.' Then, bring that silence back in on the inhale. The *Tibetan Book of Living and Dying* says meditation is one breath away."[46]

Stella rubbed her arms then stretched them overhead. Dagon couldn't help noticing how her T-shirt tightened over her small breasts as she made a circle with her arms, clasping them in namaste behind her body.

"I also need to be doing my hatha yoga practice. Without it, I bite my nails, grind my teeth and tense my shoulders. Yoga helps me consciously release tension through awareness, focus and deep breathing. I feel euphoric after I practice. Besides, it builds physical strength and makes my body more balanced and flexible. It's also how I begin meditation."

"Well, why haven't you been practicing?" queried Dagon.

"In my sleeping quarters? I can hardly turn in a circle in there. Our schedules require that someone is always working in our larger living space. I've been embarrassed to practice yoga and meditate in front of you because I thought it would make you feel uncomfortable," Stella admitted.

"So, now we have that unnecessary worry out of the way," Dagon said matter-of-factly. "Do whatever you want to do. It won't bother me."

"Thanks," said Stella.

"When did you learn these techniques?" asked Dagon.

"It's always been do or die with me." Stella drew in a shaky breath, "Given my astrology chart, I'm frequently overloaded with energy." she put her head down and sighed.

"Recently, I learned how to do energetic healing to release blocks on a deep cellular level. I had a session before I came on this journey. It," Stella's voice started to wobble, "H.h..helped. It got me on the ship."

Dagon's tried to encourage her, "Well, you are certainly doing something difficult that most people would never..."

His words were interrupted as Stella suddenly burst into tears, not the pretty kind, but the sobbing, runny nose, red scrunched-up face, kind. She reached for a tissue to cover her face.

"Stella, are you okay? Is there anything I can do?" Dagon whispered with some concern, patting her back helplessly.

"I'm sorry. It isn't anything you've done or said. I just haven't had a good cry for a while, and today, I need it." She sniffed and blew her nose.

Suddenly, Dagon knew what was absent from his life. He missed his mother, his sisters and his nieces. He'd been a soldier for too long. He wanted their easy access to feelings. The heaviness in his heart felt like a rock. It started to rise, but he tamped it down, choking on it.

Stella hiccupped, noticing how sad Dagon looked. "In our healing group we would send light to each other. You would just connect to your divine and then transfer that to another person. The teacher believed that whatever feelings came up were okay as long as you just stopped resisting and learned to accept them. I also was able to receive some divine transmissions called Blessings or Deeksha from an Avatar in the direct lineage of AmmaBhagavan. These blessings seemed to change my level of suffering, kind of emptying me out so that I felt accepting and blissful most of the time. It was so wonderful to receive Deeksha, I learned how to give it."

Stella sat quietly with her hand on her heart psychically picking Dagon up. "Your sadder then *I* am. If it's okay with you, I'll give you the Blessing." Tears of sympathy slid down her cheeks.

Dagon showed his agreement by sitting back on the cushions of the sofa. Stella placed her hands on top of his head.

She closed her eyes and imagined transferring light to Dagon asking to be a channel for divine energy.

"Lovely," Dagon said closing his eyes and dropping into a blissful silence. A sense of deep connectedness stole over both of them. The sense of oneness was beyond the words and ideas of duality. It simply was a way of being in the moment that filled them both with love.

Later, Stella sat quietly on the couch with Dagon. Floating in a deep sense of bliss. She said with a sigh, "I really had no idea it would be such a help to cry."

"Well, I never thought it would be such a help to *me* to *have* you cry," Dagon said ironically.

"Hmmm, l o v e ly," replied Stella, letting the word roll off her lips, testing it with childlike wonder. Yes, love.

It tasted like freedom.

Squeezing his hand she closed her eyes, then remembered.

"Hey, where's my candy bar!"

CHAPTER 9

✠

Talismans and tears

A bridge of comfort and trust connected Dagon and Stella, reminiscent of the deep friendships she had shared with women. Being in close proximity to Dagon was still like being plugged into a powerhouse, a magnetic attraction that electrified every contact. However there was a subtle shift. It was easier to negotiate difficult decisions. It felt great to do hatha yoga, pranayama and meditation, and she was sleeping better as anxiety eased. They were in a magical 'in-between' place, without the complicated roles and expectations of boyfriend, lover or mate. This in-between time, a time when they were literally suspended in space, was allowing them to meet each other in a new way.

As Dagon and Stella worked quietly and efficiently on allotted tasks, Stella remembered past relationships. There had been unspoken judgments, inability to have confidence, and attempts to win approval and love. She had become centered on her partner's whims, actions, or non-actions, and lost herself. Then, had come all the years alone. Late nights at the laboratory hadn't answered an aching loneliness.

Now, she was fulfilling a life long dream, making a journey to Vulcan with a man who seemed to be willing to 'meet' her.

Stella remembered a book that her mother had loved called *Knowing Woman*. The author talked about the miracle of 'meeting' someone, saying it doesn't just happen because you're in a relationship. How often when you 'try' to talk in an effort to 'meet' you are pulling something out of the other person that could damage them, because it's not fully formed yet within their psyche. That the most profound 'meetings' happen in silence. Castillejo is clear on one point. She believes that for any 'meeting' to happen there has to be a third thing present. She suggests some call it the 'Holy Spirit' while others call it the 'Higher Self.'[47]

The past few days had felt like she and Dagon were 'meeting' on every level. Their thoughts and ideas had seemed transported. Emotions were healing; body was well, great; and to top it off, Spirit, permeated it all.

What a concept! Sometimes she would pinch herself and think, Get a grip on yourself, this can't be real. Other times she just felt gripped by the heady pleasure of it all!

The next day they entered the control room and began the final countdown for entry into Vulcan's synchron belt. Anticipation mixed with dread, knowing the whole trip rested on what occurred in the next few moments. Dagon and Stella took their seats in the control room. With a 'whoosh,' the viewing port opened so that they could get an unhindered view of space. According to Dagon's calculations, Vulcan would come spinning past in the synchron belt in one hour and thirty-seven minutes. They had planned for entry into the northern hemisphere of the planet at equinox, hoping for more moderate temperatures.

What complicated entry was the fast moving synchron belt that encircled Vulcan. Computer models showed only one clear gateway for entry. Their timing had to be perfect. They had no idea yet if the spinning power of the belt itself would force them to retreat, aborting the mission.

The Golden Eagle hovered suspended in eternal night as they waited. The first sign that the Belt was approaching was vibration that gradually increased until the ship was shaking violently. Stella and Dagon were being thrown back and forth in their chairs. Stella heard a crash. Something had broken loose outside of the ship. She saw a piece of metal flying off, spinning like a top into deep space.

Then, they saw it. Whirling heavy gas and space debris, looking like a gigantic tornado, was coming straight toward them. Pinpoints of light started spinning in front of their view port, moving so fast they became a blur of streaming light. Their ship bucked violently. Dagon began to fear that the force of the belt would prove disastrous for their tiny ship. He held his breath, ready to withdraw, if need be.

"Check your straps and safety harness again," he commanded.

Two more minutes, then one, a pain gripped Stella's stomach as she held her breath. "10, 9, 8, 7, 6..." Suddenly, it opened up, a gateway through the belt where Vulcan was totally visible, so huge they could only see part of the planets surface through the haze. It was such an incredible blue-green color that Stella gasped.

"Hold on," Dagon said, launching their entry rockets.

There was a strong bump and jolt. The spacecraft shot forward on fusion powered rockets. The strong G force pushed Stella back into her seat, making it hard to move her arms or legs. Stella closed her eyes, hoping that the structure of the ship, which had been built to withstand this impulsion, would work as planned. She took a shaky breath. Yes, I can breath, she thought. The original feeling of acceleration seemed to have lessened. Now Vulcan completely dominated their view port.

She gasped, "My god, we've done it, we're in." Before them was a massive planet, where there had moments before been nothing. Now, it was only a matter of time before gravity would pull them to its surface.

Dagon gripped her hand painfully and Stella cleared her choked throat.

Amazement filled Stella and she sent up a prayer of gratitude.

Nostalgia washed over her, it was as if she had always known what Vulcan would look like from space, as if she were coming home. The urge to walk on land, to have Vulcan's soil beneath her feet, washed over her, filling her with unbearable longing.

Overtaken with emotion, shock and awe they sat star-struck. The luminescent planet seemed to glow, the color a rich teal blue, like the deep blue of the Caribbean ocean. Stella blinked back tears.

She loosened her straps. "We could use the close-up viewing telescope now."

"I've already thought of that, but the panels seem to be damaged. Remember the piece of metal we saw flying off during entry. They aren't extending properly. We'll have to use our cameras and study their images," Dagon said.

They zoomed in with cameras, studying the images, as they panned the planet.

"Do you see that dark mass over the pole. That could be a lake. Probably, hydrocarbon or methane," Stella said. "The haze that we passed through in the belt was most likely methane gas."

"Strangely, we'll never know." Dagon said as he scanned back to study their entry readings on the ships master computer. "Everything just stopped working on our data recording system at entry. We didn't get *any* information. This isn't good." He started looking anxiously through more programs.

Stella continued studying the camera images, "I see high mountain ridges, valleys, and no oceans unless they are underground. What could this color be caused from? Do you see those huge basins in the southern hemisphere? They look like meteorite craters. And, that," she pointed, "Could be a volcano."

Dagon wasn't listening. He was fully engaged in trying to understand what had happened on entry. He asked BOB for a record of any anomalies in their central computer. Since BOB could analyze information at 1.5 quadrillion calculations per second, BOB started sending thousands of data files to the screen. Dagon revised his request. "Please summarize this information for us."

"You experienced shutdown of all operational systems which analyze outside atmospheric conditions upon the approach of the synchron belt. These systems are functioning at 62% now. This fluctuation began at a random rate starting 150,000 miles from the synchron belt. There is no radio signal. All other mechanical systems and internal systems are functioning at full capacity."

Dagon sighed with relief.

"Report any change to me, immediately, BOB." He sat back for a moment.

They rested in silent wonder drinking in Vulcan's beauty and immense presence.

Dagon moved back in his chair, loosening his safety strap to get comfortable. "There is nothing more for us to do, but, wait and hope things continue to stay stable. We have six to eight hours to go while Vulcan pulls us in. I don't want to use rockets at this point unless we have to. We should probably stay strapped in, getting up only for water or the bathroom. We can take turns sleeping."

He turned to Stella, seeing he had scared her. Searching for a way to put her at ease he reached out, gently touching her pendant again.

"Vulcan's the same exact color as your ring and your necklace," he said with amazement, "How odd."

Stella smiled shakily, knowing Dagon was trying to get her to talk so she'd relax.

She began chattering away, hoping to relieve some of her tension. "Vulcan has always been an obsession of mine. When I was in my early twenties I found a reference in a book about the healing properties in stones that associated Vulcan with blue-green tourmaline. According to the author, tourmaline is pyro-electric. When heated by the sun, it develops a static charge that will draw particles to its surface. It was used in the past to draw ash out of pipes. Since Vulcan was the god of fire and ash, I thought this description rather fitting." [48]

"My mother loved crystals. She believed that highly charged electrical currents move along the striations within tourmaline crystals. Now, we use crystals for separating hydrogen isotopes in our fusion tanks. It's amazing, really."

She took off the necklace, so he could hold it. "I had this necklace made from a piece of blue-green tourmaline. It was designed to symbolize fusion and Vulcan."

They sat quietly for a few more moments, absorbing the vastness of the blue globe that filled their viewing screen, listening as the camera automatically snapped photo after photo.

Stella started a video so that their images from space could be studied in more detail later.

Dagon gripped her hand, squeezing it reassuringly, handing her the necklace back.

172

"Do you know much about geology?" Stella asked as she lifted the hair off her neck and reached behind it to fasten the small clasp.

With a little jolt Dagon noticed how her tunic pulled tight across her chest as she lifted her arms. He turned away with a little flush. "A bit," he smiled modestly "enough to know that the color of a stone is dependent on atmosphere, cooling temperatures and the mineral elements found in the composition of it."

"Right, gemstones are formed through heat and pressure. The earth's tectonic plates push up molten lava then push it down again to cool and resurface someplace else a million years later as a beautiful jewel. The earth forges stones in volcanic factories. She is a storehouse for sapphires, rubies and emeralds.[49] I believe that stones have special powers." She gazed lovingly at her necklace as she settled it on her breast again.

Dagon found himself gazing more at her breasts than the pendant. He made himself look away and fished in his pocket pulling out a peacock blue-green piece of titanized metal cut in the shape of a hummingbird. "A friend gave me last year. I told him I'd bring it with me as a talisman, for good luck," Dagon said looking a little discomfited. "Same color as yours."

"Why are you embarrassed, Dagon?" Stella punched his arm playfully. "It's okay to carry a talisman to remind you of what you believe. Remember, you're an alchemist. Titanized jewelry has had an electrical current run through it to create that deep azurite blue. Perhaps, that power and energy can radiate back to you when you call on it. I'm excited it's a hummingbird."

"Why?" Dagon asked.

"Because the Mayans believed we were in the age of the hummingbird. They associated them with the totem for high speed, vibratory light."

They both fell silent again with wonder at the unparalleled splendor that beckoned them through the porthole.   Vulcan summoned mysteriously.

"Can I tell you a story?"

"Sure," replied Dagon, "All we can do is wait now." He looked over at BOB peacefully processing information. Everything seemed normal, so he sat back to relax.

"Okay, It'll pass the time."

"When I was 26, I lost a diamond ring. It was a teal colored diamond, the same bluish-green color in front of us now. I lost the ring on the same day that I found it. Earlier that day, I discovered the solitaire in the dusty case of a local pawnshop. The stone was dull and dirty. It was only later, scrubbing it with my toothbrush, that I gasped at the flower of light blazing in its center. I pressed the stone against the glass window of my cabin. My heart thumped to see the clear scratches it created. I called a gemologist. It turned out to be a large, rare, blue diamond."

"As I drove home with my purchase, I was amazed at my good fortune. As I mentioned earlier, I'd been studying Vulcan for years, collecting stones of this color, usually Mount St. Helen's glass, or tourmaline, but, had never come across a teal diamond. I stopped the car in the sunlight, gazing into the stone's radiant center, musing about all of the possible messages this ring had in store for me."

"Then, the unimaginable happened. It slipped out of my hand dropping out of the car window. I heard the ping as it hit the pavement, rolling into the long yellow grass of the ditch. Of course, I got out of the car immediately, marked the spot and began searching."

"Bad luck," said Dagon. Stella nodded her head in agreement, continuing with her story.

"I searched for hours, combing through rocks, dirt and weeds. Nothing. I went to bed discouraged, but determined to find it. The next day, I borrowed a metal detector. Strangers curiously stopped to ask what I was doing, and shook their heads sympathetically. Every time the metal detector went off, I held my breath. Soon, I had a collection of bottle tops, coke tabs, old nails and wire, but not my precious ring. I broadened my search area even though I knew exactly where it had dropped, but still couldn't find it."

"That seems odd," Dagon commented.

"Very odd," Stella said, "It seemed to have become separated from me, lost in a bizarre way."

"I was devastated, filled with deep grief and longing. I didn't understand why I would find it then lose it on the same day. That evening, I was cleaning when an old book of my mothers fell off the shelf. Written years ago it's titled *Holder of the World*, by Bharati Mukherjee. I immediately realized that the story in the book was an uncanny metaphor that described my current situation."

Stella grabbed her Link, opening a note to read. "The first paragraph said:"

> People and their property often get separated. Nothing is ever lost, but continents and centuries sometimes get in the way... There are no accidents ... We do things when it is our time to do them. They do not occur to us until it is time; they cannot be resisted, once their time has come. It's a question of time, not, motive.[50]

"You know what was even more amazing about the story, *Holder of the World*, is that it is actually a story about a lost diamond."

"You're kidding?" said Dagon.

"No, this really happened," insisted Stella.

"Tell me the book's story, in a nutshell."

"To be brief, it's about a woman, Hannah, who ends up a concubine to an Emperor in India. A researcher does a historical search for this woman, finding her life leads to the trail of a lost diamond called the 'Emperor's Tear.' At one point Hannah had been depicted holding this diamond in an ancient tapestry."

"According to the story, the emperor is wounded in battle and although Hannah attempts to heal him, he is left crippled. Enraged, he rejects her. Hannah must hide the diamond from the emperor or he will destroy it in a fit of madness. The handmaiden of Hannah slits open her own belly and buries the diamond deep within her inner body cavity as she is dying so it will be safely protected for future generations to find by exhuming her bones."[51]

"Ughh," said Dagon, "She hides it in her own body?" he shook his head.

"Yeah, weird idea, huh, but, I had been studying Vulcan at the time and was blown away by the correlations to Vulcan in the story," continued Stella. "For example, Vulcan is the fire god, sun king/emperor, who is crippled and enraged."

"Hannah is another name for Diana, the goddess Hecate. The corpse of the feminine, through death, becomes the vessel to hold the diamond while the God is separated from the Goddess. It is in our deepest bowels, our inner gut that the memory of what we have lost resides. The diamond acts as catalyst for the transformation of energy. Like a laser, it creates the container to amplify the meeting of the polar currents. The name of this great and perfect diamond is, appropriately, the 'Emperor's Tear' because it describes the grief and separation still experienced between the god and goddess."

Stella broke out of her reverie. "I never found that diamond, but I've never forgotten the excitement the first time I saw it. That is how I feel now, looking at Vulcan."

Stella gazed with amazement at the planet that glowed like a teal colored jewel in the port hole.

"Do peculiar synchronicities like this happen to you all of the time?" Dagon queried as he checked his console again to find everything operating as normal.

"Yes," Stella said. "It makes me believe that there must be another dimension sitting right next to ours. Things materialize and dematerialize out of it sometimes when we are being given a message."

Dagon looked horrified by the thought, but then remembered his text message.

"Also, it makes me feel like there really is fate, that things happen only when it is time for them to happen."

Dagon thought about the death of his mother, and the letter that she had written him, still sitting in his locker, unread. He said with angst, "Or do we just *believe* such things because we *need* a way to survive life's hardships?"

Stella was looking pensive. "I'd answer that with another short story. Have you ever heard about Isis and Osiris?" she asked.

"No," Dagon seemed so sad. Stella squeezed his hand with compassion.

"It's a story about the grief of separation through death. Osiris is killed by Set, the evil one, then his immortal body is torn to pieces and scattered throughout the earth. Grieving to reunite with him, Isis searches everywhere to gather pieces of his body, building a temple at each place where she finds a bone. Bone by bone she puts his body back together. They are joyfully reunited. They give birth to a son, Horus, who will bring healing to mankind. Horus is like Jesus, the Christos, a resurrection sun god."

Stella turned to Dagon, with an impassioned gaze.

"*You need hope!*" she exclaimed.

"Why do I get the feeling that you are constantly reading my mind?" Dagon said.

"I do that a lot, sorry. My mother and grandmother were worse," Stella said. "But I'm only doing it because you seem so sad. I thought this story might cheer up you. It says that loss is part of a universal cycle of destruction and reconstruction. We don't have a choice. Everyone we love has to die. But, like Osiris, our sacrifices water the earth with blood. Those left behind can choose, like Isis, to exhume the corpse searching for the diamond within so that we can build temples from our hope."

"Hope for *what*, though?" Dagon said with sorrow.

"Eventual resurrection," Stella said with faith. "We are reborn again and again. Also hope for Awakening, which means we get to be with God all of the time."

Dagon felt a lump in his chest that seemed to be growing. He hadn't been able to read his mother's dying letter because of guilt. How could he have avoided this for three months?

Stella went on speaking. She could see from Dagon's face that he was struggling with something. She tried to find the right words, squeezing Dagon's hand firmly.

"When I lost my diamond in the tall grasses on that fated day, I felt like I had lost something of great value. Through self -pity, I chastised myself for clumsiness and made deals with god about finding it. I scathingly accused myself of being untrustworthy. I felt grief at the many times I have lost or hidden a part of me that needed to be expressed, grief at the times I've let a talent or gift rust away through boredom or unwillingness to face the fear of change. Our guilt confronts us, constantly."

She looked up to see a look of anguish on Dagon's face.

"What," she exclaimed. "Tell me, what is it?"

Dagon was holding a clenched hand over his heart.

Stella was alarmed and reached out to touch his shoulder.

"Four days before we left the Beta station my mother died from complications from a rare lung disease." Dagon's voice choked and tears stung his eyes at saying the words out loud. "She wrote me a message, but I haven't even been able to read it. I have felt so mad and guilty about how it all went down. I was in Special Services when I first found out she was sick. I tried pulling strings for her to get a lung transplant, but got stone-walled with red-tape. I was shipped to the planet Mars soon after for a two year stint and could only send money home or talk on video. She never gave me any idea how bad things were until I got a letter from my younger brother that she had been hospitalized. I applied for special leave, but we were in the last weeks before launch on the Vulcan probe. I decided to quit unless NASA moved her to a better hospital and agreed to an immediate lung transplant. While they said 'yes,' they took too long getting the paperwork through. She died in a small hospital with my brothers and sisters and their kids around her. Since we were four days from launch, I didn't even get leave to be at her funeral. I have been so upset, I haven't been able to read a letter she wrote me the day before she died."

Dagon unbuckled his torso, arms and legs from the web of straps, making his way out of the flight room to his sleeping quarters. He put his thumb on a keypad. With a 'whoosh' his locker opened. At the bottom of a stack of clothing was a hand written journal, yellowed with age. It was his father's diary. An envelope of light blue parchment paper was with it. He pulled out the thin envelope, sticking it in his pocket with the journal. He snapped the door shut.

"Here, this diary and letter came the day after mom died."

Stella eyes grew bigger as he pulled the envelope out of his pocket, breaking the seal on the back.

"Read it out loud for me, I don't think I can," Dagon said as he handed it to her.

Stella pulled the thin parchment paper out, unfolding it carefully, then cleared her throat. The faint ink letters made the letter hard to decipher, especially as her eyes kept blurring with unshed tears. Penned across the back of the envelop in a thick slanting cursive were the words, "Your mother asked me to make sure you got this after she died. I'm honoring her wishes. It seemed important to her that this book be kept a secret. I'll honor that too. I'm sorry for your loss. I'll miss your mom. She was an exceptional person and my best friend. Belinda Shoenecker."

Dagon, my dear son, I don't have much time and I keep seeing your face in my mind. It is the moment you turned to board your plane the day that you left for college. Your eyes were shining with excitement and you looked lit up from the inside. That is how I remember your dad. You remind me so much of him, it hurts. Your smart like he was and curious. Also, your eyes get a determined, stubborn look when you've set your mind to something. Your dad wouldn't give up either. Eventually that was the start of what happened to him. I'm giving you your father's diary because it might make more sense to you, then it ever did to me. Don't tell anyone you have this, okay. Just trust me on this. You need to know your dad loved you. He wasn't depressed, an alcoholic, or unbalanced like everyone has made you kids think. He was a genius and he left a good bit of that legacy inside you.

I'm proud of you, son. Sometimes, I look at the sky and think, 'my boy is up there, like one of those stars.'

Don't fret that you let anyone down. I know you. I could tell you felt guilty every time you wrote home. I've lived a life I wanted and that I chose for myself. I'm not dying unhappy. If this is my fate, so be it. Don't grieve me. Just think of me when you see that planet you're going to and know that I'll be with you in spirit. Perhaps, I'll even see your dad there again. I haven't ever had the freedom to travel much, but as soon as I leave this broken down body you can bet I'll have my bags packed. I love you. Forever, Mom.

Dagon took the letter from Stella, smelling it. It still carried the faint scent of honeysuckle that his mother wore all the time. He turned away, missing her so much it hurt his heart to breathe. He forced himself, not to cry. This wasn't the time, not with a landing in front of them within hours on Vulcan.

Dagon thumbed through his father's diary, then gasped.

"This can't be, Stella, look at this."

Stella took the diary and look closely at the detailed diagram. "It's a drawing for a cold fusion reactor."

"Yeah. But, look at the date. November 11, 2003. This was a year before he died and thirteen years before cold fusion was officially discovered in Russia."

"What!" Stella exclaimed grabbing the book. "Your dad did *this* and didn't publish it or get any credit for it?"

"It appears there's more here. This journal is full of tiny notes, formulas, and diagrams. What in the world?" Dagon was mesmerized by what he was looking at. His father really *had* been a genius. How could his mother have kept this diary a secret until her death? Why was it coming out now, after his dad was gone?

"I can't believe this," Dagon put his hand over his head, exhausted with a pounding headache. This new view of his dad was turning his whole view of the world upside down.

Stella got him an Aspirin and a glass of water. As Dagon gulped it back, he tried to absorb the ramifications of what they were looking at, vacillating between an odd excitement and a black, raging grief.

Stella didn't know how to help, but eventually decided she needed to do something ceremonial. "Here, Dagon, I think we need a toast to honor your mom and your dad." She opened a small bottle of grape juice, filling his water glass then topped off a glass for herself. "This seems somehow fitting."

Dagon took a moment to think then held up his glass, overcome with grief. "Mom and dad, I'm here today because of both of you. Dad you have always inspired me. And, Mom, you have been the strength that held our family together and made our lives possible. I hope that you can hear me, somewhere, when I dedicate this landing on Vulcan to you." The tears that he had struggled to hold started to fall as he choked out the words, "I'll never forget you."

If Dagon had been able to see in the ultraviolet spectrum, he would have noticed two lights hovering above him. It looked like the faint shape of a man and woman holding hands.

CHAPTER 10

✠

Landing on Vulcan

While efforts were made, radio contact with Base Command was impossible. The shaking and pressure in their small craft increased with the pull of Vulcan's gravity. Atmospheric adjustments occurred within the cabin every few minutes.

Up until now, both Dagon and Stella had spent months in a state of motionlessness, relieved only by scheduled exercise, routine and their conversations or interactions. Now, they were both aware of a new feeling of speed as they were buffeted by solar winds and geomagnetic storms around the planet.

Stella remembered past landings on earth during her space flight training. The feeling of acceleration, the bumps and jogs, all meant she would be walking on soil within hours. She had never been in space for such a long period. She could hardly wait for their final descent. The anticipation was almost over.

Their fast rate of descent and the increase in size of their targeted destination surprised them. One quarter of the planet now completely filled the porthole screen in the console room. A pole cap, covered with what appeared to be a dark surface mass, was clearly visible along with mountain ridges and the shadows of deep ravines. A light violet blue haze covered patchy areas. The land appeared light gray-brown in color, yet still uniformly tinged with the faint blue-green teal color that they had seen from farther out in space.

Stella and Dagon were each aware of an uncomfortable pressure in their body. Ears popping and head pounding, Stella laid her head back and prayed. For the past four hours they had stayed strapped into their seats, getting up only when it was necessary to drink, eat or use the restroom. While their space suits and helmets were streamlined, Stella still found hers uncomfortable and restrictive when she twisted or bent over because of the panel of buttons on her chest that monitored oxygen and an emergency parachute.

"Okay," said Dagon, "Whoa, baby, here we go!"

In the next instant, they lost sight of the planet. The spaceship was being buffeted around in a murky haze and felt like it had shifted to a nose down position. Clouds? wondered Stella. Or was this ash? Smoke?

Motion sickness began to affect her. She could see that Dagon was holding up better then her, thank god. One last attempt to radio Base, showed how alone they were. They were committed to certain death, if anything went wrong. There was no such thing as rescue, this far in space.

Dagon calmly discussed their situation with Stella, reporting the facts, as he knew them. "Loss of visibility is not expected at this distance from the planet. We should be at least 200 miles in space still. We could be in a dust cloud, methane or some other atmospheric condition that is forming a ring around the planet. It surprises me, however, since we didn't view it on approach. We are being hit by debris which is buffeting off the panels on all sides of the craft," Dagon checked the instruments in front of him one more time. "The outside metal skin of our craft is glowing hot, in the red zone. Not a good sign."

Dagon continued, "My gut tells me we are moving in faster then we planned and our equipment is giving us faulty readings because of high levels of radiation or electromagnetic fields. My north/south pole finders are unreliable. I only hope that our land scanners are functioning properly, in case we have to dock our ship without being able to see the surface. I tried to get a reading from BOB and he is malfunctioning."

Stella swallowed tightly. A heavy bump knocked them both sideways in their chairs.

"How are you holding up?" Dagon asked Stella.

"Actually, better than I thought. I think the anticipation of what could have happened is worse than being here," she smiled bravely.

"I am going to release our space probes into the atmosphere now. Hopefully, they'll make it to the surface, even if we don't." Dagon reached down and pushed a red flashing button.

"Dagon, don't say, that," Stella shuddered. She took a closer look at Dagon, "How are *you* doing?"

"Actually, I'm worried and feeling helpless since nothing is actually going as we rehearsed it on Beta III. There's not much we can do right now, but wait and hold on." He noticed Stella was looking rather gray. "But, hey, soon we'll be drinking margaritas by a tropical sea," he laughed recklessly. A rough jolt had them gripping their chairs. They decided to strap down their heads for protection.

Stella closed her eyes. Imagine you're in the palm of god's hand and he is rocking you. She repeated over and over to herself like a mantra.

A thick haze covered the view port. Soon, they both became aware of a steady pelting against the metal exterior of the ship. A light bulb went on in Stella's head. "I was worried this dense atmosphere might be nitrogen and methane. That would make this planet uninhabitable. Methane gas is broken up by sunlight and condenses to form methane pools or would vent to the surface to form hydrocarbon bodies of liquid, thus, the lake at the pole."

"And?" said Dagon impatiently as he fought to get manual control of the ship. "I know all this, what's your point!"

"That it's not methane!" Her voice rose in a combination of fear and excitement. "I think this is ash or smoke. We're being hit by burning debris. We have to be lower then we think. This is from a volcano."

The intense gravitational pull was wrenching them off course and the lasers used to help them pinpoint ravines and mountains were not working. Their targeted destination was a large open valley. Both were silently praying that the atmospheric conditions they were now experiencing would be temporary.

"We've got to find a valley or we are going to end up on the side of a mountain. We're not getting an option to go to manual control." Dagon was gritting his jaw as he frantically worked at the main computer that had just started to operate again.

"All Right!" he yelled. "We're back on, 5.1 quad per second. Atmosphere collector back on. But, that can't be right. The air reads low levels of oxygen."

Stella gasped, gripping her seat.

Suddenly, they dropped out of the haze into a world of scarlet and gold. The craft was nose down. They were hanging upside-down in their seats, plummeting into a virgin harsh landscape that was sliding into darkness as their altitude dropped.

Dagon and Stella glimpsed a network of veins and wrinkles on the surface of the land. Deep blue shadows filled ravines while a hint of scarlet touched the tops of rugged peaks. Then, with a flash the whole landscape changed to a deep red magenta that cast the terrain in an otherworldly glow. The sun powered a beam of blinding light through, the spacecraft's windows.

Like liquid molten gold, baptized with fire, Vulcan was welcoming them with a sunset unlike any they had ever experienced before. The golden glow passed quickly with descent. They were immersed in deep blue-black darkness, darker than the deep space that they had left; for there were no moons, no stars, and no spinning galaxies to, mark the passage.

It was the pitch darkness that was almost Stella's undoing, closing in around her, and suffocating her. Her body was plastered against the chair with such force that she couldn't move her hand. A high whining pitch alerted her that the ship was reaching maximum capacity as the craft shuddered, sighed and trembled. They were in the grip of the iron hand of gravity. Their frail craft was faltering.

Stella's ears were hurting and she turned her head slowly to adjust the controls on her helmet. She glimpsed Dagon. He was adjusting his body suit also. Catching his eye they exchanged a deep look. His eyes seemed to be saying something. The vulnerability and longing in them frightened her.

Then, she knew. He thinks we are going to die, she thought with panic. He is saying, good-bye.

She shook her head slightly sent a message through her eyes. We're going to make it.

Dagon read the conviction. The edges of his lips turned up slightly, nodding his head, he indicated that he understood.

It seemed as if the ship responded to their thoughts. Suddenly, the nose of the plane jerked upward. A dizzy wave of nausea went through Stella as the plane leveled off. The feeling of speed accelerated. What a roller coaster, she thought. The indicator was blinking 'alert, alert, danger,' on the console. Infrared maps of mountains and ravines blazed out over the computer screen.

They were off course, way off course, but thank goodness the laser was working again.

Oh, God, she breathed silently, please lead us home. We have been waiting a long time to come home; take us to the right place on this planet of yours.

Like an answer to prayer, the GPS on their computer lit up, flashing 31 exaflops, its highest speed, as it turned back on. It indicated a small, elevated valley between two mountains. A loud noise roared from the landing gear as Dagon gave instructions for approach.

Dagon and Stella both held their breaths. One. Two. Three. They had only ten seconds to stop before the plane hit a butte. The seconds seemed like hours as their lives hung in the balance.

Suddenly, with a thud, they were down, coasting a short distance to shuddering stillness.

"We did it!" cried Dagon ecstatically. "My god..."

Shaking from the after-effects of adrenaline racing through their bodies, Dagon and Stella unstrapped, clasping each other with joy. As they gradually calmed down they checked the condition of the craft.

"Everything looks better than expected. The inner atmosphere settings are working correctly," Dagon said with exuberance.

They sat in a silent daze, trying to re-orient themselves to their surroundings. Outside it was pitch black. Inside they saw first a green light, then a red light, then a row of green lights. BOB was waking up again. To Stella's delight his first words sent her into a fit of giggles. "It seems that you have arrived at your destination. Congratulations from Base Command. We salute the Golden Eagle and its crew. Programmed by Colonel Greene VC116794."

For an hour they talked, attempting another unsuccessful radio contact with Base Command, then reviewed the computer tapes of everything that had happened during their descent. Stella's body felt so heavy with adrenal exhaustion she had trouble even lifting her arm.

Dagon noticed how leaden his own limbs felt. "Let's try to get some sleep. We can't explore until daybreak for safety reasons." He checked the temperature readings again. "It's -72 degrees below Fahrenheit. It must hit a chilly -90 below, even though we're here in Vulcan's most temperate season. No sign of any heat images on the cameras. Nothing, no bugs, small animals, nothing. We could safely take a rest break and program BOB to keep watch for us."

"I can barely turn my head, I'm so beat," Stella said, "But, my mind is so buzzed I don't know if I can actually sleep."

"I'd like to bunk next to you if you'd like that, too," Dagon said. Stella checked out Dagon's stance, seeing only exhaustion. She reached for his large hand with her small one, noticing the deep lines of strain on his face and the bruised look under his eyes.

"It looks like we could both use some recuperation time," she said gently. "Thanks for doing such a good job getting us here, Captain."

Clutching each other for strength, they fell into bed.

Almost immediately they fell into a deep, dreamless sleep. Stella woke up two hours later. With a quick flush of anxiety, she quietly got up to monitor the temperature and atmospheric gauges in the ship. BOB was at the helm and saluted her.

"Would you like a report?" BOB said in a chirpy voice.

"Cut to the chase," Stella said running her hand through her hair.

"Everything is fine," BOB said in the same bright tone. "You can continue inactive duty."

What? thought Stella. Is he actually trying to make a joke?

Stella yawned, stumbling back into bed, snuggling into the warm back and legs of the man beside her. She awoke another time to find him gone as he did his own checks that must have been more detailed, as they took longer. It was a relief when he climbed back into bed spooning against her back, one arm flung possessively over her shoulder with his hand resting lightly beneath her breasts. She froze, almost scooting closer to the edge of the bed, and then thought better of it. With a smile she wiggled closer instead, sighing at the pleasure of being safe and warm. Pressing her head back on Dagon's shoulder, she drifted into an even deeper sleep.

CHAPTER 11

✠

Differences revealed

They slept ten hours and woke feeling groggy and content. Stella was up first, bouncing out of bed on the run, as was her usual custom. Since they still had eight hours before dawn, she began checking food supplies, tending to lab specimens and analyzing the sensors that read the atmospheric conditions on the outside of the ship.

Fixing a hot cup of tea, she sat next to the bed, where Dagon lay propped up by a pillow, to offer her report.

"The ship has some minor damage in one of the deflector panels. However, the engine and fuel supply are fine, and our electronic equipment appears to be working properly. Our food supply is low on freeze-dried meals. We may need to go on tablets toward the end of our trip. Unfortunately, I'm not receiving any communication signals and cannot get a transmission to Base. Probably, the most interesting thing I've found is that the atmospheric sensor indicates the presence of moderate levels of oxygen on the planet. Since we are in a high valley between two mountains, there could be more oxygen at lower, warmer elevations. Oxygen could mean some type of biological life forms. We have gravity out there, too, about 1.1854 that of earth. We should be able to walk around, but it will feel a bit oppressive until we adjust to it. We will need space suits, but may be some possibility of using our light gear, depending on the temperature when the sun comes out. Right now, it is a chilly -75 below Fahrenheit, a range well within the zone for life. I'm very excited about the possibilities."

Stella's fresh breeziness and merry optimism was infectious.

"So, are you ready to grow a garden now?" Dagon laughed.

"Yes, a lovely patch of carrots, lettuce and a pond of lovely trout," she twirled her hair playfully.

"I was thinking about an apple tree," said Dagon, "so we could have fresh apple pie like my Grandmother Pearl used to make. And, of course, some wheat fields, sugar cane and butter to make the crust." He was rubbing his stomach now, in an act of mock culinary satisfaction.

Stella playfully smacked his belly. "Well, aren't you industrious? Did you bring the seeds and some corn to show the natives how to harvest a crop for next Thanksgiving?"

Dagon grabbed her hand and pulled her down next to him on the bed to tease her, "No, I…" But then their gaze caught and Dagon got a bit lost. "You have a great smile."

"I do?" Stella couldn't resist, smiling up him.

"Yes," he murmured as his mouth came down to claim hers. "And, a very passionate mouth."

"I do?" Now, Stella's eyes were sparkling. Hot fire shot through her lower belly.

"And, your eyes are like sunshine."

"They are?" A new sense of wonder gripped her.

She took Dagon's large warm hand, slipping it onto her midriff.

Dagon moaned, "This is killing me."

He pulled her body full length under his, snugging her up into his body. For one moment they hovered on the edge of temptation.

Then, Dagon rested his head in her neck, breathing deeply, kissed her ear softly.

"Let's get up, before we both take this too far," he said.

Stella felt shaky all over, starting to protest. Then, the possible consequences of losing control made her scramble off the bed.

"Wow," Dagon sat up, running his hand through his hair and over the stubble on his checks. "I'm not sure even a cold shower is going to help this one."

Stella just let herself ride the wave of ecstasy that seemed to have invaded her nerve endings.

A new feeling of contentment and completion connected them as they made preparations for their first walk on Vulcan. A dim light was starting to permeate the sky outdoors and they were ready to experience its warmth.

When they were completely dressed, they entered the intermediary air lock, exiting slowly through the sliding panel doors. The view that greeted them took their breath away.

In front of them was a wide, wind-swept valley with high mountains surrounding it on one side and an unending, high plain behind. The brown-gray landscape was cast in deep indigo blue where the valley floor lay in cold shadows. The frozen plain met a sharp contrast in the scarlet sky, spreading out like a sea of blood above them. At the horizon, between the crimson and sapphire line, was a ray of golden light, a brilliant arch jettisoning over the mountain pass to impale the side of their metallic spacecraft in a radiant glow.

Dagon and Stella looked at one another, touching hands to communicate mutual joy, as Stella murmured out loud to herself, "Hmmm, Blue, Red and Gold. The three primary colors."

Dagon caught her soft words with some surprise. "What did you just say?"

Stella shook herself out of her reverie, her eyes focusing back on Dagon's face.

"I'll tell you later."

Dagon and Stella walked another twenty feet from the spacecraft, and then bent over to examine the rock-like, yet strangely spongy, surface beneath their feet. Suddenly, Stella inhaled her breath quickly in a shocked gasp.

"Oh, my god, Dagon. These are Plants! They're plants! Alive on this planet." Her voice rose in excitement as she whirled around trying to take in as much as possible. She bent down excitedly, her hand shaking as she reached out to examine the underside of the spongy surface.

"Look," she said with conviction, her words almost running into one another in her excitement, "Do you see the sepals or petals on the underside of this stem? And, the radial symmetry of the tube on the end of each head? I have no idea what genus or species we are looking at, but, you can see buds for roots near the ground, they are probably perennial. Hmmm, there is no stamen or pistol that I can see. Yet, they must fertilize somehow."

Dagon's faced mirrored the wonder in Stella's eyes, yet he took her arm and began to almost drag her away.

"Stella, we have to go back to the ship now. We can spend more time exploring when we come back out."

According to instructions from Base Command, the first walk out of the spacecraft was to be limited to five minutes as a safety precaution.   Later, barring any trouble, they would be able to increase their time, eventually, building a greenhouse outside of the craft to test any rock or plant samples that they found.

"You dope, this is amazing. Dagon..." Stella shook his hand off, refusing to be deterred.

Her voice rose excitedly. "If we have plant life here there could be animals or some type of intelligent life. Perhaps, we have just landed in a place where the climate is more unfavorable."

She peered out expectantly over the windswept tundra, willing a wildebeest to come lumbering over the horizon. All of the low-lying plants seemed to be of one type with no trees gracing the horizon or softening the rocky outcrops of the mountains.

"Hmmm, perhaps in a ravine, where there is less wind and it is warmer..." she speculated.

Looking at the sky, she was surprised to see a pale violet starting to spread above her.

"Atmosphere," she beamed, "Atmosphere and a chance of weather."

Dagon was looking at her like she was about to bolt. Firmly, he grasped her arm again, propelling her toward the ship, determined to follow protocol for safety.

Within minutes Stella was pacing back and forth in the ship with barely contained excitement.

"There is life, life on this planet! Amazing! We need to go back out. Why are we waiting two hours? Isn't that overly cautious? I mean two whole hours, really?" she complained.

Dagon watched her pace for a few moments then finally grabbed her by shoulders and forced her to sit down.

"Stella, hey, Stella. Shipmate, back to earth."

"Shipmate to earth."

Stella pushed his hand away with irritation.

"We aren't on earth. We're on Vulcan," she exclaimed petulantly crossing her arms.

"I'm sorry, it's for our own good. We are vulnerable here. We have to be very careful. We don't know how the temperature or atmosphere is affecting us. There are reasons for the rules."

Later in the confines of the ship kitchen, Dagon cornered Stella, putting his arm around her. "I'm sorry if I seem like such a wet blanket, I'm as excited as you are."

"You can make it up to me by letting me just get a sample of..."

Dagon interrupted her. "Later, I still feel we should follow protocol."

"We don't have contact with Base. If they knew how favorable this planet is to life, including our lives, they wouldn't be holding us to an old plan," she argued.

"Well, we aren't in touch, so, we go by the book."

"We just saw that there is life on this planet, perhaps intelligent life for all we know."

She sat down, then reconsidering, got up again with a huff, "Okay, I'm going to make breakfast." Slamming storage drawers she began to assemble supplies, putting liquid into their freeze-dried packets to transform it into potatoes au gratin.

"Well, what will they think of next? Gourmet meals in space," Dagon said, trying to tease her out of her black mood.

Suddenly, the air in the spaceship became very electric. The hairs on Dagon's arms rose. He gathered Stella next to him, looking around.

In the console room, Dagon saw a waving light, fluorescent and opaque. It flickered, and then blinked out. He turned to confirm that

Stella had seen the same thing and blinked, hardly believing what was right in front of him.

Stella reached out to touch his hand and saw him flinch and back away, his face pale.

She paused, waiting for him to speak to her. Then she visibly saw his face relax, as he heaved a sigh of relief. "What is it, what just happened?" Stella asked with concern.

Dagon frowned with uncertainty, trying to understand what seemed impossible.

"Stella, just moments ago I saw a source of light that appeared to be creating its own illumination from within. I saw another face superimposed over yours. Didn't you feel anything?"

"Well, the hair is standing up on my arms. I feel kind of cold and maybe a bit dizzy. And, before that I felt like something touched my hair. I thought maybe I had run into something hanging from the ceiling, but, now I can see that there is nothing there."

"What the hell," Dagon said. "Maybe I'm experiencing some side effects to this landing or my mind is being affected in some way by these environmental conditions. Perhaps low level methane gas or pollutants in the atmosphere are leaking into our air supply." Dagon forced himself to look unflinchingly into Stella's eyes as he spoke.

"Well, I'm highly charged right now. It is a bit uncomfortable, kind of like an electric buzz. Where's the EMF meter?" Stella asked

"You want to measure electro-magnetic frequencies?"

"Yes," Stella said. "You said high EMF's could create these kinds of feelings. How about Electronic Voice Phenomena? We could try seeing if we can pick up a voice digitally?"

Suddenly, one of the lights on board dimmed then popped off. At the same time all their circuitry flickered on and off.

"Wow, Did you see that, and look, my necklace feels warm. Do you suppose it could be some type of energy form, maybe gathering power from our ship or us so it can materialize?" Stella sounded gleeful.

Dagon couldn't take his eyes off her tourmaline. Just as she said, it was clearly glowing, radiating a beautiful green light. Even with evidence right in front of him Dagon still resisted, saying firmly, "That's a ridiculous idea. Where do you get this stuff?"

Stella smiled. "Paranormal research societies have a lot of equipment that they use to study ghosts. I was thinking it might apply here, since ghosts are energy trapped outside of a body."

"There has to be some rational explanation for this phenomena," Dagon scoffed, "But, still, we need to be careful. There could be other atmospheric anomalies that could affect either one of us mentally. At all times I command that you see to your safety and the safety of the ship. If I start acting out of character, there is a tranquilizer you can give me in our medical kit, similarly, I'll keep watch for you."

"You command?" Stella put her hands on her hips having trouble taking him seriously. "You said you saw an energy form superimposed over me, that isn't a sign of craziness in my book. Now, what did the face look like? A man, woman, or some other kind of extraterrestrial entity? Did you hear anything? What could it have been, a hologram?" Her mind was grappling with the possibilities, but Dagon still seemed stuck in the past.

"Well, I am first in command, you are second in command on this mission. I'm taking rank and giving you an order that I don't want disobeyed under any circumstances," Dagon said firmly.

"I think for my *safety* I should eat in another room," Stella said sarcastically as she started to move out of the kitchen.

"Wait," Dagon said, "I'm only saying this because I'm concerned. There's no need to get so miffed."

"Your emotions might frighten you. But, they don't frighten me," said Stella. "On second thought, however, since you're on the verge of an emotion, maybe I should just relieve you of first in command now and give the orders from now on."

Dagon found himself grinning.

Suddenly, they were both laughing. Dagon kissed Stella gently. "I don't want anything to ever happen to you," he confessed as he buried his face in her hair.

"We have to just go with what happens on this planet, I can't be owned or protected," Stella said gently. "I need to flow with this place, we can't follow protocol. Life changes. I will change. You will change. Let's be flexible."

"Okay," said Dagon reluctantly. "But, I still think we have some control over making things more secure."

"Maybe, to some degree," said Stella. "But, for now, we need to figure out things on a moment-by-moment basis. And, right now conditions are excellent to go for another space walk."

"Okay," Dagon relented. "I'll compromise. One hour, but then we only spend 15 minutes out."

They began to work together on their tasks. The assembly parts for the KY Land Transporter, nicknamed KYL, were unloaded in their unloading dock. Her biological laboratory was unpacked.

Dagon was already starting to assemble the complicated looking instruments and equipment necessary for Stella's workstation to function outdoors. "This stuff is pretty impressive," he said as he rigged up a better way to lift the light panels. His natural ease in assembly demonstrated that he had innate mechanical ability. It was obvious in the casual way he began constructing the platforms.

"Not any more impressive than my resilient little honey bees," Stella shifted back and forth on her feet with pent up energy. "When you think of the complicated visual and sensory system that they have and see how they are adapting within a totally different environment, you have to be impressed." she went on, talking so quickly it was hard to catch it all. "However, I wonder what the long-term effect would be of maintaining this environment. Would the lack of sound, smells and earth's atmosphere eventually destroy the regenerative capacity of their nervous system so they couldn't transmit electrophysiological signals, or would they adapt marvelously, and one day pollinate the plants that we have seen on Vulcan?"

Dagon looked over at Stella, shaking his head. She was a mystery to him.

"Stella, hand me that panel over there, please." Stella reached for it barely missing knocking the canvas off of its pole.

Dagon jumped up. "Here, I can get it." He continued working as Stella hovered over him, chattering in his ear.

"The life forms we brought from earth, including ourselves, seem to thrive here. We're making history on this journey. We've found life on another planet, the beginning of a new wave of research and discovery. Perhaps, we'll even find intelligent life!"

Dagon looked startled, thinking back on the image he had seen superimposed on Stella's face earlier. He groaned, "Stella, I need to concentrate."

Stella continued to babble as if she hadn't heard him. "We have always had 'life on other planets' in our memory and in our dreams. Perhaps, it has been in our DNA all along, this knowledge, this desire to reach out into space, the centuries of work that led up to this moment of discovery!"

Stella got into her oration as she waved her hands melodramatically. "Studded with volcanic islands, a cauldron for evolving life." Stella began to pace around. Dagon quickly rescued his knife so it wouldn't end up on the floor. "Now, we stand on Vulcan, amazed. The evolution of the atmosphere here already includes low levels of oxygen. The life cycle here is already highly evolved. Once the earth was simply a planet of blue-green algae. Now, we have encountered another blue-green world, ... Vulcan!" She threw out her hands. The tiny bag of screws went flying, putting them both on their knees to find them under the cabinets and table.

Dagon looked up from his work, wondering if she was expecting him to listen to her recital. "Stella, hand me that tiny wrench, please."

She grabbed it and thrust it towards him, practically squirming with excitement. "I'm going to write a paper about this. I need to study the RNA and DNA of these plants. RNA proteins, the first amino acids are probably still present here on this planet. If I could find some evidence of the pattern of natural selection..." Her voice petered out as she noticed that Dagon wasn't listening. He was absorbed in his task, whistling merrily under his breath.

"Dagon, listen..." she complained.

"I have been listening to you for three months, now I need to build this." Dagon said without even looking up, his fingers moving surely and swiftly.

Startled out of her mental ruminations, Stella watched Dagon instead, feeling a sudden desire to capture the moment. Was it possible to draw a picture of those capable hands? To document the way that all of his physical and mental abilities automatically became coordinated when he had a goal? This, she thought, was masculine perfection.

"My god, you are so beautiful," she exclaimed excitedly. Dagon just raised an eyebrow and kept working.

Later, over supper, Stella could see how tired Dagon was. They had spent a total of an hour and 45 minutes outside on three different walks, mostly just wandering around within sight of their ship. Dagon had insisted that they stay together in case one of them was cut by something sharp or fell down. Stella had been able to take some pictures and notes, but had noticed Dagon had been tense, guarding both of them the whole time, never really able to give in to childlike wonder like she did. After giving him a second helping of food and noticing his eyes were closing, she said, "You work so hard."

"What do you mean, I didn't do anything today," Dagon groused.

"You're constantly on guard, protecting us and being in charge of everything. You have to be so, well, 'responsible.' I guess I've never thought about how hard that must be. No wonder you're kind of parental part of the time. You think everything is your job or your fault. If you let me, I'll try to help more."

"Stella, that's just my job. You have your job. I don't always enjoy being in charge. It requires being ready to solve problems. But, it feels better than all these months just sitting in space. I'm actually happier here, even if I don't sound like it."

"I noticed that. But, it seems like you're stuck with *everything* we do, whether putting up awnings, moving equipment, or disposing of our trash. How can you stand not getting more creative time?"

"I just want to work hard and be proud of what I do. I don't think I need the same things as you, Stella. If you don't mind, now though, I just want to nap for a while, to kind of zone out and not talk for a while."

Stella left him alone then reflected on what she was noticing. She could remember her dad trying to escape her mom's talking. Frequently, he would go out on the back porch or hang out in the garage. Maybe men were actually more grounded than women were. They didn't like to talk about things. Her dad seemed to prefer just being quiet. She thought about the group of guys he met to have coffee with every Sunday. Or the way that she noticed a bunch of older guys always hanging around the barber shop in town. Men seemed to just like to pass the time in a kind of 'easy' way. They didn't have to intellectualize everything, even their emotions.

She remembered one time her dad had been really mad at her for lying to him by going to a party at a girlfriend's house that had been busted by the police. He had just gone out and started cleaning the garage. By the time he came back in, it was over. They never talked about it again. He expected her to behave better in the future and she had.

Perhaps, men could be more in the moment than women, more grounded in general. That made sense if you thought of women as the fire of Shakti and men as the calm order of Brahma. The times that she had seen men taken over by their emotions, it seemed a sign of lack of balance. There was nothing worse than a man who pouted or raged like a child.

Hmmmm. She had to stop herself from rushing over and waking Dagon up to tell him what she thought. Her mom had owned the book *Men are from Mars, Women are from Venus*. Stella had read it, but thought it a simple, antiquated and chauvinistic view of the sexes. But, the more she had watched her male friends and the men in the space program, the more the simple descriptions in the book seemed to apply. Most women experienced the world in terms of relationship and connectedness. They wanted to talk, negotiate, share duties, be heard and compromise. The majority of men saw the world in terms of a challenge that they needed to surmount. They wanted recognition and appreciation as they faced obstacles. They thought of life as something they needed to conquer alone, a woman was someone on their team to help them get to their goal.

Her mother had thought that men secretly believed that a woman might disempower them. She postulated that this was probably because men have to separate from their mothers to form their identity. They unconsciously know their mother can suffocate them and weaken them.

Women, on the other hand, keep men on their antennae all the time, hearing every little thing they need and trying to take care of it. Women feel deserted when they want someone to listen to their problems or sympathize.

Since men and women are from different planets, being together requires acceptance of these differences, releasing expectations, and learning how to have space inside of the closeness, as you believe the best about the other person. Women have to say like a mantra, 'I know he loves me,' even if he doesn't show it like she would. Men have to believe that they are appreciated and doing a good job, even when a woman criticizes them. Women need to admire their partner. Either you admire and respect the man that you are with or you don't. Women secretly want men to be like they are. So, men constantly feel judged, like they can never be enough or do it well enough.

I think I need to start journaling again, she thought yawning. I want to see if this is true with Dagon and I. The pen dropped out of her hand as she drifted into a deep sleep. She didn't even hear when when Dagon slipped into bed.

Once again they slept uninterrupted for 10 hours, waking while it was still dark to check on the ship then drawing close again under the light blanket. Stella arms and legs got tangled with Dagon's sometime during the night. She thought she was dreaming as she felt hands exploring beneath her tank top and sleep shorts, rubbing over her belly then sliding down as he lifted her on top of him so he could run his hands down the back side of her body. She woke up to find herself asleep on top of him, her shirt up with their chests touching.

"My god, I've never had a build up to sex like this. I'm ready to explode all the time, all day long. Are you *trying* to make me obsess over you? We need to get up," Stella stretched on top of his body. Dagon groaned holding her still.

"Yes, we do, but I'd like to talk a bit," Dagon said.

Stella was surprised. "About us?"

"No, everything about 'us' feels just right to me. It's more about what happened yesterday when I saw that light and the face superimposed over yours."

"I guess I've been just sort of comfortable with it. Things like this happened to me on earth too. I seem to attract entities who want to channel through me."

Dagon sat up lifting Stella in one strong movement onto his lap facing him and pushed her hair out or her eyes, his own searching her with alarm.

"Are you kidding?"

"No, what is so unusual about that?" Stella could feel herself get a bit defensive.

She started to climb off, but Dagon grasped her waist holding her in place, forcing her to look at him.

"Don't do that, I feel manhandled." Stella started to wiggle away.

"You *know* it's a bit schizoid." Dagon concluded as Stella scrambled off him.

He reached for his planner that was on the nightstand, continuing to speak. "How can you say something like that so casually, like it's normal to channel an entity?" He began bringing up his list of things that needed done for the day.

"Why is it so hard to believe?" Stella said. "What about angels, prophets, inner guides, seers. What about miracles?"

Stella grabbed Dagon's shirt and put it on, rolling up the long sleeves. She pulled her messy hair back into a ponytail. Dagon was caught off guard. Moments ago she had been as sexy as a tigress. Now, she stood there looking like a child wearing a shirt that came down to her knees. But, her voice didn't sound like that of a little girl as she started defending herself.

"If you think hard about what you believe about physics, about the properties of quantum matter, you will see it is highly probable that more evolved life forms have learned to transmit information on the particulate level. Even ancient earth mythology of Vulcan describes a god who could transport people simply with the power of his thought. Telepathy is simply a flashing-forward of light, an instantaneous electrical interplay and a direct mental communication from mind to mind, from soul to soul. It requires the ability to use the human energy force field as a transmitter and to use the chakras, the third eye, as the director of energy and force. By learning to connect to an etheric center, the mind has the ability to transform matter on the physical plane. Thought forms produce powerful effects on physical planes."[52]

"It's not rational," Dagon dismissed her, looking up for a moment from his notes.

"Why? Scientists first discovered the power of the mind when they were working with healing. As early as 1938, Max Heindel, an occultist wrote about this." She grabbed her glasses and her computer notebook, flipping it on she scrolled to the file, reading:

> A vehicle made of ether interpenetrates the dense body. This may be compared to electricity in the wires of an electric or telegraphic system. By means of this vital fluid the muscles are moved.[53]

"So, he was right," Stella insisted. He had the idea in 1938. We proved it to be true in 2020 without a doubt. Telepathy, speaking through the mind is not as unusual as you are making it out to be."

"Dagon, are you listening to me?"

"Yes."

"But, you're not looking at me, you're looking at your planner."

"That's because I need to see this. I can listen to you at the same time."

"Oh, brother. You can not!"

Dagon set his Link down with a bang.

"Well, you started this conversation," Stella said. "You wanted to talk about that light phenomena. I told you I don't think we need to be alarmed. I'll only say this one more thing," Stella said quickly, then stated her case. "Medical science supports this now. We have learned, in the last twenty years, to heal through this energy field. Why can we not also learn to communicate through it telepathically? Unfortunately, we have been sleepwalking. We have been wondering around in a daze, rooted in the thick clay of tradition, accepting darkness when we could have been learning how fly."

Dagon looked at her, blinking. "You sound like you're preaching from a soap box, you don't really believe this, do you?"

"Yes, of course, I do. I think, before we are finished here, you will too."

Dagon frowned. But Stella gulped nervously, persisting, "Dagon, remember our first encounter with Vulcan? You're are as aware as I was that our craft was being bombarded with signals at such a wavelength that communication with Base Command became almost impossible the closer we got to the planet. My own personal experience was even more profound. I haven't told you this because I knew you'd be alarmed. But, I trust myself, I'm not crazy."

Stella had Dagon's full attention now. She pulled him by both hands over to a chair, making him sit down. Then, looking into his eyes, she broke the news that she had been hiding from him. "I first began having strong thoughts that didn't seem to be my own when we were within a week of entry into Vulcan's atmosphere. At first it just felt like I was being prodded along, helped to remember and organize my thoughts. Now it feels different. This is another kind of entity. I sometimes feel it would like to speak through me."

Dagon turned pale and stammered, "The face I saw was an old, wise looking man. He was wearing a simple tunic with a gold V shaped necklace. His white hair was tied back with a cord."

"Wow, perhaps we are actually meeting Vulcan himself. Who knows?"

"Stella, that's a bit crazy. What do you mean *you've been having strong thoughts that are someone else's*?" Dagon voice rose as he reached over to the nightstand for a drink of water.

"It's hard to describe. First of all, because it's a man's voice not my own. Second because the dialect sounds old, very formal, not even the way that I speak. I haven't been listening much because I have been so excited with setting up our station. But, I know if I concentrated and was quiet, it would be different. Perhaps, we should try this. I could record what happens."

"This sounds dangerous," Dagon said.

"Well, let's not talk about it now, I really want to get outside. Today is a big day."

"Stella, I have to admit to something too," Dagon said. "I have been having some odd dreams. While I was doing some research on Vulcan, an entry appeared as a text on my Link that I didn't type and don't remember downloading."

"Wow," Stella got excited, "What did it say?"

Dagon pulled it up on his computer and read part of the message. From some odd reason he felt secretive, not wanting to disclose the whole message to Stella.

> Vulcan is a source of radiation and radium. Therefore it has the ability to spontaneously and continually emit rays capable of passing through bodies opaque to ordinary light. An intensification of Vulcan energy therefore reconstitutes and liberates electrons from solid matter, causing the phenomena of fluorescence or phosphorescence and creation of new matter.

"Cool, that second part about liberating electrons and creating new matter, that could be this phenomena we were seeing. There has got to be much more to this. Have you ever thought that this might be your dad trying to make contact with us? You should be studying his diary or let me study it. It seems like a pretty odd coincidence that you end up with it right before we lift off."

"Only because my mom died, and I inherited it. Not any other reason," Dagon insisted.

"Yeah, but it was a big secret. Now we have it. Don't you think that has some kind of synchronicity to that?"

She started to reach for the diary. But, Dagon grabbed her arm and pulled her onto his lap hugging her into his chest.

"I don't want anything to happen to you. You need to promise me that you'll tell me the next time this happens to you."

Stella wiggled, starting to protest. Dagon's grip became firmer.

"I mean it, Stella. This isn't anything to play around with. If there are other forces trying to make contact, there are risks to both you and me. Promise me."

"Okay, I promise."

"And," Dagon tweaked her hair, "The diary is mine. It's off limits. I'll look at it later by myself."

Stella mumbled an assent and quickly got up. Then she began rooting around in the cabinets for tea supplies and breakfast.

They fell into a comfortable silence as Dagon gladly continued the routine work necessary for setting up their outdoor laboratory. He was relieved to have some time alone to think about their conversation and contemplate the implications of their discussion.

Later, he approached Stella again.

"How about a walk around the ship to check on her condition? We could stay out for 1/2 hour this time, since it's almost dawn."

Dressing in their space suits, the excitement mounted.

It was an absolutely still blue-black night with the twin moons just setting behind the ship. The highest moon looked huge with a deep violet and red ring around it, the second moon about half its size was more yellow in color. They were anxious to check the temperature and to look at the plant life more carefully. "It's -67 degrees below right now, and it's morning. But, yesterday the temperature reached 128 degrees when the sun had been out for eight hours," Stella exclaimed, as they checked the outdoor temperature gauges.

"Amazing," said Dagon, "This tundra plant must be incredibly tough to withstand such an extreme temperature differential."

"Adaptation, isn't it amazing? Even here life is finding a way to evolve," Stella marveled.

The sky was lightening, showing a faint line of red on the horizon and miles of barren landscape. From their experience yesterday, Stella knew it would be a huge sun, almost twice the size of earth's sun, dominating the pale lavender sky.

Bending down, Stella touched the corner of a plant. Yesterday she had found it spongy as the temperature hit the mid range between temperature extremes, now in the biting cold of morning it was rocklike. This must be an adaptation to protect itself when it is extremely hot or extremely cold. I must check the moisture content of the atmosphere at different times of the day, she concluded to herself. It reminded her of the Dragon's Blood Tree from Socotra in Asia that was now extinct. This tree had adapted to use its upraised branches to grab moisture from highland mist.

Dagon was busy collecting rock samples in specially sealed flasks, which would be kept in a decontamination chamber, a special storage compartment on the ship. No plants or rocks would be brought into the ship for safety reasons. The climatic change could waken deadly spores or spread some type of pestilence back into Vulcan's delicate environment. Even their suits were cleaned in a special exit and entry chamber on the ship.

The half hour passed too quickly. "Let's eat something," said Dagon. "I'd like to set up the KY Land Transporter, KYL, for travel tomorrow. It will take both of us our next two space walks to accomplish this. Does that sound okay to you?" he asked.

"Great, I'm looking forward to taking KYL out and looking around," said Stella. "I think it might be time for some more photos also, so I'll get the camera ready after we eat."

"Right! So, what were you mumbling out there about colors yesterday?"

"What? Oh, you have an amazing memory," Stella said. "I was just thinking that blue, red and gold. The colors of that sunrise are the three primary colors. Yang, or masculine forces, are represented by the color red and feminine, or yin forces, by the cooler color blue. Gold, is the color associated with Kundalini, the center point of the solar plexus that creates balance. Gold is also the color associated with Vulcan, the Goldsmith. It's also cool to note that every color in the color wheel can be mixed from these three base colors. Now, I want to see something green!" Stella smiled.

The next trips out of the spacecraft were spent preparing KYL for a journey across Vulcan's surface. The transporter was equipped with advanced laser GPS, a high megapixel camera, and heat and atmosphere sensors. Getting everything connected took a bit of time. They were able to stay out longer now. But, found the work arduous because of the heaviness of gravity that slowed down all of their movements.

Stella was able to take moisture measurements, finding a small, but significant mist present from mid morning to early afternoon. Setting up a camera on one of the plants, she filmed for an eight-hour period documenting the change in the viscosity of the plant leaves and stems.

When evening fell, they were exhausted and ready for the long eighteen-hour dark cycle of their second night on Vulcan.

CHAPTER 12

✠

Two stories of wholeness

As they settled in for the night, Dagon came in to say goodnight to Stella. She had indicated she wanted a night alone. Since it was usually Dagon who had wanted that with all of his previous girlfriends, he was a bit disconcerted.

"Are you sure you want to sleep in here by yourself?"

"Yes, I want to think and dream, floating around a bit while I fall asleep and wake up. Sometimes I get my best ideas when sleeping."

"You're not going to try to contact this 'entity' are you?" Dagon immediately was on guard.

"No. But, I'm going to let myself relax, like I always do. When there is another person nearby, they're all I can feel. I like that space where you are free of another person's vibes. And, hey, you don't want me getting all needy and dependent on you, anyway."

Dagon sat on the edge of the bed. "What do you mean by that."

Stella settled back into her pillows. "I don't really know, well I guess I do. When you are psychic like me, it is as if you lose the boundaries around yourself sometimes."

"I'm sure, that's true. But, what did you mean by 'needy and dependent'?"

"The best way to answer is for me to tell two great stories with interpretations that I absolutely love. One is a Scottish fairytale called *The Selkie Bride* and is very old. The second is a Russian fairytale."

"In the first, a woman who is selkie, or part seal, is stolen off a rock when she is sunbathing and her seal skin hidden by the man who wants her. He builds her a lovely home and they have a child. But, she repeatedly tells him, 'I'm dying. I need the ocean. I can't survive out of the water. Please give me my seal skin.' He says, 'I can't, you'll leave me.' And, yet, one day when she is nearing death her young child finds sealskin on the beach, bringing it to her. She can smell the ocean and her healing, yet she knows if she puts the skin on and goes into the water she will have to leave her young son. She has no choice. Without the sea she will die anyway."

"She tells her son. 'Whenever you cry, I will be your tears. If you sing a song, I will be the sound. If you paint a picture, I will be the color. I will never leave you.' Then she slips down into the waves."

"*Claire Pinkola Estes* says this is a story about how desperately women need the feminine, represented by the ocean, to simply survive. They need constant connectedness to their sealskin or soul skin, which is experienced through feminine things like art, nature, color, music, other women, community, family and children. If they try to go to men or the masculine to get what they need they dry out and slowly die. Their dependence becomes poisonous. Worse, some men possessively try to keep women from getting their seal skin back."[54]

"I know that one of my ocean sources is meditation, inner connection to the divine, silence and the waters of deep sleep. That is why I am making sure I don't make the mistake of depending on you. I know that you can't give me the nebulous thing that I want. I get that by being more of what I am in my deeper nature, not less."

"Fascinating," Dagon seemed to be deep in thought, "What about men. Is the Russian story for men?"

"Yeah. This is a fairy tale that I heard on a tape read by Robert Bly. There was a prince who saw a long boat row up with a beautiful woman in it. He said to himself, "That's it. She is my destiny. Tomorrow, I'll leave with her." He tells his mother the queen. But, she secretly tells his tutor to prick him with a poison pen the next day so that he'll go to sleep, missing his rendezvous with the long boat. This happens. The prince falls asleep, but when he wakes he finds a note from the princess saying, 'Your mother has betrayed you, lop off her head.' "

Dagon breaks out into an involuntary laugh.

"Well, it's a Russian tale," Stella smiled. "The prince confronts his mother. Sure enough, she has all sorts of excuses for doing it, but she betrayed him. He takes out his broad sword, cuts off her head, starting on the journey to find the beautiful maiden by himself. It is an epic journey. He has to face the Cyclops, sirens and a host of other evils and ends up finally at the hut of the Baba Yaga, a witch woman whose eyes hang onto her checks, whose breasts hang down to her knees and who has the heads of men on stakes around her hut. She asks him a riddle. Only when he successfully answers it is he united with the beautiful maiden who is inside the hut."

"So, what do you think this story means for men?"

"Robert Bly says that it's important that men have a quest. That they have to confront their addictions and ways of falling asleep and wake up to journey toward their challenges and fears. To do this they break dependence on their mothers and face any negative aspects of the feminine represented by the sirens and the witch woman. This is how they finally are united with their own feminine to become complete. They have to decide to be heroes on a quest, bucking society and convention, with the only final goal being their own sense of wholeness."[55]

"I can see why you think of men and women as from two different countries," Dagon said.

"Yes, our needs are so different, we can't even express them well to each other. My cousin and his wife divorced because she wanted him to express love and affection while he thought he was loving her by working harder to bring home money and remodel the house. They have a daughter named 'Maris,' after me. It's so sad; I *know* they really love each other. They are just so different they can't *hear* each other. Every time she expressed dissatisfaction, he became more exhausted, like he could never do enough. But all she wanted was a kiss and a hug."

"It's like the story of tomato soup. A woman is sick and pleads for a bowl of tomato soup so she can get well. Her husband brings home a gallon of chicken noodle soup. She asks again, begging this time, all I need is tomato soup. He sells part of his business to bring her home a truckload of chicken noodle soup. You have to feel sorry for both of them. They just can't understand how to get what they need."

Dagon said thoughtfully, "I like the Russian tale. We are on a quest now. We have no idea what will happen, what dangers we face."

"A nice thought to go to sleep by."

"I know, it is, isn't it?" Dagon smiled wryly.

"Things would probably be different if we were back home," said Stella. "Your adventure would probably be hours spent at the office or new research. Either way, I have to meet my own deepest needs and you need to be filled with the conviction that your accomplishing something that matters, that you're doing it on our own."

"Which reminds me, what will we do when we are back home? I live in Wyoming and you live in Washington," Stella's voice seemed vulnerable as she broached the sensitive topic.

"We can fly the Mach III. If we go by Concord, we are only half hour away from each other."

"You know what I mean?"

"I don't know, yet. I can't think that far ahead. We'll figure something out."

"Okay," Stella said with innocent trust. "Good night, sweet dreams."

They gazed deeply at each other for a moment, soaking each other up before Dagon left for his own sleep quarters. Dagon noticed how dark and mysterious her eyes looked in the half-light. He could almost see the Egyptian woman of his dreams. She would be wearing a soft silk wrap, tied at the shoulder, a gold belt around her slim waist.

CHAPTER 13

✠

The fool and creation

Dagon wandered in a trance-like way toward his bedroom noticing that everything looked a little different, more intense in color, more heavy with sound. He touched his bed cover, finding himself just stroking it, enjoying the warmth. His body felt heavy with the need for deep rest, for 18 hours of darkness.

Sleep came quickly and he was dreaming again, vividly, in bright color. First he saw a Magician with a long black beard and a maroon robe with pointy toed shoes. The man winked, gesturing toward the ground to indicate a sword, a scepter, coin and a chalice. "These are your armor: air, earth, fire and water. They are keys to wisdom that keeps unfolding. Follow this owl, she will take you to the beginning point, the place that the initiates call 'The Key.'"

Without warning. Dagon felt himself being hurled through the air on the back of the immense bird. He clung to the feathers straining to stay on until his body began to ache and his fingers cramp. Below him, he could see the gray evening landscape of patchwork fields, hills and trees. Then, they dove down silently, landing in a high grassy field on top of a band of cliffs.

He heard a man whistling in the distance. Suddenly, in front of him, next to a path, stood a man dressed like a jester. He carried a knapsack on his back, and a dog was yipping at his heals. The man was grinning broadly, slapping Dagon on the back with a friendly gesture.

"So, you've decided to take the journey."

"I don't know what you're talking about."

"Relax, just follow, you'll see."

Whistling a jolly tune and skipping down the path, the simpleton seemed harmless. Dagon followed cautiously.

Suddenly, the sides of the path dropped away. It appeared that they were both balancing on a precipice, the sides dropping away to an abyss on both sides of a narrow walkway. The jester seemed totally at ease. In fact, he began to balance playfully on the edge.

Dagon tried to clutch his arm, to pull him back. But, the reckless fellow just began to call out in a singsong voice.

"Everything is possible here. Here is the power of the unknown. Here is the mystery beyond chaos, the place in-between the positive and negative energies. It is no-thingness, samadhi, muhkti, and nirvana. To be here you, must surrender. *Are you brave enough for this quest?*"

The fool then pulled a rope out of his pocket and cast it into the air. It seemed to float in a large loop above him. He looked at Dagon, grinning broadly.

"You must become like a little child." With that, he playfully pushed Dagon over the edge into the abyss. Terror stricken, Dagon flayed his arms, screaming as he plummeted toward the rocks rising beneath him.

"Play," a voice resounded loudly in his head.

Tentatively, he tried to tuck in his feet to slow the free fall. It felt good. He did a somersault, putting out his hands.

Giddiness swept over him. "I can fly."

Rising on the current, euphoria filled Dagon, he felt spontaneous, trusting, innocent and totally fearless.

In front of him he could see an ancient city, carved out of rock on the side of a high cliff face.

Something disturbed him. He came out of the dream, back to his dark room, feeling the hard plastic base of his mattress-covered bed. He got up and went over to the mirror over his locker, but noticed that it was cracked down the middle and the overhead light wouldn't turn on. The bedcovers began to wave in ripples. I must still be dreaming, how odd.

Dagon became aware then that his body felt frozen. He was in bed still asleep. Wow, he hadn't had a hypnogogic dream since he was a teenager. It is a state where the dreamer is consciously awake, yet, still dreaming in full REM sleep. As is true with all deep sleep, the body can't move. This is very scary if you don't know what is happening. In this dream state you can travel by just telling your mind where you want to go. Dagon decided to be brave and experiment.

As he sunk back into a dreamy half sleep, the dream seemed to continue, hypnogogic or almost real, full of color, feeling and even, consciousness.

After a long night of fitfully going in and out of these REM states, he finally woke up exhausted. He quickly grabbed a piece of paper, trying to write down what he remembered, then fell into regular sleep. When he woke again, it was still dark. He could hear Stella calling out in her sleep as she tossed and turned. But, he decided not to wake her.

The long day and night cycle of the planet made it necessary to spend more time in the ship than either would have liked.

Stella came into his bedroom, looking sleepy. She cuddled, spoon style next to his warm body.

Surprisingly they both said at the same time, "I had a dream."

"You go first," said Stella. Dagon quietly described his dream of the jester and flying.

"How wonderful. You were dreaming of the Greater Arcana, of the Tarot. Oddly, I dreamed of it to. Only, I was watching it and observing a boy who came flying out of the sky. It looked somewhat like you, but, different. Younger maybe, more like a teenager."

Stella continued, "He flew forward and landed on a stone-lined street. What he saw captivated him completely. A number of ancient looking males and females wearing long robes with gold necklaces were walking in orderly rows toward a temple. They seemed to see him, nodding to him as if he was somehow familiar, and then walked into the white pyramid shaped temple. He could see elaborate carvings in the white limestone of murals or panels that seemed to glow with unearthly phosphorescence."

Dagon squeezed Stella tightly and sat up. *"That is what I dreamed.* I was that boy. I remember looking at the murals, fascinated. I turned and found a nondescript woman standing next to me in a simple, gray robe tied with a gold cord. Her hair was knotted in an intricate crown of braids and she wore the golden V necklace of the monks. She quietly gazed at me expecting questions."

"You asked what the temple was," Stella interjected and sat up too, pulling a pillow behind her so she could lean against the headboard.

"Yes," Dagon said with amazement at what was happening between him and Stella. "She explained they were students of a way of initiation and spiritual evolvement. They were pacing out the four directions in front of the Temple of Rejuvenation and using the akashic records to open higher consciousness."

"Right" said Stella. "Her voice was so amazing when she answered your question it was like music, it resonated with all sorts of layers of harmonics."

Dagon nodded, starting to get nervous about what was happening between him and Stella.

Stella continued. "She said more. I wrote it all down this morning so I wouldn't forget. Stella read:

"Their journey is into the inner paths of the mysteries, a world beyond this relative reality. This secret was given to your world through Atlantis and Egypt. But, it came from Vulcan. It is hundreds of thousands of years old. In your language would be called, the seven sacred principles of creation."

"Seven principles?" Dagon said. "I don't remember any of this."

"I remember thinking that the boy in the dream wasn't paying attention. He was studying the murals on the panels one by one."

"Yes, I remember doing that," Dagon said.

Stella read out of her notebook, "These were the principles:"

1. The principle of Mind. Words have power to create. Empty mind therefore creates endless possibilities

2. The principle of correspondence: As above, So, below

3. The Principle of Vibration: That nothings rests; everything moves and vibrates

4. The Principle of Polarity: That Everything is Dual, everything has poles, everything has a pair of

opposites, that extremes meet, that all paradoxes may be reconciled into non-duality.

5. The Principle of Rhythm: That everything is always flowing in and out, rising and falling

6. The Principle of Cause and Effect: that every cause has an effect. That there are many planes of causation

7. The Principle of Gender: that every is masculine and feminine." [56]

Dagon looked at Stella with astonishment. "You actually remember these? How?

"I've read them before somewhere. Perhaps in my alchemy research. I just know them. We should see if BOB can find a source," said Stella.

"Okay, now, this is really getting out there," said Dagon. "How could we have the same dream?"

"Maybe one of us had it and telepathically sent it to the other person, or maybe we are both getting the same message from the extraterrestrial force we seem to be coming into contact with. Tell me the rest of *your* dream," said Stella with excitement.

Dagon thought about it. "The woman went to great length to tell me about the Fool, she said, 'He is the only key to entrance.' "

Stella heard a noise and looked over to see BOB standing at the entrance to their room.

"You called me?" he asked.

"No, oh, I guess I did. I have something I want you to look up in your databanks. It is called the Seven Principles of Creation."

There was a moment as BOB's lights flashed and he said, "Yes it is also called the Seven Hermetic Principles of Universal Cosmic

Law. The Universe exists by virtue of these laws which form its frame and which hold it together. They are considered the master keys of ageless arcane wisdom. Please hold for a minute." BOB turned, looking into an empty corner of their room, then turned to look back at Dagon and Stella. "I have been given information for Dagon."

"Go ahead," said Stella, curious about what could possibly be going on.

> The Fool is Zero, a sacred key, and the eleventh path that stands before the face of the cause of causes. Bordering on the source of the cosmos it is initial potential to transform the world with the word or thought.[57]

> You know it as the unified force field, the holistic field that makes up the universe, the place we come from, the place that we return. As an initiate you can see the panels. It is your choice. Before you stand mysterious thrones. *If you choose, step inside; you will be given inner instruction from your own guides as to those paths necessary.*

Stella looked over at Dagon who seemed shaken to his core.

"BOB," asked Stella. "Who gave you this information?"

BOB, however, seemed to be trying to provide other data.

> An experiment was conducted by Cambridge University utilizing a lead shielded and airtight Faraday chamber for particle research. In theory, if the internal chamber was pumped down to a vacuum environment such as in space and the temperature reduced to absolute zero, all particles should stop vibrating and there should be no energy present in the chamber. What was discovered instead was enormous energy, enough in a 100-watt bulb to bring the earth's ocean to boiling point. *There is omnipotent and infinite presence in the universe. It exists within the place in-between. The Zero-point or the Fool is the key.*[58]

Stella turned back to Dagon. "He said 'you'd be given instruction from your own guides to those paths necessary.' Did you step inside any of the panels in your dream?"

"Only one, I woke up soon after," Dagon had his head in his hands.

"Wow, which one!"

"The Lady in gray called it the Wheel of Fortune," Dagon said.

"Tell me about it," Stella's face was flushed with delight.

"There was an intricately carved picture like a mural on the wall of the temple. It showed a revolving wheel with symbols all around it. I just stepped up to it and suddenly I was inside the panel. I was standing directly in front of a spinning wheel. Millions of colors were flashing out of it as it contracted and expanded. The center was deep black and the outside edge white. I sensed that each color was emitting a vibration and sound, but knew somehow that it would overwhelm me to hear the music. Then, before my eyes all the colors shifted to a gold light so bright that it hurt my eyes. I fell to the ground in a stupor, overtaken by the majesty of it, then woke up laying in my bed."

Stella said excitedly, "The Wheel of Fortune in the Tarot represents fate or destiny. It must be a place of creation because black and white contains all other colors within them. Your experience of it reminds me of stories in the Old Testament where a prophet would see a vision of God or an angel and would have to turn his face away, 'least he be consumed by the glory of God.' "

"Also, the wheel of fortune and your description of it remind me of the sun," Stella said with excitement. "I spent six months helping with data from NASA's *Solar Dynamics Observatory*. The solar plasma is packed with electrified magnetic fields, which emerge on the surface in a dance with solar wind flinging plasma outward.

Meanwhile, the plasma spheroid at the center fuses 700 million tons of protons in helium nuclei every second so that the core throbs and contracts with a deep slow heartbeat. This nuclear furnace makes a lot of noise, ringing like a bell in millions of distinct tones. It's like the Wheel of Fortune you described just now."[89]

Stella had a pensive look on her face. "Hmm, a golden ball."

Dagon had gotten up and was pacing back and forth still trying to understand what was happening to them.

"I can't believe this. How is this possible? We had the same freaking dream!" Dagon ran his hand over the stubble on his chin. "And, The Seven Principles of Creation? Even worse. A dream, I could relegate to fanciful thinking. Getting this kind of information download during sleep?"

Dagon sat down hard, holding his hand to his forehead.

"Not so unusual for me," said Stella. "I often dream and get messages when I'm studying something. The dream seems to give me the lesson in such a way that my inner psyche has to shift it from just words to an experience. Once I dreamed all night over and over, 'God is in Everything.' 'God is in Everything.' 'God is in Everything.' I woke up with a completely difference sense of what that really meant through 'knowing' it."

Stella's eyes sparkled. "This dream is describing the tarot. They are sacred images on cards that have been handed down for centuries to describe to initiates the mysteries of the universe," she said reverently.

"But, I've never looked at or used the tarot. I don't know anything about it!" Dagon got up and began to pace in frustration.

"Calm down, Dagon," said Stella. "This has to be a phenomena connected to Vulcan. Maybe here one of us can pick up the other person's dreams. I would be the one most likely to be dreaming of the tarot and you said you had never heard of the seven principles."

"Or," Dagon said ominously, "Maybe this is an example of us being manipulated in our sleep by whatever force exists here. We must be most vulnerable to it when we're sleeping."

"Sure," said Stella, "That's when most psychic experiences happen, in dreams when the conscious mind isn't resisting."

"Or it's possible *your* unconscious was trying to teach us something," Dagon said frowning, frazzled by the thought.

Stella looked sheepish, "Well, there *is* a lot of important symbolism in the tarot. The tarot contains the ingredients the alchemist uses to create the world. Fire/wands and Air/swords are masculine while Water/cups and Earth/pentacles are feminine. The elements are in suits are numbered 1-10, with a page, knight, king and queen. Each number represents a harmonic vibrations or frequency in creation."

"The Greater Arcana of the tarot is a very complicated set of symbols on twenty-two cards that each represent stages of spiritual initiation. If you examine for instance the first four cards, you see something profound. Card one, the first stage of initiation is the initial spark or seed for life, the power to create something with a Word and is represented by a Magician carrying a fire wand. The second card, number two represents a joining of opposites, which first created duality, or consciousness represented by the sword or air, the High Priestess. The number three represents, the Empress, a creative dynamic force that draws things together uniting and merging like water or cups. Finally, the number four represents physical manifestation, the coins, earth and the Emperor. So, you can see that it two pairs of consorts priest/priestess, empress/emperor, fire, air, water, earth, the essential elements for the creation of all life. And, if you use the tarot for divination there is an unlimited number of combinations that you can get from the cards."

"This all makes very little sense to me," Dagon complained.

"Well, it would mean more to you if you were interested in these types of things, just like quantum physics might not mean much to someone who isn't a scientist," responded Stella.

"The main thing to learn is that the tarot, numerology and astrology are all connected. There is a pattern running through esoteric systems that explains life, creation, masculine and feminine, balance, transformation and union. Within them you see the Seven Principles of Creation."

"For example, the ancients knew all about the zero point, represented by the Fool. To them it was a point of unity, describing unbounded and expanded consciousness."

Dagon found himself staring at Stella as she spoke, becoming disconcerted when he noticed that her face blurred out as he gazed at her. In place of her face, he could see another face superimposed over hers. It was the face of an old man, the wisdom evident on the gnarled high forehead and the kind eyes. He seemed to be looking directly into Dagon's eyes.

A high level buzzing started in Dagon's ear, a tone that was at once both sweet and piercing. Suddenly, Stella's words came back into focus. Shaken, Dagon tried to concentrate on the concepts that she was speaking about.

Dagon blinked hard. If he squinted his eyes, he could still see the old man superimposed over Stella's face.

The next moment, she looked directly at him, her gaze piercing.

"You have been avoiding the truth within you. This is all actually very familiar to you. You simply have to remember your past. By insisting on what you call rational logic, you blind yourself to the building blocks of matter that you need to do your work."

Dagon was startled by this confrontation and squirmed.

"Your dream is a memory," the old man admonished.

Dagon left the bedroom and went to stare out into the black night through their view port.

Stella followed him, standing behind him. She rubbed her hand on his back in a comforting gesture.

"How could this be a memory?" Dagon said. "I keep getting that message, 'remember.' Some of the things we've talked about feel like I've known them before: little bits of Hindu text, dreams that take me back to Egypt, familiarity when you talk about Atlantis, and now this odd dream of the Tarot and the akashic records. The Temple that I saw in my dream seemed to be located somewhere on Vulcan."

Stella patted the back of Dagon's heart, then hugged him from behind.

"It will come clear to you in time. We must trust that there is an intuitive intelligence in nature that moves things in the best direction. You must be remembering for a reason."

For a while they both stood silently looking out into the pitch dark. There was no man made light in the distance, no stars shining through the haze of the synchron belt and the moon had set.

"It is seems so dark, black and empty. But, it isn't." She sought for some way to comfort Dagon. "That darkness is like your dream of the Fool. It holds endless power for encoding new knowledge that can change all of the possibilities for our future. But maybe your dream was trying to tell you to relax, play and fly. All of this mystery will reveal itself in time."

If Dagon had just looked behind him, he would have seen Stella gazing at her hand with a dazed expression. Are these my hands or somebody else's? she wondered. Through half-closed eyes she could almost make out the image of a serpent and a dragon on a palm that wasn't her own.

CHAPTER 14

✠

Dreams of dragons

As daybreak came, Vulcan welcomed Dagon and Stella with another lovely sunrise. A bright ray was shooting a luminescent arc of gold across the frozen indigo blue of the tundra. Deep in individual thought, each watched the dramatic changes in color, the sky first crimson, and then gradually lightening to pale lavender above the exotic, silent vista. The rolling hills spread out in swelling waves as far as the eye could see with mountains on each side in the distance.

Stella reached across the gulf that had been between her and Dagon since their early morning discussion about their shared 'dream.' She tentatively took Dagon's hand, finding it cold and unresponsive. With determination, she squeezed and imagined warmth passing from her hand into his. Dagon looked up from his reverie and his eyes seem to brighten a bit. He pulled her toward him, putting his arm around her.

Standing arm in arm, the sunrise looked even more beautiful.

Stella and Dagon had packed emergency supplies, food and water in KYL. With an awkward tangle of arms and legs, they sandwiched themselves into the cramped interior of the cab that was set high above four wheel extensions, which could be manipulated to propel them forward. BOB had been left to monitor and send them reports from the ship.

Fiddling with the series of dials and knobs in front of him, Dagon frowned with concentration. They would have to move more slowly than expected as the force of the planet's gravity field weighed KYL down. Fortunately, the surface of the tundra offered little resistance. The smooth covering of plants cushioned their trek as they maneuvered around large rocks, boulders and unexpected ravines.

Stella felt a frightening lurch in the pit of her stomach as they began moving, her fear of the unknown haunting her.

Why was it that the simple act of movement had this affect on her? She could remember having the same feeling as a teenager. When all of the other kids piled into the car with excited expectation, Stella had shivered in the back seat, hoping she wouldn't get carsick.

It had been the fight against her fear that had propelled her into the space program. She had spent years exercising courage about the simplest things, like flying or taking an unplanned detour on a vacation. Someone once told her that your greatest gift is what you fear. She had worked for years to train her mind to release thoughts of anxiety and had learned gradually to enjoy spontaneous, changing situations. The fear had served her well, for it had become a pathway to spiritual study. It had led her to yoga, breath work and meditation. In the face of fear you had no other choice.

Settling back on her seat in KYL, she noticed that her deep breathing was making her feel giddy and lightheaded. A stifled giggle escaped, seeming out of place in the army camo atmosphere of the cab. She gripped the seat to stop herself.

Dagon looked at her alarmed.

"Sorry, I get the giggles sometimes when I'm working with the energy in my body. The release of tension just makes me laugh. Don't you ever do that? Hmmm, obviously no."

Dagon was the picture of intense, serious focus.

For as far as they could see, the landscape stretched out endlessly, a desolate, monochromatic ocean of cryptograms. The sky, now a pale shade of violet, contrasted only slightly from the muted browns and grays around them. Stella became mesmerized by the endless silence, punctuated by the rhythmic thud of the long octopus-like legs, as KYL plodded forward.

Suddenly, Stella realized what she was seeing. "Wow," she exclaimed as the thin air reverberated with a loud crash. Dust puffed up in a small cloud in the distance. Rocks tumbled down the stark mountain slopes, and a soft gray dust appeared to be eroding away from the hilltops, the cloud of it wafting out in slow motion.

"This is erosion we are seeing. There has to some type of weather here for erosion to be occurring. I wish we could stay longer than seven days. We won't have an opportunity to see any seasonal changes," Stella felt an incredible sadness. She softened her voice to a whisper, the absolute silence affecting her.

Dagon looked at her quizzically, his face a mask of professional concern.

"How are you feeling?" His gaze was quietly intent.

"Fine." Stella crossed her fingers behind her back. "Why? Are you okay?"

"That's a good question to ask yourself, I think," said Dagon. "You look pale right now. You went to sleep early. But, when I woke up last night, I could hear you talking in your sleep and tossing and turning. Have you felt sick again?" He tested the waters gently.

"Actually, I've been having crazy dreams like the one we both had last night for weeks now. My dreams feel totally real. I had to pinch myself this morning to make sure I was awake and not dreaming," Stella admitted.

Dagon gripped her wrist. "You've been having hypnogogic dreams *every* night?"

"Ouch" Stella said shaking him off, "Too tight." She rubbed her wrist as she explained it. "Once, I thought I was awake. When I tried to move it felt like there was a weight on my chest pinning me down. An inner voice said 'You're just dreaming.' So, I tried to relax and accept my paralysis. You woke up and came over to shake me out of my sleep. We talked and I got out of bed, beginning to prepare breakfast. But, as I was cooking, bizarre things kept happening to me: odd distorted images, the egg floating up, then turning into a chicken, vivid colors, super powers. I finally had to shake myself internally and realize that I was still dreaming. It was like being caught in a time warp that looped back endlessly. I couldn't get out."

"It sounds a little more intense than what I experienced, more frightening."

Stella turned her exhausted gaze to Dagon, drawing a shaky hand over her brow, twitching slightly as he reached for her hand, this time, gently. Her sensitized skin felt the tender, sure stroke of comfort.

"I know these are dreams. Yet, they seem so real."

"Can you remember any of them?" Dagon asked.

"Yes, but now isn't really the time to talk about it," Stella said.

Dagon playfully grabbed Stella, pulling her close to him. He was surprised to find her body stiff and taunt as a board.

"You're trembling, are you scared?"

"Let's just concentrate on the scenery."

"What scenery?" Dagon asked sarcastically. Then, he firmly grasped her hand again as if reluctant to let her go. "Stella, you can tell me your dreams. I might be able to help." With an almost imperceptible shrug, he focused his attention back on his responsibilities.

"Don't worry, I spent years traveling around Mars. KYL's an old friend." He patted the dashboard.

The red instrument light blinked in steady periodic bleeps on the computer console. "You have already traveled 12 kilometers," KYL's GPS system reported in a robotic voice. "According to the scanner we have gained 686 feet in elevation. This canyon dead-ends at .548 miles. There is an opening into the next valley we can pass through."

"Good, let's head there and see if we find anything interesting,"

Within the hour they were deep in the canyon climbing steadily. Rocks towered high on either side of them. The ground cover had changed color. It was browner with small patches of dull grayish green. Bone white stones could be seen scattered in groups, and occasionally a band of these stone ran through the otherwise gray rock around them.

Dagon used the robot arm of the KYL to take a sample of the stone, putting it in the sealed storage bins at the back of the unit.

As the pathway narrowed, both Stella and Dagon began to get a little tense. There was no way to see in front of them. Every bend just seemed to lead to another bend through the maze of rocks. Their only lifeline was the laser scanner, which actively programmed each step to allow them to retrace their paths should they get lost. KYL reported that their had been a rise in air temperature of 10 degrees and in ground temperature of 5 degrees. It was reassuring to note

236

that the spacecraft was still sending out a homing signal, which allowed them to measure distances and their coordinates. They had successfully made one contact with BOB who had given them a positive report on the condition of the ship.

Unexpectedly, they passed through a stone gateway into another valley. From their elevated position on the plateau, the panoramic view was breathtaking. Just ahead the ground dropped steeply. In the lower portion of the ravine, they could see with telescopes that the tundra was a slightly blue-green in color.

"My god," Stella gasped. "They must have some type of storms here. These plants respond to the smallest amount of moisture. Perhaps heavy mist?" she speculated.

Dagon barely heard her. He was busy looking into the distance through the spotting scope.

"Stella, I'm sure I just saw the flash of some sort of prismatic color. I wonder if we should follow in that direction?" he said, adventure shining in his gray eyes.

A sharp pain settled in Stella's stomach. She brushed away a mental picture of how far they were from the safety of their spacecraft, and from the safety of planet earth. Emptying her mind of the scary image, she focused again on her breathing and his voice.

"If we are seeing some type of atmospheric disturbance, it would be worth pursuing," Dagon said. "Perhaps, it is a rainbow from some fine mist. Whatever it is, it could lead us to a pot of gold."

"Gold," Stella repeated, her adrenaline making her feel altered. "Gold," she repeated in an absent, dazed manner, looking at Dagon with dawning awareness. "I'll tell you some of what I dreamed one night last week. It was a strange teaching about gold."

"I was going down into a deep cavern to meet Vulcan who was a goldsmith there. Dwarves lined the sides of the pathway guarding it. I could smell a wet dank mold as we dropped down, entering into a large cavern. I thought I was supposed to meet Vulcan there. Instead, I saw a Dragon curled up like a snake on a nest. In front of it was a circle of druids chanting. I couldn't wait to get out of there, but got lost as I was trying to find my way out of the dark passages. I ended up following a young woman wearing a gray robe who was holding a lantern. When I finally came out into bright sunlight, I fell down on my knees with relief and gratitude. Somehow the dream felt like something that would happen to me in the future."

"It did?" Dagon was looking startled.

"I wrote a dream poem," Stella said.

"A what?"

"A dream poem. I quickly tried to describe the images in a poem."

"I would like to hear it," said Dagon as he wrestled with the wheel of KYL while they traversed a rocky section of the valley floor. "But, first let me stop. Then, we'll have a little picnic and a break from this infernal bumping and jolting."

Rubbing the back of her neck, Stella settled back with a sigh, enjoying the stillness after they stopped moving. Some simple organization and moments later they had laid out a simple meal of sandwiches on their laps. She ate, hungrily licking the crumbs off her fingers before she settled back with a small moan.

"Every muscle in my body hurts. Who said four-wheeling was fun!"

"Sore, huh?"

"Aching and to top it off, I'm kind of crampy. I have taken medicine to stop my periods while in space, but I still get PMS symptoms when I would have normally had my monthly flow. Unfortunately for us, I'm still ovulating and am fertile. I wish every man could spend one day inside of the body of a woman. Then, he might understand why she gets emotional, fragile and bitchy."

Dagon felt a softness start in his chest at her willingness to talk so intimately with him.

"Maybe that's why I dreamed about a dragon last week."

"What?" Dagon looked confused.

"Dragons seem universally feminine to me. Primitive like a woman's moon cycle is. In my dream I knew she was a female dragon. She had ancient eyes and her tail circled a nest filled with golden eggs. Her scales were like hummingbird wings. I couldn't help thinking of the goddess, Kundalini. She was a snake goddess because she represented the power coiled at the base of our spine that can rise through the chakras, as we are enlightened."

"And, your poem?"

"Yes, my poem." Stella pulled out her Link and began to intone the words of the poem, her voice rising and falling as she let her voice play with the music of the words.

DRAGONS, DRUIDS, and DWARFS
Earth energy is cool, yet strong. Polarities have cold spaces, too. We pull our coats around us. The north wind is at our back, the moon a lamp. Passive, yet enduring, soft and malleable, near zero, forever, forever, forever.
DRAGON
The dragon's lair in the dark moist earth harbors a water creature, cold-blooded, reptilian. Blinking she pulls her scaly tail behind her and coils it around her treasure.
GOLD,
Breath of fire, the lair a nest of metal, its egg the captured light of the sun, glinting even in darkness.
DWARF

Gnarled hands and woody skin, with pick and shovel he sings to the bowels of earth and dark subterranean passageways of mud and rock.

The caves drip, moist, and watery pools reflect the wavering light of the smallest of men with the smallest of beards.

Gold,

He smiles for his luck to craft such beautiful jewels.

Wrought in magma, the deepest caverns hold the forgers fire.

DRUID

Smoky incense, within a moonstone circle, soft footfalls on dewy pathways to secret places, where trances and altars wait, with talismans, cauldrons and blood.

Gold,

Bowl of rebirth, dance of ecstasy, in bird headdress he flies with the fire to heaven

VULCAN

Dragon, Druid, Dwarf - Otherworldly power, deep in the caverns of this world. The dark birth canal of knowledge, cauldron of subconscious ancient memory

Dwarf, Dragon, Druid he works the gold, breathes the fire and rises as a phoenix from the ashes to heaven.

She glanced up at Dagon when she had finished to find him looking disconcerted.

"Dagon, what's wrong?" she asked, startled.

He shook himself. "I don't know. I'm just thinking about how bright the light was in my dream last night. It was like getting a glimpse of the golden light that fuels creation. I was so overwhelmed by the immensity of it, I passed out. Your talk of Kundalini reminds me of it. You dreamed about it as a deep primal feminine dragon. I dreamed of it as a bright transcendent light."

Stella looked excited. "There is an alchemical image of a world tree. At the root of the tree is a dragon; in the high branches is an eagle. They represent the same thing in opposites. Kundalini travels from the root chakra to the crown chakra. In Jewish mysticism the tree of life defines the nature of the universe by diagramming attributes of God with pathways between them. At the root is Malkhut, the Kingdom with a pathway to the crown, Keter, Remember what BOB said, that the Fool card in the Tarot is the 11th pathway. To get from Malkhut to Keter in the Tree of Life you go through the 11th pathway." Stella felt a tantric rush as she thought of kundalini flowing up through that pathway.

"You have that dark, mysterious look right now. Maybe it's just your Plutonian Scorpio nature. Do you know that the both the dragon/serpent and the eagle symbolizes Pluto. You're such a Plutonian person. Perhaps, you have a dragon coiled up within you too," she said seductively as she stroked the long length of his vertebrae.

She felt his immediate response. Amazing, she thought, Sex, Dagon, dragons, kundalini, gold, and Vulcan all in one ecstatically loaded moment.

Dagon looked away, pretending to concentrate on his food, as he willed himself to focus his sexual arousal into conversation.

Dagon and Stella began to put away the remains of lunch, getting out of KYL to walk around. Without their spacecraft, Stella felt a bit disoriented.

"How did you deal with two years on Mars," Stella said.

"Oh, you get used to it after a while. I guess it's not much different then living at the South Pole. You start to depend on the people around you and your routines for simple daily chores. I enjoyed myself most of the time."

Dagon got his video camera and took some footage of the scenery around them. "This planet" said Dagon musing. "could support a human colony. It is much more forgiving then Mars. It will be interesting to see what Interspace Research does here in the future. We might be standing on prime real estate."

Stella threw her empty plate down on her lap with disgust.

"I don't like that idea," began Stella angrily. "Money and economic endeavors are setting priorities for our mission. A large corporate structure, like Interspace Research, only wants to get its greedy hands on Vulcan's natural resources before the Federation of Nations can protect them. That's just plain wrong."

She went on passionately. "My hometown is in Wyoming's Rocky Mountains. Over the years I watched Wyoming politicians decide it wasn't important to protect our pristine wilderness. I saw ignorant people treat nature like to was something to be conquered. I don't want to be a part of doing it here. We flew here in a ship called the *Golden Eagle*. We need to be like the eagle, more visionary. We *have* to do something different here!"

"I'm just warning you, Dagon. I'm not going to go along with *anything* that compromises this planet. I've met the heads of Interspace Research. They have no sensitivity to anything outside of the god of money. They don't realize yet that everything that we do to others we do to ourselves. Fishermen who bash in the heads of endangered seals are bashing in their own heads. People who trap and kill intelligent animals like wolves are killing themselves. It would be only too easy to do that here. As a toxic bi-product of gluttony, another planet could get trashed, like Mars and the Moon."

Stella's voice rose in distress. "How could we have allowed mining on both of those planets!"

Stella continued. "I feel guilty enough, now. KYL is walking over fragile plants that took, millions, maybe billions of years to grow."

"Oh, really, Stella," Dagon rejoined with brusque impatience. "Isn't that a bit strong? What is your intent? Mine is to produce life, not, destroy it. I'm here because I'm trying to use my talents and skills to build a new colony for earth. I'm not trying to take away anything from other life sources that I make contact with."

"Can you really say that, Dagon? How can we justify exploring a planet so that it can be used for material resources that would pad a corporate pocketbook?"

Stella's cheeks were bright red with passion.

Dagon retorted. "Corporations funded this trip, yes. However, the benefits will eventually filter back to all of mankind. How come there isn't any place for 'mankind' in your philosophy? We deserve to live just like these plants. Are you the judge of what is moral, or ethical? It's very complicated, not as black and white as you're making it. Discovering something isn't a reason to feel guilty. Maybe the West *wanted* to be discovered by pioneers. Maybe space *wants* to be explored!"

They were facing each other nose to nose now, hands on hips, squared off, as if in battle.

Dagon's voice softened when he saw the sheen of tears behind the anger sparkling in her eyes.

He said, "As long as we put ethical values back into the formulae, things will work out. We can disagree about what to do with this land, how it should be developed, how the resources should be used or even about what organizational structures we each think are 'okay.' But, fighting each other, like this, doesn't help. And, who knows, perhaps the debate will eventually lead us to better solutions. There has to be a reason, even for our differences."

"Still, don't you see," Stella almost pled for his understanding; "It hasn't been 'abundant life for all.' We have been suffering in a hierarchical system that doesn't even honor the dragon that guards the gold, the feminine, and the earth that provides the resources. Sure, we have been slowly moving toward more cooperative efforts, but business is still the center of our lives instead of 'life' being the center of our businesses."

Dagon countered, "Don't you think there is some reason for this hierarchy, too? Maybe it's for information, for evolution, for growth. Hell, I don't know. But, neither do you. And, you have to admit our world economic systems have changed dramatically since Vulcan was discovered. Cooperative horizontal management systems are now the norm. They weren't in that past, sure, but they are now. Even those big nasty corporations have to be more responsible to the values of the people that support it or they can't exist. Corporations are just people. As our values change, the corporation's change. Interspace Research will change."

"What will happen to Vulcan in the meantime?" Stella asked tremulously, "It is so fragile."

"Stella, this planet isn't fragile. We are. You and me. We are the ones that could be snuffed out in moments, who are risking our lives right now. This planet will still be here in 100 million years. You're not responsible for it. It is bigger than you. You can't control it. I'm sorry it hurts you. However, you can't control things bigger than you."

"Well, we can learn from our mistakes. We can change and be responsible for the things we know hurt, even the smallest insect. I won't pretend I don't see something hurting, I won't stop my heart from having compassion for suffering by saying, 'Oh well, suffering is always with us.' "

"Stop it!" Dagon had had enough.

"Stop what?"

"Stop looking so broken-hearted." Dagon turned around as if to shut her out.

Stella's sadness turned to anger. She knew her claws were coming out, the part of her that felt ferocious if she saw a lost dog or an animal being abused. Eris was alive in her, the part that didn't care what kind of discord her emotions caused. She almost felt the dragon in her starting to breath fire.

"I don't care if my emotions about this are inconvenient or uncomfortable. I don't care if it interrupts order if I throw a fit about this. I don't care if it feels good to you or anybody else if I say this. We have been acting like cowards on earth; acting like mankind is an animal instead of a conscious being. I haven't changed my mind. I don't want to tell them there is life on this planet so they can come strip mine it," Stella said bitterly. "I'm glad that the radio system hasn't been operative."

Dagon's eyes widened slightly, but before he could speak, Stella corrected herself.

She shook her head helplessly. "I realize that eventually all of this information has to be public. Finding the cryptograms is going to create a storm of press and speculation." She put her head down. "But until that day arrives, I prefer to put off the dirty deed. Vulcan is untouched, and it's vulnerable to the rotten side of mankind. Just by being here, you and I are changing this planet forever."

She paused for a minute and took a deep breath to calm herself. Her eyes were pleading as she looked up at Dagon. "Let's stop arguing. I hate this disharmony too. What's gotten into us? This is kind of weird."

"Well, you started it," Dagon said firmly.

"I agree with you about that," Stella turned abruptly away and began to restlessly clean up the rest of the mess from their little picnic. Tiredness descended over both of them as they silently contemplated the barren landscape in front of them. The spirit of adventure had been snuffed out, dulled by their argument and by the food sitting heavily in their stomachs.

It was with unspoken mutual agreement that they began to turn around. Pausing to telescope down the steeply sloping valley floor, Dagon's disappointment intensified. The prism lights seemed to have vanished with no other reoccurrence of the odd phenomena.

"We can try a different direction tomorrow. We'll also need to work with our laboratory specimens in the greenhouse station. Then, we'll only have four more days," Regret lowered his voice to a husky pitch.

Dagon maneuvered the craft around and set the direction finder on autopilot. He sat back in his chair with his hands behind his head. The dejection in his posture, stirred Stella. Being a passionate fiery person, meant emotions came and went easily for her. She felt better just because she had spoken her feelings out loud. Maybe she needed to be more careful, if it took Dagon longer to get over an argument. She stroked a lock of hair off his forehead.

"I'm sorry, did I bum you out."

Dagon squeezed her hand with a little half smile. "I'm starting to get used to your outbursts."

They sat in comfortable silence together for a while lulled by the rhythmic movement of KYL's leg extensions as they lumbered along.

Then, Stella said softly, "Do you know what I miss most in this landscape? Animals. I guess I always took the sound of birds for granted. At home if I went for a walk I would hear wild geese or see a bluebird, my god they are so bright blue, their iridescent feathers, jewel-like."

Dagon reflected, "We had red winged blackbirds near the farm where I grew up. They make a great trilling racket. Sandhill cranes came into the fields seasonally, when they migrated through. Their call sounds hauntingly ancient."

Stella nodded. "I agree, like you're hearing a pterodactyl or something. I often hear them when I take morning runs along a dirt road, which borders the National Elk Refuge, the winter-feeding ground for elk herds that migrate down out of the mountains. I guess you kind of take for granted sound and animals. There is no sound here other then that kind of creaky howling of the wind sometimes. I miss it. The sterility is shocking."

Dagon stroked Stella's cheek, his tension easing.

"I grew up in Midwest farmland, moving to the city when I went to college. I never looked back," he mused. "Nature, now, is trees planted along the boulevard with little fences around them. The weather has become clouds, rain and color reflected off the windows of tall skyscrapers."

"What city?"

Dagon was interrupted from answering by a huge jolt to their craft that threw them forward in their seats. Carefully checking the terrain, Dagon noted that there had not been any obstacles in their path. The thumping happened again, just before the ground started to sway beneath them.

"It's a quake," Stella gasped. "Whoa!"

A wave of dizziness gripped her as the hillside moved in front of them. To their right, rocks avalanched down the slope. A crack opened in the hard-packed soil only 150 yards north of their transporter. Fifteen seconds passed while they held their breaths, shocked and disoriented. No sooner had the tremor passed than an adrenaline reaction made Stella's legs quiver and her heart race.

Barely discernible in the distance, they could see smoke rising in the sky. Fear turned to excitement at the sight.

"An active volcano," said Dagon, after observing it in the scope. "You were right. Vulcan is a volcanic planet! This might explain the light prism. Perhaps, there are hot pools nearby from underground vents. This had to have been the ash and fire that was in the atmosphere when we were landing our ship."

The implications were profound.

"This could be part of the cycle that has brought vegetation here. Now, if we could find water," Stella said excitedly.

Feverishly dictating notes into their Links, they recorded the approximate coordinates of the wisp of smoke that they had seen in the distance. Then, swinging wide of the cracked soil and staying away from the base of the unstable hillsides, they began their trip home again. They each breathed sighs of relief when they found that the boxed canyon they needed to pass through hadn't slid.

Stella and Dagon were now anxious to get back to the spacecraft as quickly as possible. The earthquake reminded them that their spacecraft was their only lifeline in this isolated station.

Dagon initiated communication with BOB. They were happy to hear his cheerful British accent. "Our meters currently register normal here, although we experienced a significant tremor, reading 5.2 on the Richter scale exactly 1 hour and 23 minutes ago."

Fear was balanced with a high pitch of excitement that was leaving them burned-out, but high-strung. Stella sighed, "My god, I feel like I'm standing on a knife edge."

The rest of the trip passed without mishap. An hour later, the spacecraft was spotted, apparently unharmed. Stella almost collapsed with relief to be home.

Later, as they prepared supper, Stella said brightly, "I feel like saying grace tonight. I'm so grateful for the safety of this ship. I am grateful for you. I'm grateful for BOB," she saluted the robot over in the corner. "I am just grateful," she ended on a high exuberant note, as she opened a package of freeze-dried vegetables and reconstituted some apple juice.

Stella waved the box effusively in front of her, "I've thought about what you said, Dagon. Here is my prayer. Alice Bailey once said,

> From the point of light, within the mind of god, let light stream forth into the minds of humankind. Let light descend on earth. From the point of love within the heart of god, let love stream forth into the hearts of humankind. From the center where the will of god is known, let purpose guide, the purpose that the Masters know and serve. Let the plan of love and light and power restore the plan on earth.[59]

"Perhaps, our presence here *is* part of this planet's evolution," Dagon said softly, amazed at the possibilities before them tomorrow.

Stella filled her glass and Dagon's for a toast.

"To true gold, true power!"

Raising his glass so that the light sparkled through the amber liquid, Dagon joined her.

"To gold, to the Golden Teachings of Vulcan."

CHAPTER 15

✠

Perception and magic

As planned, Stella spent the morning working in her laboratory gathering information on Vulcan's plant life. However, by late in the afternoon they found time to pack up KYL again for a bit more exploration. The coordinates were set to move as closely as possible to the site where they had seen smoke on the previous day. While it seemed to be a greater distance away than they could possibly travel in six hours, they hoped to get close enough to get a better sighting of its source through their telescope.

The journey turned out to be a hot one, without much relief from the monotonous scenery that surrounded them. Stella began fidgeting around, adjusting the scope and getting a bit goofy from the heat. She began singing the following simple children's round in a lilting, sweet voice:

From the Garden window
we see the falling leaves.
By looking through the window
we touch the hanging boughs.
The boughs touch our hearts
Our hearts move our hands
Our hands play the notes
And the music sings this song

Dagon looked over at her, stroking her cheek. "What are you singing about?" he asked.

"Just perception. This children's song seems appropriate right now. Just think, we're on a new, totally undiscovered planet looking through a telescope to gain an even different perception of points off in the distance, at objects we are totally unfamiliar with."

Dagon rolled his eyes at her.

"I'm serious. We look with our minds, decide what it is we are seeing, and then our imagination fills in the rest. The simple act of seeing moves us from a flat, two-dimensional experience of life, like looking through a window or this telescope, to the garden beyond. Our vision creates a sensory experience of the object of focus. We look through an arch in a garden wall. By looking we feel our hands touch the leaves. We remember that they are cool and smooth. We can taste their freshness and smell the pungent loam of the soil. Still, we never know if it is really real or a figment of our imagination. Like this smoke we saw. We both think we are headed for a volcano, right? We can see it in our minds. We have pictured it before. But, what if that smoke was a campfire? What if it was actually steam?"

Stella laughed up at Dagon, the corners of her mouth crinkling as she noticed he was getting nervous about her subject of discussion. Playfully, she winked at him. "Maybe this isn't happening. We are just dreaming it all." Then, she had the grace to look contrite, when Dagon shuddered.

"I agree. The mind creates, defines and also limits things," Dagon said. "I went to a meditation group once that a friend talked me into. I had just spent a year at the outpost in Mars in almost complete silence. We chanted, 'I am that I am,' over and over again. However, the next day I found the words themselves separated me from the simple emptiness I had been enjoying before. It brought home to me that words often separate us from 'experience' because they have human effort behind them."

Dagon continued, "Everyone in that group wanted Awakening. Yet, the language and forms of religion seem to be the greatest barrier of all. I wouldn't mind going back to that outpost."

"You seem to have really spent some time learning about this."

"Not really, I just crave inner silence," Dagon said as he jerked the wheel to navigate around a boulder.

Stella was holding on tightly as she got thrown around. "I like that little song because it says that by simply looking through the window, a certain magic happens. What was in our mind becomes real."

Dagon looked up at her with a frown. "Stella, things are what they are, not, what you make them to be."

"What makes you nervous about a reality that is as fluid as our perception?" Stella asked adjusting her seat again as a large jolt threw her into Dagon's side.

"I don't know. It just seems like a recipe for chaos. I prefer things to be a bit more ordered," Dagon said as he adjusted their visor to keep the glare of the sun out of their eyes.

Stella considered what he had said, "Well I kind of thrive on chaos, but I suppose that, underneath, I hate change, and have more fear than most people. My Dad used to say 'Things can be familiar, but, they won't be exciting. There are times in life when everything should get drawn on a clean slate.' You, by the way, seem to be a great traveler!"

Dagon slapped his hand on his leg. "Speaking of traveling, I forgot to tell you that we are headed in the wrong direction."

"What do you mean, headed in the wrong direction?" A jolt

of fear shot through her causing her voice to rise in a squeak.

"Just that. I programmed KYL to move toward our coordinates from yesterday, and a few moments ago, I looked down and the dials were spinning. There appears to be a flux in the geo-magnetics. It could be caused by any number of things. I'm not sure if we can trust any of the coordinates we put in this baby." Dagon patted the steering wheel of the transporter, affectionately. As far as Stella could tell, being without the GPS, wasn't bothering Dagon at all.

Stella drew in a sharp breath turning a little pale. "Does that mean we could get lost?"

"Lost? Well, I suppose so. But, not if the homing device is working properly, as it seems to be doing."

"How bizarre, I don't like the idea of wandering around without knowing what our actual position is."

"As you so aptly pointed out, one of the realities of travel. How often do you really know exactly where you are, anyway? As soon as you think you have figured it out, you're already somewhere different."

"Dagon," Stella laughed wryly, "I feel some kind of 'I told you so coming,' or are you a budding philosopher."

"Yeah, that's me. Zen and the art of interplanetary travel."

"Amazing," Stella grimaced, suddenly changing her tune. "Do you think this is fun? We don't know where we are. We could be lost. We are headed out to look for a puff of smoke that could be almost anything."

"Breathe," Dagon smiled a little cocky grin. "Remember to flow with it. As you just told me, it's not that bad. If you think about it, life is one long journey." Stella knew that Dagon was playing with her and couldn't help smiling. "Let's see," Dagon said, "Oh yeah, don't forget that we are actually traveling all of the time.

Every moment is a zero, a new moment with every possibility present. The key is to act like the fool and play when you are scared."

"Not bad advice," Stella said.

"Oh," Dagon continued. "I once read a little saying on a restaurant blackboard. 'We will always do foolish things. The important thing is to do them with enthusiasm.'"

Stella laughed a high sweet laugh. Dagon watched her closely, harboring dark thoughts. *She is probably on the verge of hysteria.* Yet, she seemed to simply be jubilant, changing her fear into joy in an instant, her face as mischievous as a nymph or a fairy.

"There is another way to end that children's song," Stella said.

> From the Garden window
> we see the falling leaves
> By Looking through the window
> we touch the hanging boughs
> The boughs touch our hearts
> Our hearts move our hands
> Our hands move the world
> And, the ***magic*** sings this song

Stella laughed, "I'm standing by what I said before, perception is fluid. If matter is also energy, why can't forms be changed in the blink of an eye?"

"So, what are you trying to say?"

"That magic is real. If you read the story about Vulcan, it tells you he was a magician. Hell, maybe there is magic on this planet."

Dagon was focusing on driving and tried to ignore her.

"It's already happening," Stella insisted. "What about our shared dream, the mysterious text message you got, and this light form that you've seen. Everything we see is only made up of energy anyway. Solid form could metamorphose right in front of our eyes."

Stella continued, "In your dream, you met the Magician because he symbolizes the ability to initiate through fire, using alchemical magic. He is pictured with the four elements of fire, water, earth and air because pure elements are the tools of the druid. He was also called Thoth. The origination point of Thoth's magic was simply 'mind' or the 'word.' Words have magical power. Genesis says the world was created that way. 'And God said, *Let there be Light*.'"

They fell into silence, giving into the rhythmic rocking of the transporter.

"Perhaps, magic happens over long periods of time, too," Dagon gestured expressively to rugged mountains and valleys surrounding them. "It is a one-in-a-billion chance. Yet, Vulcan is maintaining life. That's magic enough for me. Some cycle of regeneration and order is at work here. We don't understand it yet. However, someday, we will."

Hours later, Dagon and Stella sited a small waft of smoke or steam rising in the distance.

Training her glasses on the smoke, Stella looked back at Dagon with amazement. "I could swear I'm looking at something green back there." Dagon took the glasses and checked himself.

"Perhaps, it's some type of mirage caused by the sun and its angle as it reflects through the telescope."

"Well, I, for one, prefer to believe that it really is something green." Stella looked at him with disgust. "Are you always so skeptical?"

"Are you always so willing to believe something that isn't proven as true?" returned Dagon.

"I do see green, and I trust my eyes are seeing something real."

"Well, as you said, real, is in the eyes of the beholder," Dagon countered. Looking up they caught each other's eyes and shared a slow grin.

"Actually, I'm sure it must be a great big green oasis," she said playfully.

"And, I see a mirage, the green is simply a spot on the lens," Dagon reciprocated.

"I just wish we could get closer," said Stella wistfully.

"The condition of the world," said Dagon cynically. "Well, I think we should try to get as close as possible, if only to satisfy our curiosity on this matter."

Dagon checked the time and the angle of the light. "We will probably have to return home in the dark. But, I agree. Let's go on. Even if we had to travel after the sun sets, we should easily have enough power to light our way back."

They set off across the valley floor at a more rapid pace, the scanner in place.

Soon, the going began to get rough. They were steadily gaining altitude, and large boulders were strewn in their path. The startling sound of rocks crumbling and falling in the distance became a familiar sound. Twice they actually saw rockslides, and as a result, they began steering clear of the base of the more steeply sloping hills.

The steady hum of the KYL and the regular extension of its mobile legs were comforting. Even so, anxiety was building. They had committed themselves to a long journey home in the dark and to an unknown world that could crumble away or simply swallow them in a fissure.

Turning back was not an option now, for the column of smoke in front of them was growing larger and drawing them inexplicably forward.

It was Stella who heard it first, a gurgling bubbling sound accompanied by hissing and popping noises.

"Stop! Now!" she gestured wildly.

Hearts beating loudly, they waited in absolute silence.

"There, there it is again. Listen. We are either approaching some type of hot springs or a volcanic lava flow."

They made the decision to proceed around the next bend on foot, not wanting to risk losing the transporter to soft ground. Armed with a battery of equipment, including laser guns, they began to gingerly walk around the large boulders in front of them.

Dagon's arm snaked out as he jerked Stella to his side.

"Stay close to me. I want you to walk behind me."

Reluctantly, Stella agreed. However, her natural aggressiveness rebelled at following. Soon, she was walking beside him in total disregard for his orders. Moments later, she wished she hadn't been so foolish.

A jolt and tremor threw them both to their knees. Stella's right leg slipped into a narrow crevasse. Panicked, she began to flail around desperately, losing her laser down the gaping hole as she struggled to pull her leg out. She felt herself being jerked upright by the armpits.

"I told you to stay behind me. We are going back. Now!" Dagon's face was a mask of fury.

"No," Stella clamped her jaw stubbornly. "I can see steam rising just around this rock. I have my camera. We can take photographs, then leave as quickly as possible. We'll analyze the results on the way back."

"*You* will not take any pictures, *I* will. Stay here and don't move. I mean it, Stella. Do not take one more step or you'll have to answer to me later." Dagon slung the digital camera around his neck and began to go forward carefully.

Stella found herself holding her breath, counting to ten to get her anger under control. Then, she began praying silently as the minutes seemed to stretch into hours.

When Dagon finally rounded the boulder in front of her, Stella knew immediately that he had seen something significant. His face looked transformed and incredulous.

"There is what looks like a pond there. It is not a hot spring. Instead of water, the pond is bubbling with what looks like molten gold, churning molten gold. It must be some type of superheated plasma."

"I have to see it myself," Stella said.

"It's too dangerous," Dagon held her back. "My feet were sinking down into the ground with each step. The mantle is totally unstable."

"But, I'm lighter... I could..."

"No, I have the photos. You can study it. I'm sorry, Stella, I will have to pull rank on you here."

Disappointment flooded her, showing on her face.

"This is for your safety," Dagon said firmly, "The crust has already been compromised by my weight. You could fall through. You're going to have to trust my judgment in this."

Another shudder from the ground beneath them, settled the question. As quickly as possible, they made their way back to KYL and reversed direction to backtrack, following the same footprints that had led them to this spot.

"We can come back here someday." Dagon squeezed Stella's hand trying to comfort her.

"Sure," she turned away with disgust. "Sure. Someday I will come back here. I only traveled, literally, 48.8 million light years to see this spot, or rather, not to see it."

Stella turned her back on Dagon. She was blaming him, yet she knew she wasn't being fair. He had been acting to protect her and, had she been first in command, she probably would have done the same thing.

She swallowed her resentment. The light outside was beginning to dim and an overhead light had been turned on in the cab of the transporter.

Dagon was outside of the cab working on their headlamp. While she waited, Stella laid her head down on her arms. Exhaustion was stealing over her. She imagined how nice it would be to curl up in the worn goose down blanket that she loved at home, listening to the wood crackling in the wood stove, its light casting flickering reflections on the glossy weathered logs of her little cabin. The snow would be drifting down softly, cocooning the sleepy town, bending down the branches of the trees, touching the earth quietly, reverently...

With a nod, she brought herself back. She had fallen asleep. She needed to fight this exhaustion. Dagon shouldn't have to be responsible for getting them back home in one piece. They were in this together. He might need her to help out in some way.

A gentle touch on her arm cut off her worried thoughts.

"Stella we're almost four hours from home. We are on course, simply following the homing device back. It's already dark. I see no reason why you couldn't stretch out and sleep in the cab."

"But, the pictures...they..."

"I know, I'll just leave them until we can look at them together."

Stella gazed up at Dagon with relief. Sometimes it is nice to have a man in charge, someone to drive the car at night, or to lift the heavy things. He looked so alert and capable. She let her shoulders sag, allowing herself to snuggle into the arm he had put around her shoulder.

"I am very tired. Do you think you can stay awake?"

"I'm fine. Believe me, I feel like I've had three cups of coffee. I may be awake until tomorrow morning, the way that I feel right now."

Stella gave in, laying her head on the back of the seat, awkwardly curling her feet up on the wide seat. Within moments, her body felt like a dead weight being jostled and bumped around. Her last thought was, How did people ride for months on covered wagons?

While Stella slept, Dagon's mind raced. He fought to calm himself down by breathing deeply and rhythmically. Why was he so buzzed? If he closed his eyes he could hear a sound like gongs resonating in his eardrum. The sound changed pitch, sometimes so low it sounded like Tibetan monks chanting. Other times it sounded like cymbols vibrating in multiple harmonics. Perhaps, the atmosphere around what he now thought of as the 'golden pool' had been charged with negative or positive ions.

He couldn't seem to get the thought of the molten gold out of his mind. The rolling, bubbling cauldron of glistening beauty had seemed seductive. It was only concern for Stella that had kept him from going forward. His tie to Stella had been growing stronger every day. When she almost slipped into the crevasse, he had been gripped by a panic so painful, it had hurt to breath.

He looked over at her slight body curled up on the seat, her hair a wild red halo around pale, freckled skin, her hand clutched in a fist. The yellow light of the cab made her look so small on the huge leather seat. A wave of protectiveness filled him.

How did other men do this? How could his dad have actually left his mother and his sisters? Why had he gone? Dagon thought of the diary that he hadn't started to read yet. There was something mysterious about all of this. His dad been found dead, an apparent victim of alcohol and poor judgment. Now, Dagon wondered about the truth of this for the first time. He had never actually seen his dad drink. But his dad had seemed helpless when it came to raising children or working the farm. Their security as a family had always rested on his mother's back. She had been the strong, silent type.

Stella was the exact opposite. She seemed to be able to talk non-stop. The thoughts just bubbled up out of her, as if she was channeling them half the time. She seemed free of ego, yet full of passion. It was a fascinating combination. Her thoughts seemed to come out of an empty mind. Was that actually possible?

He could hardly wait to see the pictures. He hoped they had captured even a little bit of what he had felt and seen. Maybe it really was molten gold. He thought of Vulcan, the goldsmith, the artist who had shaped creation from molten gold. He wished again that he had gotten a sample from the pool.

He was anxious to view the photos. However, he had promised Stella he'd wait to see it with her, so he just focused on the goal of getting home in the dark. It was important that this happen without mishap. What would kill them on Vulcan were extreme temperatures. Going out it had been 131 degrees, coming home it was already -59 below. A malfunction of the transporter, and their lives were history. KYL plodded on, stepping back over exactly the same track they had made earlier in the day. Eventually, even Dagon became tired. He was incredibly relieved to see the lights of their spacecraft, and gently shook Stella awake.

"We're home," he said.

"Home," she sighed with pleasure.

"Yes, home."

They both fell into a deep sleep as soon as they entered the ship. Dagon's body felt drugged with exhaustion. He instinctively fought dreaming. But, it didn't seem to matter. The dreams came again, this time even more real, more poignant. When he woke, six hours later, it was still dark. Stella was sleeping soundly so he got up and went into their main room. The dream was still vivid in his mind. So, he dictated everything he could remember into his Link, then lay back and fell asleep on the couch trying to sleep for another two hours.

CHAPTER 16

✠

A trip to another dimension

Stella woke up groggily. Turning over with a moan, she reached for Dagon, finding his side of the bed empty. She staggered out into the main room to find him lying with his feet hanging over the couch. He was sporting a four o'clock shadow looking as exhausted as she felt.

"My whole body is sore." Stella did a forward bend then rubbed her back. "I feel like I've been beat up. It's KYL. They should have given us something that could travel above ground on an air cushion." She did a little backbend then rolled her shoulders.

Dagon just watched, enjoying the view of her standing in her camisole and sleep shorts. "You're right, hmmm, not a smooth ride, hmmm."

"Dagon", Stella did a little jump in excitement, "The pictures!" "Let's check your camera." Stella rushed back to her compartment to throw on some clothes and brush her teeth. She could see the anticipation in her eyes as she checked the mirror and ran a comb her through her hair.

She came out to find that Dagon had pulled on a sweatshirt and made them both a cup of tea. They carried it all into the conference room, the eagerness mounting as they connected the camera to their big screen to examine the photos.

"I only had time to snap off three shots," Dagon said.

Nothing could have prepared them for what they saw. Each picture looked as if it had been taken at a different location.

The first photo showed blue-green plants beside a large steaming pool of hot water.

The second was simply of barren rock, nothing else.

It was the third image that was most shocking. What appeared to be the shadow of a huge creature was hovering over a pool of boiling golden magma.

"Dagon, did you see all of this?" Stella looked at him with amazement.

"Definitely not. I saw a bubbling golden pool of what appeared to be some type of molten lava. I felt intense excitement. It seemed to have some type of magnetic attraction. I found it difficult to leave. My physical and mental state was highly charged for hours afterwards."

"Do you remember our discussion about perception and magic?" Stella said. "It appears that the camera caught the ghost of some other type of creature above the pool. But, more importantly, it actually photographed three entirely different images. Wow, Dagon, Vulcan is magical. What we perceive to be true may actually come true here. It's like my dream. If I want to share a dream with you, it automatically happens."

Stella gestured with animation. "Do you remember me saying that I saw green through the spotting scope? The photo captured what I imagined was around the corner of that boulder, a steaming pool of water with blue-green plants around it."

"No, that is too fantastic. We'll find another explanation." Dagon seemed desperate.

"What other explanation could there be?" Stella clapped her hands with glee. "The green plants in the photo are amazing; the gold magma looks mesmerizing; and the rocks appear real. Why can't more than one thing be real at one time? Why can't there be many dimensions of reality, your reality and my reality."

"No," Dagon protested, "The camera didn't have a reality. It didn't have a mode of perception. It is a simple mechanical device that recorded what was there."

"Perhaps on Vulcan, spirit or thought can manifest easily into form. The camera must have picked up my thoughts."

Stella said with animation, "Wow, remember, I had mentioned a dragon earlier. You must have been carrying the image in your mind. The dragon symbolizes highly sexual kundalini energy. That was the charge that you felt, the excitement and draw you felt to the pool. Dragons are real. They are created inside of us. Elves, dwarfs, and druids are real. Tree people are real. Spirits and ghosts are real."

Dagon sat down hard in his chair. "I feel like I've just entered a nightmare."

"Then, you're creating a nightmare. Why don't you create some breakfast for me instead?" Stella smiled taking a sip of her tea.

"How can you be so happy about this?" Dagon seemed disgusted.

"Because it is life." Stella eye's sparkled. "It is simply life. I have been watching magic on earth for a long time. You just have to be watching. You have to be looking. You have to be expecting it. And, wham. It happens. It happens every day. Every single, blessed, solitary day." Stella got up and began walking into their main room. "So, I'm not shocked. Maybe it is a bit more dramatic here. Still, I've seen some pretty dramatic things on earth, too. I've been given answers to questions by internal voices, I've watched seeming coincidences unfold in a very deliberate planned way. It's just happening here, too. That's all."

Dagon shook his head in amazement. It was the first time that it had ever happened to him. Then, another thought struck him. What will I tell NASA?

They started breakfast together, each reflecting silently on what had just transpired. Dagon cooked and Stella cleaned up after him and set the table. Breakfast was a plate of gray dried eggs with onions and spices. Bread and juice was reconstituted and looked slightly more appealing. Dagon was morose, Stella contemplative, and BOB sat quietly blinking in the corner.

Finally, she couldn't stand it anymore. Stella walked over and sat in front of BOB.

After explaining the details of the photographs, she asked his opinion.

"Hmm," said BOB turning his head from side to side and holding his metal fingers on his chin in a look of contemplation. "Highly unusual yes, but possible, based on the theory of multiple dimensions and multiple realities. In this case it was a camera, a piece of programmed metal that experienced multiple realities. This might have positive implications for all artificial intelligence including robots like me. The question would be, can the machine have its own perception. Examined from the theory of the unified field, yes. In practicality, it is a rare occurrence. It is, however, common for people to use pendulums, dowsing rods, and divination tools such as stones or cards to receive information and to reveal reality."

"Thank you, BOB," Stella said while Dagon just groaned.

Later, after breakfast Stella and Dagon talked.

"I have this uncanny feeling. Almost as if someone was listening in on our conversation, then decided to play an April Fool's Day joke on us. Don't you see the bizarre sense of humor displayed here?" Dagon mused.

"You could be right. It's almost like someone was trying to teach us something by illustrating it graphically. It's either that or BOB's idea." Stella joked. "We have to go back, back to the same site and look again."

"Too far, not enough time," Dagon said with disappointment. "We have only three more days left. It'll take two long workdays to finish in the laboratory and the last day to prepare for lift off. If we miss this phase in the rotation of the planet, we would have to wait six months to get a safe launch again. Being cut off from Base Command, we don't have access to data we would need to even calibrate the exact launch time correctly. With no extra food or supplies, and no protection from extreme changes in weather, we would die out here over the winter."

Stella pondered for a moment, then brightened as she thought of a possible solution. "Maybe we can make the trip here, in this room? If it could happen out there, maybe it can happen anywhere on Vulcan. We could set up a test experiment."

"Get the camera," Dagon said, reluctantly warming up to the idea.

Stella went into the conference room, and then came back to their living area. "You first. Visualize something, an apple, and a tree over in that corner. Okay, do you see it in your mind's eye?"

Dagon became very still and wide-eyed. Then, he said softy, "Take the picture, now," without breaking his gaze from the object of his concentration.

Stella snapped it. Then, she glanced at Dagon with concern. He looked visibly shaken.

"What happened?"

"I tried to imagine an apple. Suddenly a whole different image started to appear. It was like being on an LSD trip. I saw an open window, which seemed to open into another world. Behind the window was movement and changing color, and it seemed to beckon me to step through, as if by stepping through I would have all truth revealed to me. I would have incredible powers. I would be connected to ancient wisdom."

"Why didn't you go?"

"I didn't know if I could come back. I didn't want to go without you."

"Let's look at this snapshot, then decide what to do." Moments later, Stella was opening her photo program with shaking fingers. She drew in her breath quickly.

It was there in the picture. A window suspended in space in the corner of the console room. Vivid colors blurred together in a psychedelic pattern. Another world was inside the window.

Dagon turned pale and looked shaken as he continued to stare at the image. How was this possible? His mind couldn't put it together. Could something be manifested from the mind that quickly into physical form? This was like a long extended trip on mushrooms, that he couldn't control. If he imagined it, it happened. Like the dreams that both he and Stella had been having. The whole thing seemed very seductive and dangerous.

"We should go. Go there together," Stella began speaking quickly. "The photograph is telling us that this magical world is 'real.' I can remember at home on earth when a bright ray of light from the prism that I hang in my window would seem to illuminate my computer, encompassing my hands as they flew over the keys. It usually happened when I was researching or studying Vulcan. I always felt as if some special blessing were happening. The creative flow was coming to me from Vulcan itself. We are being asked to step into the prism and experience magic, as real." She looked at Dagon, expectation and faith shining on her face, her aura suffused with a powerful blue-white light.

"Okay, Okay." Dagon relented. "But, this is perilous. We are taking all kinds of chances that could jeopardize our life and our mission. I don't like the fact that it seemed to offer unlimited power. That feels like being 'tempted' by some other force. I have no desire for 'power.'"

"Good, then that won't happen to you. We should surround ourselves with allies to protect us. Call the angels, Raphael, Gabrielle, Michael, and Uriel to ward off anything that might hurt us," Stella said with confidence.

"I don't know anything about those angels."

"Well, then, what do you believe in? Call forth that as protection."

Dagon hesitated. "I believe in myself. I want to wait for a half hour. This force is pulling us forward with too much potency. We are acting rashly. If I still feel like this is something we can do in a half-hour, then we'll do it."

Now, it was Stella's turn to groan. She tried to concentrate on her research, but her heart was beating too fast. She was over-excited and captivated by the psychedelic colors in the window. It seemed to be enticing her to step into it, even though she was resisting out of respect for Dagon.

Dagon didn't even pretend to work. He seemed frozen as he just sat and thought, not wanting any interruptions or conversation.

Stella looked longingly at BOB, wanting more of his knowledge and reassurance. Dagon had the full right to decide NOT to do this, she thought. He was the commander, and *she* sure didn't want responsibility for this decision.

When Dagon looked up Stella noticed he looked very calm. He had always been fearless, fighting in a terrible war and confronting horrors she couldn't even imagine. She trusted him to take care of her.

"Okay, I'm going in. By myself."

"What!" Stella wailed. "You can't. Not without me."

"Actually, I can! You can fly this ship if it becomes necessary. Everything is set for re-entry. If I don't make it back, abandon KYL and the outdoor lab station. Follow the flight manual with exact precision. I want you to stay behind and observe what happens to my body when I'm in this altered state. Record everything with video. This will give us more information about what is happening here."

Stella gripped Dagon's hand, closing her eyes. "Please, I don't want to do that!" The tears were coming and she couldn't stop them.

"Stella," Dagon's voice took on a gentle, comforting quality. "If it all seems fine, you can go on the second journey with me."

Stella was mollified and said reluctantly, "Okay, let me set everything up." She got a timer and the video-camera put on a tripod in position. Then, she moved BOB to he was nearby and got Dagon a jacket and his daypack. She filled the backpack with emergency provisions: a rope, matches, energy bars, a water bottle, a light weather jacket and a knife.

"Well, we don't know what will happen. You might need this," Stella insisted.

Finally, they were ready.

"Okay, let me visualize the window, then we'll just take it from there."

The window appeared immediately in front of both of them. They looked at each other with anticipation.

Dagon walked forward towards it while Stella made herself stay seated at the table. With each step, the window seemed to grow larger, his focus looking more deeply into the window. As Dagon got close to it, he realized it was quite tall. Then, he simply stepped through into a swirl of prismatic color and entered another world.

In front of him was a landscape softly lit from an unidentified light source. He turned his head and saw Stella standing next to him.

"How did you get in here?" Dagon was furious.

"I swear, Dagon, I wasn't trying, I was watching you, and then suddenly I was just here with you. I guess I couldn't stop myself from *wanting* to come."

They were standing at the base of a small hill. To either side of them were low shrub-like bushes with greenish-silver leaves and pinkish-golden flowers. An unusual sheen covered everything making it appear sculpted and metallic.

Dagon and Stella quickly comparing notes. They were seeing exactly the same thing. "Okay, since your here, you'll have to come with me, but stay behind me."

They began to walk up the hill together, conscious of a sweet smell, like gardenia, wafting in the air. The atmosphere was balmy. The moist sweet air moved over their skins lightly, a soft breeze that was sensual and soothing. The climb up the hill was not arduous, but it was steep enough that Stella found her heart beating with exertion. Placing her feet down carefully so that she wouldn't slip on the springy grass that seemed to cushion the ground, she noticed a path winding up the side of the slope. In places, it had been worn down to the ground, the ground itself seeming to be some type of shiny amber stone.

Automatically, she turned and began traversing up the slope on the path. Dagon quickly stepped in front of her so that he was in the lead. She noticed he was carrying the laser gun from their ship. Rather than taking them to the top the trail, it appeared to be leading them to a gully that wound through some odd looking knobby trees, then up to the top of a cliff face.

Dagon glanced behind him to make sure Stella was okay. Suddenly, he heard an inner voice say, 'You must stay on this path so that you can find your way back.' Looking back, he realized that he couldn't see the window from this side and a tremor passed through him. Would they be trapped in here? Not if he could help it.

Dagon's steady presence was calming to Stella. She noticed he focused on following the path and on memorizing landmarks, noting any forks in the path as they traveled upwards.

When they reached the top of the slope they were not greeted with a view, but with the continued winding of the path up another hill.

It was then that she caught the glint of gold on the hillside. To the right of their path, through some trees, low against the hillside, a flashing glint beckoned. As Stella started to move it that direction, Dagon firmly grabbed her arm.

"No, it's off the path. We'll get lost."

"But, it's not far. We can find our way back."

Dagon tested this against his internal intuition and felt his skin crawl in discomfort. "No, I don't feel good about it. We must call it to us, not go to it."

Stella interrupted impatiently, "You're creating fear."

"Stella, I asked for protection and I got a clear message that I would know, inside of me what was safe or not. It's not a good idea to go off this path. We must call it to ourselves, if it is willing to be known, not step into its power. Think of all the people on earth who get lost in dogmatic religions, cults, and addictive substances. Our power is in discernment and self-knowing. We must review it inside of our own knowledge, test it, then make our decisions, freely."

A new warmth filled her as she registered Dagon's words.

"Of course, you're right. Let's imagine it together and bring it to the edge of our path."

They closed their eyes and suddenly, near the path to the right of them, they saw a solid gold door carved with an intricate pattern of hieroglyphics. It appeared to be the door to a cave dwelling set in the hillside. The path led directly to the entrance.

Dagon sighed with relief.

Walking up, they tentatively knocked on the door which simply swung forward silently into a dimly lit cave. Sitting in a corner, his hands folded in his lap, eyes half closed, sat an old man with a white beard that seemed to touch the ground. He appeared to be meditating. However, when they discretely coughed, he gestured them over with a gnarled hand. "I have been expecting you."

"You have?" they chorused in unison.

"You said you wanted to understand magic, understand the power of Vulcan. Well, I've been sent by the old ones to tell you its story."

CHAPTER 17

✠

Astraea speaks

The sage grinned, "Isn't this who you would expect to see in a cave, an old man with a long beard, meditating?"

His wizened eyes sparkled with mischief.

"Or perhaps, better if I were a golden child?" he said with humor.

Before their eyes his body faded as the image of a child took its place. The child could have been a boy or a girl. White skin accompanied dark, long, thick blond hair. Black eyes sparkled with the same humorous wisdom. A robe made from animal fur with a beautiful clasp of gold in the shape of a V on one shoulder, was fashioned around the child's body.

"Or perhaps a warrior, the commander of a fleet of spaceships who faces you for battle?" Before their eyes, the child shape-shifted into a tall, strong woman wearing a metallic tunic fashioned like a suit of armor. The torso was inscribed with a pattern of intricate geometric designs. Her bold face, high cheekbones, well chiseled lips and commanding eyes were those of a Valkyrie. Her low resonating voice, powerfully full, rich and melodic, echoed in the cave.

"I am old, young, man, woman. Manifesting many of the forms that I have been in reality."

And, then she gestured casually to a small table in the corner of the cave.

"Would you like some tea?"

The offer seemed so ridiculous in light of the occasion that it took a moment before Dagon caught the teasing glint in her eyes.

"What I would like is an explanation. I want to know how this is happening, whether I can trust this."

"Accept my offer of hospitality then. Do you think I would drug you with tea? After all, I am a figment of the imagination. But, then again, perhaps you wish to subconsciously betray or harm yourself." She cocked her head pretending to consider this ludicrous suggestion while Dagon felt his anger rising to the surface.

"Don't play this cat and mouse game with me."

She turned to Stella catching her eye and holding the contact. "And, what do you think, child. Hmmm, I see, 'Real.' "

She paced forward and Stella got a clearer view of how truly tall, strong and vibrant this warrior woman was.

"I will speak. You must remember this and write it down later in that book of yours. It will come in handy for the battles you desire to wage on behalf of earth." Her expressive black eyes held Stella's forcefully for a moment. Suddenly, Stella pictured a board table at Interspace Research with a black cloud hovering around it. A pasty faced, overweight man sat at the head of the table counting out large bills into little piles. His accountants were looking pleased with themselves.

"You can call me Astraea," The regal woman spoke with measured politeness. "I am a being of the stars, my people are from the star Arcturus which is your own soul seed's birthplace. You were both children of the DNA of our colony of Atlantis. Both of you were once priest and priestess of the sun temples. Later you served Ptah and Sekhmet. Even now, you both embody their energies. It is why you were brought together again for this journey. I have been studying your earth for eons and even lived there long ago. I have become most interested in fairly recent developments."

"You earthlings have done very well with each crisis that you have faced. For example, the discovery of evolution shook the foundations of religion, but freed you. At the millennium, a majority of people began to believe you had been granted free will to save your planet. Through the Oneness Movement you reached critical mass in awakening higher and consciousness, staving off destruction of the earth in 2012."

"Unfortunately, however, your world is still split between those who embrace this acceleration of higher consciousness and those who would like to go back to the old ways of superstition and fear."

"The collective has power to create reality. Your thoughts, emotions, body, create the story being played out on earth. The only real absolute is the inner Atman or Self that actually *is* God."

"You see when god made humans she put a part of herself in them. Why? I don't know. We have all wondered that. But, never the less, it is within you. Every one of you, every last human is part god. If you destroy yourself, She is destroyed too."

Astraea moved her hands purposefully. "There are answers being supplied for your dilemma. Beings such as I have been in communication with earth for over 130,000 years, watching over the development of civilization."

"The greatest danger your earth overcame was from radical fundamentalism. By creating a religious scenario of 'antichrists,' diabolic incarnations of evil, and radical martyrdom, the extremists bred an explosive perversion of truth. Their beliefs spawned dissidence and strife that carried the third world nations to the brink of apocalypse. We have watched with gratitude those bodhisattvas, which reincarnated during that period in your history to change the hearts of those who were born in poverty. These great avatars allowed all humans to know they were created equal."

"Mankind has found the answers by searching within. Your DNA and your archetypal memories hold the truth about reality. Great teachers have been born in the field of science, art and religion that have led the way toward your collective god-mind."

"Now, you are entering another time of acceleration within the Golden Age. It is time to understand magic. I have been playing these little games with you to teach you that energy and matter is the same thing. God is in matter. God is energy. She has the ability to magically reshape your physical world."

"Evolution is not moving from evil towards light, it is going back to the original first essence or pattern that underlies all of life. In a sense evolution is going back to our archetypal memories of the primary source that underlies matter and spirit. Thus ascension is actually expansion of our reality to encompass a broader experience of Source."

"With this knowledge you have your hands on the tools to radically transform the world in an instant. However, humans must catch on to a few simple principles first."

"The most important truth is that You *are* God. There is a faster-than-light form of communication that links particles. This enables transformation. Fast, complete, transformation."

At this she stopped and smiled, a slow sensual smile.

"Your mind is very easy to read, Dagon."

Dagon looked startled and defensive.

"Of course, you've always been skeptical."

She continued, "Scientific theory now addresses the possibility of a higher dimensional reality which explains the mysterious connection between subatomic particles evidenced by the wholeness and implicate order within matter. When you apply these theories to the mind's influence on matter, you suddenly see a vindication of miraculous healing, paranormal experiences, alchemy and stories about beings like Vulcan."[60]

"There is a highly evolved, greater intelligence linking all of life, a communication network from Source which leads us each into a path of evolutionary growth that runs at 'time warp speed' when compared to this transformation within the chaos. From the perspective of primal source, creative variety just makes things more fun!"

"During your travels on Vulcan, you experienced the magnetic lines of force of this planet. However, what you didn't realize was that those forces were in flux and constantly changing. The poles of the planet break in half periodically, then instantly reorganize themselves into two complete fields. Magnetic fields always try to reconstruct themselves to wholeness."

"You were allowed entry into the Vulcan's atmosphere during one of these solar storms. We've been waiting for you for eons. I have seen your faces many times and knew you both intimately on earth."

"But, there is more in store. Dagon, you already have this information. Vulcan will be eclipsed, and the electromagnetic patterns of the earth will be completely shut down when this happens. Your father had been studying this possibility and has written about it in his diary. You will find it very helpful."

"The eclipse creates an opportunity, one of the places in-between, in the void, when all things are possible. It's possible for your planet to align with a totally different vibrational sound frequency, a sound that encourages awakening to the Magician within. I have simply been giving you a taste of it in the past few days."

There was silence as Stella and Dagon took in what Astraea was saying.

"Dagon, I see from your expression that you need some proof that I have connections to earth," Astraea smiled teasingly, "You used to have a stuffed giraffe that you called 'Bolo' if I'm not mistaken."

Dagon was flooded with discomfiture then exclaimed, "How do you know?"

"Let's just say I knew your parents when you were a toddler," she replied mysteriously.

"Stella," she turned her piercing gaze, "You have a big secret you haven't told Dagon." And, when Stella blushed uncomfortably, she gave her a commiserating look. "I won't give it away," she whispered with exaggeration. Suddenly, the Astraea's eyes blazed.

"How is that you trust this man, but haven't been willing to speak the truth," she accused, pointing a long expressive finger. She then smiled compassionately. "I'm sorry to shock you, dear, but these are your own thoughts."

Stella shuddered involuntarily.

Astraea continued turning her penetrating gaze to Dagon with a tone of accusation, "What is stopping you from believing what is right before your eyes. You have understood the scientific explanation for magic for lifetimes, you know you could holographically encode and create the experience that we are having right now."

Her aura seemed to expand with an otherworldly glow crackling with a neon green light as she paced toward the back of the cave and then turned around. She drew her mantle around her with a pensive look.

"My mother was Vulcan and my father was Arcturian. Vulcan's tribal memories are in my blood calling constantly. It is rather annoying. And, what's more, you are part of the royal blood. You are both in direct lineage to Vulcan through your ancient Egyptian ancestors, who originated in Atlantis. I guess that would make us related," Astraea laughed.

"This heritage is both a burden and a gift because it connects you to the seed of origination through Vulcan, creation, and the seed of compassion through Arcturus, love for mankind. You have no choice really. You have a job to do."

Unexpectedly, Astraea's image began to waver as they felt a deep tremor rocking the ground beneath them.

"I would say more, but the time is not now. Hear the voice of the belly of this planet. He is rumbling his dissatisfaction. His strength is magnetic. He is pulling the earth and sun in his wake."

Stella swallowed a tremor of fear. "Our ship, is she safe?"

Astraea seemed to look off through space.

"Yes, you are both sitting safely within her, your eyes closed as you journey with me."

"Do you mean, this isn't real?" Dagon asked.

Irritation crossed her face and her voice boomed out echoing in the cave.

"Have you learned nothing yet? Life is linked moments. In the moment lies the encoded information that is the truth of existence. Every moment is real."

Her voice became lower, "Do not misunderstand." With grave sadness she intoned the next words using the measured cadence of a prophet. "The miracle that will save your earth from its pattern of destruction is encoded in the akashic records from the past, records, even now, which are being misused and misconstrued. It all hangs in the balance."

Stella began to feel a sense of panic. She could feel that their interview was closing and there was so much more information needed.

Astraea looked at them intently. The golden breastplate that she was wearing, dazzling, with twelve jewels set in a circle, mesmerized Stella.

Astraea's image began to fade away, yet her words still came in disjointed phrases, full of portent. The sound vibrated in a deep echo off of the walls of the cave. "Revealed at last,...seven x seven seals...twelve ships to come...fusion... lunar and solar...ten thousand times ten thousand times brighter...gold."

A faint presence of her seemed to come back into the room. "Come with me," Astraea beckoned. "Are you willing to walk within the bowels of the earth? To crawl on your hands and knees to the darkest pit? To see the master forger at work?"

She seemed to grow larger, and then to shrink back, her face becoming gnarled and wooded, her bones the short squat body of a Dwarf.

Dagon and Stella blinked, astounded.

A rough croaking voice cackled. "Have you ever seen a dragon?" Then he bent over to laugh a belly-laugh deep into his scraggly, unkempt beard.

Without warning they felt themselves spinning as if they were in a film being re-wound. A force of energy was sucking them back down the path, pulling them like a vacuum to the surface.

Stella resisted for an instant, holding on to the branch of a tree that seemed to be bent in a howling tornado of wind. Grasping at a limb, she saw two gold stones wedged in the crook of the trunk. She gripped the gold stones, holding on tightly as she was propelled along the path. She was literally lifted by the force of the gale to spin up and out, flying backward down the amber lined path, backward down the hill and sucked back out through the window into her chair in their spaceship, The Golden Eagle.

The clock read 11:11. Barely ten minutes had passed. The remains of breakfast were still on the table. The console lights blinked. The sun had still not risen.

Dagon sat numbly, his eyes covered by his hands. Stella was holding her hands in a tight fist, her fingers turning white with the pressure. For in her palm she was still holding two golden stones. She slipped them carefully into her pocket and made her decision then to keep them a secret, too.

"Whew, I can't believe we just did that," Dagon exclaimed later as they talked about their experience together.

"Amazing, wasn't it?"

"I still feel disoriented. What are we going to tell NASA about this? They'll never believe us, never."

"Do we need to tell them?" Stella slipped her hand into her pocket gripping one of the stones..

"We should."

"Then, we should be prepared for a media freak out. Maybe that's what Astraea meant when she said we would get a chance to tell people that there are ways to shift reality, to use magic to create protection during the coming earth changes," Stella shivered violently.

Dagon just frowned. "Yeah, but all that talk about destruction of the earth, that's frightening. People don't want to hear about that."

"Humanity has always known about these things. It seems to me her message was completely positive. I mean, after all, she's saying we can create a new world in an instant by learning how matter and spirit connect."

Dagon drew hand across his brow, "I've always believed that knowledge is power. I generally feel that to find truth, we have to be fearless of the complications. Still, this kind of information is like being initiated into the mysteries of the universe. Is the world really ready for knowledge like this?"

"Who are you to make that decision for others," Stella said. "I think so. This wisdom has been in our collective subconscious for eons, surfacing with the Gypsies, Gnostics, Egyptians, Templars, Free Masons, New Agers - always there. Now, science is validating these ancient mysteries, what better time for them to be public?"

"Did you notice the clock when we got back", Stella said. "It was 11:11. Only ten minutes had gone by. We left at 11:01."

Dagon stretched his long body and studied the clock. "How odd, look the clock is flashing 1:11, 11:11 right now, like it's trying to give us a message." Dagon went over to fix it. However, it corrected automatically showing them the normal time of 11:26 again.

Stella was buzzing with excitement. "There must be some code to the gateway between dimensions, a doorway opening at the time 11:11. I remember at home the odd synchronicity of noticing the clock every time it was 11:11 or 1:11. I began to believe that it meant that I was at the right place, at the right time, doing the right thing. I have always been fascinated with how numbers have symbolic meanings. In fact letters are assigned numerical values, so that each word has meaning. Double numbers are called master numbers and have special meaning. I added the value of my birth name and it was 77. The value of your name was 88. Seventy-seven is a number representing completion of cycles, scholarship and knowledge. Eighty-eight represents actions, responsibility, leadership and being a spiritual warrior."

Dagon shrugged impatiently, "Well, I had better start leading soon or we won't be ready for our launch off of the planet." Dagon stopped himself, thinking, I need to balance my negative thinking, if we can really create what we think.

"Astraea said you should read your dad's diary," Stella said.

Dagon's eyes brightened, his eagerness visible. "I think that I'll start that this afternoon when we rest."

While they wanted to talk in depth about their experiences over the past few days, their work was calling. They both dug into their tasks and were soon engrossed in research. Stella was busy testing her biological samples, taking specimens and placing them in special decontamination containers. Dagon was measuring the iron content of rocks, weighing some of the white rocks they had discovered when they were in KYL.

Later in the afternoon, they went out for a long walk to film and photograph the landscape again. Evening came. They were preparing supper before they got a chance to talk again.

"Did you find anything interesting in your dad's diary?" Stella asked.

"Interesting isn't the word for it. It is unbelievable! There are diagrams for the formula for fusion, a perpetual motion machine, and his formulations on what he called Galactic Mathematics, a new theory on particles within black holes. It's all in tiny handwritten print. I'm sure I'm going to find something about Vulcan. Vulcan was discovered around the time the journal was written and I'm guessing he had his own theories about it."

"You look tired," Stella said.

"Yes, after those trips out on KYL and another night of poor sleep, I'm hoping to really sleep hard tonight. It looks like we both need it."

"I wrote some notes so that I would remember exactly what Astraea said to us. I think they'll come in handy later."

"Good", Dagon put his arm around Stella and pulled her into a comfortable hug. Cuddled together on her bed, they relaxed, enjoying the intimacy of the moment.

Naturally, they fell into a meditative state simultaneously and noticed a sensation of profound centeredness, feeling relaxed and balanced, with unlimited energy. It was so peaceful and at the same time enlivening that Dagon gave up all effort. He was flowing, yet exquisitely still.

Dagon said, "I've never really felt this way before. Sometimes when I'm with you it feels like we are in the center of the yin and the yang, moving and resting at the same time."

"I know what you mean. I have never had that balance by myself and I know my spiritual, physical and mental health have suffered because of it."

"My mother worked with people who were sick. She said all life whether star, plant, human, animal, or particulate, automatically seeks homeostasis. It is how we metabolize, grow, reproduce, rest, regenerate, dissipate and renew. These processes are very sensitive, but reliable. When 'out of balance' life automatically corrects, sometimes crashing the system."

Dagon hugged Stella closer. "I once saw a sign that said *'Awakening is recognizing you are God. Balance is understanding how God ticks.'* "

Dagon lightly stroked Stella's hair and soon they were gently kissing. The energy and passion grew until all they could feel was the ecstasy, waving and rolling toward them on a tide of bliss. Exhausted they feel asleep, still holding each other.

CHAPTER 18

✠

Cryptograms and our shadow

The next day they began their work photographing and researching the Vulcan plants that Stella had dubbed, cryptograms, because she was still trying to decipher them. Suiting up, they went to their outdoor research station to begin their examination of the specimens.

It became readily apparent that these hardy plants were almost indestructible. They could only be pulled out of the soil with great effort, for they had a strong, vine-like root system that, in the heat of the day hardened to stone. Furthermore, when they were cleared from a small area, other plants filled in that space very quickly. It was possible to watch this amazing feat without special time-lapse cameras.

"Dagon, I've been thinking that it would be interesting to perform an experiment with these cryptograms," Stella said, concentration puckering her brow.

"Over the past few days we have noted that they adapt to very small moisture changes in the air. What have you discovered about the oxygen content and elements which make up this atmosphere?" she asked.

Dagon had been analyzing computer print outs and came over to stand next to laboratory table set under the bubble dome of the greenhouse.

"We could probably simulate Vulcan's atmosphere on earth," he said. "Many of the properties are similar, however, there is much less nitrogen and oxygen, and a bit more carbon dioxide, hydrogen and argon. These mixes fluctuate during the day because of the extreme temperatures of hot and cold."

"What if we gently mist a plant with water and see its response?" Stella was tapping her pencil against her tablet excitedly.

"Well, it could grow seven feet tall and start walking," Dagon said with a smile.

"You're kidding, I know, nevertheless anything is possible. I'm a little bit nervous about interfering too much when I see how almost 'animal-like' the plants appear when you dig one of them up. It was rather eerie seeing them scramble to fill the empty spot."

"These plants seem to have an incredible ability to find a balance between energy lost and energy supplied. That's why they can survive in extreme conditions," Dagon said.

"Let's take a break and decide what to do then." She pulled off her gloves and adjusted the oxygen valve on her suit, stepping out of the greenhouse laboratory.

They walked over to rock and perched on the edge of it, sharing a flask of warm broth between them. Stella began postulating out loud.

"The plants on Vulcan are a good example of the search for equilibrium within extreme conditions. By introducing another stimulus, a fine mist of water, we would be requiring the plants to adapt. Even the presence of our spacecraft sitting on other cryptograms, and the pathways that we and the KYL have made on the planet's surface, have left a new environment in our wake. We impact what we touch. This planet is accommodating our presence amazingly well."

"So, does that mean you feel comfortable hydrating one of the plants in a controlled environment?"

"Yes and no, yet, somehow, I think we should try this little experiment."

Later, in the outdoor station, they prepared a solution of pure H^2O and Dagon handily rigged up a way to spray a fine mist over one plant. The sun beating down on the cryptogram made it rock hard to the touch. In fact, if they hadn't known better, they would have thought it *was* a rock. A camera was set in place to film the plant's response.

Stella found that her heart was beating and her hands slightly unsteady as she prepared to begin the experiment. "I wish I knew if we were doing the right thing by interfering with this ecosystem."

Dagon looked at her steadily. "If not us, someone else. We won't be able to keep this world all to ourselves."

Stella sighed, "I suppose you're right. By providing these plants with a rich supply of H^2O we'll be upping their 'power supply.' If they're healthy they'll try to find some creative way to respond to it. Evolution is a natural desire of most species."

Stella smiled apprehensively at Dagon, then, very carefully she sprayed fine mist over the plant before them. What happened next was something they would never forget.

The cryptogram quickly started to change color from gray-brown to a dull green. Then, a vibrant, almost luminescent blue-green color seemed to glow from the inside of the plant. What had been hard was now soft, eventually it seemed to flutter or vibrate before them. It became visibly larger in front of their eyes and in the space of 10 minutes, had sent out a small tendril with an egg shaped bud on the end of it. The petals of the bud were transparent gold filaments.

As the sun beat down through the netting, the inside of the filament seemed to heat until it was glowing like a golden globe. Then, without warning, it disintegrated into ashes.

No more mist had been sprayed, and over the next eight hours, in between their other duties, Dagon and Stella watched the plant gradually shrink back into its rock-like, gray form.

Later they discussed what had occurred as they watched the film they had taken of the experiment.

"I analyzed those ashes," said Stella excitedly. "They are rich in nitrogen and iron. That plant was fertilizing itself and releasing nitrogen into the atmosphere. In the presence of moisture, the plant sends out a bud. Because it is a spherical, transparent globe, the heat of the sun is intensified until the nutrient-rich petals become ashes. What an incredible example of adaptation!"

"I'm sure now that this species exists on other parts of this planet, that, during certain times of the year, it receives enough moisture to go through this process. A complex adaptive process like this probably took millions of years to evolve. It didn't happen for the first time just now," she continued with conviction.

"Given what we've seen, I wouldn't be surprised if there weren't other forms of life on this planet already. Animal life is very possible. We have a host plant here for parasites. We are standing on a possible garden of Eden!" Stella looked dazed, stunned by their discovery.

"Even more than that, we are looking at an immense powerhouse," Dagon exclaimed.

"What?"

"A powerhouse, in all of these plants, on this planet." He gestured around expansively. When Stella still look puzzled, he expounded.

"Energy, in essence, is the act, ability or potential for transference of heat, sound, light or any other form of energy from one form to another. On earth we measure power as force exerted and describe it in units such as volts, megahertz, or gigabits. But, power can also be 'potential' which hasn't been released yet. Look at what is covering this planet!" He gestured to the plants, which covered the ground as far as the eye could see.

Stella nodded. "These plants have evolved a way to harness the power of the sun. When those filaments were glowing with golden energy, it reminded me of a light bulb. The transparent filaments created a container where the energy of the sun could be amplified."

"It's reminiscent to me of lasers and how they work to amplify energy," Dagon looked pensive.

She gestured toward the plant from their experiment. "Today we watched this powerhouse create the elements necessary for its continued evolution. It was in the cycle of dissemination, its transformation into ashes, that the nutrients are released for future proliferation of the species."

"Come on, let's get out of here and go for a walk again," Stella pulled at Dagon's arm. "I need to think about all of this."

They began a slow stroll away from the ship, the silence between them comfortable and reflective.

After a few moments Stella noticed a look of sorrow flashing across Dagon's face.

"Dagon," Stella spoke softly, "A penny for your thoughts."

He shook his head, looking up with glazed eyes, "Oh, sorry, I must have been daydreaming," he said.

"Your face looked sad, what were you thinking about?"

"How my dad would have loved to see this."

"I wish that my mom and dad could see this too," said Stella. "You must miss your dad," she continued.

"Actually, I've just been mad at him. Though now, I certainly respect him more." said Dagon a bit gruffly, clearing his throat. "Still, I miss my mom. Tell me about your family, Stella," Dagon quickly changed the subject.

"Right now my family is a seventeen year old black and white cat named Merlin. He's very old, but still thinks he is a kitten. A friend is keeping him until I get home. The day I left, he jumped onto a pile of papers I'd just sorted out, slid, tried leaping from the kitchen island to the table, skid across the table and crashed into a potted plant. My caretaker had just arrived. The kitchen was a wreck."

Dagon smiled at Stella's expressive description. He seemed to relax and took Stella's hand affectionately as they kept strolling

"Okay, now *you're* looking sad," Dagon said, "What is it?"

"I was just thinking about my lovely cabin and my great life. I am so fortunate, one of the elite 16% who can read and write, has a computer, has food on my table, and has been educated with freedom of religion. Except, what do we do about the other 84% of the people on the planet that don't have this? Or even worse, what about the animals and those creatures weaker then us that we are supposed to be championing? They are lucky to get *any* consideration when everyone is struggling to use up all of the earth's resources. Yet, once when I was meditating about this dilemma, I saw an image of the earth from a distance. All the death and destruction seemed inevitable, maybe perfect, in its own way. It is very mysterious."

Dagon shoulders seemed to droop. "It's recently become clear to me, that I've been angry most of my life. I've tried to be that perfect person that my dad wasn't and have been stuck with unvoiced judgments and disappointments toward myself. Maybe perfection isn't what we need."

Stella nodded sympathetically. "I can relate, I joined a group who started praying for the healing of the world and became disheartened pretty quickly. It all seemed so pollyannaish. Especially when we are naturally so greedy and selfish as a species."

Dagon, fell silent for a moment, "What would utopia look like? Is that really what we should be striving for?"

"Or is it possible this world is already an expression of God." Stella joined in, "That limitation is this world's 'perfect' signature. I mean look at Vulcan. These plants produce ash and fertilize themselves through a process that includes death."

Dagon thought for a moment. "There was a children's story that my mother used to read to us as kids. It was called Beauty and the Beast."

"Oh, I remember that story."

Dagon let himself get into telling the tale. "There was once a king with a beautiful daughter. She asked him to find and pick for her a black rose. The king happened on an empty castle. Looking in the garden he saw a black rose. As soon as he had picked it, however, a beast came out and said that he must now give him his beautiful daughter for this trespass. The king sadly went and got his daughter who was at first horrified by the beast. However, gradually she began to see the beast really had a good and kindly nature underneath. When her father the king was dying, she left the beast to go nurse her father. The beast missed her so much, however, he began to die from grief. Fortunately, while looking in a mirror at her reflection, Beauty saw that the Beast was dying and rushed back to his side. Her tears and a kiss changed him back into a handsome prince. They, of course, lived happily ever after."[61]

"My sister used to ask my mom to read the last part over and over. I'm not really sure why."

Stella hit Dagon's arm. "I would have like to have known you as a kid," she said.

"I have an idea what this story could mean." Stella cocked her head thinking.

Dagon turned towards her "I expected that you might."

"The story is about loving yourself, both your good and bad sides."

"You said there was a black rose and a mirror, right." Stella pulled her hair out of her collar and put it in a rubber band as she spoke.

"Yeah?"

"We can interpret the story like a dream. At the beginning of the story the princess is looking for a black rose. The black rose symbolizes her desire to find beauty in darkness. So, her father, or the wise part of herself, leads her to the beast."

"It was while the princess was seeing the beast in a mirror, a reflection or a pool that feelings of love for him come over her. The mirror indicates that she is seeing a reflection of the shadow side of her own self. With the full recognition of the beast within herself she learns self-love and compassion. In the end she is able to marry the beast in herself, to view her animus as a wonderful prince. Utopia comes from that realization, i.e. she lives happily ever after."

"Pretty good," chuckled Dagon.

Stella continued. "The story shows that the princess found wholeness, but only in acceptance of imperfection. Most people who are highly spiritual are constantly searching for 'light.' They believe that they should ascend out of darkness to find a more perfect world. Not realizing, god is both light and darkness. It is both polarities that make up the unlimited energy of this world."

Dagon threw an idea into the discussion. "Perhaps, as Astraea suggested, we are like holograms. A hologram is formed by a laser beam, which projects two images. Those images collide and seem to break everything apart into a chaotic picture. However, if you look at each individual component part of the picture you see that the whole still exists, complete and perfect within the image. All you have to do is shine a light through one single cell and you see the whole image. This world is like that. It is only that sometimes all we see is the darker parts. Wasn't it Christ who said, *'now we see through a glass darkly, but then we shall see face to face.'*[62] He taught that god was in him and he was in god. In other words, that we are all part of the boundless consciousness that created this world. Viewed like this the story of Beauty and the Beast could be a holographic model."

Stella started to get excited, "Remember our discussion about Vulcan. He was born deformed even though he was god. His fall woke up the artist in him because he landed in the ocean."

Dagon stopped their stroll, turning her to face him so he could concentrate on what she was trying to convey.

"You see," Stella said, "There is creativity within imperfection and chaos. Life requires mutation to break down old forms and make way for the new forms. It has always struck me that the word 'evil' is 'live' spelled backwards. Evil is simply our 'fear' of the beasts. There is sensuality in darkness. At the root chakra there is a 'black' lotus flower, with one thousand petals. It's the dark nurturing mother, womb of the universe, the deep black expanse of eternal night where planets explode and galaxies are birthed." Stella threw out her arms widely then twirled around. "The passage of millions of human beings through death could be a great burst of blissful, pleasurable energy being sucked back into Source."

"Hmmm" said Dagon smiled at her antics. "I'm remembering the Wheel of Fortune. Black is a composite of all colors mixed together. White also contains all color. The positive and negative current is equal as well as equally necessary."

Dagon continued. "Then, you could say the problem is not duality, it's the judgment that we make about it. We create right and wrong. We decide we are being punished or victimized when misfortune happens even though the rain falls on the rich and the poor. And, look at these cryptograms. They rise from the ashes just like the story of the phoenix."

"Yeah, the phoenix, cool!" Stella interjected.

Dagon got excited at a new thought and smiled. "On one of the trips with on KYL you talked about the world tree. It strikes me that a tree grows strong only because of its ability to move in opposite directions simultaneously. It reminds me of a few words from *The Hitchhikers Guide to the Universe:*"

> Standing silent and alone in a dark corridor
> His one head looked one way
> And, his other, the other
> And, each decided that the other way
> was the way to go. [63]

"Ha," Stella laughed. "That's a great quote. And, I like your tree idea. Gravity pulls down and the root seeks the nutrients of the earth. Sunlight pulls the plants leaves up seeking needed light for photosynthesis, yet both directions of movement are necessary for the plants health and growth."

Dagon continued to think out loud. "Then, duality is the modus operandi of the earth. Duality becomes painful only when we try to choose one way as better or above another way. Choosing one direction over the other is the judgment of mind that spawns pain in separation. It is not necessary to shrink the universe into a manageable size. Nature creates life from death. Her cruelties actually strengthen the evolution of the life forms that she sustains. Yet, if we look deeper, look within the chaos, we see the holographic imprint of a perfect, united world."

"Yeah," said Stella. "It is in the total acceptance of and embracement of duality that we experience complete unity." Stella flipped her link out of her pocket and scrolled to some excerpts from the Tibetan Book of Living and Dying. Rinpoche says it better than I can." She read:

> Fear disappears when brought back to the human and universal context. By moving through duality to unity we give up projected or falsely perceived external reference points… With total acceptance of duality we have no need to manipulate, assert, validate, confirm, fragment or solidify our experiences. The deeper essence or nature of mind, which exists in a state of unity, connects matter and spirit. This essence of mind can rest in the present…the true nature of mind is "skylike." 'It is simply your flawless, present awareness, cognizant, empty, naked and awake. [64]

Stella concluded. "He says that being in the present brings simple skylike awareness embracing the greater patterns and all aspects of life as necessary and important. Accepting duality therefore is releasing fear and distrust of others or yourself."

Dagon was looking surprised. "I am beginning to remember something from my past about the akashic records."

"You are?" Stella said, "What?"

Stella checked her notes from their meeting with Astraea. "Astraea said the miracle that will save your earth from its pattern of destruction is encoded in the akashic records from the past, records, even now, which are being misused and misconstrued. It all hangs in the balance."

Dagon was looking thoughtful. "I'm not sure where I learned this, but Akashic records are the supercomputer or mind of god where the library of all information past and present is stored. If we go back in the library and really study our origins we could find that evolution is not moving away from evil to light. Instead it is going back to the original first essence or pattern that underlies all of life. In a sense evolution is going back to our archetypal memories of base energy. Thus ascension is actually expansion of our reality to encompass a broader experience of Source, remembering who we originally were. From this view we could learn to manipulate and co-create, changing matter with spirit, using the magic that she describes."

"Wow!" Stella said amazed. "And you don't remember where you learned this?"

"No, I don't know. I just seem to remember this. Oh, odd."

Stella turned to walk back toward the greenhouse, finding the little plant lying where they had left it, as hard and apparently lifeless as a stone.

She put on gloves and picked it up. "There is a very powerful principle represented here. The golden globe reminds me of a picture in alchemy books of the philosopher's stone, the secret to immortal life."

"When Vulcan was sighted mankind discovered fusion, a source of unlimited, clean energy, a powerhouse. Now, we're looking at potentially unlimited energy in these little cryptograms."

"On top of that they burned to ashes, like the phoenix, that archetypal bird said to rise from ashes to new birth. In Greek and Roman mythology, Vulcan was the great metal forger who puts everyone into the furnace and by burning away the dross, gets down to the essence of our being. Perhaps, like you're suggesting, this is all to take us back to original Source. To find out how we can re-create the world and access immortality."

Stella set the cryptogram on the table and stripped off her gloves. She laid her head on Dagon's shoulder, sighing. "Sometimes I feel so tired and overwhelmed with it all."

Dagon pulled her in a close embrace, hugging her silently, understanding what she meant. The rest of the day was spent putting away their equipment and double-checking all the safety locks and coordinates for their launch back into orbit the next day. It had been a bittersweet day, as both were feeling sad about leaving.

CHAPTER 19

✠

Soul mates

Dagon pushed the side panel button to slide open the door to the decontamination chamber of the ship. The heavy metal snapped open with a thud. Under his arm he carried a shiny bundle. Wrapped in layers of plastic and thin aluminum sheeting lay the cryptogram they had used during their experiment, prepared now to be transported with them back to earth. He carefully strapped it into a box designed to replicate the atmospheric conditions they had found on Vulcan. After he had placed it on a shelf in the small square room, Dagon walked over to push a video screen, which displayed the outside of the ship. He could see Stella throwing their equipment haphazardly in boxes and winced. Reaching for some of the green bags with the logo of Interspace Research emblazoned on them, he rushed back out.

"Here, let me do that." He rescued a delicate piece of their equipment and began painstakingly packing it. "You can put all of those rocks in these bags."

Stella grimaced at his commanding voice and wandered over to the rocks, which she soon began tossing around playfully.

"Here, Dagon, catch," she teased without throwing it.

"Be careful," Dagon snapped. "This equipment is very fragile and you could easily destroy it."

"Why are you being so tetchy?" Stella groused.

"Well, you should be careful! We are part of a team that worked hard generating this scientific technology over five years."

Stella shrugged, then sat and listened for a moment. "You really are serious, aren't you? Hey, sorry. I'll tip toe around a bit more."

Dagon ignored her and began rolling up the long series of cables that attached to the electronics of the ship. Then, he reached up for a clipboard and punched in the code to switch the video to the ship's flight room. "BOB," he said, "Please, check all the coordinates again for our launch tomorrow."

BOB's calculations were showing they were quickly approaching the window in the rotation of Vulcan that would allow them to launch safely. It would be touch and go, as exiting the synchron belt had to be timed within minutes to correctly align them on their homeward navigational path. If everything went well, the next three months would be spent in deep space as they made their way back to Beta III, the Interstellar Space Station on Mars, then, finally, home to earth.

Dagon switched the video back, and saw that Stella was just finishing her task. He activated the microphone in his headgear and spoke, watching her look toward the ship on hearing his voice. "How about some supper?"

"Are you cooking?"

"Yeah, we'll make it something special, the last supper."

He saw Stella's shoulders slump, wishing he hadn't said anything or that he was out there to put his arm around her.

"I'll see you inside," was her downhearted reply.

Dagon switched off the video and entering the decontamination room shed his clothes, putting on fresh clothes hanging in a nearby locker, his mind already on how to make a celebration supper out of dried food.

Stella just stood frozen, trying to capture the quickly fading light, her face a mask of grief. It would probably be years, if ever, before they were allowed to make another journey to Vulcan. She cringed at the thought that tomorrow they could be saying goodbye for good. She shook her hair out of her eyes as the last golden rays of the sun sunk under the horizon, watching the sky turn a blood red crimson before the deep blackness descended. The words to one of her own long a forgotten poem came unexpectedly, *Shrouded in the gray, cold death of winter, is life. Hidden it springs beneath the frozen plain, waiting for the blood red resurrection dawn.*

Later, changing her clothes in the decontamination chamber, she had a chance to compose herself again after her moment of sadness.

She opened the door to the main living area of the ship to see Dagon at the kitchenette with a wide assortment of cooking supplies stacked on the counter. He was reading the recipe book, trying to figure out how to mix the various dried powders.

"What are you trying to make?" Stella smiled at his seriousness, "You're not going to put in a pinch of this and a pinch of that?"

"You mean toads and potions," Dagon shot back, "I'm not a witch like you."

"You shouldn't make fun of witches. White witches and high magic were what kept the goddess faith alive all through the Dark Ages."

Dagon looked up briefly, then pulled a box toward him examining its the back of it as he replied. "I just remember hearing about the evil witches, the ones with the broomsticks."

"The broom was a stick carved with phallic symbols and used for ceremony and feasts honoring fertility and the cycles of the moon and earth. Witches knew how to use spiritual symbols in sacred ceremony for healing. Fortunately, all the ancient codes required they were never to use that spiritual power for selfish ends."

"But, I mean, really. You can't believe that you were a witch in a past life?" Dagon chided as he lined up all of his ingredients."

"Yes, I do. I also think these powers are passed on through heredity. My mother and grandmother are both intuitives. My grandmother was a well-known clairvoyant and my mother was a natural Seer. We just don't have initiation ceremonies anymore to pass these things on to our children."

"Yeah, well, you have to admit it's a pretty wild idea," Dagon said abstractly, as he began to mix powdered parmesan with freeze-dried red pepper rings.

Stella turned away abruptly, thinking about the secret she had been carrying. It was time to come clean. She whirled back around again to throw out, "well, how about this idea for 'crazy.' I have known for years that I knew you before in many lifetimes. It was a kind of love/hate thing! Now, that's a wild idea. I seem to remember really hating it when you would get so technical about everything!"

Dagon reached out to pull Stella under his arm as she stalked behind the kitchen island. "How could I be 'technical' in a past life, what were we doing, some wild alchemical experiment? Besides, this is a crazy conversation, not, logical at all." Dagon turned back to his recipe.

"Oh, blast you," Stella fumed, "You infuriate me. It's obvious that we're soul mates. How else do you explain the odd coincidence of us making this trip together?"

"Soul mates?" Dagon sounded incredulous.

"Yeah, like twin flames, blah, blah, never to part unless it is through curses, misfortune, or stupidity," she said sarcastically.

"My, my I can feel the flames now." Dagon teased, moving Stella out of his way so he could read the ingredients.

"Simmer briefly, add tomato paste and herbs," he muttered.

Suddenly, he was startled by a soft hiccup and noticed that Stella was hastily wiping her eyes with her sleeve. With a groan he reached out, pulling her against him again.

"I love you," he told her softly.

"You do?" Stella said, "In a twin flame sort of way?"

"Oh, brother," Dagon sighed, "Didn't you hear me?"

"Of course, I did! But, we've known each other for eons, been together in countless lives, and you didn't contact me this time until I was twenty-eight. Even then, you practically ignored me for two years and three months. If we hadn't been stuck together on this ship, you probably wouldn't have come to your senses at all!"

Stella looked up, flushed from her outburst.

Dagon looked angry. "This is a ridiculous conversation. How can you scold me for not remembering something I don't even know is true anyway."

"How can you say that it's not true?" Stella ranted.

Dagon's eyes had that steely gray look that didn't bear good will. Gripping her arm he pulled her with him into the main living area of the ship.

"I don't seem to remember you saying that you 'loved *me*' in all this time." His face softened as he took in her defiant stance.

"You used to be able to read my mind."

"Stella, this has gone far enough."

"I'm not going to kiss and make-up."

"Did I ask you to?" Dagon was smiling.

"Of course, you intend to. Remember, I know you." Stella folded her arms smugly over her chest.

"Oh, you do, do you? Then, you probably also know that I'm intending to ignore this ridiculous outburst, not kiss you," Dagon said through gritted teeth.

"That's the way you always used to start," Stella sniffed smugly. "The kissing followed soon after."

Dagon found himself grinning again. "And, then what would we do?" he teased, starting to warm up to the idea.

Dagon's eyes opened wide then narrowed as he gazed at Stella's stubborn expression.

"If you are making this up Stella, so help me I will..."

"Well, I'm not, so there," Stella stalked out of his reach. "I've kept this a secret. Astraea knew. This was 'the secret' she referred to that I didn't tell you. I've always known who you were. The first time I met you, I knew you." Gazing at his startled expression, she relented.

"You see, years ago I began to realize that I was very unhappy in my love life. I'd been in and out of relationships with men, but always unhappy. I'd spent years alone and independent, but been lonely. I found myself fantasizing about a great passionate romance where I would finally meet the man who could love me and whom I could love in return."

"Then, one night I had an amazing dream. I was standing on the edge of a cliff and a voice asked me if I wanted to fly. I did, and I flew to a Mediterranean villa. The dream was so detailed I could see the scrolls on the shelves and the tapestries on the walls. As I walked down the stone hallway through arched columns, my heart started to beat faster. I opened the door to one of the rooms and standing there was a tall, Greek man with dark hair and unusual gray eyes. I knew his name immediately. We fell into each other like two halves of the whole finally finding each other. I didn't want to wake up from my dream. When I did, I found that his spirit or presence seemed to be with me for weeks. I could literally feel his hand touching my cheek or hear his voice in my head."

"A month later I found a book with a symbol of the Rosicrucian rose on it. As I opened the pages and began to read, I was startled to hear the author describing the place I had seen in my dream, to the last detail, even talking about a man by the same name. I tried contacting the author. However, found he was already dead."

"A couple of weeks later, a friend of mine had a party, and a psychic was there who did past life regressions. I made an appointment and began a four-month journey, seeing lifetime after lifetime, of being with this lover. I can tell you, I got to know him rather well."

"In most of the lifetimes, I was a student or teacher, always involved in debate, research and philosophical study. I was somewhat stubborn and impulsive. He was a rationalist, a warrior and builder, with the deeper soul of a poet. We fought often and of course, had wonderful discussions in and out of bed."

"When I first met you, I knew immediately who you were. You have the same eyes, the same commanding and bossy nature. But, what clenched it for me was when I learned your middle name is Gideon. It has been the same name in every lifetime."

Dagon had been listening incredulously, but now he interrupted her.

"It seems I may have known you before, too," His eyes glinted dangerously. "I have this memory of a know-it-all, who was part super nova and part mermaid. I could never correctly guess which part would win out."

Stella rolled her eyes and tried to draw away from him, but he went on in a low seductive voice.

"Yes, red hair, you haven't changed at all, you used to bait me then too, at least until I lifted all those layers of linen..."

"Stop... Now!" Stella's voice rose tremulously and she began to pull away frantically. "You didn't do that in my regression or I would have remembered it."

"Are you sure, sweetheart, it seems that I'd be the one to remember those details," Dagon reached for her wrist, pulling her into his body.

"I will not let you win this argument."

"Who said we're arguing? Dagon dropped his head into her neck and smelled her skin."

"You completely slay me," he said.

"Dagon, stop," Stella gasped pulling back "You're still making fun of me and I won't have it, I won't, I..."

Her protest was forgotten in a deep passionate kiss. Dagon picked her up, wrapping her legs around his waist and pushed her up against the wall.

"Wait," Stella wailed momentarily stopping Dagon who looked up with glazed eyes.

"You're forgetting supper," Stella caught her breath as she motioned toward the mess on the kitchen cabinet.

"I'm not hungry for food anymore," he started to unzip her tunic kissing the column of her neck, letting her slide down his body.

Stella sighed and gave in completely. "It was always meant to be like this," she whispered as she ran her hands down his back.

He backed them into the couch.

"We have had enough foreplay," Dagon said. "I hope you're ready for this, because I don't care what the consequences are."

"I have been ready for a long time. In one life we…." She gave a little gasp as Dagon nipped the top of her breast.

"Stella" Dagon said, "Be quiet, I'm concentrating."

CHAPTER 20

✠

Micah explains

Later they sat satiated and happy at the dinner table snacking on anything left that was still edible. Stella blushed at some of the things that Dagon had done to her. She had never had such a demanding lover or felt so consumed. My God, if it were like this all of the time, she'd never manage to work around him.

Dagon, on the other hand was focusing on food. He was still hungry and grimaced at the gray dried food packets as he searched for crackers and cheese.

Stella opened their only remaining bottle of wine.

He poured her a glass, and then lifted his glass in a toast. "To a safe launch tomorrow and to Vulcan."

Stella's eyes misted as she thought about leaving. She put her head down on her arms.

"Many mysteries of this place are still unsolved," Dagon commented as he sipped from his glass.

"What do you mean?" Stella looked up from the table.

"Well, the prism for one. We never discovered the source of that. And, the volcano smoke. Was it really a volcano? How did Astraea know about our pasts? What about her enigmatic prophetic words about the seven seals and the seven times seven? Even stranger were those wild magical trips we made through thought transfer, the times that it seemed some other entity was channeling information through you."

"Our experiences here have been mind-blowing," Dagon continued, as he reached for his glass and moved his plate aside.

They left the clutter on the table and moved over to the living room. Stella was wearing sweats and a long shirt of Dagon's that reached past her knees. Dagon pulled her near and absent-mindedly picked up one of a stack of pictures from off of the worktable. It was a photo taken on Vulcan of the sun setting behind their ship, the signature sunset and sunrise of Vulcan, brilliant primary colors of red and blue with the sun shining like a golden center between the extremes. He stared at it, lost in thought.

"Well, what is your most burning unanswered question?" Stella took the photo away setting it back on the table as she drew him to the sofa where she created a nest of pillows for them.

"I guess if there are really extraterrestrial beings and if so, how they've interacted with earth," Dagon said seriously.

"Shall we try another experiment?" Stella squirmed in her seat flushed with excitement.

"Now, what do you have up your sleeve?" Dagon turned toward her noticing how small her wrists looked in his rolled up sleeves.

"I want to try to contact the entity we've felt present with us on Vulcan. You can ask questions and I'll consciously submit to letting him take over my voice," Stella said quickly.

"No," was Dagon's immediate answer. "This is not something to play around with. What if you find yourself under alien control?"

Stella looked up at Dagon with sadness. "You'll have to trust me with this. I know they're guides and friends. If I didn't believe this, I wouldn't be willing to go so far with the whole thing."

Dagon sighed with resignation. "How do you propose trying to do this?"

"I would simply close my eyes, right here, and offer myself as a channel. It's as easy as that. I've done this before on earth."

Dagon began to protest, but Stella put her finger to his lips. "Shh, I feel his presence very close to me. His home is Vulcan," Stella whispered.

"Stella," Dagon tried to stop her, but she was already drifting off, her eyes glazing and her body getting limp.

"Later, tell me later." Her voice dropped to a whisper.

Dagon startled when he saw the face of an old man superimposed over Stella. The old man's body seemed to hover in the soft glow of the living room lights. Dagon felt a prickling of the skin on his arms, like a cool breeze had passed through the ship's cabin.

"So, you would like to know more about your universal relatives?" the old man said with a kind smile. "Don't worry about your mate, she's fine, just resting. She'll wake up feeling refreshed."

Dagon felt a little shock go through him at the rich resonant voice coming out of Stella's throat.

"Who are you?" Dagon asked with alarm.

"I AM a soul sent from source to voice an ancient memory. My origin lies before the creation of the world you call earth. I AM one of the Old Ones that watched as the waters rolled over the deep and the firmament separated. I AM one of holders of the truth about the fundamental composition of life, witness to the beginning when the most elemental structures found form. I AM here to help you access cosmic information encoded in your DNA. The source of the information is intergalactic, coming from what you call 'God.'"

Dagon found his throat constricting at the soft authority in the old man's voice.

"What's your name and rank?" Dagon said with a frown.

"You can call me Micah. Don't worry," he smiled, "I'm harmless."

Dagon peered at the apparition, relaxing a bit at its obviously human form that was "floating" in front of Stella's body.

Micah seemed to read his mind.

"I appear human to make you more comfortable. We are actually beings of energy that would appear to you normally as bands of white and gray light. In our world, we speak through resonant tones or vibrational frequencies. To speak in your language is very limiting as 'words' do not accurately describe cosmic realities."

Dagon swallowed hard. "Why are you trying to contact us?"

"We have decided that earthlings are ready for more information because of the coming crisis."

Dagon looked around him rather distractedly. "Would you mind if I recorded this conversation?" The face of the entity seemed to fade back then suddenly billowed forward making Dagon draw back into his chair. "You do not need to. You will remember." The old man began to speak slowly and carefully, gesturing occasionally as he made his points. "I can hear your questions without you saying them out loud. I'll try to give you as clear of a picture as I can." Dagon settled back to listen as Micah began speaking.

"The earth was a stroke of creative genius. God found in man and sentient animals a way to integrate emotions, intellect and spirit within physical matter. Each sentient being holds within them the seed pattern of god Her/Himself. God is both male and female. God is all that is. We each have memories that are hundreds of thousands of years old. These memories are not just archetypal collective unconscious. They are the memories of a conscious Higher Self, a part of your eternal soul that is God."

"You have known us as guides, angels, inner voices, intuition, ascended masters, avatars, bodhisattvas, or saviors. We contact you, through synchronicities and internal guidance. We originally came as tribes from different places in the universe. Earlier you asked if there are other extraterrestrial beings in this universe. The answer is yes. Not only that, but the earth itself is a gene pool of many of these entities or galactic tribes."

"The birth of the human race, through evolution, coincided with the entrance of these celestial entities onto the earth plane. In some cases they bred with human's improving the genetic pool of the race. This was true with Atlantian, Mayan, Egyptian, China, India, Greek and Roman civilizations among others. The Bible speaks of great tall men who lived for 150 years. The Greeks called them the Titans. Almost every culture has a story about them. Abraham, the father of the 12 tribes of Israel was among these great men. They were humans who had been influenced by the special molecular and behavioral characteristics, strength and weaknesses unique to extraterrestrials."

"The Argon or Canopus tribal members were gifted with intense gravitational resonance. Argonians are psychically magnetic, masters at understanding energetics. They were attracted to sacred centers of power on the earth, and contacted earth in order to create channels for vortex energies. They activated the earth's star grids. These star grids intersect to form areas where mental vibrations can be targeted to galactic points within the universe in fractions of seconds. Argonians worked with a magnetic blueprint to foster evolution.[65] For example they carved the Sri Yantra on a lake bed in Oregon and are responsible for crop circles."

"The Arcturians live primarily in an 'essence of bondedness.' Their focus is relational and they are concerned with uniting humans with the interconnected web of the macrocosm. Humankind experiences them as 'angels' because of their expressions of love and their illuminated chakra radiance. Mother Theresa and Jesus Christ are direct descendants of this race. So, are whales and other gentle sea mammals."

"These beings suffer great grief as humans. They cannot understand a less than perfect world. Astraea is part Arcturian as are both you and Stella."

"There are many more from the Pleidian system. Pleidians concentrated on holding the physical form and keys to the original creation of humankind. They watched the evolution of man from an ape to an intelligent being. They have been helping to seed and expand the DNA code. They are natural scientists with a strong rational logical mind. Stella's father was Pleidian and her mother Arcturian. Your father had ancestors in Orion and your mother was Arcturian. Their tribal roots have influenced your genetics."

"It took the energy of both Orion and the Pleides to create the first evolutionary steps for humans.[66] The Pleidian code is evolving just as the DNA is now evolving. The 11/11/11 phenomenon was Pleidian seeding which was to proceed a 12 helix DNA matrix connecting mankind to other universal life forms and intelligence."

"The earth served perfectly as a midway station by beings from other planets. It had good potential for the growth of plant life because of its ideal location from the sun. The earth had already formed an atmosphere and was ripe for the fruits of this introduction, having already started its own slow evolutionary journey."

"Are you amazed at this, Dagon? You shouldn't be. All human art, mythology, legend, history tell of humankind's understanding of these other life forms. There are many unexplained phenomena that have been witnessed by mankind including ancient drawings of flying machines, landing strips in the high mountains and perfectly mapped on the desert, laser cut rock, advanced galactic astronomy and mathematics, the Phoenix lights, documented UFO sightings, crop circles, and shared world mythology that crosses cultural barriers."

Dagon's mouth dropped open. "Wait a minute, you're saying that Human's were moved along in their evolution by space aliens? My god!"

"Yes, your God." Micah smiled. "Unfortunately, some humans are direct descendants from Neanderthals. The more primitive humans resolve crisis through animalistic, fight or flight modes. It is still survival of the fittest for them. They even look like their ancestors, quite ferocious." Micah smiled and Dagon couldn't help smiling back.

"What you are not understanding is that Everything is God. All aliens, angels, guides, avatars, ascended masters, humans, nature are actually God. You, the earth, every form of life on it, the air you breathe are God. God is Everything! So, the fact that other beings of the macrocosm have interacted for thousands of years with humans should not come us a great surprise. The earth is not the center of the galaxy, God is! Your mistake as humans comes often from a runaway ego."

"The earth has just passed into Satya Yuga or the Golden Age in the last century. During the golden age mankind can experience peace, harmony, stability and prosperity. You have already met Astraea. She is the goddess who presides over the golden age.

Thousands of years ago she fled to the stars to find refuge in Virgo until the time that she could enact a path of justice on earth. She is talking to you for a reason."

"The time is auspicious for taking awakened consciousness and beginning to re-create the earth. Your father had many ideas about this, which you should read about, in his diary. He has been trying to help out a bit recently, but is ready now to pass on to the stars. He is with your mother. They both want you to know that they are proud of you."

"He would want you to draw the strength from each community that has been trying to help. Argon brings earth wisdom, Orion power of mind, Arcturus, the ocean of emotion, and Vulcan provides the last missing element, the golden fire of creation. This is what Astraea was referring to when she spoke about the Golden Teachings."

"Vulcan is where can take the action of fire to embrace dualities creating new world life using the golden light of kundalini."

Dagon was feeling a bit overwhelmed, but kept listening carefully.

"As for your other unanswered questions. The prism, the golden pool, was 'real,' but also created by your mind. You each have an amazing gift of being able to actualize your thoughts. The nature of personal reality is that you are the co-creators of everything that you see and hear. Be careful then what words you use. They are powerful!"

"So, Stella and I, what are we to do from here?" Dagon asked, just holding it together.

"Share your most recent dream with Stella. You are headed back to earth, of course." The old man smiled then relented.

"Your tribal seed is from the Old Ones. You are descendants of the original synergy, the first male/female form of order and chaos, of Vulcan. That is why you are here."

Dagon was confused, "There are no people here. How can we be from Vulcan?"

"I don't qualify as 'people'?" the old man chided then continued firmly. "You mistakenly see only the surface dimension of Vulcan. There is a fifth dimension just beneath conscious awareness. That is why you could travel to meet Astraea. It is why you could see a prism of light. It is why we are having this conversation. I am Micah, a priest on Vulcan sent to inform you of our presence and purpose."

Dagon sat back bewildered. "Give me a moment." He ran a shaky hand over his trouser leg then asked the burning question on his mind. "What is the purpose of the experiences which we have had for the past six days on Vulcan?"

"To wake you up, my son, so you can save the earth." Micah said this with conviction, but then gave a little laugh.

"We had to put you through some schooling so to speak. You seem to have forgotten the most basic galactic tenants, the creative power of thought for instance. You are being prepared for a work that you must do when you return to earth. As Astraea said, the story of Vulcan is encoded in mankind's secret alchemical doctrines, which are even now being misconstrued and misused. Vulcan is twin to earth. We are coming to a rare occurrence, an eclipse of Vulcan that will affect the sun and therefore earth. It will destroy life on earth unless you begin to understand the Golden Teachings, the Alchemical Wedding of the sun and moon."

If anything, Dagon looked even more confused.

"Don't worry about all of this now, fate will lead you. Some answers you must wait for."

Dagon felt as if his whole life was exposed before the truth in the old man's eyes.

"You are an old soul, too." The old man said gently as if answering an unspoken question. "You are just waking up to your root memories. Do not abandon what you know deep within you because of fear and skepticism. This is your greatest test."

"Evolution happens as the images or pictures of Higher Mind are encoded and materialized in energy and matter. This pulsation of intelligence finds expression in our time and space dimension, even though it is better understood in other dimensional realities. These pulls toward energy embodiment resonate through the human energy field or chakras. During the 11:11 opening, the eight and ninth chakra vibratory levels opened. The eighth level unites the energy of the 1st to the 8th by controlling the magnetic line of force. This power is represented by the symbolism of Vulcan."

"The Vulcan principle means the uniting of opposites and the power inherent in the movement between. Thus far, this has allowed the earth to find a way to survive by creating cold fusion. Survival meant learning how to recycle resources, to find unlimited energy sources, to restructure social and economic systems so that they were continually revitalized. It was a crucial period for the earth because it hovered on the brink of annihilation if those lessons were not learned."

"Now, in the year 2033, your task is again critical. It is to help mankind see the pathway through the great earth changes that are coming in the near future, to be an Alchemist for the Earth."

Dagon had been so immersed in Micah's words; he had stopped watching the time. He glanced out of the viewing portal of the ship.

The night was unusually clear, blazing with stars and the twin moons that hung pendulous and heavy on the horizon.

"Micah, who are you, really?" Dagon asked quietly, the question spoken from some deep instinct.

The old man responded instantly. In front of Dagon's eyes he seemed to change shape until his weathered face and twisted hands became the gnarled branches and roots of a great oak tree, his beard now flowed down like branches, his voice like a whisper of leaves in a soft breeze.

"The month of June or the month of the summer solstice is the month where a person can look two ways, both forward into the second half of the year, and back toward the first."

Micah's leaves fluttered and he continued in a soft voice, "The Oak, Duir or 'Door' tree, sacred to the month of June, is symbolic of those deities whose powers extend both to the Underworld and to Heaven, the Overworld. United we become the summer solstice, the meeting place in-between where the year turns, literally, The Door."[67]

"Who am I? I AM the Door." His last words seemed to gradually fade away as the image of the great oak faded away. Dagon could just make out the last words as they became softer and softer. "I AM the Door."

The old man's voice faded to silence and the wavering image of the great oak disappeared.

Stella sighed, stretching sleepily.

"Where am I?" she murmured.

Dagon gathered her close to his chest.

"You're with me, home with me."

CHAPTER 21

✠

The alchemical marriage

"It's hard to believe that today is our seventh day and our last morning on Vulcan. What is the exact time for launch again?"

"11:11 a.m."

"Of course, it would be 11:11," Stella cleared the lump in her throat, sighing wistfully, "I wish that we could stay," she mumbled as she walked away, "What would the Lady of the Golden Stone do?"

Dagon raised his eyes from his instrument board, asking with a tense voice, "What did you just say?"

"Nothing," Stella looked away guiltily.

"You said 'Lady of the Golden Stone,'" Dagon came over assessing Stella's remorseful expression. "I think you should explain yourself." Dagon's mouth was set in a grim line.

"I'm beginning to think you should explain yourself! What are you so upset about all of the sudden?"

"I'm not upset," he shook his head impatiently, "Just surprised."

"Where did you get the phrase 'Lady of the Golden Stone'?"

"From a manuscript called *The Alchemical Marriage* that dates back to the 15th century A.D. penned by an alchemist named Johan Andrea. The story is about a seeker, Christian, who goes on a journey to an alchemical wedding and witnesses the creation of the world. He and his female companion are awarded by the goddess Virgo by being made Lady or Knight of the Golden Stone."

"Tell me more," Dagon grimaced.

Stella went and got her computer out of her locker and turned it on so she could read her notes. "Here, I'll send them over to your Link. The Alchemical Wedding is a great mystery that takes place in seven days."

"Day one, there is a violent storm and the alchemists are magically transported to a secret ceremony."

"Day two, they are weighed to determine their integrity."

"Day three, they pass another test and are gifted with a symbol of immortality, the Golden Fleece."

"Day four, they go up a long winding staircase to the top of a tower. There they meet the king and queen of creation. Before the queen is a mysterious book, a celestial globe, the sands of time and a glass vial containing blood red liquid. A white serpent crawls in and out of orbit nearby. They are told they are to be wedding guests at an alchemical marriage."

"Day five, the wedding guests are taken to a laboratory where plants, stones and matter are distilled into their essences and placed into glass vials."

"Day six, the white haired keeper of the tower examines the laboratory work and finds it satisfactory. The assembled scientists are now called 'Artists who have ascended.' Now, awakened as gods and goddesses, the artists reduce their bodies to liquid states and that fluid is drained into an immense golden globe and arranged so that the sun's rays can cause it to become very hot. Later, the sun's rays are deflected and the globe permitted to cool. It is cut open with a diamond to reveal a beautiful white egg. This great egg gives birth to an ugly bird, which is fed blood. After each feeding its feathers change color until it becomes beautiful. The bird is then fed with the light of the white serpent, and at its request, burned to ashes. These ashes are used to mold a new human race, one male and the other female. Virgo Lucifera then appears and, through a tiny hole in the dome of the tower, a ray of light descends to give them each fully awakened souls."

"Day seven, Virgo announces that each of the wedding guests has now become 'a Lady or Knight of the Golden Stone.' They are each given a sailing ship that bears a sign of the Zodiac. The newly created 'Knight and Lady of the Golden Stone' are instructed to go home and teach mankind what they have learned."[68]

"You've got to be kidding. This a *real* manuscript written in the 15th century?" Dagon sounded incredulous.

"Yep, its real. I got it from BOB's data banks. I had been thinking about how our journey here is taking place in seven days and said the words out loud. BOB was listening and spit out a copy of this manuscript. I was floored. Bizarre story, huh!"

She looked up and noticed that Dagon had visibly whitened. "What's the matter? You look like you've seen a ghost."

Dagon said, "Micah mentioned we needed to talk about my dream and said we will become Alchemists for the Earth. Now, here it is right in front of me."

Dagon continued, "I dreamed this Alchemical Wedding story three days ago in Technicolor, everything, all the details you just read. I know I've never seen this manuscript before."

Stella's eyes lit up as she tried to keep her excitement in control. "Hey, maybe you were this Andreas guy in a past life. Sorry, not trying to freak you out, but spill it. I want the details."

322

Dagon looked flustered as he brushed a lock of hair out of his eyes. "It was all there, the lab, the king and queen, the egg, the tower. Everything."

"Wait", Dagon grabbed a pen, taking some notes. "Look at this!" He started to draw a timeline that looked like a graph, making brief notes over it. "Our trip here to Vulcan parallels the seven days of the story. It's as if we've been living out the details of the 'Alchemical Wedding' ourselves through some bizarre twist of fate."

Dagon continued, "We come in on a violent storm, and are leaving on a ship with a message and a mission to save the earth. Those Cryptogram experiments almost exactly mirror the alchemical wedding down to the egg, the ashes and the phoenix. The old man in the story is Micah and Virgo is Astraea. They have been proving us fit for this journey by reminding us and teaching us. The golden pool was the golden fleece."

Stella jumped in seeing the correlations. "We became 'awakened artists' when we realized that we have power to magically transform matter with the power of mind. As alchemists we are the fifth element that channels air, earth, water and fire to create new life."

They both froze for a moment silently contemplating the chain of connections. Stella was the first to speak.

Dagon's keen mind went back to the heart of the matter. "So, why now on the seventh day have you referred to yourself as a Lady of the Golden Stone."

"Yes, why?" Stella croaked, "Eehmm."

Dagon looked at his Link. "The story says that those who witnessed the alchemical birth of life were sent home, journeying on zodiac ships or starships, entrusted with a message for the world, Ladies and Knights of the Golden Stone."

Suddenly, a loud warning buzzer sounded. "One hour to lift off."

Dagon took Stella's arm and drew her over to her chair, strapping her into her seat and life support. His movements were smooth and efficient. This moment had been practiced over and over back at Beta III during their flight simulation training.

The revolution of the planet was at maximum rotation for lift off. The time had come to commit to the launch. All systems were ready. They had spent the day before storing equipment, sealing the ship, and logging into a flight record in case their ship failed on re-entry. Dagon had left detailed records that future scientists could find in case of such a disaster. Now, it was a matter of waiting for launch.

"I want to stay here," Stella burst out, emotions making her irrational.

"That's crazy," said Dagon. "We wouldn't survive one month. We would have no food or oxygen. We would run out of medical supplies. Eventually our energy core on our ship would fail." He gently touched her back in a comforting gesture. "We aren't like Micah and Astraea. We're human, we have to go back."

With resolve, he made sure that BOB was strapped down and fastened his own belts, setting the launch sequence.

"I have a present for you," Stella said.

"Now...while we are taking off?" Dagon looked at her with consternation.

"We have a moment." Stella insisted. "I need to give you this, now." She reached down into the side pocket of her chair and handed him a black box. Nestled inside wrapped in a soft cloth were two golden egg shaped stones.

"Where did you get them?" Dagon asked, amazed as he picked one up. It fit perfectly into the palm of his hand and felt warm to the touch.

"I found them in the crook of a tree as we were flung away from the cave where we saw Astraea. We each have one."

"You found these here on Vulcan?" Dagon practically shouted. "And, didn't put them in quarantine, or record them in our research log! They materialized from our astral travel!!" He sounded angrier at each question.

"Yes," Stella clutched hers for strength then said resolutely, "I'm not going to give them to Interspace Research. The fact that you dreamed of the Alchemical Wedding reinforces it for me. We are Lady and Knight of the Golden Stone. They have some purpose. I just don't know what it is yet."

Dagon gripped the stone and it seemed to respond to his touch, glowing with an inner light, a warm, pulsing radiance. He had a sudden flash of what the future held for them: a battle with greed, large corporations, hidden secrets, a mission for the earth and danger. The stone gleamed in his palm, seeming to speak to him. "You have a job to do. Remember this! You have a job to do."

Except, now wasn't the time to think about it. That was for another day. He had to concentrate.

"Okay, but you can bet we are going to be talking about this later." He slipped the stone in his pocket and went to work, while Stella closed her eyes and tried to relax.

The time went by quickly and soon they were at final countdown.

11:07, 11:08, 11:09, 11:10, 11:11.11 - Engines ignite.

A huge tearing sound and inner pressure pressed them back in their seats as the rockets ignited and the ship shook. Lift Off!

CHAPTER 22

✠

Return to earth

The rumble of the spaceship taking off was ear splitting. The G force compressed Stella's body, pinning her head back in the seat. Her straps and belts were so tight she couldn't do anything but grip the armrest tightly. She could hear Dagon breathing through a microphone in their helmets. Her adrenaline was racing.

"Tell me again, why we didn't get a new ship," she said trying to put some brevity into the situation. "This is like being flung up in space in a bucket of rocks."

She heard Dagon chuckle.

"Whoa baby! Feel that vibration?" he teased.

"It's that damn synchron belt, it wants to take us with it." Stella said, trying to holding her breakfast down, as she turned pale.

"Only a few more minutes," Dagon assured her. "Like riding a green colt, it'll be over soon."

"Yeah, well, I don't ride horses...ever!" Stella tried to quip to keep her mind off the noise, rattle and shake.

"I'll have to teach you," Dagon murmured sounding preoccupied.

There was something incredibly calming about Dagon's voice as he said this. Stella snuck a look at him as he focused on the flight panel.

The fear began to shift into excitement with an edge of thrill. She gave up, letting herself lean into the vibration, relaxing her tense body.

Her grip on the armrest softened.

Poise, capability, confidence and strength were innate to Dagon. That's why it was easier to put up with his bossiness and rigidness. Some men seem like boys. They never really grow up. Some men are never boys. They are warriors. Stella wondered what in the world they would do when they got home and Dagon didn't have a battle to fight.

What an incredible trip this had been. It felt like they had been on Vulcan for seven years instead of seven days. Time had slowed down, almost gone backwards.

Stella wished she could hold on to this altered state of languidness. She supposed it was a lot like camping. Time slowed down when you were more in the moment. As soon as you arrived at your campsite, it felt like forever before it was time to light a fire or climb into your sleeping bag. Vulcan time was like cat time, totally Zen. A goal to work towards, she reminded herself.

The ship dipped and swayed to the side. Unconsciously, she gripped the golden stone in her pocket, and then surrendered to her breath. One breath in, one breath out, drawing the breath through the belly up to the chest, a long slow inhalation, a long slow exhalation. Breathe. Oh, there, she sighed inwardly, starting to feel better.

Acceleration jerked them free of the synchron belt. The sense of motioned stilled. The ship's artificial gravity now held her body from floating to the ceiling. Stella peered through the view port, catching one last glimpse of Vulcan as it vanished, curving into the distance then out of sight. Through the haze surrounding it, the crystalline blue-green beauty was so mesmerizing she had an overwhelming urge to follow it, and never come back.

Within minutes Vulcan was thousands of miles away, whipping by on its orbital path in the synchron belt. The darkness of space and their aloneness gripped her. All that remained was the tracing tail of a geomagnetic storm. Lightening sheets of iridescent, prismatic colors, waved around them in a spectacular display, gradually fading to darkness.

Stella closed her eyes, willing the rainbow color to stay, drawing on the memory of the northern lights on earth. It was a cold winter night in Wyoming, the stubby sagebrush poking up out of snow that was about six inches deep. Because she walked it almost every day, the snow was packed in a series of little steps that led to the top of the knoll behind her house. From there she had a great view of the Big Dipper and the North Star, Polaris. She pulled her coat around her and tied the earflaps down on her hat, awed by the immensity of the sky and the millions of pinpoints of light in the clear, cold, moonless night. She knew many of the constellations by heart because her dad had started pointing them out to her when she was only five.

"Look Stella, that's Cassiopeia, let me tell you the story," he'd spoken in his big deep voice grabbing her in a bear hug, "You know he had said as he twirled her around, "Your name means 'Star.'"

This particular night she was up on the hill alone, her family warm in their beds. She had read in her astronomy magazine that there was a good chance to see northern lights because of x-class solar storms a couple of days before. She'd almost given up when the first waves of blue and grey banded across the sky. A green ray had shot across the middle of the Dipper and out overhead.

That was the moment that Stella had decided that she would travel in space some day. She'd been fourteen years old, yet was already recognized as an upcoming researcher. Her science project had won an international award and a pharmaceutical company that had seen a possibility in the plant antigens that she had isolated was taking her research seriously.

Stella floated out of her memory then blinked back into the ship in time to see a thin double ribbon of light shoot across the dark sky of space. Red and blue this time, like the signature sunset on Vulcan.

"Wow!" she cried trying to catch Dagon's attention. What was he feeling now? Like a shutter snapping tight, Dagon had seemed unapproachable as soon as they had pulled free of Vulcan's gravity. Seeing the synchron belt disappear made everything they had gone through in the last seven days seem like a figment of their imaginations.

Soon they were able to unstrap and begin setting up their stations on the ship. As the day went by she forced herself to concentrate on the work at hand, praying that, whatever was eating at Dagon, he'd get over it soon. There was plenty to do. She lost herself in myriad projects, recording her specimens and making notes. Pointed focus for days, weeks even months at a time were natural to her work.

At first it was okay. The hours ticked by with both of them so busy they skipped sharing lunch or dinner. However, after a long day of silence, hurt and anger started to build. Distant, professional politeness was painful.

That night, Dagon went to his own quarters to sleep, barely saying good night. Stella kept working into the wee hours of the morning. Exhausted, she slept when Dagon got up to do the ship maintenance and repair chores. When she did wake up, she was too hurt and confused to talk to him. It was as if they were back at the beginning of their relationship, business as usual. The loneliness was like an arrow in her heart. And, they still had three months of space travel left to get home.

After a second day of isolation and frustration, Stella decided to confront Dagon. The moment to talk came over supper as she was making a sandwich.

"Dagon, what's up? Are you mad at me about something? Why this distance?"

Dagon looked down at his coffee cup with a hangdog expression that made her want to pull his hair.

"We stepped way out of line by compromising the mission with all the crazy stuff that we did together. I'm just trying to figure it all out. I needed time to think. Also, I've been reading my dad's diary and it has given me a lot to think about."

"Did you consider this might be hurting my feelings? That I might want to *share* what you're thinking about?" Stella said tremulously.

Dagon looked even guiltier. "I'm sorry. I guess I haven't been thinking about 'us' so much as about what happened."

"Maybe it would help to have someone else to share this with. I mean we *both* went through the same thing."

"Yes, but I feel like we're going to be on a completely different pages about what we need to report to Base Command. The communication system is working. We'll be able to make contact tonight."

Stella felt a deep crawling dread. She had been putting this off, not even wanting to think about what she would tell Command.

"Also, I got a transmission from Starship #819 on its flight back from Galaxy M5545. They will be intersecting our flight path tomorrow. Their ship is a space station big enough to dock this ship for a piggyback ride to Earth instead of Mars. They are equipped to quarantine our specimens and begin processing data. We may be requested to board by Colonel Greene."

Stella felt a wave of shock run through her.

"When did you find this out?"

"This morning."

"And, why didn't you tell me right away instead of giving me the cold shoulder," Stella's voice was beginning to rise with accusation. "Don't you think that I'd want to be preparing for what I want to say to them too?"

Dagon looked sheepish.

This was too much like it had been before, during that excruciating two years, as she waited for him to see her and acknowledge her while they were doing their space training. It felt as if their new relationship was doomed. He had told her he loved her, even been vulnerable, yet the old skeptical Dagon seemed to be surfacing again the farther away from Vulcan they got. It was all too radical for him.

She hated the performance required by the space team to satisfy the public. Upon arrival on earth, they would be bombarded with questions, television interviews and debriefings. She realized they had to decide now what could be ethically told of their experiences and what should be kept secret.

Secrets, ugh, she shuddered, thinking of the danger of letting the information that they had go public. Alchemy was full of secrets.

The mysteries of ancient teachings were now fading away on fragile scrolls and tablets hidden in private collections. Most would *never* see the light of day. They included cryptic messages warning that the uninitiated faced certain death should they stumble on arcane formulae.

Alarm caused her hands to tremble, unexpectedly.

This is ridiculous, she chastised herself silently. Why am I getting scared all of the sudden? Profound synchronicity brought me here. Didn't my psychic say I would be in the public eye, with information to share? Why should I be frightened now? Yet, she knew in her heart that something sinister was waiting for her.

She comforted herself by recalling the day there had been a total eclipse of the sun on her birthday. Looking up at the sun through a pinhole on a cardboard paper, she had been flooded with knowledge that seemed prophetic. It was a glimmer of what the future held and what she would sacrifice for it. Events had unfolded according to a greater plan. Now, she knew that her only real choice was to sit back and try to trust the ride. In the meantime, she knew with a certainty that almost everything they had experienced on Vulcan must be kept secret, until the right time came to reveal it.

Someday, she vowed, I will go back and live on Vulcan. Perhaps, we would have been able to materialize what we needed for food and shelter over the winter through the power of our thoughts. We could have made it our heaven in the universe. Instead, like it or not, they faced going back to a world full of skepticism and disbelief. Dagon's skepticism was the hardest to face.

"Dagon?" He looked up, then quickly away. Stella ignored his distance and plunged in.

"Regarding information for Base Command, I feel that the best thing is to relay the physical data from the plant experiment, soil, atmosphere and gravity tests, but omit anything about the other experiences we had with translocation, shared dreams, telekinesis, and our contact with extra-terrestrials."

"I believe those experiences were for our personal edification, to set us on a personal mission, not, for public consumption. While we might share it all at some point in the future, the time hasn't come for that yet."

Anger bubbled up at the subject. Dagon tried to swallow it, along with his guilt, for acting like a heel.

"I suppose you're right. We wouldn't want anyone to think we're crazy," he said between clenched teeth.

Stella looked at him searchingly and frowned, then quickly swallowed her own angry retort. If he wanted to doubt his own experience, she couldn't stop him. She pulled her sweater tightly around her and turned away.

This felt familiar, a guy thinking her philosophy was too radical, and breakdown of relationships over courage of belief.

"Promise, no matter what pressure is put on you, you'll hold this and your golden stone a secret!" The words burst out of her in a rush.

Dagon twitched with shocked. "You mean make some kind of vow or pact between us?"

"Yeah, that's what I mean," Stella's tone was sharp. She tried to cool her temper by taking a deep breath.

Dagon closed his eyes for a moment then shook his head slightly. "Okay, I agree, although I don't know why you're being so dramatic."

Inside, he knew. They both knew. This information was potentially explosive. On top of that, they faced court martial from NASA if they withheld critical findings.

"We have to erase our conversations from BOB's memory bank. He'll be downloaded," Stella said. "We will need to say he malfunctioned as we got closer to Vulcan."

Dagon shuddered, but nodded approval. There was no other choice.

Stella erased the history in BOB's data bank and spent a bit more time doing some maintenance on his data bank, something he seemed to appreciate. At least BOB didn't take this personally.

Dagon hated this. As a trained physicist, he was used to looking at the world through the eyes of proven constants, laws and principles that could be replicated in experiment after experiment. If the world was created through individual perception, it opened the door to chaos. Another voice was arguing within him. Ah, but would it really be chaos? There is a pattern in human consciousness. Humans themselves are made up of the same elementary component parts that are constant in the universe. He knew he still believed that it could all be amalgamated into one universal principal, one universal truth.

The strong forces, the forces that hold together the nucleus of atoms, were the same forces that seemed to be drawing them along some mysterious path of its own design. The weak forces, the forces of decay, which brought transmutation and change, were at work too. In their presence, he was being forced to let go of everything he had once believed in.

The powerful forces of magnetism and electricity, had, from the beginning, drawn Stella and himself together for this journey. He had to trust this.

The stones are powerful, dangerous, his inner voice warned. He closed his hand over the warm, smooth stone. Last night, he had held it up in the dark and noticed that it had a thermogenic, phosphorescent quality, making it glow in the dark when heated against his body. This meant it probably had a half-life and was radioactive.

To be truthful, it was how they had gotten the stones, not, the stones themselves that alarmed him. They had come out of the world beyond the window of his imagination. They were positive proof that matter could be materialized through the power of mind. He'd tried to examine his discomfort, even writing his thoughts in a private journal, as he went in detail over each of their days on Vulcan.

So, what was frightening him? Why did he feel so frozen inside, afraid to move? In seven days they had walked through what seemed like years of spiritual teaching. It had been a 'private initiation.' Yet, another part of him wanted to shake it all off as grandiose, psychotic thinking. Who was he to think he had any answers to life's greatest questions, that he had been singled out to save the world. If there was a god, let god be a mystery, he found himself praying. He believed in the mystery, not really wanting a pat answer.

In the end, his final act of self-denial was to turn off all his thoughts, pretending nothing had happened to shake up his world.

After a shift change, Stella and Dagon both began procedure to try radio communication with Base Command. Transmission equipment repaired, short-circuits rewired, and out of range Vulcan radio interference, they couldn't wait any longer. With one deep look to seal the pact of secrecy that turned on their feed.

"FLIP on," Stella gave the voice command.

A weak signal began turning into a discernible rhythmic pulse, the numeric code and sound frequency of Beta III. Stella's eyes flooded with unexpected tears. They were of both joy and grief.

This was home. The green light started to beep. They began to receive a blurry video transmission of Colonel Greene. His face was wreathed in a broad smile. They could hear cheering in the background.

"You made it! Congratulations! Golden Eagle."

"Thank you, sir," Dagon said.

"What happened, what broke our transmission?"

"We couldn't get out a signal once we were in the synchron belt. We tried again after landing, but found our equipment had been short-circuited and needed repair. Even BOB went down."

"Are you okay?"

"Yes, both of us are doing fine. We had a rough landing, but our land scanners pulled through at the last second. The exit went just as planned. Both of us are in good health and looking forward to getting home."

Colonel Greene was radiant. "Were you able to release the space probes to Vulcan's surface?"

"Yes, sixteen out of the twenty five made it through the atmosphere and are in position now, although we haven't received any information from them yet."

"What's the condition of your ship?"

"Excellent."

Now, the Colonel was visibly beaming. "And, your report on Vulcan?"

Dagon looked at Stella, and then he said very clearly, "We found a living biological organism on Vulcan."

There was an astounded silence, then the excited sound of other voices interrupting.

"Would you please repeat that?"

The world was listening.

Stella stepped out of the shower, toweling herself dry slowly, rubbing the soft thick cotton towel over skin that had been denied this sensual pleasure for four months. Keeping clean on the ship during their journey had been a much more efficient process. She sat down on the edge of the tub, enjoying the steamy room and the sweet scented oil that she slowly applied to her legs and arms. Then, she began to brush her hair, making each stroke a luxurious ritual.

Her mind started to drift over the past couple of weeks and the intensity of their re-entry to earth. As Dagon had suspected, they had been asked to piggyback a ride on Starship #819. Since it was a self-contained space station, there had been days in decontamination units, medical tests, and hours of interrogation and debriefings about their findings. Fortunately, being together during the debriefings helped them work out all the details of their story.

In one of the more horrible moments, she had been questioned over video feed by Emilio Fauntis, the head of Interspace Research, a pasty faced, obese man who was the picture of greed. All she could think of then were Astraea's warnings. It seemed wrong to show them tapes of the complex adaptive life form on Vulcan. The cryptograms had probably evolved over millions of years, and her testimony could wipe them out if Interspace upset the delicate balance on the planet.

The probes were beginning to send in data that was being analyzed by computers. The Vulcan samples were being matched with DNA blueprints of thousands of other earth organisms, viruses and diseases to look for microbial life. The small plant that they had brought back with them was encased in a decontamination unit, awaiting further experimentation.

Many of her colleagues had expressed true joy at their discovery. Dagon had said that it was the challenge to find life that had propelled him into the space program. She saw that same idealism in others, yet it was exhausting to be around the feverish excitement of the space technicians who asked endless questions. Stella cringed at memories of the strident interrogation of the investigative team of Interspace Research.

"How much of the product was there?"

"Repeat again the exact manipulations done in the experiment."

"What was the result? How much energy did the plants produce? So, they seemed to grow with mist only?"

Looking back she was grateful she and Dagon had agreed to keep many of their experiences from Vulcan secret. That information would have made them subject to extreme religious sects and worse, corporate greed. Some would be looking for a way to make magic a tool for power and domination. She was grateful for Colonel Greene. He had trusted them, refusing to allow them to be submitted to neural brain scanners on the basis of principle.

These scanners would have read their most recent memories, processing all their feelings and sense images through a computer learning station. To Stella, this adaptation of the computer to augment mental cognitive reasoning through attachments to thoughts was a dark invasion of privacy and human dignity. She shuddered to think of the ethical ramifications of these neural networks. She knew she preferred 'spiritual magicians' to 'mental logicians' any day. The world of politics baffled her.

Yet, a strong pattern was emerging as they went through the exhausting process of television and video performances. Most of the public seemed to fall in one of three categories: the Conservationists, Starseed, and the Skeptics. The Conservationists recognized that global progress required recycling all products, energy, and human resources for reclamation and redistribution. Even social programs were valued by their degree of efficiency.

Starseed was the global unification of a wide range of religious groups that believed that future answers would require leaving planet earth to colonize the universe. Finally, the Skeptics were scientific in orientation and pessimistic about the future of earth. They were currently focusing on trying to find solutions for earth changes that could not be ignored: massive earthquakes, weather changes, changes in the magnetic poles, gradual extinction of species and the holes in the o-zone. It was Starseed that had formed TTL, the Think Tank Laboratory where the greatest minds could explore the links between history, geography, biology, language and physics. TTL bred idealism, and a mixture of contention and ego, as each scientist fought for his or her school of thought. TTL ideas had become very influential in the space program.

News of the cryptograms had spread like wildfire through these intellectual circles. Already an international meeting had been scheduled to take place at the end of the month. There a panel of scientific leaders, and the heads of the various research laboratories around the world, would meet to ask first-hand their questions about all of Dagon and Stella's experiences on Vulcan. Stella swallowed, gripping her towel around her belly, nervously.

She had always hated public appearances and, although she could speak professionally, and seemed cool on the exterior, she usually felt butterflies and a sense of inadequacy. After giving the speech for the International Science Fair, it seemed she hadn't had a moment of rest. To sit on a towel, enjoying the warm vapors of the sauna, made her sleepy. She wanted to curl up like a cat, forgetting all of the intensity and greed that had hounded her since their return.

Dagon was getting out of a lot of the media pressure, she thought, But not, for long. For now, the focus had been the cryptograms, on biological life, because of the financial gain it represented. Soon, however, the scientific community, and the skeptics who were slower to make their voices heard, would be probing the possibilities of utilizing the radar capabilities of the synchron belt.

Unconsciously, she found herself looking over at the black velvet bag where she had placed her golden stone. Thank god they didn't know about the stone, she thought.

A chill went through her as she remembered the words of the physician, *John Schweitzer*, better known as *Helvetius*, a well-known scholar and author of many learned tracts. One of his writings described an event that occurred in December of 1666. Helvetius was visited by a stranger who drew a handsome ivory box out of his pocket containing three transparent, yellowish crystals the size of small walnuts. The material was heavy and had a sulfurous glow. The man said, "I am a brass founder and student of alchemy." Helvetius examined the crystal, wondering about its power to heal, to extend life and to transmute base metals into gold. He begged for a tiny fragment of the crystal.[69]

Later, Helvetius wrote he was able to melt lead and put fragments of this crystal into it, turning lead into an ingot of the finest gold. Years went by before another mysterious stranger, Compte St. Germaine, claimed to be using small portions of the philosopher's stone as an elixir that granted immortality. His well-documented life seemed to support this bizarre claim.

Hieroglyphics of the ancient Egyptians depicted alchemical experiments as early as 200 B.C. Even more alarming, kings and queens, through two thousand years, reportedly held a variety of alchemists in prisons, demanding the secret to this power.

Hitler's right-hand man, General Ludendorff teamed up with a gentleman named Tausend who reportedly could transmute base metals to gold. The effort drew investment funds that diverted 400,000 marks into the Nazi party, continuing until Tausend was sent to prison for fraud. In the 1960's there were still reports of groups of practicing alchemists.[70]

Stella looked at the golden stone in her hand. It had a strangely heavy feeling and sulfurous glow. What if the stories of the alchemists were true? Sure there had been frauds, but what if these secret societies had actually found a way to alter molecular structure using rarefied solutions of chemical compounds.

Modern scientists were still trying to transmute properties by bombarding atoms at higher and higher pressures to separate particles. This allowed the atom to form new arrays. Quantum physicists were still trying to changed lead into gold. Perhaps there was a circle of ancient initiates who knew the formula to do this as a chemical process. This was information that could radically change the world.

She had found the stones on Vulcan, the planet's namesake being a great alchemist and gifted goldsmith. Perhaps, the teachers Micah and Astraea were the souls of spiritual alchemists. Stella took her stone out the velvet bag to gaze at it. It seemed to pulse with energy in her hand, glinting mysteriously. She knew that somehow it connected her to an underground river of information. If her dreams were correct, it would lead somehow to the lair of the dragon. The dragon was an ancient symbol of alchemy. If there was a society of alchemists alive today, she sensed, they would come to her. For some reason, the thought both terrified and thrilled her. -

She could feel a mighty power rising around her, something wild and uncontrollable, was in the air. And, she was alive to witness it.

She wondered if Dagon was thinking about any of this. For someone so brilliant, she thought was sure acting stupid. He could see how the laws of the physical world worked, scientifically categorizing things into their component parts. Yet, if he tried to figure *this* out, he'd need more abstract theories. He was missing one whole half of the equation, magic. Suddenly, Stella was filled again with the overwhelming urge to contact him. The sadness brought tears to her eyes again and she brushed them away, tired of the heartbreak.

Two months had gone by now since their last day on Vulcan. It was as if the tender moments they had shared had not existed. That last night on the ship they had slept in separate bedrooms and she had cried herself to sleep. Once aboard Starship #819 they had been kept apart by necessity. She'd secretly taken a pregnancy test as soon as possible. It had been negative. She wistfully rubbed her hand along the soft towel, down her leg to the sole of her foot, then leaned her body forward and hugged her knees, overwhelmed by deep, gut-wrenching loneliness. With effort, she shook it off and briskly towel-dried her hair again, thinking, I want to go home to Wyoming. I miss my cat. I want to sleep in my own bed. I wish that I could hate him.

She heard the phone ringing in the inner room, but let the answering machine pick it up. A face appeared on the video screen. It was her assistant, Gary, listing her scheduled meetings for this week. She stayed where she was, not willing to be seen. Her vulnerability couldn't show, somehow that had to be hidden from everyone.

Dagon gratefully sipped the warm tea that had just come out of the dispenser. He stretched his back, looking around him at the mess. His apartment was trashed with clutter, his desk overloaded with papers. Take-out containers of old food littered the kitchen cabinets. His hair was standing on end and he was still in his sweats. He hadn't even gone running in a week. Instead all he had done was study his father's journal with its tiny diagrams, mysterious mathematical formulas, and questions that he couldn't answer. He had taken some of the ideas and begun his own research. On one page of a fat notebook were his notes on the quantum electrodynamics of chemical reactions.

He was studying chemical transmutation in the light of the electrical impulses that existed between the electrons, particles, and quarks within the atom. He wondered again where he was stuck. The formulas kept showing error. Perhaps, he was approaching it from the wrong direction.

He had been searching for an elementary quantum theory to explain transmutation in chemical reaction, following some intriguing notes in his father's diary. Perhaps, the missing piece was beyond fundamental laws about the mechanics of photons, quarks, or superstrings.

What if you examined all rules of physics in the light of what he had always thought of as medieval or superstitious theory? He considered the power of delusion vs. the intolerance of the Skeptics. He had been a Skeptic. Except now he was realizing that by treating paranormal experiences as pseudoscientific events, he had narrowed his view, closing the door to new information. To experiment in the field of the paranormal would be difficult. Yes, the results would be considered cloudy. There was chance for falsification, fraud and suggestibility. But wasn't his *skepticism* his *own* area of weakness and suggestibility?

Where had the religious sects gotten their information anyway?

The first philosophers knew about atoms and could explain the life and death of stars. How was this possible? Micah had said that there were extra-terrestrials who had intermarried with humans, who understood the laws of the universe, referring to the advanced scientific civilization on Atlantis. What if you did genetic experiments believing that it was true? What would be the results?

On Vulcan, Dagon had experienced some form of atomic translocation. His inner thoughts had materialized into matter. What if he experimented as if this was possible? As difficult as it was, he had to trust his experiences on Vulcan. Either he was totally delusional, or all of his experiences had happened. He had to have the courage to listen to his intuition, to base his theories on wider possibilities. For example, to posit that, 'All is Mind,' one of the Seven Principles of Creation.

A little quiver of guilt passed through him as he remembered how cruel he was being to Stella. He hadn't made an effort to be intimate with her since leaving Vulcan. Yet, he thought about her day and night.

What was he so nervous about? Just the thought of talking to her made him feel exposed.

I have to believe this stuff because *I do*, not, because *she does*, he thought. When I'm around her, I get swept into her philosophies.

The memory of their shared intimacy, in and out of bed, kept coming back. He had told her he loved her. He had never said this to another woman. Still, was all part of the confusion of his fantastical experience?

He thought again about their agreement not to show the stones to anyone. He knew he should perform some kind of experiment to test the properties of the stone. Because of secrecy, he couldn't enlist the aid of any other technicians or a supercomputer.

The intrigue made him wary. He wouldn't break the vow he had made to Stella, but he felt as if he was caught up in something bigger than him. The light and dark were moving, swirling around him. He was idealistic enough to want to protect the world from darkness.

Dagon looked back again at his notebook. It was full of quantum theory, ideas forming a pattern. His father had also been exploring the question of how matter could be transmuted from one form to another. But, Dagon's intuition told him that his father had missed an important piece, the spiritual principle behind the process.

He impatiently threw down his pen. I need to call her, he decided. It's been too long since we talked. Standing up, he stretched his hands overhead. Hmmm, so good to be back on earth, he thought. Perhaps, now that the interviews are slowing down, I'll start running in the park again.

It was like a fog was clearing. He looked around at his apartment a bit shocked. This isn't like me. He started to pick up crumpled pieces of paper off the floor but got waylaid by the view out the window of thunderclouds.

The sky was heavy, the air getting thick. It looked like a spring storm. He sighed thinking, Stella, are you seeing these clouds now? Are we both going to be in a thunderstorm so powerful, so dark, we'll be swept away by it?

He shook off the alarming thought and looked down at one of the crumbled papers in his hand. There were numbers doodled on the page.

It was Stella's phone number.

CHAPTER 23

✠

Supercomputer

Stella and Dagon dreaded the next day because they were to meet with the technicians who had inputted their Vulcan data into NECSA, a Neural Ever-net Computation System programmed to evaluate complex questions.

The computer had the ability to 'learn,' processing information on logical and conceptual levels. Learning required that the computer rate millions of possible solutions per second for strengths and weaknesses, then access parallel informational formats, like historical or scientific data, to brainstorm and invent new solutions to problems. NECSA Learning Centers had been operating extensively in the last decade to discover cures for diseases. While the supercomputers had originally been housed in large buildings, they had now shrunk in size and increased in speed. This computer operated at 2 zetaflops, 100,000 times faster then the original petaflop computers. The net computation outputs were relayed to the programmer from a digitized voice box. The computer could graphically display its findings on a video screen, or print out historical data from its memory banks.

Traveling to the NECSA offices, Stella straightened her skirt and uncomfortably hitched up one stocking. The day was perfect, a magical spring day in Washington, yet, for some reason, she was miserable. She glanced at a reflection of herself in the passenger mirror. The little crow's feet around her eyes seemed pronounced to her. Her hair, just washed and squeaky clean, seemed to be popping out of every pin in disarray. She blew her bangs off her forehead and turned up the radio. A blues tune was playing, 'Oh, baby, baby, you've put out my fire and left me cold.' She grimaced, aware again of the ache in her heart.

Checking the front of her suit and noticing wrinkles, her shoulders slumped. I hate this part! I just hate it! she thought. Arrival at the ultra-modern steel pillars that towered in front of the entrance to the NECSA high rise happened all too soon.

Her driver got out and opened the door for her, gingerly assisting with her briefcase, as if sensing her disgruntled mood, then drove away, leaving her standing before the ominous entry. As she walked through the foyer to the elevator, her heels echoed on the marble floor and off of the high, unadorned walls and ceilings of steel and copper.

I feel like I'm in a wind chamber, Stella complained inwardly, annoyed by the inhumanity of the architectural design. After she punched floor fifteen, the elevator opened to a comfortably furnished lobby, the smell of coffee wafted towards her from a corner of the room.

Great! Following her nose, she found herself hurrying towards relief, only to be stopped in her tracks, her heartbeat painful, as she saw Dagon pouring himself a cup, his back to her.

Her first instinct was to go the other direction, yet she seemed frozen, drawn instead to study his wide back and shoulders, his height and the way his dark hair, now neat and trim, touched the back of a crisply starched white collar.

Sensing her presence, Dagon turned slowly. Gray eyes met blue, searching, then dropped.

"I thought I'd have some coffee, too. What a beautiful day out there," Stella uncomfortably began making small talk, aware of a light tremor to her voice.

She pulled down at her skirt, which seemed to be inching up. Dagon followed her movement, then stopped, arrested by her slim ankles and long legs. He coughed, turning back to the station to reach for a packet of sugar.

"Can I pour you a cup?" he offered politely.

Damn, can I pour a cup over your head? Stella thought. She made a face behind his back. "Sure, so where is this meeting taking place?"

"Follow me," Dagon efficiently handed her the cup and napkin and escorted her by gently touching her elbow.

Rounding the corner, she saw two huge steel doors. Dagon placed his identity card in the security gate slot and they swung open silently. Inside was a round table with a dozen people, all dressed in similar blue or gray suits, all waiting on her.

"I didn't realize I was late." Stella excused herself, sitting down quickly.

A handsome gentleman across from her smiled with instant reassurance, sliding a packet of prepared material across the table.

"Hello, Dr. Miren. My name is Lawrence Statton. I'm one of the administrators of the NECSA division and am the head technician in charge of this project. The other people in the room are wearing their company ID badges, which should help you to keep them all straight as we work together this morning. Most are either NECSA staff or Interspace representatives."

349

Stella was surprised by the man's well modulated, rich voice and found her self taking a little better look at him as he talked. He seemed too young to be the head of a department like this. His sandy, blond hair was combed back from a model's face: square, clean-shaven, high cheekbones, blue eyes, and a high forehead. The eyes flashed with sly intelligence and overt flirtatiousness. All in all, he seemed a little too perfect to her, like the Barbie doll 'Ken.'

Stella brought her mind back to the present and realized that Lawrence was aware she had been examining him, noticing the smug smile he hid from his colleagues.

"All right everybody. Shall we get to work? Please open your files and turn to page two with me."

They all became business-like, reviewing together the exact input that had been entered into the computer before they went into the control room for results. The first three pages were a list of facts discovered about Vulcan: the atmospheric condition, the results from the soil samples, the findings from the rock samples, the medical studies of their own physical adaption to the climate, a breakdown of the cryptogram into its organic properties, gravity and radiation readings. Also related in detail were the cryptogram experiments, examining their response to moisture and its adaptions to temperature changes from night to day on the planet.

It all looked correct and complete, so, Stella found her mind wandering soon after the meeting had started, her gaze straying to Dagon again. To her, he seemed so much bigger, so much more 'real' than all of the blue suited figures around her. Everything about him was solid, strong and rugged. She could imagine him working a ranch in Wyoming, or fighting in Afghanistan. She noticed that the other people in the room seemed to naturally defer to him, while they politely avoided her restless intensity.

A question was sent her way. Stella quickly brought herself back from her daydreaming, looking up into Dagon's quizzical expression, catching the glint of humor that he quickly shuttered.

"What was that?" Stella flushed.

It was Lawrence addressing her, his gaze going from Stella to Dagon as if trying to guess the nature of their relationship.

"Dr. Miren?" he began.

"Stella, please," she waved his formalism aside.

"Very well, Stella," he conceded, buttoning his shirtsleeve fastidiously then tapping his pen on the desk with a banked impatience, "It's key that all of the components of your experiment with the plants be exact. We have the video of the procedure and would like to show it to you again to refresh your memory and perhaps bring any new information to light that may have been missed."

Stella felt her heartbeat quicken. She hadn't seen the film since her first review of it on her Link while in space. The room was darkened and a screen panel dropped down, covering an entire wall. The color and sound were excellent and the image so large, Stella was automatically mesmerized. The filming began just prior to them setting up their equipment for the experiment.

Stella blanched, feeling slightly sick with nostalgia as she saw the camera panning the Vulcan landscape, moving close to rocks and plant features, and then shifting to a wide angle of the barren landscape. The film could never capture the immensity of the place, the unbounded silence and the subtle, shifting colors under that pale violet sky.

The outdoor pan stopped and the next scene was of her makeshift workstation with Dagon standing by observing and assisting her as she worked. Seeing him like that through the eye of the camera, she noticed how respectful and attentive he was to her, following her instructions carefully and giving her complete charge within her domain.

A corner of the spaceship could be seen on one side of the film. Center to the camera was the cryptogram, which was lying like a hard, little wrinkled knot on the table before them. The microphone came on and off with Stella speaking in terse detail.

"We will be using a solution diluted 1 to 100 of pure H^2O applied through a diffuser in a fine mist for 1/2 second. The specimen chosen for this experiment measures 8.45 inches and was extracted using a probe 4 minutes ago with all of its tuberous roots."

Then, there was silence, while the camera focused on the plant, as Stella and Dagon conversed, their bodies just visible in a corner of the picture.

Lawrence reached out for the remote and froze the screen.

"Stella, why are you turning on and off the microphone instead of recording all of your conversations with Dagon? It would help to know what all of your concerns were as you were doing the experiment."

Stella's cheeks flushed red as she worked to control a quick retort at this a subtle violation of her privacy. She noticed Lawrence was curiously studying her response to his question.

Putting on a professional mask, she said easily. "There were seven days of taping to do. It seemed important to keep any personal conversation off the tapes. Only the pertinent information was recorded."

"Yet, this seems an important dialogue," he panned to an image of Dagon and Stella, froze it, enlarging her face on the screen.

"You look quite concerned. What were you talking about in this instance?"

Stella looked sharply at him, noting that, although his question had been voiced mildly, Lawrence's expression seemed accusing.

Dagon interrupted. "Mr. Statton, this is not a debriefing. We have a limited amount of time in our busy schedules to spend with you. To answer your question, I remember Stella being concerned at that point about a generator we had left running in the ship. We knew we were going to be outside with the plants for most of the day and were discussing whether we should turn it off to conserve energy. Now, if we can move on, I'm anxious to see the results that this input gives us."

Stella gave Dagon a grateful glance. He had used his influence in the room to embarrass Lawrence into stopping this line of questioning.

She looked back at Lawrence, his only visible annoyance was to gather his papers rather forcefully and straighten them with abruptness.

She sank back in relief after Dagon's rescue, remembering their discussion now in detail. She had been debating with him the ethics of an experiment such as this. Was it violating the ecological laws of the planet? Would it be better to simply not tape it or show Interspace any of this research? She remembered their argument the day before about the financial greed that she felt was motivating the whole trip to Vulcan. Harvesting marketable goods from space put a political pressure on all of NASA's decisions, changing the priorities of the mission from environmental ones to monetary goals.

Her stance would have been paramount to mutiny to this group she recognized, they all seemed to be taking the party line. In fact everyone around her was dressed so much alike, she didn't see any humor, or individuality in any of them.

Stella felt transported as they watched the rest of the tape without interruption. Seeing the whole event again filled her with the same excitement she had felt on that day. She watched the cryptogram change color from a dull gray to a vibrant blue-green, its hard surface becoming soft and mobile. Then, within minutes an egg-shaped bud began to form with transparent petals. The sun heated the inside of this globe, turning it golden, and then without warning, it disintegrated into ashes that were rich in nitrogen.

Lawrence ran the film back and froze the screen on the moment that the spherical, transparent globe was glowing golden. He enlarged the pod on the screen until the light and heat waves that it generated were visible. From this view, it seemed you could look within its egg-like shape and see the faint dark outline of a stamen and pistol, in their odd way, appearing like the shadow of a man and woman waltzing.

"What is your take on this picture?" Lawrence asked Stella. "It is possible that the plant is fertilizing itself for reproduction. However, in the original plant there was only a stamen, no apparent pistol."

"This could be an isolated phase of its life cycle. Of course, this is all speculation," Stella replied.

"Did you measure the heat emitted by the plant?"

Stella sighed, sick of answering this question for the hundredth time.

"We had no idea what would happen and were not set up for that type of measurement."

"Why didn't you repeat the experiment? Didn't you have a robot that could have measured this for you?" Now, Stella found her temperature rising.

Dagon however stepped in, saying very coolly, "Our robot was out of commission. We had limited time on the planet, and that type of experiment was beyond the scope of our work." He gestured a little impatiently, cutting off the viewing of the film. "It seems as if we have all of the information here, let's see what the computer does with it." He started to rise, and Lawrence had no choice, but to follow.

One by one they cleared the table and walked through another door into a medium sized room dominated by a supercomputer that sat on one side of the room. The computer was connected by high-speed express to a video screen and there were seats set up at another table in front of the screen for the group. Water pitchers, glasses and computer pads with the NECSA logo sat on the white tablecloth.

Stella turned to Lawrence as they took their seats. "Have you already seen these results?"

"No, this is an interactive program. As soon as we start the loop, the computer will begin asking questions, then respond to feedback as it learns or 'thinks.' It seemed best to have you present with the information for its first run."

Stella noticed video cameras were recording their meeting, that their conversation was being taped.

She turned back in her chair, somewhat uncomfortable with the whole procedure and with the insidious antagonism she had sensed from Lawrence earlier. Why? She shuddered, wanting to reach for Dagon's hand in the darkened room, recognizing how childish that would be.

An efficient looking young woman with dark framed glasses stepped in front of the group. "Data entered, Rudy processing."

"Rudy?" Stella nudged Dagon.

"It's the computer's name," he whispered back.

A few more seconds went by, before, a pleasant baritone voice came over the audio system. "Hello," said Rudy.

Lawrence returned the greeting.

Lawrence began asking a series of questions. The computer confirmed that he had a reading on a planet named Vulcan.

Lawrence gave Rudy an open-ended question. "What information do you see as important about this planet?" Rudy began to 'talk,' randomly listing an odd list of qualities it considered 'important.' The list turned out to be a confusing hodge-podge of facts pulled out of the computer's inner memory banks.

"It is the first planet discovered by human's since 12,000 B.C. that has a living biological life form on it. It is a planet that emits high levels of radiation because of galactic polarization to the sun. The god, Vulcan, held significant importance in mythology and human history. It is the first project funded solely by Interspace Research Program outside of international guidelines."

Since 12,000 B.C.? Stella thought. What in the world? Was this going to be a complete waste of time?

Lawrence became more specific in his questions. "Please look specifically at the rock samples, atmospheric samples and other planetary data. What information is unusual here?"

"Vulcan is similar to other planets in most aspects, but different in the high content of iron in the soil which makes the mass and gravity unusually high. However, the fast orbit within the synchron belt keeps this planet from becoming a super nova."

"Please carry this thought farther," Lawrence said.

"In theory, the planet is moving past the speed of light and therefore does not exist in earth time, however the gravity field holds what is actually a wave in a particulate state giving it the properties of stable matter."

Stella sat up on the edge of her chair and Lawrence looked at her.

"Do you have a question?"

"Yes," Stella looked at the group. Lawrence nodded, but seemed surprised by her next question.

"How would that wave-state affect a human organism that was on the planet?"

"Following fundamental laws of physics, the human electromagnetic and atomic frequency would be stimulated so that the two wave patterns, would be in synch. There would be no limitations in terms of time. There could be the possibility of dematerialization of the body and movement through time and space."

There was a little giggle of disbelief in the room, and then one of the other team members cleared his throat. Stella grabbed Dagon's thigh under the table without thinking in her excitement. Dagon gripped it over his leg refusing to let go.

Stella stammered out her other question hoping nobody could see what was going on. "You said at first there had been no life discovered on other planets before 12,000 B.C., what did you mean by that?" A flush spread up her body and her breathing quickened as she tried to pull her hand away from Dagon's leg but couldn't.

"The Atlantians were from another planet and brought biological life forms to earth. The Mayans met with travelers from other galaxies who gave them information about the galactic time cycles. These extraterrestrials were worshiped as gods and are pictured in Mayan rock paintings. Prior to that, the Greek and Romans worshiped gods from other planets. An extensive list of 20,000 of those known gods is available to be printed. Would you like to print it?" the computer asked.

Someone in the room sighed.

"No," Lawrence answered impatiently. Then, he spoke to the room and Stella. "You must recognize that this computer has read most of the books in print. It gathers its information from a very wide source. We have to filter out these kinds of answers on almost every question, even simple ones like, 'What is the significance of an apple?' The computer starts talking about Adam and Eve. Let's continue with that in mind, not encouraging this line of reasoning."

"Hmm, Adam and Eve?" Dagon whispered in her ear, circling his hand around Stella's wrist as someone asked another question in the darkened room. Dagon asked the next question with cool efficiency. "Rudy, How does Vulcan affect the sun, and the earth through the sun?"

"It keeps the sun in homeostatic balance between energy stored and energy emitted. Without it there would be no life on earth."

With a little tussle Stella broke her hand away knocking the table and spilling her water. "What are your proofs for this reasoning?" she said as she gripped her hands primly together. Glad the room was dark so nobody could see her red face. Dagon casually threw his napkin over the mess with a slow smile.

"The studies of galactic polarization completed by Dr. Thomas dated December 14, 2023, and a list of the above 81 papers and books. (The printed list could be seen on the screen.) Also, ancient mythology about Vulcan describes this from the cultures of Greece and Rome. It is a known concept in the teachings of the Rosicrucians."

A heavyset man at the end of the table said impatiently, "Why hasn't this computer been programmed to see the religious answers as less desirable solutions?"

Lawrence looked a little flustered. "Only, to give it free reign to make those judgments, itself. We have given it 'free will,' so to speak. There appears to be almost an equal amount of religious as scientific literature in the libraries of mankind."

Lawrence asked the next question. "What possible benefits to mankind do you see in the cryptograms discovered on the planet?"

"If liquefied, they would be nominally digestible as all of the ingredients in them are edible and nutritious for humans. The high level of the above listed 87 mineral compounds make these plants unusually rich as a source of food, however high copper, mercury and sulfur compounds would need to be leached from the plant to avoid poisoning at higher quantities. This unusual combination of minerals has the potential for promoting longevity for humans."

Lawrence broke into the computer's comment, his face showing his excitement.

"List your proofs for this reasoning."

On the screen came all of the studies showing that humans could live to be 120 years old in some cultures because of a diet rich in minerals. It included the autopsies of animals and humans who had died of mineral deficiencies and provided proofs that mineral deficiency was the primary cause of 65% of deaths related to diseases in humans.

"How abundant is this resource?" he asked.

"In theory, there is an endless supply of the plant, because it propagates quickly, and requires no food or water from a human source."

Stella broke in taking a defensive posture. "How could humans impact the ecological system of Vulcan? Would they destroy this delicate balance?"

"Humans require temperatures and moisture at different rates than these plants do and they could create false environments that would affect these gradients. Unless the plant could adapt quickly, it would become extinct. Based on Constant Law, any small effect could create a profound change."

Lawrence was looking a little bit annoyed as he went back to his own line of questioning.

"What other benefits could these plants have to mankind?" A long list appeared on the screen that included a huge variety of things, from automobile parts and soles for shoes, to jewelry and the landscaping of gardens. Lawrence was printing out the lists and looking at them excitedly.

"What about the flower? What benefits do you see for mankind in it?"

"The ash by-product of its transmutation could be used to make a jewel which would be highly valued."

Lawrence looked excited again. "Describe this jewel."

"This particular combination of metals in an ash form would create a blue-green stone of rich hue similar to stones made from volcanic ash, however the stone would be as hard as a diamond." Stella gasped noticing Dagon sit forward to.

"What are its scientific uses?" Dagon asked.

"The stone could be used in laser technology and in prismatic spectrographs. The carbon has many scientific uses. They are listed below."

Dagon looked at the list being spewed out of the printer.

"*Amazing*," he said under his breath catching Stella's eye as he remembered their conversation about this.

Lawrence was flushed, "What about the value of the energy emitted from the flower before it burned to ash?"

"The plants are an example of biological perpetual motion because on a quantum level, through increase of pressure and heat, they move the plant from solid to gaseous forms, then recycle that carbon and oxygen into a new arrangement of atoms with the same energy potential. There are possibilities for harnessing this power as a source for light."

Another scientist in the room threw in another question. "How could this be used as a light source?"

Surprisingly the computer switched gears in its line of reasoning as it considered the question. "The flower is a symbol of immortality which has the value of providing spiritual light to many believers world wide." What had been an excited murmur in the room came to a sudden hush as everyone tried to understand this unusual response.

"Please explain this statement," Lawrence asked.

"The flower is pictured in alchemical texts as a source of spiritual light. See list in memory bank #111. It was called the philosopher's stone, a cosmic or world egg, from which was created, out of chaos, heaven and earth, the first male and female. The golden egg gave birth to a phoenix, which burned itself to ashes, so that it could be reborn again, out of the ashes. The phoenix is called the sun or solar bird, and is symbolic in Christianity of Christ who died and was resurrected. The process of transmutation is called transubstantiation in the Catholic Church. The Church celebrates the meeting of the solar and lunar essence, Christ and Mary, in the Eucharist." On the screen a graphic symbol began to appear, an ancient alchemical symbol. It was an egg with a flame in the center of it, and joining hands in its center, were the silhouetted image of a man and woman.

A sigh sounded in the room and most of research team began to talk again, dismissing the last bit of news as they poured over the other computer printouts that detailed various economic products that could be produced from the cryptograms. Stella just looked at Dagon, both of them staring at the graphic representation of the philosopher's stone, awe struck. She looked up just in time to catch Lawrence looking away, slyly. I don't like that guy, Stella shuddered silently. He really gives me the creeps.

Hours later, the meeting was drawing to a close. Everyone was satisfied that they had achieved a great deal in a short time. The Interspace Research representative walked over to Dagon and Stella to shake their hands.

"Hello, sorry we didn't get introduced before, ya know. I'm Ernie Flannigan, my friends all call be Flanny for short."

Stella looked down at the stocky, short man in front of her. His smile seemed real, behind a bristling mustache, and his handshake was warm and firm. She noticed he had dressed up his blue suit with a little shamrock tie pin, and his rounded head, though balding, sported hair a little too long to be fashionable.

"I hate this stuff," he blurted out.

He laughed, a generous sound in such a stark room.

"Well, the boss'll be glad about some of this news, he really stuck his neck out on this one."

Stella looked up with interest. Perhaps, here was a way to get more of a scoop than they usually got at formal political dinners.

"Cost a pretty penny, ya know," he rambled on. "Now, here's a way ta' hedge his bets. However, it'll cost a mint to go back and harvest the stuff. Fact is, it'd probably cost billions, question is, can they make billions?" He scratched his belly. "Don't matter much to me, I sure as hell wouldn't want to go work there and leave my wife 'n kids at home. It'd take some kind of religious fanatic to do it and rumor has it," he continued to confide with a kind boisterous bravado, "There's plenty of those types around." He looked around him, and then whispered dramatically, "Starseed." And then, waving his hand, he made a quick exit.

Dagon looked at Stella and they both started laughing at once. Impulsively, he reached out lightly touching her shoulder and gazing intently into her eyes.

"Would you like to have dinner tonight?"

"I'd love to," Stella said, grimacing, "But, Lawrence asked if I could stay late with him to discuss some important things. He said he would feed me supper."

Dagon's jaw tightened. "Watch that guy, I don't trust him. He'll probably be all over you, once you're alone with him."

Stella grinned at Dagon's discomfort. "I can take care of myself."

Nevertheless, Dagon was looking serious, not amused, at all.

Good. Stella thought. I hope he's jealous. Maybe, I should have a few dates with Lawrence. Would that get Dagon moving?

"I'll try to call you tomorrow morning, if I don't get in too late," she said airily. Dagon looked like he was going to shake her, then seemed to draw himself together and gathered up his papers.

"I'll call you at 9:00 a.m.," he said with some asperity. "If you don't answer, I'll be there at 9:30 to wake you up. We have some talking to do." Stella felt a sense of loss as he went out of the room, gradually realizing she was alone with Lawrence. It felt decidedly uncomfortable.

CHAPTER 24

✠

Secret circle

As the room emptied, Stella became aware of the ominous stillness of the building, broken only by the occasional beeps being emitted by Rudy, as his row of green and red lights flashed in a colorful sequence, to indicate he was still processing information.

Stella forced herself to look directly at Lawrence, aware of his predatory gaze. "Does Rudy ever sleep?" she asked stiffly.

"Of course," Lawrence smiled, perfect teeth shining. "But, not, often. By tomorrow, the questions, we asked today, will have been examined from every angle and new learning will have occurred, which will be stored in his super banks. Let's find a more comfortable place to chat."

Lawrence pushed a small button and a panel of the wall at the far side of the octagon room slid back, revealing a large sitting room and library behind it. He gestured for her to lead, and once she had stepped into the room, snapped the sliding door back in place. Stella glanced around nervously at the closed door, realizing how alone they really were for the first time. She found herself rubbing her palms nervously, and made herself put her hands behind her back.

"So, what did you wish to talk with me about? I'm afraid, I can't stay for supper," she lied, "I made plans to dine with a friend tonight."

Lawrence's smile seemed to waver, but he pasted it on again. "Fine, this won't take long, then. Please, take a look at this library, and then I will tell you why I wanted to speak to you."

Stella glanced at the titles of the books on the oak shelves that lined the walls from floor to ceiling. *Oh my god*! She began to read the titles in earnest, chills running up and down her spine.

All the books had ornate covers, some scribed in gold, the titles handwritten on leather and parchment. A stack of rolled up scrolls were organized in a series of cubbyholes along the side of the room. In the center was an ebony table with reading lights, stylus and blank paper. It was obvious that the copies were valuable, and very rare. Stella began to scan the rows, becoming even more excited: *Le Mystere des Cathedrales, Alchimie, The Eight Immortals, the Alchemist of the Golden Dawn, Integra Natura, Speculum Artisque Imago, The Kabbala, the Ancient Druidic Alphabet, Magus, Secrets of the Occult*. She turned to Lawrence with surprise. "Yes," his sharp eyes were gauging her reaction, "It's an extensive library of original manuscripts, all pertaining to metaphysics, specifically relating to alchemy. Some of these manuscripts are on microfilm, and some, are not. This is the only place in the world, today, that they, now, exist."

"But, why? How...?" Stella started to stammer.

Lawrence motioned to a comfortable leather chair around the writing table. "Sit and I'll tell you."

Stella sat down heavily, her legs a little shaky. Lawrence seemed to be enjoying her discomfort. His smiled seemed nasty as he began to pace in front of her. He threw his blond lock back, in a vain gesture, as his voice took on a quality of sneering importance.

"This collection is the result of four generations of work. They were passed down to me from my father, via his own grandfather, and prior to that from my great grandfather's mother. I come from a long line of scholars who were students of the occult. My ancestors had both the money, and the inclination, to obtain rare, antique manuscripts from private auctions and dealers."

Stella passed a hand over her brow. She was a bit overwhelmed as she fought off a wave of dizziness.

Lawrence continued, throwing out his chest in pride as he gestured at the fragile bindings. "Some of these books are from the library of Sir Isaac Newton. On his death, it was discovered he had a library of 174 alchemical texts. For the right amount of money, these reached the private sector in secret transactions."

Lawrence picked up a particularly old manuscript opening the page to delicately rendered artwork of dragons, angels and geometric symbols.

"I've had these records privately scanned into Rudy and have used him extensively to evaluate and analyze data."

Stella began to look alarmed.

"Why, for what purpose?"

Lawrence continued ignoring her question, "I've done some research on you too. I know about your thesis and your area of interest, in parapsychology. I also know about your research on whether or not biological organisms are sentient. Your grandfather was an alchemist, your father a chemist, and you are continuing your mother's research. In fact, I have seen the books you've downloaded on your Link through the NASA library program. It seems, we have a similar interest."

Stella gasped. "How dare you invade my privacy!"

Lawrence just ignored her as he turned his cold eyes to hers, tightening his hand into a fist.

Stella found herself nervously watching his fist open and close.

"What did you think about what Rudy had to say about the philosopher's stone?" Lawrence stopped pacing, moving close to her, as he demanded her answer.

Stella scrambled to come up with an answer that wouldn't give her away. "I understood some of what was being said. That some of the oldest creation myths describe heaven and earth as created from a large cosmic egg. For instance, to the Egyptians, Geb was earth and Nut was heaven. In mythology, they were born from a golden egg. I didn't understand what Rudy was referring to when he started talking about the Catholic Church and transubstantiation."

Lawrence smiled like a cat licking cream off its paws. "Rudy was drawing together widely diverse sources of information and making connections between them. If you read Catholic theology on the Eucharist, you will see that millions of devoted Christians practice alchemy every time they take mass."

Stella remembered her self-defense class and snuck her hand into her purse looking for something sharp, a pen perhaps. She felt her cell phone and impulsively hit the dial for Dagon's phone, turning on the speakerphone.

"You see," Lawrence explained as if talking to a child, "Myths of death and resurrection can be found in many cultures. These 'Christos' stories describe the rebirth of the sun at the winter solstice and its resurrection at Eostre, dawn or Easter."

Stella smiled. "Yes, it is wonderful. Christian churches all celebrate this transmutation of light through the life and death of Jesus Christ."

"True," Lawrence nodded importantly, "However, the Catholic Church being the oldest church also carried forward the secret liturgy of alchemy. In the Eucharist, Mary, the lunar essence, brings them to Christ the solar essence. They believe, that during the ceremony, the bread and wine of communion are transubstantiated or actually changed into the real body and blood of Christ. Because of this, only a priest can only perform the sacrament. Alchemy is the process whereby one substance is transmuted into another substance. The meeting of the male and female is seen as a holy union. This is why marriage is a sacrament in the Catholic Church, and the egg produced from that union, sacred. Contraception is not allowed because it defiles the egg, symbol of the World-Egg."[71]

Sneaking her hand back in her purse, Stella made sure her speaker was turned up on the phone.

"How did you get all this information?"

Lawrence rose to the bait and began to brag. "There is more. I have copies of many encyclicals, the Papal writings and the visionary writings of various nuns and priests through the centuries. Studied in depth most of the relics, and sacramental symbols within the church have pagan origins."

"But, why?" Stella probed, "Why are you studying alchemy?"

"I am attempting to replicate certain experiments that were conducted by alchemists in the 14th and 15th century."

Lawrence smoothed his hand over the back of his flawlessly formed head and reached out his hands to either side of Stella's arm chair, moving in closer to pin her to her chair.

Stella found she was growing angry at his latent aggressiveness and leaned back in her chair in an effort to get away from him.

Lawrence looked at her in a calculating way then walked over to the right wall and selected a book from one of the middle rows, setting it open in front of Stella.

"Have you ever seen these images?"

Stella gasped. It was an original copy of the *Mutus Liber*, a wordless book that was a series of fifteen plates of enigmatic pictures, alluding to the chemical recipe for creating the philosopher's stone.

"I see you do know of it." Lawrence looked pleased.

"Again, I have to ask, how did you get this?" Stella demanded.

"Never mind how," Lawrence seemed scornful, "My question to you is: What *really* happened on Vulcan?"

Stella was not prepared for the directness of his attack. "What are you talking about?" she pretended confusion.

"It's obvious to me, that, you haven't been sharing all of your findings about Vulcan with the research team. The very nature of the questions you asked Rudy, and your attitude with Dagon, indicates to me you share a secret between you. Since you can see my interest in alchemy, and you yourself are familiar with some of the most obscure treatises, you will recognize, that, to the alchemist, anything discovered on Vulcan would be important."

Stella quickly chose ignorance as the best response to his probing. "Why important? I don't understand." She attempted to sound innocently confused.

Lawrence shook his finger at her and moved a little closer saying, "Now, now, why do you play games with me? We both know that it's a waste of time. Are you and Dagon lovers?" he asked suggestively running his finger up her arm as she flinched back.

"I really don't know what you're talking about." Stella felt panic starting to take her over. She had been raped before and recognized perversion. This man had the same psychopathic quality.

Her heart was beating in her throat as Lawrence walked away again. He picked up another scroll and unrolled part of it, the medieval images unveiling themselves in colorful intricacy before her. He spoke quietly now almost reverently. "It's eighteen feet long, the Ripley Scroll and one of only 20 copies in the world." The elaborate drawings drew the eye to a Latin inscription that began, 'The mysterious stone is shrouded in a secret source.' Next to this was a picture of an alchemist, brooding over a flask, with an inscription on the arms of the vessel exhorting him to 'make water of earth, and earth of air, and air of fire, and fire of earth,' a reference to the complex process of transmutation, described on the rest of the scroll. Within the flask was a symbolic picture of the prima materia, the raw material that made up the world, along with various alchemical metals, which would be used in the experiment.

Lawrence slowly unrolled the scroll. On the next four feet was a tree of life with a dragon-woman and radiant youth, with the Latin words, 'for spirit and soul, sun and moon.' Above, an eagle or phoenix was perched, which would create the philosopher's stone out of fire. Beneath it was a dragon, the common alchemical symbol for aquo fortis, or nitric acid. The next image was even more graphic. In the center was an image of blood, dripping from a wounded dragon, falling onto a winged sphere that represented the philosophers' stone.

"You see this inscription. It's Latin."

Stella stood up and looked, reading it quickly, while she pretended to be clueless. Beneath the sphere, in Latin, was a poem explaining that only the blood of a dragon can dissolve the stone.

Beneath this was a picture of an impoverished alchemist, raising his hand in protest at the fruitless pursuits that have consumed his life, his constant search for the fabled philosopher's stone.

Stella was dazed, but managed to keep her pose of bewildered innocence. "What does any of this have to do with Vulcan?"

Lawrence began to explain to her in a condescending tone. "You heard Rudy describe the cryptogram flower as having the characteristic of perpetual energy, as containing possibility for longevity. We are searching for an unlimited source of energy. What do you know about a stone that could contain this power?"

Stella gasped, this time truly shocked by the shrewdness of his line of reasoning which was hitting so close to the truth.

"Lawrence, you're crazy," she protested, noticing her voice was slightly wobbly. "Unlimited power. It's the worst kind of greed."

"These alchemical texts were given so that the experiment could be replicated," Lawrence countered importantly. "Then, they were kept a under lock and key for thousands of years. Think about it. Even the secret liturgy of the Eucharist is unknown to most who take Mass every Sunday. I, however, have access to these texts."

Stella protested again her voice rising with conviction. "The Church teaches that to celebrate the Eucharist you first confess your sins and commit all of your motives to a higher good. To misuse power is black magic. The true alchemist prayed that he would be transformed, reborn into a spiritual body. Alchemy was transmuting base matter into spiritual matter, the same way that a Christian would feel after experiencing baptism. True power is having a mystical connection with the Divine."

Lawrence face darkened, a slow rage beginning to simmer beneath the surface.

Stella continued. "Our trip to Vulcan was a scientific journey, our tests merely routine. You have become obsessed in your quest for hidden treasures, and are asking me the wrong kinds of questions."

Lawrence looked a little doubtful now. "Then, how is it that you recognized some of these texts, for instance the Mutus Liber?"

"Because I have a book on alchemy at home, even if I have only glanced through it. That doesn't mean I'm really interested in any of it. I'm a biologist, all of my work has been concentrated on scientifically provable research."

Lawrence smiled slyly. "Come, come, Stella. We both know that isn't true. Is astrology scientific? Some of your research has been on how plants and animals respond to various phases of the moon and planetary orbits."

Stella flushed angrily. "What have you been doing, investigating *me* or your theories?"

Lawrence didn't seem upset at all by her anger. "It's common knowledge that you dedicated two years of lab research trying to reproduce Lilly Kolinskies' capillary-dynamolysis experiments using filter paper to soak up solutions of metallic compounds like gold chloride to study whether earthly metals are influenced by the sun, moon and other celestial bodies."

"So, what if I did? Astrocartography, astrological predilection, and planetary influence have been studied and proven now in a number of experiments."

"Yes, but those experiments didn't work specifically with metals and the planets."

"Kolinskies work was ingenious, it deserved further study," Stella maintained.

"I'm not disagreeing, only pointing out that you've had an interest in alchemy for a long time and have shown a bent toward metaphysical philosophies all of your life, for example, your English paper at Middelton Junior High School." Stella looked at Lawrence sharply.

"You can't possibly know what I did when I was twelve?"

Lawrence scoffed, "There is no privacy in this digitized, computerized world. Your life is an open book to anyone willing to look."

"I still don't understand what you're trying to get at," Stella insisted.

Lawrence slowed down, exaggerating like he was speaking to a very dense and willful child, "*I want to know what happened on Vulcan*, if there were any events that would elucidate any of these ancient alchemical texts, some which describe Vulcan as the key to understanding them."

Stella passed a shaky hand over her eyes. Lawrence seemed to notice her discomfort for the first time and softened his approach to manipulation.

"Listen, Stella. You, really, must trust me. I'm a fellow scientist and friend with similar interests. I'm part of a group of people who have dedicated themselves to the betterment of the world through our search for knowledge."

Stella looked up now, wondering at the truth of his words and studying his face for some sign of this high purpose he spoke of. His face was handsome, but strangely devoid of integrity or human warmth.

Lawrence persisted, his voice now oily with persuasion, the tones low and honeyed, "Tonight is a special meeting of a confidential inner circle. The circle includes some of the most esteemed scientists in the known world and powerful politicians who influence global policy. We would like you to come to this meeting and give us a chance to talk to you further. You must trust that we have only the earth's welfare in mind. Afterwards we could go out and have a drink together, just you and I."

Stella recoiled, wondering if she were just being foolish by doubting Lawrence' motives, but her intuition was insistent. Something isn't right about this man, she thought. I need more time. I don't believe in 'secret circles,' it sounds like a great chance for a whole lot of grandiose, delusional thinking, and possible misuses of power.

"Listen, Lawrence, I will think about what you have shown me, truly I will, but you will have to give me some more time to decide what to do. I won't come to the meeting tonight. However, I will stay in touch with you."

Lawrence looked disappointed and somewhat disgruntled. An angry sneer, started to form with his next words, but was quickly hidden with a smooth smile. He grasped her hand gently, squeezing her with cold fingers.

"Well, don't keep me waiting. I look forward to working with you. I'm sure we'll be seeing each other soon."

Stella shuddered at the sexual overtones and threat in his manner and moved towards the door. "I think, I must go, now," she said firmly.

"Just one more thing," Lawrence stopped her. "You must vow not to tell anyone about what you've seen here. You were brought here in an act of trust and you must honor that."

Stella thought quickly. Hopefully, Dagon was listening. She crossed her fingers behind her back, and then said simply, "I won't tell anyone who doesn't know anything about any of this." There, she thought, I won't be breaking my promise. Dagon already knows and he can tell anyone he wants. Lawrence looked skeptical, but then shrugged his shoulders. "Okay, I can easily ask NASA to do the Neural Brain Scan. Colonel Greene was outside of his jurisdiction to veto it before. Let me show you out, you'll be leaving by a different exit."

Stella looked around her, realizing that the room was somewhat confusing, large enough that you could easily feel lost in the maze of shelves and books in the odd, octagonal shaped room.

As Lawrence walked her to the elevator, she felt her tension lessen, anticipating the freedom of being outside again.

Phew, she breathed, at last standing on the sidewalk and looking up at the sky. Maybe I'll walk home, and stop at that Italian place on the corner of 13th and Grover for some pizza, then catch a movie. She hit the, 'on,' switch on her phone and it immediately rang. "Dagon," she sent a quick text, "I'm on my way." Dagon's face started to come up on her Link, but she hit 'disconnect.' She would be there in five minutes.

She started off at a quick pace, not noticing the gentleman who had been reading a magazine at the bus stop who casually began to follow her.

Back in his apartment, Dagon was working out on a punching bag in his weight room. "Shit," he grimaced, as his knuckles began to sting from an especially vicious hit. He could imagine Lawrence's face in front of him, so he took another hard swing. The sweat was beading on his forehead and trickling down his bare back before he stopped and mopped his face with a towel. He glanced at his watch, 5:00 p.m. Where was she? Out having dinner? Maybe, she just went home. Without thinking about it, he picked up the videophone for the third time, punching in her confidential code number, Eris. Nothing. Nobody there. A quick shower followed. Then, another call. 6:30 p.m. She said she was on her way. Something must have happened.

Impatiently, Dagon pulled a rough cotton crew neck sweater over his faded blue jeans, pulled on his oldest sneakers and headed outside. The evening air was cool, luscious with the scent of flowering trees and spring flowers. The mellow sweetness reminded him of wonderful evenings outdoors as a kid. He could hear children screaming as they played in the sand around the park swings. Mother walked by with babies, and young people lay in the grass reading or holding hands. It all seemed so normal when Stella's conversation had been so otherworldly. A nervous restlessness made him start to jog on the path. He texted again in caps, "WHERE ARE YOU?"

This time it beeped back immediately. "Sorry, a bit of window shopping on the way and I got lured into a sale. I'm standing in line. Where are you?"

"At Capitol Park, by the rotunda. I'll meet you at the hotdog stand in 15 minutes."

"Might take longer."

"No, 15, no excuses," Dagon dictated impatiently then went back to a slow jog, studying the people all enjoying a perfect March evening.

Usually this kind of scene calmed him, lulled him. What was wrong? Why had hearing that conversation with Lawrence made him so jittery?

He trotted across a side street, jay-walking through the rush hour traffic to make his way to a vendor who sold soy hot dogs and pretzels at the corner.

"Hi, Jer," Dagon smiled at the burly guy in front of him.

Jeremy reached out a large, hairy arm and gripped Dagon's hand in a painful handshake. "Dag, long time, no see."

"Yeah, I've been a long way away."

"You're not kiddin,'" Jeremy looked up at the sky, meaningfully, "a looong way, bud."

"So, did you save any dogs for me while I was away?"

"Not one," Jeremy smiled his shy, lopsided grin. "But, I can give you one fresh made today."

Dagon slathered it with mustard and relish, took a deep bite and sighed, contentedly. It had been so long since he had had real meat, he didn't miss it. "In space," he said, chewing absently, "you eat food that doesn't really look like food. You know, salmon mousse that looks like scrambled eggs, or ham that looks like blended green spinach."

Jeremy blanched. "What did a hot dog look like?"

Dagon thought about it. "They don't include hot dogs on the menu. It's much more French, if you know what I mean."

Jeremy looked doubtful. "So, hey," Dagon smiled pulling the titanium hummingbird up on the long leather cord that hid it under his shirt.

"I took the old hummer with me."

Jeremy broke out into a bright smile. "Well, did you now? You said you were gonna take it and you did."

Dagon looked down at the little totem Jeremy had given him. "So, how have you been lately?"

Dagon suspected Jeremy was part of some type of fraternity.

"You're not involved in anything dangerous, are you?" Dagon had once warned.

Jeremy smiled innocently. "Whatch you talkin' bout? These here hot dogs?"

Dagon wasn't buying it.

He suspected that Jeremy ran with some kind of secret group that might have access to defense equipment and transports, yet somehow it just didn't compute with the simple, kind man he had known and liked for years.

Dagon tucked the hummingbird back in his shirt thinking; it has seen things you couldn't even imagine.

After exchanging a few more bantering words, Dagon took up watch again and realized Stella was a no show. An email beeped in.

"Will meet you at your apartment later. Got caught up in supper with a friend that I met at the sale."

Dagon couldn't believe it. His hair was standing on end and she was having dinner with a friend.

He began to saunter down the sidewalk toward home. 7:45 p.m., he thought. He buzzed her again. Damn, Not home. Looking at his watch, he made a quick decision.

I'll stop at the museum. I have an hour before it closes, and just check out the paintings of Vulcan that Stella told me about. She should be home by 9:00. Dagon paid the small fee at the gate and made his way to the directory of paintings, Floor 4, West Gallery. Within minutes he was looking up at an amazing scene. It was four highly detailed oil paintings by sixteenth-century Flemish artist, *Jan Brueghel*, of the four elements, fire, air, water and earth and the deities associated with them. Vulcan or Hephaestus was the god of fire at a smith's forge. A smoke-belching mountain could be seen in the background. Dagon thought about how Aristotle and

Empedocles had believed with most thinkers that the basic ingredients of all life consisted of these fundamental constituent parts.[72]

Next to these pictures was another painting by Michelangelo. It was of Venus and Mars lying in a passionate embrace, a fine web-like net cast over them as Vulcan angrily looked down on them. The pair was ringed by all of the other Olympian gods, some of them laughing, some looking concerned.

Dagon felt a little rush as he studied the svelte lines and soft roundness of the artists rendering of Venus. He found himself remembering his conversation with Stella about this. Mars and Venus, body and soul, united through the demiurge, Vulcan. Vulcan creating a net that would link them forever. He looked down at the little place on the wall describing the artist and date then stopped surprised by a simple symbol in the right hand corner of the card. It was the Egyptian symbol for infinity or immortality, a serpent biting its own tail.

He was still wondering about it when a young woman, obviously an employee of the museum, walked up to him and said quietly. "It's a beautiful painting, isn't it?" Dagon was surprised to be addressed by a stranger and sized her up with a quick look before answering.

She appeared to be about 26 years old and was conservatively dressed in a simple blue suit. Probably, a uniform, Dagon thought. Her hair was pulled back in a practical style that emphasized her pale cheeks and dark, serious eyes. Dagon frowned. There was something familiar about her, but he couldn't remember what. "Yes, it is interesting. Do you work here?" he countered with a question of his own.

"I'm a guide, just checking through the rooms as we are getting close to closing time." She glanced at her slim wrist, noticing her simple watch, and short, manicured fingernails. "If you would like," she said quietly, "We have a resource library where you can look up information about your subject to get more details."

Dagon was surprised and pleased by this news. "Yes, I'd like to do that," he said.

"Follow me, then and I'll show you how to get into the computer." The resource station was one floor up. There was only one other person working at a computer. She turned on the computer and showed him a simple menu. "Simply type in your subject or artist and you can read some of the historical data on the painting."

"Thank you," already Dagon was engrossed in the computer. When he looked up, he noticed she had quietly left him. He pulled up the file. Thinking, Simple enough. Hmmm, info on the artist, a short sketch on Vulcan mythology. Then, he noticed it again. In the right hand corner was the same little icon, the infinity symbol. Acting on impulse, he clicked the symbol with his mouse and was surprised when the screen changed. In front of him was a request for a password to get into a different program. Dagon began to type in words quickly, whatever came to mind. 'Vulcan,' 'Venus,' 'Gold,' then, without really knowing how the series of word associations had led him to it, 'Dragon.'

Instantly the screen came alive, flashing a new menu in front of him that included an index. As he started to scroll down it his heart was pounding. They were all metaphysical subjects and at the top '*Alchemy.*'

Just then, a pleasant canned voice said over the museum speaker, "The Museum will be closing in five minutes. Please begin to make your way to the nearest exit. We hope you enjoyed your stay."

Dagon blew out his breath impatiently and clicked the button.

Aegean sea, Alchemy.... It contained a list of subjects, which he scrolled through quickly, *Feast day of Vulcan, Fires, and First matter.* He clicked '*Feast day,*' reading:

'Current societies still practice rituals to celebrate Vulcan's feast day, which in 2016 was set as March 30 of each year.' Dagon looked at his watch. Today is March 22, only eight more days, he thought. Then, he quickly began scrolling again only getting to the P's before a second warning came over the loud speaker.

Phoenix, Philosopher's Stone, Philosophy, Pillars... He clicked '*Philosopher's Stone,*' and was amazed to see before him the same image that Rudy had shown them earlier, drawn graphically on the color screen.

He was scrolling down the page when he heard soft footsteps behind him and looked up to see the serious-faced young woman who had led him to this room earlier. She started to explain to him that he needed to leave, but stopped, when she saw the computer screen.

Dagon acted quickly while she was off guard, "What's your name?"

"Katherine Grant," she murmured softly.

"Who programmed this information on your computer system?"

The young woman just stood calmly saying nothing, her demeanor somehow mysterious.

"You really must leave, it is closing time," she said, softly, but looked at him steadily waiting for a response.

"I would like to meet the director of the museum," Dagon said immediately.

"He's not usually here at this late hour, perhaps you could call and make an appointment tomorrow," she deferred.

Dagon insisted. "No, I'd like you to check first and see if he is around this evening, please."

With an inscrutable smile, she went to a small phone on the wall and made a call, then nodded her head for him to follow her, ushering him into an empty office toward the back of the building. It was 9:15 p.m. Dagon buzzed Stella quickly. Nothing. His blood pressure rose.

What in the hell was she doing, anyway? Hopefully not spending time with some other jerk face like Lawrence. He checked himself, surprised by the slow, burning rage he felt. The door opened silently and in walked an old gentleman, his white hair and lined face, radiating a gentle peacefulness. As Dagon gazed at his face and eyes, he saw ancient wisdom. He reminded him of Micah from Vulcan.

"How do you do," the man reached out his hand for a courteous greeting, his voice formal and genteel. "My name is Lucian Westfield, and you I already know, Dagon."

There was a slight pause as they studied each other.

"So, now you know," the old man's soft tremolo seemed to echo in the basement room. "Know what?" asked Dagon.

"About the Secret Circle. Members of a society, which is still studying and learning from alchemical texts that are centuries old, use these computer files. We are having a meeting right now in the basement of the museum, you are welcome to join us."

Dagon felt a rush of adrenalin, his mind racing as he took in what the old man was saying. This must be the meeting that Lawrence was telling Stella about. The old man seemed to read his feelings. "I assure you it will be quite elucidating and perfectly safe."

He turned and began leading Dagon down a winding corridor farther down into the bowels of the huge museum. They walked through some heavy double doors. Dagon saw that a large round table was in the center of the room. He guessed there were over 40 people of all nationalities there. He recognized a few well-known politicians from America and the head of one of America's wealthiest families at the table. There also seemed to be men and women who were famous scientists from around the world.

Sitting to the back of the room, watching him intently was Lawrence Statton. Dagon immediately bristled, but then decided to ignore him.

At least he knew now where Stella wasn't. Each person there ritually bowed to the old museum curator, showing unusual deference as they made a symbolic gesture of hand to heart. For some reason, this alarmed Dagon.

Who was this guy!

Lucian began speaking in slow, measured tones to the whole group after having someone draw up a chair for Dagon.

"We have a new member in our group tonight, Dr. Dagon Andrew. For his sake, I will quickly recount to him this group's goals and purposes before we begin discussion about new business." Lucian began to speak slowly and clearly.

"My real name is Comte de Saint-Germaine. I have been granted a long life and good fortune, allowed extensive knowledge of the world, its languages, its culture and art and I have watched the growing wealth of scientific research lead us from the renaissance, through the industrial age, to the space age."

"In April of 1942, we reached a critical junction in our earth history with the onset of World War II with the production and use of the Atomic Bomb. At that time, this council was formed as a private United Nations to safeguard the moral and spiritual development of each of our respective countries."

"Many of the members of this group are practicing alchemists or scientists who come from generations of spiritual scholars. Others are figures with great political power that believe in a higher purpose for humanity."

"It is our goal to work toward the betterment of the world. To that end, we have gathered here tonight for our bi-annual meeting."

"The meeting is open for discussion. Are there any specific concerns which need to be voiced tonight?"

A German gentleman said he would like to speak and rose to his feet. The audience seemed to sigh collectively, as if they already knew what his complaint would be. The man rambled for a few minutes about the immorality of the younger generation, intermarriages that he felt were diluting culture and his private grievances with the latest International Conference decisions. St. Germaine cut him short and looked around the room.

"Any other pressing concerns?"

A very neat woman in a three-piece suit stood up introducing herself as Elizabeth Tieback. "There is still a 25% starvation rate in the third world countries. I feel we should take some time tonight to reallocate funds to cover these needs. I have written my plan up in this document." she began passing around a thick stack of papers Lucian, or St. Germaine, nodded his head. "So, Miss Tieback, you have suggestions for a better way of organizing this distribution of funds also?"

"Yes, I would like to start an agency called, MITE, The Meek shall Inherit The Earth. Those benefactors here with funds can put them in this holding organization which will distribute the monies on an 'as needed' basis, rather than through group decisions of this counsel. All distributions will be reported to the counsel."

There was a general nod of approval. She had obviously been preparing for this moment, because everyone had received the documentation months before and had been lobbied for their vote. It was moved to take the vote after recess.

A hand went up. It belonged to a well-known politician from China. He gestured to Dagon and spoke quickly. "It seems we have a guest who was the scientist present on the latest space journey to the planet Vulcan. We have now received information that there was biological life on this planet and have learned of Mr. Statton's NECSA findings. The discovery of plants that can use miniscule amounts of water and sun in a transmutation process, which can create perpetual, endless energy, holds great promise. I am interested in hearing more about these findings and how they could benefit the Starseed program whose goal is to use atomic power to build greenhouses on planets outside of our solar system. Using atomic power, we propose creating our own suns to power colonized planets. It is our hope that there are some clues which can be provided to us from the results of the Vulcan space mission."

Dagon looked around the room in alarm. "You must let me fill Dagon in or he will be totally confused," Lucian interrupted.

"Dagon, the trip to Vulcan was funded by an organization called Interspace Research which is a front corporation for a few of the members of this group. Our purpose in funding this trip was to explore a planet long held in reverence in Alchemical text as holding the key to understanding immortality."

"We have not been disappointed. You have achieved more than any here thought possible. Now we have learned that the cryptograms on this planet may hold keys to longevity for mankind. However, we have other concerns about your research there. We need a full and complete report from you on all of your experiences in order to examine clues for our theosophical research."

"Mr. Statton," he indicated Lawrence, "Has expressed concerns that you and your space mate, Dr. Stella Miren, have not been forthright in providing all of the information needed for us to ascertain whether or not the program was completely successful."

"Let me say here," St. Germaine, cleared his throat, looking around the room meaningfully, "That I personally believe that it is dangerous to take atomic power into the universe without clearly defined purposes. There is danger of uncontrolled chain reactions, ultraviolet catastrophes and contamination of our universal food and drinking supplies."

There was some shuffling of feet and papers at the table as tensions rose. Dagon shot a look of dislike to Statton. For a moment they challenged each other with their eyes. Lawrence was the first to look away. Dagon could see that the group seemed to be divided on how they felt about the Starseed program. Dagon shuddered thinking, god help us if something as ridiculous as Starseed ever won national approval.

He realized that, unbelievably, this momentous decision was happening in the basement of a museum, hidden from public press. The future of the world was to be decided by the private agenda of 40 people meeting secretly.

A squat man with rheumy eyes hidden behind thick spectacles stood up asking for the floor to speak. St. Germaine nodded, but asked that there be a five-minute limit to all comments as they continued their discussion.

The man began by looking at each member of the group as if he were reading their minds. In fact some of the members actually seemed to squirm under his gaze.

He nodded with faint approval as he looked at Dagon. Dagon felt slightly alarmed as he felt the telepathic invasion.

"The psychics and prophets of this world have been speaking through living avatars reincarnated to give this message. 'Karma requires that we create practical programs which benefit humanity and which address current, real problems, on this earth plane. Every action has its consequence. We created all of our problems. Every problem we are facing comes from previous actions, which must be reversed in order for tranquility, focus and compassion to reign around us. We are not called to create heaven off of earth, but to roll up our sleeves and work out the problems of earth."

He sat down suddenly as he had nothing left to add and was not a long-winded person by nature.

A cheerful woman named Lynette Davenport with short hair and a large smile stood up next. "The churches have united in an interdenominational message, however, they are divided on the direction they feel God is calling. Some call for apocalypse and exodus to a new land, the promised new Jerusalem. This group supports Starseed. Others have focused on social programs and healing of the sick and poor. It would take very little to rally them to one united cause, but there have been no strong leaders coming forward at this time. Christ was their greatest Teacher. Many are waiting for a reincarnation of Christ again on earth."

"However, in the last decade there is a rising spiritual movement that sees the mind as a powerful tool if it is connected to Divine

Mind. This has resulted in some unusual miracles as of late." She sat down heavily, the smile still beaming through a row of large straight teeth.

Lawrence stood up, saying proudly. "Starseed now has over 30 million followers and is continuing to grow. It has captured a large portion of the New Age generation because of its visionary promises. We feel, strongly, that we will create the future for earth."

Dagon looked down quickly to hide his alarm at this statement. Any physicist could see the potential disaster of using nuclear power indiscriminately in the universe. Weren't there other scientists represented in this room? Why were they keeping still on such an important issue?

He looked around the room and counted five genius-level scientists in the room. He recognized immediately that they hated the political aspects of this meeting. Dr. Fartham was actually doodling calculations and drawings on his computer Link, completely ignoring what was being said. The others looked equally bored.

It was Lucian who stopped the discussion with a small sign. "It's clear it will not be decided in this meeting tonight, but by fate itself. As yet we do not know how to create the mega energy source that Starseed requires to power its proposed colonies."

A small woman with a soft voice stood and the group seemed to become more hushed to hear her. Dagon could tell she had the respect of everyone present. "You can fill a bowl over and over and it will just empty out. It is not what is in the bowl that is important. The more important question is what the bowl itself is made of. What is the essence of the container and how is mankind like that clay? Only then will you find that endless source of energy that you are all chasing."

Dagon was amazed by her profound insight that was so close to the conclusion that he and Stella had come to on Vulcan.

Another gracious looking East Indian woman added quietly, "We do not yet know the secret of the fabled philosopher's stone that Starseed is enamored by, but we do know that God is in everything and God is immortal, unending, limitless energy that is beyond life and death."

Lawrence looked impatient. "This conversation is a waste of valuable time which should be spent on more useful purposes." There was a general grumbling in the room, as some people were scandalized by his criticism and other wanted to rally behind him.

"We will ask that everyone review again the papers provided by Ms. Tieback over recess." Lucian broke in, effectively stopping disagreement. "Thank you." Dagon got up to go also, but Lucian detained him for a moment.

"I want you to leave now and forget what you have seen tonight. It would be better if you were not here for certain factions to raise questions in the second half of the meeting, we have much to attend to and very little time to meet."

Dagon simply gazed at the old man, and then asked the question that was burning in his mind.

"How did I get here? Was it a coincidence that I stopped at the museum?" Dagon shook his head bemused. "And, more then that, I knew, I knew inside of me the code word to get into the computer! Then, there is this meeting. It only happens twice a year and I bring my own self to it! Why is all of this happening to me?"

Lucian smiled, a small smile of hope. "You may have asked the most important question anyone has asked all evening."

"I must think about this. Thank you, son."

CHAPTER 25

✠

A package arrives

Dagon found himself in the hallway being shown the exit by Katherine Grant. He couldn't help asking her as they walked down the hall. "Are you related to Lucian Westfield?"

"Yes, you could say that, indirectly." Katherine spoke carefully and Dagon looked up with alarm. She seemed so controlled, so peaceful, yet so mysterious. Because he worked with strong, goal-oriented women in the space program, her quiet air struck him as odd.

"Are you a member of Starseed?" he probed. She just kept her head down, "The exit's this way."

He turned around to wave goodbye to her, seeing for a fleeting moment a young woman in a simple robe, standing before huge rock carvings of the tarot, the woman in his Vulcan astral travels. Then, he shook away the illusion and stepped back into the real world.

As Dagon stepped out into the brisk night and sounds of the city he breathed a long sigh of relief.

What a day! Almost an unbelievable one, yet everything was still normal out on the street. Cars flew by on the airstream in traffic layered four rows deep. Partygoers braved the streetscape laughing as they gazed at festive shop windows. A cat ran down the alley.

The superconductivity SCD bus barreled by noiselessly filled with passengers reading their papers in the overhead lights.

Dagon found himself walking with purpose down the sidewalk, his stride lengthening to a half-jog as he made his way through the street people, eating up the ten blocks to Stella's apartment. He stopped on the darkened sidewalk and looked up to her window. It was lit so he punched in a security code and went into the foyer of the building.

It seemed to take forever to run up the four flights of steps to her door, yet once there he was struck by self-consciousness. He looked at his watch 10:37 p.m., too late, but hell. It was too late in general. He should have been here months ago. He knocked firmly and saw the peephole open. The door flew wide.

"Dagon," Stella pulled at his arm. "Come in. Come in." Her face was a radiant smile of welcome.

"I won't stay long, just wanted to get caught up on that crazy call you sent to me and give you some news," Dagon began.

Stella ushered him in. "Come and have a drink with me, I'm watching Braveheart, an old Mel Gibson movie that I found at the downtown flee mart." She took one last longing look at the beautiful eyes of the man on the screen and turned it off. "I love that guy."

Dagon chuckled. "You," he chucked her under her chin, "Are a sucker for a pretty face."

"Mel Gibson's not 'pretty,' he's handsome like you are." Stella immediately looked embarrassed.

Dagon playfully tweaked her hair and drew her a little closer so he could study her flushed skin. Suddenly, he had a longing to push her up against the wall again, to completely dominate her sexually so she couldn't text him with excuses while he paced the floor. He could tell that one move on his part and she would give in. It was such a temptation that Dagon had to close his eyes to slow down his ragged breathing. He looked up to see Stella watching him with a look of consternation.

"So, you went to see Lawrence?" Dagon chose the safe route.

"Yeah, did you hear the conversation through the speaker phone?" she shuddered, hugging her arms around herself.

Dagon nodded looking at her sternly. "Where have you been?"

She countered, "It's been a long day and I walked 10 blocks and up five flights of stairs to see *you* and *you* weren't there!"

Dagon's smile became dangerous as she tried to turn everything around. He asked again more quietly, "Where were you?"

Stella didn't like being pinned down. "Hey, this feels a bit like the inquisition. Do you want to know when I put on my lipstick or if I stopped at the ladies room after I had a drink with my friend?"

Dagon moved in closer crowding her back against the couch. "It's just that I waited six hours to see you after that nasty phone call. I worried about you. I paced around. I looked at my watch. I called you about 20 times. And, all I got back was that you were shopping with a friend or having dinner. If you don't want me to worry, don't press the speakerphone when you're at a scary rendezvous with a creep. So, where were you?"

Stella reached out both hands and put them on his upper arms to push him back, but then thought better of it. His upper arms felt warm and hard. He felt like the strength she had been wanting earlier.

"I'm sorry about that." Stella smiled and shrugged her shoulders. "I'm not sure what got into me. One moment I was all intent on seeing you, and then it was like I was taken over by a shopping demon. And, I hadn't seen Cassie for ages. She was just there, one of my oldest friends buying lacy underwear out of the same sales bin. We grabbed the same skimpy and pulled, then started to laugh, hysterically."

Dagon smiled, but still looked thoughtful. "Does she live here in Washington?"

"Yes, but on the other side of town with her two twin two year old boys, meaning she *never* gets out of the house. And, she had a half off certificate for Broudies Happy Hour. Which was already half off. And, guess who we saw there, two old friends from college who *did* just happen to be in town. I swear, it was like I *couldn't* get to your house. The force was stopping me. I was just having too much fun!" Stella had the grace to look sheepish as she said this.

Then she became suspicious. "Where were *you*?"

"At a meeting of a Secret Circle where a group of powerful people were deciding the fate of the world."

Stella grabbed his arm and shook it. "Are you kidding me?"

"No," Dagon explained what had happened.

Stella shared what had happened to her in the beginning of her meeting with Lawrence.

"I was invited to go too, but it seemed too creepy to me. I don't believe in powerful, select groups making decisions for everyone else behind closed doors. Lawrence is definitely one of the bad guys if there are any."

Dagon went rigid looking ready to fight. "What did he do to you?"

"Nothing, really, just threatened me with his deceptive tongue, and pinned me in the chair to frighten me. He's a double-tongued viper. I don't like him at all. I'm sure he's a sexual pervert, too."

"Well, I told you so."

"Oh, please," Stella drawled out, "What could you possibly be saying 'I told you so' about. You didn't tell me anything."

"I told you not to stay and have supper with him."

"I didn't have supper with him."

"Well, you saw him alone, that was bad enough. I'd like a few moments alone with him!"

Stella looked interested. "Oh, really? What would you do to him?" Then, she looked again and saw this wasn't really something to encourage. Dagon looked like the Special Services Air force pro that he was, all stony anger and combat attitude.

Dagon ignored her.

Stella followed his lead not wanting to wake a sleeping tiger.

"Dagon. This is really big stuff. We have those two stones. I have a feeling about this. Maybe they're the Philosophers Stone everyone's looking for. Secondly, what we experienced on Vulcan was totally mind blowing: translocation at will, discussions with extraterrestrials, spiritual guides, dreams of dragons and gold, alchemical experiments, matter appearing, then matter disappearing at will. These are teachings similar to what you said the last two women in the Circle brought up. This committee wants to know all of these things. What would they do with the information?"

"Well, Starseed would send a colony to Vulcan. The church might decide Vulcan has become their New Jerusalem," Dagon said.

Stella jumped in. "Even more importantly, why is this happening to us? To us, Dagon? There has to be a reason, a purpose, some kind of plan trying to unfold. We are central figures in it."

"I know," said Dagon. "That is my big question too."

Dagon closed his eyes and shook his head. "Stella, it was uncanny how I got to that meeting. It was like each step was led. And, when I think about how I ended up on this mission in the first place…"

Stella squeezed his hand. "Perhaps, there really is a God and it's all bigger than us, this committee, or Lucian Westfield."

Dagon looked skeptical. "Or perhaps we are the victims of mind control. There was one guy in the group that seemed to have that power. He looked right into me, like he was reading me. It was very uncomfortable. Don't you suppose people with those gifts could misuse that power and use it to try to control others?"

"Yeah, but you said his message to the group was to take care of business at home, create a better world here."

Dagon looked at his watch. "One more thing, Stella. I feel like something is winding up to a climax. Today is March 22. There will be a worldwide celebration of Earth Day and Vulcan's Feast Day on March 30th."

He continued, "There are strong factions making their voices heard right now, and the political atmosphere has been violent. In the meantime, there are a lot of people wanting information and I feel we are targets, so I want you to be extra careful. Lock your door and call me tomorrow. Do you promise?"

Stella remembered again how upset Dagon had been when she unthinkingly walked into danger at the volcano on Vulcan. "Yes, I'll try to be careful." Dagon looked at her doubtfully, noticing the glint in her eye and her restless excitement. He shuddered knowing she was a magnet for trouble.

Stella went on to describe some more details about the books in the Stratton's secret library. "I don't trust him at all," she concluded, "Still, I would love to see his book collection again." Her eyes lit up with mischief.

Dagon put an arm around her protectively. "Don't even think of it," he said.

Suddenly, her eyes went serious and then angry. "Dagon, I've missed you. What in the hell have you been doing? You've been ignoring me for two months and it hurts."

She pulled away from him, straightened her shirt and started to stalk towards the kitchen. "I'm getting some hot chocolate, do you want any?" she called over her shoulder.

Dagon shook his head no, having a hard time taking his eyes off her tight jeans and simple, white pullover that slipped off one bare shoulder only to be pulled primly back into place again. Stella had tied her unruly chestnut hair away from her neck to beat the heat and it emphasized the slimness of her neck and small ears.

He walked behind her into the kitchen and pulled her closer to him, nibbling on the back of one pink ear.

She jumped, and then half-heartedly pushed him away. "Talk first," she said.

"I can't," his eyes teased. "I'm struck dumb by you."

"Oh, bullshit," Stella pushed at his solid chest reaching around him for the milk. "You can't just come on to me in my kitchen."

"Why not?"

"Because, I'm an old-fashioned girl."

Dagon's eyes glinted dangerously. "Really, what naughty things are you thinking about?"

"My nasty feelings about you just ignoring me, then showing up and not even being willing to talk to me about it."

Stella jerked open the spoon drawer and threw a few forks aside. "Where is that stupid spoon anyway?"

Dagon tried to soothe her by rubbing her arm, but she pulled it away.

"Don't spit at me," Dagon said

"I'm not spitting."

"Trust me, your like a cat, where is Merlin anyway?"

"You're coming dangerously close to getting this milk dumped all over you." Tears sprang unbidden to her eyes and she turned away.

"I'm sorry."

Stella blinked once and sniffed. "What did you say?"

"I said, I'm sorry."

"You don't look sorry." Stella studied him.

"Well, I feel it, inside. I don't know what's been going on with me."

"It looks a lot like cold feet to me."

"Sweetheart, if you would just sleep with me you would see that I'm like a furnace. You're the one with the icy hands and toes."

"Dagon, you know what I mean. Don't kid right now, I need a little honesty."

"Honesty, then. Yeah, okay," Dagon maneuvered Stella away from the stove, through the small opening out of the efficiency kitchen, past her cluttered table and to the overstuffed white coach.

"Sit still for a minute, so I can really look at you, then I'll tell you."

He studied her intently until Stella felt like squirming under his scrutiny.

"I've missed you, too. I've just never done anything like this before and I'm used to being alone. I've spent the last two months trying to make scientific sense of everything we went through and have been studying dad's diary."

Stella blinked twice. "That's it, that's your whole explanation?"

Dagon began to look a little uncomfortable. Stella got up and walked into the kitchen again to get the pan off of the stove and fill her favorite mug. She sat down on the couch with him and her steaming drink. Dagon wasn't looking at her now, his long legs were stretched out in front of him and he seemed to be sinking down lower on the coach, his eyes flickering shut.

He reached for her with one lazy arm, set her drink down on the coffee table and pulled her next to him, his arm wrapped around her shoulder, his finger stoking her cheek. "We can talk more tomorrow."

"What, you're spending the night, now?"

He reached for her and slid his hands under her shirt, up her bare back, running his large hands around her ribs, thumbs under her breasts. Then, one warm hand moved up to cover her left breast his thumb rubbing her nipple lightly. Stella felt her knees begin to quiver and her insides turn to molten heat. He lifted her, settling her on the couch beneath him and put his lips on her belly, pulling her shirt up with hands that spanned her entire rib cage.

Stella came back to herself, and pushed him away, sitting up primly as he groaned.

"You're making the leaving harder," she touched his crooked nose. "Go, now, you big lug."

"Why?"

"Because," Stella said with a hint of moisture in her eyes, "It isn't enough to just say to me you don't know why you've ignored me for two months. I don't want to get more involved with you, and then get hurt. You're going to have to give this more thought and really decide what's going on with you and talk to me about it. We both went through an experience that was mind-blowing, but we went through it together. I don't understand you being okay with simply stopping all contact with me. I wouldn't even do that to a friend and we were much more then friends."

"Okay, okay. I know that what I did is wrong. And I have missed you and thought about you every day. I also knew that I was being a heel. I just felt like I had to get my feet under me by myself, without your influence."

"Well, if you had trusted me you would have known that I would have let you figure this out without trying to dominate you in any way. It isn't in my nature to dominate."

"I know that too. Ah, hell."

Dagon took one last long look. "I will think about this more, so I can explain myself better. I'm exhausted anyway. Stella," he took her hand again as they walked to the door and kissed her fingertips. "I really am sorry, and I really do care about you."

"I believe you, Dagon," she said holding back tears that threatened to spill. "We'll start building again and see what happens."

After a long quiet hug, she let him out of the door. She was just turning around when he scared her by popping his head back in the door.

"I didn't hear the dead bolts." Stella pushed him out with a quick kiss.

"Okay, Okay and hey, I didn't get to show you the lacy purple thong I bought."

Dagon groaned as she pushed him out and with a smile slipped the deadbolts in place, listening at the door this time as he took the stairs two at a time and headed home.

Outside in a dark car, a nondescript looking man picked up his phone, made a quick call and settled in for the night. At around three o'clock in the morning, he drew on dark gloves and quietly left the car, being careful not to slam the door. A compact tool kit and a few wire clippers took care of the security system at the front door. The small flashlight wavered in the dark as soft-soled shoes tread lightly up the stairs, stopping in front of Stella's apartment door. The gloved hand reached into his dark jacket and pulled out a package tied with brown wrapping paper and a simple white string.

He leaned the package against the door, leaving quickly and silently, going back to the car to wait for the next call.

CHAPTER 26

✠

Alchemy in the tarot

Stella rolled over in bed, stretching luxuriously against the soft, silky sheets. The sun was making patterns through the window slats and across the tiny straps of her pale yellow camisole and pajama shorts. She jumped out of bed and threw open the window, remembering why she felt so good.

Dagon. She would get to see him again today. Jumping in the shower, she turned up the hot water full blast, soaping her skin and enjoying suds running down her back.

Great day! She put on a pair of black chenille leggings and a long blue soft cotton shirt as she towel dried her hair. Then she found her pink elephant slippers and started the coffee.

First the paper. She opened the door, ready to head down to her mailbox, when her foot knocked against a brown paper package.

Bending to examine it, she lifted it to her ear. No ticking. What if it was one of those mail bombs? She laughed at herself and pulled at the string, before she had time to think about it. A couple of tarot cards fell out, slipping down to the floor with a little note. "Herein lies the key."

She was captivated to see that she was holding a deck of richly engraved antique tarot cards that must be priceless. They even appeared to be hand drawn and painted with elaborate symbols and rich colors from hand ground pigments. She clutched the precious deck close to her heart as she moved into the living room and carefully laid them out on her coffee table one by one. The cards were all of the 22 cards of the Greater Arcana.

She had studied the tarot and the kabbalah for years and even done readings for friends. Each tarot card not only had symbolic meaning, but was also associated with a planet and those planets in turn were associated with various minerals and elements. The key to the tarot was considered to be the Fool or Zero card.

Stella shuffled the cards, and then laid them out in numerical sequence wondering immediately how they could be related to alchemy and the creation of the philosopher's stone.

Then, it hit her. Her blood started to race and her heart pounded. Somebody had left these cards at her door during the night. Who could have had any idea of the experiences she and Dagon had had on Vulcan. Why the Tarot?

Then, the next thought came clear. The philosopher's stone, perpetual motion, unlimited energy. Of course, the key would have to be the Fool or the Zero card because it is the symbol for infinite possibility within the unified field.

She began to ruminate about the story of Christian, the seeker who had wanted to find the secret to immortality. Dagon had dreamed of this when they were on the planet Vulcan. Dagon and she were the Knight and Lady of the Golden Stone, asked to bring this information back to earth in their starships. They were sent back with some important formula that could save the world.

Stella began to remember the story again. The goddess, Virgo, had taken Christian to a tower where there was an odd experiment taking place, a distillation that required the souls of each of the participants to make an elixir that would bring rebirth and awakening

So, what were the compounds used in the experiment? The answer was in the elaborately symbolic cards that were laid out on her coffee table. Traditionally each tarot card had a metal or element assigned to it. Cards 1 through 4 appeared to be a list of the formula's ingredients. First came the *Magician*, the ultimate Alchemist, who could create something out of nothing, *Mercury*. Then, came the *High Priestess*, Venus, the conduit between heaven and earth, positive and negative charges, *copper*. The *Empress* was the third card in the series. She represented the importance of *water* or hydrogen and oxygen. Finally, the *Emperor* represented Saturn or the element of *lead*. This planetary influence was interchangeable with Mars or iron. *So, here were the ingredients: mercury, a copper conduit, water, and lead or Iron.* The list sounded familiar and brought an immediate image to her mind. Vulcan was unusually rich in these metals, iron especially.

How was the experiment to be performed? She began turning the next tarot cards in the sequence and saw a pattern. Card #5, The Hierophant was the alchemist or chemist himself. His job was to join heaven and earth through his body. The body, the body, she thought, wiggling with excitement for this mental treasure hunt. Of course, 'the body' must be a container. She visualized a container; through it was running a copper conduit. In the container would be placed pure H^2O. Alchemists often collected dew or rainwater for their experiments then distilled it to purify it. It was placed in the Athanor, the container. She turned over the next card. It was the Lover card showing the male and female being joined. Somehow a positive and negative current was created along the copper conduit. Card #7, the chariot showed movement along a perfectly balanced path. The yin/yang symbol on the card implied a calm center where the positive and negative current could meet. A light went on in her head as the answer came. This could be an electromagnetic field created by placing something highly magnetized like heavy lead at the bottom on the container.

What would happen if you did this? Did Mercury and water with a magnetized ground started an electromagnetic field? The answer was so simple when it came to her that it took her breath away. The mercury chemically cooled the helium present within the hydrogen molecules to zero degrees yet kept it fluid. The molecules would then be set in motion or heated by the magnetized lead then cooled again by the helium in the water. This would cause a refraction of the photons within the atom, spinning off the electrons of some of the atoms to create light. The constant changing of amplitude through refraction and the resultant interchange between photons and electrons would spin particles away from the atom. Eventually the conduit would become so charged this would start the atoms moving in a synchron radon pattern, whipping around at high speeds on the copper conduit and creating radiation or radioactivity. Of course, tarot card #8 was Strength. Wait a minute. That was exactly what was happening on Vulcan. This was like creating a miniature synchron belt. The synchron belt on Vulcan did the same thing, whipping around at high speeds until it was virtually invisible to the human eye.[73]

What were problems in doing this or what parameters did they need to follow? she wondered. She turned over the next card and sat puzzled for a moment. It was the Hermit, the image of a spiritual adept who goes into seclusion and is instructed, 'to wait.' This experiment would have to be performed in a private place for some reason and a period of waiting and timing was involved.

What could that timing be? Card #10 was the Wheel of Fortune. Stella thought about Dagon's dream. It was the place where God entered the equation, funneling creative force according to mysterious timing that was out of our control. So, what would happen if radiation were being bombarded on atoms trapped within H^2O? If left alone, the heat being produced on the conduit would gradually increase in strength. She turned over the next card, #11.

Justice which showed two scales being kept in perfect balance. The experiment must not only require a wait period and perfect timing but also that the elements be kept in absolute balance.

If all that happened what would be the result? Her mouth went dry after she got out a piece of paper and scribbled some notes and equations. That's it. Oh my god. Her heart began to pound and her palms became sweaty. Of course, the next step in the Tarot was 'The Hanged Man' saying that everything had been turned upside down. In other words the electron would separate from particles from the atom. The protons and electrons would be naked bringing about the next step, card #13 Death or transmutation.

This was starting to sound scary. Naked transmuted atoms meant fission.

She examined the remaining cards closely. After Death came Temperance, the Devil, The Tower, Star, Moon, Sun, Judgment and the Universe in that order. Perhaps, the next nine cards were to describe simply how careful humans should be and the spiritual lessons they must learn in order to correctly use this valuable elixir.

If you weren't temperate with this power and instead followed human desire represented by the Devil, there would be a huge fiery explosion represented by the Tower. This transmutation would affect the stars, moon and sun. It had far reaching affect within the solar system and galaxy. It was up to us to exercise finally proper judgment. On judgment day are deeds would bring us karma for our actions. There was an opportunity to connect to universal power or to be destroyed and absorbed back into the universe.

Stella thought about it again. By tradition the general public thought the alchemist was trying to create gold out of lead. What if instead the gold was golden light? The copper plate would turn a rosy hue of gold because the molecules in it had been super heated. It would be a source of light similar to the filaments on the plants found on Vulcan. It would not be real gold, but would be more valuable, priceless in fact.

Then, another thought grabbed at her. What if it the last eight cards were a continuation of the experiment, a sequence of events, which took place *after* the molecular structure of the atoms, had been transmuted in step #13? The Temperance card, #14, traditionally was the card of the tarot showing an alchemist mixing two substances in a vial in front of him.

In one hand he held a lunar essence, in the other a solar essence, above him were the symbols for the four elements of earth, air, water and fire. The two elements were being mixed over a fire. *At the foot of his worktable was a man with a woman's head and a woman with a man's head.* She looked at the picture on the card more carefully, interpreting what she saw. The element had already been transmuted. *Lunar was solar. Solar was now was lunar.* These two elements were being mixed together in a second distillation that was being heated. That would mean that the helium and nitrogen compounds, that were a byproduct of the prior process, would be subjected to further experimentation. Her mind went blank and she sat there for a moment just drumming her fingers. Then, it hit. The next card, the Devil, was a warning card. It was like seeing the skull and cross bones. It was at this juncture that some alchemists must have been either killed by noxious fumes or blown up.

What would make this step dangerous? Perhaps, there were other residues from the first distillation that were poisonous. *No, No that can't be it.* She looked at the Devil card, noticing that the now familiar image of the male and female symbols in balance were there, too. Here was also the bizarre image of them trading and sharing anatomical parts. Devil was the word 'Lived' spelled backwards. In the image he was huge, a monster. She walked over to her shelf, rifling through her books found an old book on alchemy. In it was a photo representation of the Mutus Liber, the Wordless Book, the series of fifteen plates that showed how to create the philosopher's stone, the original had been in Lawrence' office. In many of the plates was an image of what looked like a tower. A fire was burning at the bottom of it and inside could be seen a symbol representing Mercury. Card #16, the Tower was the next card in her sequence. Traditionally, in the tarot this card represented a possible catastrophe or accident. Later it came to be represented by Uranus, that electrical planet that represents sudden, sometimes violent change. Perhaps in this case it meant a radical shift of energy. Then, she shuddered. Oh, My God, of course! The next card, #17 is THE STAR. *A star is a sun. The property being acted upon was helium. They may actually have found a way to create an explosion so big it could create a star like our sun through a chemical process*! Stella was shaken and dumbfounded.

The alchemical marriage had talked about a red compound. What was the missing element, that when added to rarified helium atoms, could cause an atomic explosion? She got out her alchemy book. There were numerous references to a red mysterious compound being mixed with shavings from the philosopher's stone.

Supposedly this was how gold was created. It was the race for gold that had propelled thousands to try these experiments. This had eventually led to other chemistry research, birthing science, as we know it today.

Perhaps, someone had hit upon a dangerous formula, which had been concealed for hundreds of years. She remembered reports that in 1937, a man called Fulcanelli performed a demonstration witnessed by two physicists, a geologist, and a chemist. He sprinkled 'an unknown substance' into half a pound of molten lead, which allegedly changed to 1/2 pound of gold. He then supposedly transmuted silver into uranium.

More than two decades later, exiled Polish scientist, Jacque Bergier, claimed to have met Fulcanelli.

Stella searched through her computer file, frantically calling up a passage in Bergier's book that she vaguely remembered. In a book published in 1960, Bergier said his work was interrupted by the sudden appearance of a total stranger. The scientist said the stranger spoke in a 'metallic voice' announcing he knew Bergier was involved with experiments in nuclear energy. He also knew that Bergier's work focused on producing radioactivity with plutonium by electrifying a bismuth rod sunk in deuterium under high pressure. The stranger said, "You are on the brink of success. May I be allowed to warn you to be careful? The work that you and your colleagues are undertaking is appallingly dangerous. It imperils not only you, but it is a threat to the whole of humanity. I am telling you this point blank. The alchemists have known it for a very long time."

The stranger went on say that alchemists were not ignorant of the structure of the nucleus, "Certain geometrical arrangements of highly purified substances are sufficient to release atomic forces without recourse to vacuum lines." The stranger then reportedly picked up a book by Frederick Soddy on Bergier's desk, opened it to a certain page and read, "I believe that there were civilizations in the past that were familiar with atomic energy, that by abusing it they were utterly destroyed."[74]

A sinking feeling hit her in the pit of her stomach at reading this. Her first thoughts were of stories of a highly evolved scientific civilization called Atlantis that had been destroyed. There were also stories of the deluge, the great flood that supposedly destroyed mankind in ancient times. Was there a large scale catastrophe back in their past? As a student of mythology, she knew that almost every culture had a similar story of a flood. Geologists had actually found some evidence to support this. What seemed to resonate in her was her archetypal memory. A psychic had once told her that she had been a priestess in Atlantis during a past life.

Then, her mind flashed again to present day. Currently propaganda was being distributed in the scientific community encouraging a project called 'Starseed.'

These scientists were proponents of using atomic power in space to set off super nova explosions to create new suns or stars that could heat planetary stations located at ideal distances for colonies with greenhouses. It was an idea that had been gaining popularity and had received wide publication due to the coming of Earth Day. The thought of it made her shudder. Interspace Research, the same company that had funded the trip to Vulcan was considering a proposal for this now.

What about the mysterious teachings about a philosopher's stone? What about the two stones that she and Dagon had in their possession now? These stones had somehow been formed on Vulcan, a planet that was a synchron radon planet emitting high levels a radiation. She looked through her alchemical book, reading the oldest reference to the philosopher's stone.

Zosimus of Panopolis, a town in Upper Egypt, in about 300 A.D. described it as a 'stone that is not a stone, a precious thing which has no value, a thing of many shapes which has no shape, this unknown thing which is known of all.'[75] The wheels of her mind kept turning.

Hmm, A stone that was not a stone.

If the stone itself was a solidified form of concentrated helium and nitrogen it would not really be a stone, it would be precious yet have no value in the world. It could take many odd shapes depending on how it had cooled; it would be unknown, yet known to the All.

If alchemists had stumbled onto a way to mimic Vulcan's synchron radon field in a laboratory, with such a simple list of elements, they would be in effect be producing a miniature synchron belt capable of casting off particles in the atom, weakening the defenses of the nucleus and allowing fission. This was breathtaking. They could create a sun like our own star, which was even now releasing, through explosions of helium, billions upon billions of units of energy every moment. Stella picked up the Mutus Liber tablet again and studied the small symbol in the left hand corner for the Philosopher's stone. It looked like an egg or a round sphere. Sectioned and seen from a front view it appeared to be a nucleus with rings circling it. My God, she was seeing an ancient drawing of an atom.

Stella held her hand over her eyes, noticing that her hands were trembling. Laying the cards aside, she lay down on her back on the soft carpet, and took a deep, shaky breath.

I have to get ahold of Dagon. She scrambled up feeling panicked. *It may be that our Vulcan stones are a solidified form of the first distillation. Mixed with say arsenic sulfur or some other red compound they could destroy the earth.*

Her next thought was even more alarming. I must find out what that 'mysterious compound' is that must be avoided. A more uncomfortable feeling came over her.

Someone had placed the deck outside of her door. Someone else was hoping that she would discover this secret in the tarot, perhaps already know the final compound necessary.

Could someone actually know she had the stone? She took it out of its black velvet bag and looked at it again. It seemed to be glowing from an internal light.

I must keep it in a safer place, she thought. After a moment's indecision, she took the dried flowers out of the vase on her bookshelf and placed the bag in the bottom of the vase, putting the flowers back in again. Then, she picked up Dagon's phone and dialed his number. No answer.

Punching in an access number, she placed in their shared code number that accessed his computer terminal.

"Dagon," she spoke quickly to the voice-activated keyboard of the terminal. "I may have discovered something important regarding the objects in question. Meet me at my apartment, as soon as you can. I'm afraid to go out, as there have been some new developments. Keep your gift very private, and very safe. Extremely important."

After a moments pause, she added, "I missed you last night, Stella."

After leaving her message, Stella settled down on the couch to wait, drifting before long into a fitful sleep. A slight noise wakened her, startling her as she tried to open her eyes. However, a hand went over her mouth and a dark cloth was put over her eyes before she knew what was happening. She felt a prick of a needle and immediate grogginess. *Dagon, Where are you? I need you?* She tried to relay telepathically.

As a last desperate act, she slipped off her Vulcan ring, dropping it onto the cushions and kicked the box of tarot cards on the floor under a corner of the couch. Blackness won out over her struggles.

CHAPTER 27

✠

Kidnapped

The darkness moved from total black-out to a foggy blur. She felt herself being carried, like a sack of potatoes, over someone's shoulder. They were walking up steps. Then, came the noise of an engine and a plane. Another prick of the needle brought total night again.

Her next confused memories were of bumping along a rough road in the back of a truck. It was horribly hot and difficult to breathe. A rope bit into the back of her hands. Her old feelings of claustrophobia overwhelmed her until, gratefully, she fell into a faint.

She came too again, with a bandana around her eyes, recognizing the horrifying feeling of dropping down, down, down. She was on some kind of elevator that seemed to go on forever. At least thirty minutes must have gone by as they continued to drop.

Oh, my god. What's happening? Stella thought. The horror of the situation overwhelmed her.

They must be in some sort of mineshaft, going down miles beneath the surface of the earth. Stella fought panic. She gulped in deep breaths and focused on her inhalation and exhalation.

I will conquer my fear, she said to herself, repeating over and over the verses from Dune that Dagon had taught her. The elevator finally stopped and she was pushed, stumbling, forward. Tripping and falling on her knees, she was jerked up roughly and taken between two heavy steel doors.

The sound of the doors shutting heavily behind her was almost her undoing. Trembling and quaking, she was thrust down in a corner, and then left alone to silence. It seemed that only moments had passed when she heard another sound, a sinister chuckle from someone nearby. She tried to hear where the sound came from, but found it impossible. Then, there were soft footstep and he was in front of her. Though she tried to hold herself still, she jumped and screamed when he touched her.

"Boo!" then laughter. "Shall we take off your blindfold, so you can see how much trouble you've gotten yourself into?" The knot was quickly undone and she blinked her eyes uncertainly trying to adjust to the dim light. "It's you," she whispered.

Before her stood Lawrence Statton, his eyes slightly wild, and his face set in a leering grin. "Lawrence," she began "You can't do this. You can't just kidnap a public figure like me. You'll be caught, you'll..." He waved to her impatiently, signifying that she stop talking immediately. "You may call me Esrom, my name as High Priest and Elder of the Brotherhood. You can't speak unless spoken to." He sounded like a nasty boy making rules on a playground.

Esrom, what kind of ridiculous name was that? she thought. It was hard to take him seriously.

"Can I say one thing?"

Esrom was looking annoyed.

"Just one thing?"

He looked flustered and nodded his head slightly.

"I could use a restroom and a drink of water. I don't know how long I've been out, but I can tell you I am not very comfortable right now."

He nodded toward a door in the corner.

"It's there, you can't escape, since you're three miles underground."

Stella gulped visibly, but held onto her air of bravado.

"My, my, what a dungeon, simply marvelous." She staggered a bit on her feet, then began to walk gingerly toward the restroom closing the door and sinking with relief to her bruised knees in front of the commode, where she proceeded to throw up what little she had in her stomach.

After washing her face and using the restroom, she got a drink of water out of the sink and found she felt better. Reluctantly she left the room to go face Lawrence again.

"So, where on earth are we?" She noticed the little flicker of pride cross his face before he replied.

"As I said over 15,000 feet below the surface."

"There is no place that deep," Stella started to say, and then stopped. "You mean we are in some type of mine shaft?"

"Not just *any* mine shaft." Lawrence mocked.

She looked around her for some type of clue, but the room seemed quite empty and stark.

"Well, let me just guess," she answered rather smartly, "Is it gold?"

"An excellent deduction. We only hope you have been as good with your other research."

Stella studied him more carefully. There was a bulge on his left hip, probably a laser of some type. He was wearing a metal gray jacket. She noted that on the right hand pocket of the jacket was emblazoned an image of a red dragonfly biting its own tail, the alchemical symbol for immortality.

That red dragonfly, however, made her shudder. It had a violent look about it. Stella decided to try a little trick with Esrom to make him nervous. She had learned in a self-defense class how to deduce truths and speak them with power, modulating her voice to make the perpetrator feel powerless.

"Well, Lawrence. Others and I know a few things about you."

He looked a little alarmed so she continued, "You're leading a violent segment of your sect that bases its creed on a distortion of old alchemical theories. You believe that you have been called by god to pass judgment on the rest of the Order and are seeking ultimate power so you can do this."

He seemed visibly startled and uncomfortable.

"How did you know?" he began, and then stopped himself.

I was right, she thought to herself.

He caught himself. "You're the one who is going to give us all the answers we want and very soon. And I promise you it won't be pleasant."

Suddenly, another image flashed through Stella's subconscious. With a white wig, he would look just like the man from her past life, the one who had sentenced her to die as a witch. She shuddered. Well, karma had brought them together and that meant he would be the one to learn a lesson this time. She relaxed slightly. Seeing her look more comfortable rather than frightened only added to the look of unease that was growing in his, now nervous, mannerisms.

"By what authority do you accuse me?" Stella let her voice be stronger, deeper, as if she was the one questioning or interrogating him.

"By the right of my lineage," was his defensive reply.

"And, what might that be?"

Esrom drew himself up proudly and began a long line of begets. And, Jared begets Heth, and Heth, Shez, then way down the line to Cam, then Esrom.

Duh, Oh brother, thought Stella, even as she listened carefully. Was he just crazy or what?

Surprisingly, he opened his jacket and pulled a small, antiquated book out of his pocket. He began reading fervently: "Behold, 0 Lord, thou has smitten us because of our iniquity. 0 Lord, look upon me in pity, and turn away thy anger from this, thy people, and suffer not that they shall go forth across this raging deep in darkness, but behold these things which I have molten out of the rock."

"Therefore touch these stones, 0 Lord, with thy finger, and prepare them that they may shine forth in darkness and they shall shine forth unto us in the vessel which we have prepared that we may have light while we shall cross the sea. Behold, 0 Lord, thou canst do this. We know that thou are able to shew forth great power, which looks small unto the understanding of men."[76]

Stella tried to get a look at the cover of the book. *Geez what was his gig!*

"Behold thou shalt not suffer these things which ye have seen and heard to go forth unto the world, shew it to no man, seal them up, that no one can interpret them; for ye shall write them in a language that they cannot read."

"And, behold, these two stones will I give unto thee and ye shall seal them up also with the things which ye shall write."

"For behold the language which ye shall write I have confounded, wherefore I will cause in my own due time that these stones shall be invisible to the eyes of men 'til I chose to magnify them."

Now, Stella was feeling seriously spooked. The prophecy was actually talking about the two stones that she and Dagon had. How could that be?

Esrom continued in a monotone sing song voice, "And, it came to pass that the Lord did cause Cam to put forth the stones into the vessels, which were prepared; and behold, they did give light unto the vessels thereof. And, thus the Lord caused stones to shine in darkness, that the faithful might cross the waters of destruction."

Esrom stopped reading and looked up somewhat expectantly. "This prophet was in my lineage. As you can see, by lineage, the stones belong to me."

Stella began to think quickly. He can't know I have the stones. He's just referring to the stones in the prophecy. The stones must be a reference to the philosopher's stone coveted by the alchemists. According to this text they were 'sealed' only to be revealed should God choose to magnify them.

She would have to bluff her way to some position of power with him. It amazed her that the text was talking about two glowing stones being put on a ship to save followers from a great deluge.

She lowered her voice and began to speak with authority. "God has been displeased with your Order. He has taken the stones and given them to the worthy. They are sealed according to his plan only to revealed at his will."

Esrom looked startled, then began to listen carefully as Stella quickly bluffed her way through the prophecy. "Stones that glow, still light the way, but you can't use force to take them. The Great Power will only give them back to those who are righteous followers of the Kingdom of God."

Esrom looked relieved. Not the look that Stella had been hoping for. "I won't be using force. You're scheduled to have your memory read by NECSA. I assure you it will be very painful."

Stella faked a stern expression. "The language has been sealed, you will not be able to understand what has not been magnified by God himself."

"Oh, quit the bullshit," Esrom bit out suddenly. He reached out suddenly and slapped her hard across the face. Stella fell against the wall shocked. "Do you think I really believe all of this stuff? My followers do, but I'm a scientist. I know *almost* what you know and I am going to find out *everything* that you know, soon."

We're sitting on a gold mine." He laughed to himself at his own pun, "Sitting on a gold mine." His voice seemed crazy as he got up and walked out, locking her in.

Stella let the tears fall, going in the bathroom to put some cold water on her swollen jaw. This was an abandoned mine, what did he mean? One thing she was sure of, however, they didn't have a stone. They were following other leads, other alchemical texts trying to create a stone.

She had to get out of here somehow, quickly. Everything was at stake. If she got an opportunity to face the Brotherhood, then she would have to bluff her way out some how.

However, as a last resort, before revealing everything to NECSA, she would have to find a way to commit suicide. If she didn't, it might mean the death of everyone on earth. She bit her lip. That was, if her tarot theory was correct. She started a little internal debate. You don't want to die for a theory, do you? Yeah, well, if I'm right, everyone on earth would die.

Stella wondered why she felt so little fear about suicide. Instead it felt like a steely purpose within her. During one of her past lives she had vowed 'even her life as a priestess' and she knew when it came to it, she could do it. It was just a question of how.

Esrom had locked solid, steel doors behind him and there were, of course, no windows.

She looked around her and noticed for the first time a totally unexpected sight. A small white butterfly was fluttering near the ceiling light as trapped as she was in her prison.

Then, it hit her. How could a butterfly be this far below the surface? It must have had a way in from the outside. There had to be airshafts, tunnels for circulating air down into the mines. Instead of going straight down, perhaps they angled out, following the shortest distance to any valleys or lower geographic features of the area.

Tears leaked from her eyes. She had read once how 33 Chilean minors were trapped for 69 days 2300 feet beneath the surface of the earth. Two of them were saved by a white butterfly that led them away from a huge slab of rock that would have hit them during the cave in. The butterfly should not have been there, so far beneath the surface of the earth. The story had spread to those above, giving hope to frantic relatives.

The butterfly seemed be trying to get her attention. She watched it float towards a corner then slowly start crawling down the wall behind an empty metal shelving unit.

Hurrying over, Stella pushed the lightweight aluminum shelf aside and smiled. It was a grate and the butterfly was crawling into it. She placed her face close to it. Yes, fresh air. She pulled at the bars of the grate. It didn't budge. Oh darn, she thought, A crow bar. She looked around the room. There was just the chair she had been sitting in. She put the metal leg of the chair between the bars and pushed on the chair with all of her weight. It didn't budge.

Damnation, wouldn't you know it? She thought with ironic disgust and a bit of humor. I need a screwdriver and I left my Leatherman at home.

She heard the door opening again and rushed to carry her chair back to the center of the room, hoping Esrom wouldn't notice that the shelving had been moved.

She was determined that he not see her fear. So she feigned a casual bored look. Esrom looked suspicious.

I wonder how I could have been fooled, even for a minute with this guy, she said to herself with disgust.

What a fop.

He handed her a plastic container with spaghetti and noodles in it, a plastic fork and threw a piece of foam that was rolled up under his arm into the corner. "You'll be staying here for a couple of days while we get the computer equipment moved here for the test."

"I'm the only person that you will see, so try to be friendly. You'll get three small meals a day, so eat all of it. Any questions?"

"Only one," Stella smiled weakly, "Where's the TV? Internet?"

Esrom turned around and walked out disgust, leaving Stella to the deafening silence that had been her undoing so many times before. She began breathing deeply, praying for strength and following her inner voices as she fought the fear that threatened to engulf her. She made herself eat a few bites of food, but immediately began to feel groggy,

Shit, they had drugged the food, was her last thought before falling into a deep sleep. She dreamed of a different kind of alchemy. In it the Seeker was transmuted to become the Star, a glorious Awakened Being full of the unlimited light of God. She didn't want to wake up.

CHAPTER 28

✠

A rescue operation

When Dagon got home he noticed that the red message light on his computer was flashing. He was alarmed to read the ominous message from Stella.

His first thought was to try to contact her by phone, no answer. He jumped on his motorcycle, driving at break-neck speed to her apartment.

What he saw there had him even more concerned. The apartment was empty, the door neatly shut, but unlocked. There was no note, no sign of any struggle, just an intuitive feeling that someone had been there and that something was wrong. Then, he saw something sparkling on the couch, Stella's Vulcan ring. She never took it off.

It had to be a desperate message. On the floor just under the corner of the couch, he saw a deck of tarot cards loosely wrapped in brown paper with a little note, "Herein is the key." One look at them told him they weren't your run of the mill playing cards.

My god, this has to have something to do with those alchemists, he thought. Someone's kidnapped her.

The first house call he made was to Lucian Westfield. He was at the museum at his office desk. Dagon pulled him up into a stranglehold.

"Where is she?" he demanded. Lucian choked, then sputtered hoarsely, "she?"

"Stella, you know who I mean."

"Is she missing?"

Dagon pulled Lucian around, holding him up higher by the collar.

Lucian seemed mildly annoyed, but not, in the least bit alarmed. "If you will kindly let me down, we can talk about this in detail."

"I don't trust one word that comes out of your mouth."

Lucian smiled slightly and waved his hand. "Still if you put me down, I can help you as much as it is possible for me to."

Reluctantly, Dagon released his hold, but not, the pent up tension that was coiled to strike, should Lucian reach for a weapon.

"So, Stella is missing?" he said mildly. Dagon started to reach for him again.

"No, no, not, again." Lucian sat down quickly. "I will tell you everything I know."

"Which is?" Dagon said gruffly.

"We are missing someone, too. He is a young alchemist who is part of the Brotherhood. I have had some doubts about his sincerity recently. His name is Lawrence."

"You mean Lawrence Statton?"

"The very one," Lucian looked at him with gentle, questioning eyes and suddenly, Dagon began to feel ashamed of his rough treatment of the frail old man.

He began to apologize, but stopped mid-sentence. "Let's not waste time."

"If Statton is a traitor to our cause, he's very dangerous. He has been let into the inner circle and is privy to most of the information that they have gathered about the alchemical process which can produce the philosopher's stone."

Dagon began to look impatient again. "I'm sick of hearing about this stone. How important can it be? I mean..."

"More important than you can yet imagine. The fate of the earth, and possibly the universe, rests on it."

Lucian turned away. "I would have trusted no one in the old days. It was such a lonely path watching generation after generation come and go with nobody to share it with." He shrugged a defeated shrug. "It's time that I left this earth plane. I wish that I could."

Dagon looked at him puzzled, then angrily. This was ridiculous, how could this man be as old as he claimed?

"I will help, but I must tell you at this point, I have no idea where Lawrence could have taken her," Lucian said. "But, you must promise me one thing."

"What?"

"I have guessed that you must have two stones. Make sure that no one else knows about this for now."

Dagon was surprised that his request was so similar to the Stella's frantic message.

"There are only two other stones on the earth. I have one of them and the other is held at a sacred island far from civilization."

Lucian reached out for Dagon's arm. Dagon shook him off.

"I'll find her myself." He stormed out of the dark interior of the museum, striding forward with great purpose, then stopping abruptly.

"Find her?" he chided himself, "How in the hell am I going to do that?" A couple of plans surfaced. Tail Lucian, perhaps he would lead Dagon to Lawrence, or better yet, search Lawrence's apartment first for any possible clues.

It was easy to find Lawrence's apartment by following the address in the phone book. When he arrived he found the door locked without anyone in sight.

Quickly Dagon slipped a credit card out of his pocket and began to jimmy the lock. Finally he gave in with frustration and blasted it with his laser. He looked around again. Nobody had seen or heard him. Opening the door, his weapon raised to his chest, he quickly scoped out each room, seeing that not only was the apartment empty, but all of Lawrence's personal items of clothing were gone from the closets.

The place had been swept clean.

Shit, Dagon stomped his foot. He was wasting time. In the meantime, Stella might be hurt, or even dead.

He stopped the horrifying thought and renewed his thorough search. It caught his eye just as he was leaving, a little glint in the carpet. When he reached down to retrieve it, he saw it was a very fine, flake of gold. What in the hell?

Then, his foot ground into something else. It was a small pebble that was just the size to wedge into the tread of a pair of sneakers. It was some kind of ore. Gold-ore, gold-ore, he thought. A mine?

He turned away, hurrying from the apartment. He had left fingerprints everywhere and blown down the door. That would mean the police. Well, let them come, I might need them.

The next stop was Lawrence's office. It was evening and very quiet. He could see NECSA humming in the background. A small hall light threw a greenish glow on the ultra-modern desk and terminal in front of him. He tried to turn it on, but found the desk locked.

Now, where would a man like Statton hide a key? A small plant on a window ledge drew his attention. On a whim, he picked up the pot. There, shining in the faint light was a small key.

Dagon was startled by the immediate answer to the inner question. Something odd was happening to him. It was if his mind was working in overdrive. His intuitions were pointing out probabilities almost faster than he could act on them. The odd thought struck him that perhaps Lucian was helping after all.

He turned on the computer, concentrating on the file server, personal files first. Okay, now for the password. Gold, Mining, Ore, Mines. Nothing was working. Then, following an inner voice again, he typed in the letters, SSR. Why? He didn't know.

It seemed important not to doubt the inner voices now. Perhaps, he was getting help him in some weird, metaphysical way.

The letters SSR sounded sinister reminding him of Hitler, the swastika, and tyrannical power. To his shock and almost horror, the file opened as *Starseed Reclamation Program.*

A quick glance told him everything. This was about atomic power. No wonder Stella had told him the stones were dangerous. He scanned the index under Starseed and saw the category he wanted.

Mine. Hitting it with the mouse, a graphic picture of a map began to spread out over the screen. It was in South America, in the jungle and mountains of Draesbran, a mountainous basalt escarpment between Chili and Argentine in the Andes mountain range. Taking out a flash drive from the drawer, he began downloading the whole Starseed program, slipping the drive into the inner pocket of his jacket along with his pocket Link.

He left as quietly as he came in, just missing the truck that pulled up in the back. It was a large van with the initials NECSA filled with dollies, robes and moving people. Walking out into the afternoon sun, Dagon paused for a moment on the steps of the high-rise.

On the street in front of him was a blind preacher with a crowd of street people gathered around him. A young woman seemed to be leading him. She was wearing a gray robe with a cowl. "The good Lord says that the meek shall inherit the earth. That means you and that means me. See, the meek are those people that are poor, blind, and sick. God didn't intend immortality to go to the greedy. He intends it to go to those who understand that the immortal lies within. Look deep within. Search past the ego, the mind and emotions. You will understand who you truly are. We are each god. God is in everything. That is where your true power lies. That is the true alchemy that you seek."

Dagon looked at the preacher assessing him. Then turned away quickly and headed for his bike. His hand reached for his keys in his pocket. Instead, he found the titanium hummingbird he always carried with him.

He held it up briefly to catch the light as an idea shot through him. The meek, the simple, Jeremy!

Dagon quickly reached for his cell phone and was pleased when Jeremy picked up the line after the first ring.

"I need your help. There is a big problem and someone that I care about is in danger."

Jeremy's voice came back in its unhurried easy manner. "Sure bro, where shall I meet you? Oh, by the way, you need any other reinforcements?"

Dagon thought for a minute remembering his days in the Force on special missions: "Four good men that you trust, a terrain vehicle, some rope, sleeping bags, food, knives, weapons, compasses, headlamps and other caving gear, water, camouflage clothing, night goggles, night binoculars and a fast transport pod craft."

"Oh, and," Dagon continued, "I don't want any of those men to be nervous about snakes."

"Shoot." Jeremy groaned. "How soon?"

"Yesterday."

There was a pause and he heard some voices in the background.

"Well, how 'bout late this afternoon? Where we goin'?"

"I'll tell you when you get here. Meet me Arbor Point Airfield at 017:00 hours." Dagon looked at his watch. That was only four hours away. "Okay and Dag," there was a pause before Jeremy said, "I'll bring the hot dogs."

As soon as they signed off Dagon found himself pacing back and forth. He hurried back to his apartment and plugged in the drive.

After reading a number of files, including those on the mine, Starseed, and the financial sheets of Interspace Research, he was sure he must know at least as much as Stella did when she had called him frantically.

His next step was to devise a plan for getting down into the mine without being seen. The solution came to him after studying the ventilation system for the mine. Air vents supplied fresh air down into the mineshaft from two locations on the valley floor. The problem would be locating the vent openings in the thick jungle forest of the Draesbran valley. The map would get them to the general area. Then, it would be a matter of luck. He packed an assortment of dynamite and detonation packs in his backpack and included his computer so he'd have a good GPS system and topo maps. Then, dressing in dark clothing, he brought charcoal to blacken his face.

Thank god for my combat training. At the time, working for the Special Services had seemed like the only way to work his way into the space program.

Now, he was glad he knew strategic defense tactics and had spent some time on black ops.

He hoped Jeremy was getting him some tough guys. As he took one last look around his apartment before leaving, he noticed the wooden box with his stone in it sitting on his dresser. *I'd better hide this.*

Seeing a vase with some dried flowers in it on the fireplace mantel, he pulled out the flowers, put the stone in the bottom of the vase and put the flowers back in.

There. Hopefully it'll still be here when I get back. For a moment, doubt assailed him. *What if Stella hadn't been taken to the mine? What if she was nearby?* He shook it off. He had to follow his intuition. He had nothing else.

The late afternoon sun was beating down on the airfield when he got there, mirages ribboning down the runway.

Jeremy's burly body and quiet stance was calming.

"Thanks," Dagon gripped his arm in a firm wristlock. "Anytime, Bro."

"So, who have you found to help?"

"Mo, Joe, and Henry."

Dagon moaned inwardly. Mo and Joe were giants, as simple-minded and military looking as Jeremy. But, Henry was a skinny little runt of a guy with glasses so thick his eyes look distorted and huge behind them. His hair was balding and sticking out in odd places. There was a slightly greasy look about his clothes.

Ugh, thought Dagon. He turned to Jeremy, speaking in a whisper. "So, why Henry?"

"He can blow up anything, using just 'bout nothin' and he wasn't afraid of comin,'" Jeremy shrugged.

Dagon looked at Henry with new respect, and then, gathering them all close, he shook each man's hand with ceremony.

"Thanks for responding to my emergency. I'll tell you more about it in the transport pod and give you my proposed plan of action."

Dagon was the pilot of the F67 *Starbright* so he had to brief them in the crowded cockpit while keeping one eye on his flight panel.

"Okay, we're gonna try to blast into the air vents of this mine. To get there we go cross-country through a valley in the Los Lagos region of Chili. This is a mountainous area. The valley starts from a river in Argentine traversing the Chocamo jungle. This is a virgin temperate rainforest with climbers, vines and undergrowth, wild boar and an occasional puma. We will be flying out from an outback lodge in the lower La Junta Valley. The mine is situated over a rough mountainous area, so most of this has to done on foot."

"After we're into the air vent on the mine shaft, it's probably 1/2 mile of crawling in the tunnel to get to the inner chambers of the mineshaft. There are only a few really big rooms. My guess is that they have Stella in one of them. If we encounter this guy," he flashed a picture of Lawrence, "We shoot to kill." It was only when he said this that the group began to look a little uncomfortable.

"I won't shoot anybody. I'll grab him though, and tie him up for you, if you want." Mo smiled a large gentle grin.

Dagon looked up at Jeremy, startled to encounter the same resistance in his expression.

"Okay," he gave in, "Everyone who gets in the way, gets tied up, okay?" he patted his laser beside him. "Or you can stun them or knock them out. That won't be a permanent." He saw the guys nod approval.

At least if we need it I'll have a gun, Dagon thought.

Jeremy spoke up. "So, exactly what's this place called again?"

"Draesbran, meaning Dragon Mountains for the volcanoes in the area. An Aztec king named it. The back of the Dragon Mountains is called the Battlement of Spears. They are sheer, jagged peaks above jungle floor. The Northern and Central Draesbran are National Parks. The Central is called the Giant's Castle. We'll be in the Southern Draesbran, a huge, undeveloped wilderness area."

The F67 handled well and was fast. They were there in two hours and with the time difference arrived during the steamy hot of early evening. The landing was quick and smooth and the transport immediately camouflaged itself to blend into the jungle. Transportation had been arranged by phone and they found a Terrain vehicle waiting to take this as far as they could go by road.

Dagon had time to ask a few questions of Jeremy. How did you get this stuff?

"I'm not supposed to say, but I work for the good guys. Don't worry 'bout that."

"Not worried, but this is a lot of expense."

"Well, these chaps are rolling in it. A drop in a bucket for them," Jeremy shrugged.

Dagon didn't know what to think, but it wasn't for him to question, especially now when he was getting needed help.

Within twenty minutes the gear was unloaded and reloaded without ceremony. They found themselves bumping along a potholed road that seemed to climb up forever, dropping into deep gullies only to start its ascent again.

They had been driving for four hours in the dark when Dagon saw they were approaching an important landmark.

"Slow down," he yelled to Mo over the sound of the grinding engine. "There it is."

A narrow riverbed that widened into a watering hole was marked by a tall basalt rock shaped like a cone. Prayer flags were tied around the bottom of it and road signs with arrows stood at its four corners.

Quentha's Gatehouse, said Dagon pointing out the landmark. The road turned there into a rough path up a jungle ravine. There were jagged cliffs were on either side.

"This is where we hide the vehicle and walk," he motioned.

Mo and Joe stepped out of the transport, putting on their heavy packs of rope on with ease. But, Henry blinked and just looked around with curiosity, not even remembering his pack. Dagon cringed inside. What a rag tag army.

If he was right, Lawrence could have as many as 100 followers with him living in the mining headquarters above the mineshaft. One misstep and these good-hearted men would be dead.

They refused to carry any weapon other than a stun gun. Probably, for the best. Dagon was pretty sure they'd hurt themselves with it, if they tried.

They began trudging, first south, and then following Dagon's pocket computer, they made a sharp turn east. The jungle was getting thicker. Huge tangled roots tripped them and wild calls from the trees made Mo look upward warily. Large red and black horse flies bit them as they crossed bridges and went past felled Quele trees and giant Alerce trees. At one point Joe ducked and said, "Gunfire!" It turned out to be a large rare woodpecker.

Then, came the thorn bushes and rocky gullies that were impassable or had rickety rope bridges over them. Henry almost gave up, but Joe took his pack. The last straw was the deep mud. Jeremy got stuck past his waist in a hole and had to be rescued with ropes. In the process he lost a boot and turned his knee. Fortunately, Dagon had one extra pair of shoes. The extra shoe, however, was too small so Jeremy was limping along with a pinched foot.

The biting flies were feasting on any open corner of flesh. It was so hot, even in the dark, that Henry had started to fall behind to wipe away the sweat, which made it almost impossible to see out of his fogged up night glasses.

Eight grueling hours had already passed before they came to a cold clear small lake that he had been hoping to find at the base of rock cliffs. Everyone stopped for a drink feeling discouraged about finding the mineshaft vents in country this rugged. A couple of the guys walked into the water to cool off, while Dagon studied his map. We have to be close, he thought. It's near this lake.

That's when he saw it, a flash in the dark. "There, did you see that flash of light on that rocky hillside. It's from something metallic." He jumped up and began to scramble up, using the huge tree roots as steps in the steep slope to make headway. "We're close. It's somewhere up in those rocks." He peered through his night goggles more carefully. "It looks like there might be a cave up here." He began to scramble up again, dislodging first pebbles and then some small boulders in his excitement to reach the top. It wasn't until he turned around from the top that he saw his mistake. A rock had knocked Mo off balance. Sliding down slippery vegetation on the slope, he had taken Henry out too. When everyone got untangled they found that Mo had a badly sprained ankle, which effectively put him out of commission.

Dagon grimaced. It was like going on a commando reconnaissance mission with some good church folk. It took Jeremy dragging and pulling, even though he had a gimpy knee, to get Henry all the way up the hill to the cave. In the meantime Dagon had to make his own decision. He looked down at his Laser and then dialed it back from 'Kill,' to 'Stun.' Thinking, I don't want responsibility for killing anyone anymore. I've done enough of that.

Jeremy pointed to a hollow where the rocks dipped into a shallow cave. "Look, a rock painting." They stood in silent awe captured by the figure of a moon goddess on the weathered rock.

"The Mayans lived here centuries ago. There are numerous sites like this all through the Draesbran," Dagon told them.

He said a silent prayer to the goddess, then, turned to Henry. "We need to blow up this grate." Henry reached into his backpack for wires and tape, and set to work. He seemed quite capable as he set up a plastic explosion with a silencer to muffle the noise. This went smoothly.

The next obstacle was the small size of the vent hole. Henry and Dagon could fit in it, but Jeremy and Joe were far too large to crawl one-half mile down a pipe like that.

Henry seemed to be backing out on his desire to come along. "I thought I'd just be blowin' stuff up not crawlin' through holes," he complained. It took some talking, but he finally agreed to go as far as the opening to the room and help Dagon get in, then he said he was hightailin' it out as he didn't like tight spaces all that much.

Okay, braced Dagon, It's just going to be me. I will still get her out! In order to manage the steep descent in the airshaft, they had brought along magnetic suctions, which could hold long, lightweight ropes to repel them safely down. On the slippery metal, through pitch black it seemed to take forever, but it was probably more like an hour before they saw the first glimmer of light, which showed them, they were reaching the rooms within the mining shaft.

The pipe split, dividing into two directions, and Dagon squirmed his body uncomfortably around to mouth silently and point, "that way." He didn't know how he knew which direction to go, but like everything else that had happened that day, he just knew.

Then, suddenly they were there. He could see clearly through the vent the back of a metal shelving unit and part of a large, sparsely furnished room. In the corner was Stella. She was lying so still that his heart almost stopped. Was she hurt? Or worse?

No one else seemed to be in the room, but it occurred to him that their might be bugs or sensors planted. Picking up a little piece of pebble inside of the grate, he tossed it through the opening, trying to get Stella's attention.

She moved and rolled over, then started to look around. At that moment, he heard the door open, and he dropped back a little farther into the darkness of the vent. It was Lawrence.

"Okay, Stella. Times up. You get to gaze into a crystal ball now." Dagon felt his blood rising as a rage filled him. He tried to hold his temper in check, straining to hear everything.

"We have NECSA and Rudy set up in the next room. I'll be giving you a truth serum in a few minutes. So, do you want to voluntarily tell me what you know or shall we just plug you in and drain your brain?"

Stella pushed her hair back from her eyes and stood up swaying. She held her arms around her body defensively. "I don't know anything so there's nothing I could tell you."

"It isn't good to resist. Bad children are punished." Lawrence shook a finger at her and then his face darkened with evil intent.

"I've decided to remove all of your memories, from birth forward. You'll be left a vegetable."

"You, Esrom, are like a bad guy in a bad cartoon. I only laugh when I think of you. History will spit in your face for this act of cowardice. So much for your lineage." Her eyes looked like flint. Suddenly, she felt no fear at all.

Esrom's face turned almost purple with fury. He punched her so hard she doubled over and dropped to her knees.

Dagon gritted his teeth, his body tightening with deadly control. Henry was still setting up the explosive. He had no choice but to watch Stella be brutalized.

Grabbing her arm, Lawrence started to pull Stella toward the door. "Will you come, or shall we carry you. My men are just outside of this door."

"Wait," said Stella, "I need to use the restroom first."

Esrom looked at her suspiciously, and then dragged her to the bathroom door. "Two," his voice rose, "Two minutes, that's all you get."

Dagon didn't feel good about this. He knew Stella. She had some kind of plan or she wouldn't have asked to use the restroom, but what could it be?

Now, was the time to get Lawrence out of the way, and then get her out. Within five seconds, the silent detonator was on the grate and Dagon was posed to jump through. It went without a hitch. Lawrence turned and raised his weapon, but Dagon had hit him square in the chest. A look of stunned surprise was all that he was allowed before he hit the ground, unconscious.

Henry looked startled, but then pleased as he dragged him behind the door.

Dagon rushed for the bathroom door, trying to open it, but he found it barricaded.

"Stella," he yelled, "It's me." Then, he kicked open the door.

What he saw was a nightmare he would never forget. "Oh, my god." Stella was hanging from the showerhead, her shirt wrapped tightly around her neck and her feet dangling. She was already unconscious, maybe dead. Dagon lifted her immediately taking the pressure off her throat. He felt his knees give out with relief when he heard her gasp and gag as her oxygen starved body painfully pulled air into her lungs. He checked her pulse. It was faint, but there, the rasping an answer to prayer as she drew air through blue lips.

Henry stood helplessly at the door watching.

Dagon was rocking Stella back and forth as he hugged her to his body. "We have to get her out of here. Bring me that blanket and we'll wrap her in it. I'll tie the rope around her body and pull her behind me up the vent. You follow and watch our backs."

Henry nodded, his eyes bugging out at the beautiful, half naked woman in front of him.

"Sweetheart, you're safe now, I have you," Dagon crooned. "You're going to be all right."

He gently put her shirt back on, wrapped her still body in a blanket from the bed and tied the rope around her waist and under her armpits. Then, they carefully put her body in the airshaft and Dagon began the slow, laborious ascent, lifting her body and his, straight up hill. He accomplished this by using the ropes that he had set as pulleys. It took everything he had to lift her through the cramped tunnel. When they reached the outside, Joe and Jeremy enthusiastically greeted them, dragging them the rest of the way out of the grate. Dagon lay on the ground his shirt soaked with sweat from his herculean efforts. Panting he rolled over to cradle Stella.

He rubbed her cold hands between his fingers, trying to bring her back to consciousness, rocking her against his chest. She still hadn't stirred but was breathing normally. "We'll need to carry her," Dagon gasped out.

Jeremy noted Dagon's exhaustion and immediately picked up Stella in his large brawny arms. Dagon noticed he had split open the front of his makeshift boot so his toes, stuck out. Good idea, but bad if there were snakes around. Slipping and sliding down the steep slope, they joined Mo, who was waiting anxiously at the bottom cursing his sprained ankle which he had wrapped in a bandana soaked in cold water from the lake.

"We've got to get out of here."

Jeremy carried Stella. Mo leaned against Joe with a stick for a crutch. Dagon helped Henry as they hurried into a clump of trees and undergrowth. Within twenty minutes they heard the sirens of the mine go off.

"Okay, guys, they've found Statton and they know how we got her out. We only have only a few choices. Our best bet is to keep heading for the transport. It's really our only bet. It is located higher in the valley at the La Junta lodge. Somehow, we have to speed up the pace."

He looked around at the mud-smeared, anxious faces of his compatriots. They nodded and hit out as fast as they could.

Dagon turned back to see Henry struggling valiantly along, but getting caught in the tangled roots of fallen trees that the others were able to step over. "Go on without me," he panted. "I'll set a series of explosive booby traps, then you can pick me up in the truck over at the base of that bluff."

Dagon hesitated. It made sense, but he knew somehow he was looking at Henry's death, if he let him stay behind. It didn't take long to make a decision.

"No, get your butt up here and stop falling behind. We need you with us." Henry looked relieved and pushed his way through the undergrowth, a new look of determination on his face.

An hour passed before they heard the first shouts of the enemy nearby. Stella still hadn't stirred. It was as if she were drugged.

Gasping for breath, the exhausted group hid behind a large fallen log. It was then that they saw it. A huge black helipod hovered silently over the nearby meadow. A crimson red band was painted across the side of it, and at the tail was an image of a red dragonfly, biting its own tail.

Dagon motioned for his companions to stay under cover. Had they been spotted? He pulled Stella closer to his body, at last feeling her stir beside him. Within moments, she opened her cloudy eyes, her expression gradually clearing to one of surprise, then wonder.

"Dagon," she rasped, "Am I in heaven, or are you real?"

"You're alive, sweetheart," he ran his finger lightly across the angry black and blue mark around her throat, "We broke into the mine and took out Lawrence, just in time."

Then, an angry look took the place of his loving one and he shook her gently, "How could you try to kill yourself? I could kill you." She smiled painfully at him, drawing her long blue shirt around her tightly, noticing that she was still wearing one of her fuzzy elephant slippers.

"Where are we? Who are these people?" Stella looked around at the group of sweat-stained men that were huddled nearby.

"We are between the borders of Chile and Argentine. This is my makeshift army. However, we're not in the best of positions." He motioned to the field. "It looks like they're trying to find us with thermal sensors. We're sitting ducks anywhere in these woods."

Stella sunk back, fighting a wave of dizziness, and let Dagon wrap his arms tightly around her. He put his face in her hair, breathing her in. "My god," he groaned, "I thought I'd lost you."

He pulled her against his chest, and she could feel the rapid beating of his heart. Looking down, he gently took her chin and raised her eyes searching them, finding what he wanted. "We have a lot to talk about." A single tear slid down her cheek, which he caressed away with his thumb. Then, his eyes hardened as he turned away. "But, first we have to get out of here."

Stella closed her eyes thinking, and then blinked them open suddenly, hope making them bright. She began to whisper in a hoarse, strangled voice, "Dagon, listen. I have an idea. What if we just go out to greet them, walk right out into the meadow? They won't kill me, because they know I have the information they need. I'll say that I want to talk to them, that their leader betrayed them, that I'm a messenger from God."

Dagon look startled. "What are you raving about?"

"I don't have time to tell you the whole story, but these guys are part of a radical religious sect. I know their prophecy. I think I can win them over."

Dagon thought it through out loud. "It's a good idea. The Helipod is our best way out of these woods. Except, I won't have you risking yourself. I'll go out as a decoy and wave a white flag. My men can sneak up from behind and take the pilot silently while they have their guns on me." Dagon was thinking quickly. "If it doesn't work, you stay hidden. Don't move. We'll bury you in underbrush and leaves, before we go out."

Stella wished she hadn't said anything, but she simply nodded. Forming her own plan, even as Dagon started to map out the strategy with his men. After a few moments, they started to slip out, moving in place around the perimeter of the meadow. Dagon turned back to Stella, giving her a quick hug before he dragged some light branches over her. "I love you," he said softly, squeezing her hand. "Whatever happens, remember that."

He was up and walking forward, a white handkerchief tied to a stick, before she could respond. The men in the Helipod saw him immediately and turned around, setting down silently in the meadow. Dagon could see a pilot and co-pilot. After they landed, the hatch opened and four other men came out, carrying automatic weapons. Behind them came Lawrence Statton an evil grin on his face.

Lawrence gave them the command to shoot just as Dagon's men stepped out of the forest. Statton darted forward towards the front of the craft with his gun, firing towards the woods. At the same time his men started firing the same direction. It all happened so quickly that Statton was the first to go down, hit in the back by one of his own men. He was dead. There was a few seconds of stunned silence before the men turned their guns back on Dagon, pointing them at the center of Dagon's chest. Dagon's reflex made him jump to the side just as a laser scorched the grass where he had been standing. Damn. He was a sitting duck. It's over. Suddenly, however, Dagon noticed them gesturing to each other to put down their weapons. He looked over his shoulder and saw Stella walking out of the woods. She had tied a scarf around her bruised neck and walked forward her head held high, with a stride of self-confidence.

She greeted them with a smile, as she held up her hand in an ancient symbol of brotherhood.

The enemy soldiers looked at each other quizzically and waited for her to walk up. Dagon reached for her hand as she started to walk by him, almost wrenching her shoulder as he pulled her angrily to his side. Stella's smile didn't waver, but she pinched Dagon's wrist, and tried to twist her arm out of his grip.

"Greetings to my tribe. She said with a low, hoarse croak, "I have waited many centuries for this moment to come. We are at last reunited." She placed her hand over her heart, making a symbol for the sun. The men looked at her suspiciously. Stella closed her eyes for a moment, asking for the voice of prophecy, submitting herself to the words that began to form and flow through her. "You have been betrayed by Esrom as was prophesied in holy writ. He was beget of lineage of Cam, yet his ways were evil, and in his iniquity he has brought a curse upon himself. His death his punishment for his darkness."

The soldiers were listening carefully now, their postures showing respect for her words. "I have the stones that you have sought these many years. I have them because God has chosen to reveal them in his infinite goodness, in his own way, at his own time."

"They were passed to me through the lineage of a High Priest who is not of this earth. Perfected by the eternal, they have been kept hidden from the eyes of the wicked. Who are ye?" she pointed her finger at them, "that you would doubt the words which shall bring in the kingdom of god. Repent now of your blindness or die also in your sins." The soldiers began to put their guns on the ground. Clasping their hands over their third eyes and bowing their heads in supplication.

Dagon could see his men starting to walk out of the woods, ready to overpower the pilot. He motioned for them to move quickly, but saw the stubbornness in Mo's eyes and groaned inwardly as he remembered their refusal to carry any weapons. Instead of overpowering anyone, the men simply came out of the woods and silently joined the others by taking the same attitude of supplication.

Dagon was shocked. It seemed Stella had a following now. She had become the High Priestess of a whole Order. Dagon knew that the Starseed group numbered globally at 30 million. What did she think she was doing? After they had been ushered into the safety of the dragonfly helipod, they were whisked off to living quarters on top of the Draesbran. The spacious main hall of the quarters had been ingeniously designed as a temple with symbolic images painted on the walls, including Mayan symbols, a red serpent, and geometric patterns depicting alchemical drawings of the cosmos. The main hall was large and spacious, but simply furnished, the focus being an altar.

Stella was separated from the men, immediately. They were taken to private quarters, where they were offered baths, clean simple white robes and a vegetarian meal.

Dagon knew that Stella was meeting with the leaders of the sect by herself. He found himself pacing in his quarters, worrying about the turn of events. By the time the soldiers, who were guarding his door, stepped aside to allow the entry of a party of interrogators, Dagon had come up with his own plan, and knew what he was going to say. It seemed to go well. A restless night of disturbed sleep followed. The next morning, he found that the guards had been removed from his door.

He walked down the spacious hallway looking for some sign of Stella, amazed to find her sitting in a sunny room, enjoying a breakfast that looked more like a banquet. She was alone, the sun creating a halo around her fiery hair. A white chiffon scarf was tied gracefully over the black and blue bruises on her neck. Other then a slight bruise on her check bone, she looked fine. Dagon strode in angrily, breaking up the peaceful scene, to admonish her.

"What in the hell do you think you're doing? How could you just walk out of the woods, pleased as pie with yourself, and proceed to put us in this mess?" he blundered.

Stella wrinkled her nose, defying him. "Would you rather be dead, or maybe have those soldiers dead?"

"You didn't give it a chance to work, if you had just waited, we wouldn't be in the position that we're in right now."

Stella looked at him as if he was crazy, and then offered him a croissant, motioning to the feast in front of them trying to keep from smiling. "Some mess!"

Then, she began in a more serious vein. "Oh, Dagon, I know it seems ridiculous, but these people have been misled. They're seeking a new order for the universe. They desire to base it upon spiritual principles, yet have been using the old 'power over,' domination principles of the old order. There are scientists and wealthy, politically influential people who are a part of this group. They will make a difference in the future of this planet."

"Now, consider this," she paused for effect. "These people have been following an ancient prophecy that predicts that at the end of time, two stones will be revealed by god. According to ancient holy texts, they believe these glowing stones will power a sun that will provide light for them after the great deluge. Don't you think it odd that you and I have two golden stones given to us through magical

444

circumstance? Am I supposed to just walk away from this responsibility? I have begun to believe that our golden stones are rarefied helium, which through simple chemical processes offer unlimited, access to nuclear power that mirrors the furnace of the sun."

"What?" Dagon exclaimed and Stella hastened to catch him up on what she had learned from the tarot cards before she went on.

"Starseed members number in millions. Their plan involves using atomics in the universe to create new suns. We both know what a bad idea that is. We can help these guys stop from making this mistake. I can't just walk away from this responsibility."

Dagon shuddered as he remembered her hanging by the throat only yesterday. She was willing to die for this. He recalled Lucian's plea that the stones stay hidden. "We could just get rid of them. Hide them somewhere."

Stella looked up, her expression tortured. "Then, why were they found? Why did we go to Vulcan, and encounter an extraterrestrial presence? Why were we led to the stones? What if this really is God's work and guidance? I can only trust my experiences, my own inner voices and guides. I know that there is a reason why we have been asked to confront Interspace Research, to confront the Starseed program. I just can't shirk whatever responsibility I've been asked to take. We have cold fusion now to power our way into the universe. However, this plan could destroy stars, planets, and whole galaxies. If we don't nip it in the bud, it will just come up again. They'll figure out a way to use Vulcan to do this."

Dagon looked disgruntled. "But, you'd do this by pretending to be some kind of High Priestess." He gestured towards the flowing white robe she was wearing. "Isn't this hoax a way of taking power over people, the very principle you're fighting against? After all, if people follow some guru and not their own inner guide and inner soul they are like drugged automatons. They can't grow spiritually. They are simply devotees of some dogmatic religion."

He looked away, wanting to hold her, yet shocked by the turn of events and angry about the stance that Stella had taken. Stella caught his eyes, her gaze reflective. "It isn't a hoax, I have been a High Priestess before."

Dagon watched and his pupils widened as he recalled his past-life dream, memories of her when she had been a priestess in Egypt and Atlantis. He saw the strength and grace in her queenly stance and shuddered.

"I agree with everything you have said," Stella sighed. "It's better not to have intermediaries to god. In this instance, I'm praying that any act of leadership will be submitted to divine will. I have no desire for this role. I wish that it had passed me by. I don't enjoy the homage they show me, although these croissants are pretty good," Stella smiled. "I vowed my life for the betterment of mankind. If this is what it requires, I can't run away from it."

Dagon shrugged helplessly. "Did you rescue stray animals when you were a little girl, too?" Stella looked up, a little wounded, her eyes big and for a moment vulnerable. "I'm sorry," he said, squeezing her hand. "I don't need to ask that, I know you did." Then, he gently pulled on her hand and drew her into a sheltering embrace speaking softly into her hair. "You're brave, but you are in a danger. There are plots, political intrigue and death lurking around the corners of this job you've taken on." He paused, and then broke the news without preamble.

"I might as well tell you now. I have informed the guards, that I am the High Priest. That is why I'm here talking to you now. We will be married, body to soul, at a temple ceremony tomorrow in front of your congregation."

Stella gasped in shock.

"I was interrogated yesterday by the church father's and announced our intentions to them at that meeting. So, you can't get out of it." Stella started to struggle out of his grasp kicking him in the shin, but Dagon held her easily until she quieted.

"My intentions are good, little bird. You have to trust me, too. I've made my own vows."

She looked up angrily. "And, what vows are they?"

Dagon shook his head, his eyes like flint. "I vowed to protect you. Matrilineal rule through a priestess cult will not cut it with these bozos. We'll demonstrate co-rulership between man and woman as equal partners. As quickly as possible, we will introduce democratic principles, then step down from this fanatical throne."

Stella couldn't help but smile, as she heard the voice of Apollo in his words. "You sound like Apollo. He was the god who was twin brother to Diana or Artemis. He got tired of following his mother and sister around like a dog, so he gave birth to the sages, music, and poetry, and through them science so that the masculine would get equal time to rule with the feminine." Dagon shook his head at her change of topic, but then sharpened at her next question.

"And, how do propose finding these democratic representatives and setting up a decision making process for the group?"

"We will start with a council, then elections," Dagon said.

Stella began to smile, "What a great idea. I am so glad you're going to do this with me." She began to squeeze his arm, a wave of euphoria and relief washing through her. Dagon shrugged off her excitement with briskness, "We'll see if it was a good idea, later."

CHAPTER 29

✠

The prophecy

Stella looked at herself in the mirror, amazed at the transformation that Sarah, her handmaiden, had been able to create with her hair. It had been coiled up in an intricate twist of braids into a coronet on her head. Tendrils of her curly hair were pulled loose from the top, and then the whole creation threaded with ribbon. A filmy veil of black and gold draped down her back from the center of the braid. Her dress was a simple, pale amber shift with an overskirt of transparent chiffon that had a copper braid pattern down the front of the dress and around the hem.

The color drew attention to the red highlights in her auburn hair and her alabaster skin. The dress itself was so soft, it naturally settled on her slim hips and small breasts, emphasizing Stella's femininity, yet still appearing royal.

Stella gazed at the young girl who was helping her, her heart contracting at the air of innocent perfection on the girl's face. Sarah could not be more than 15, yet she had the silent, solemn quality of a much older woman. Her long blond hair was kept in one braid down her back, and her soft, calm voice was soothing to Stella's high-strung nerves.

"Sarah," she asked, stopping the hand putting in the final pins. "How did you end up in this place?" Sarah looked a little alarmed at being addressed with a personal question, but sat down her brush and dutifully began to answer.

"I was raised by my mother. Five years ago she joined the Fellowship after beginning a relationship with a Bio-Engineer that was a Follower and who invited her to a meeting. Two years ago, when I was thirteen, I was sent to a special girls' camp in the mountains of Vermont. We studied the teachings there, and I was baptized into the Faith. Because of the prophecy we saved our money to come here. Now, praise be to the Creator, we are seeing the Word unfold before our eyes in you my Lady."

Stella turned her head sharply at the formal tone of address. "Please, recite to me what you know of the prophecy, so that I can test your aptitude as a pupil of the Truth."

Sarah looked a little uncomfortable and stammered with a blush, "What would you have me recite, my Lady?"

Stella squeezed her hand and smiled. "Don't be nervous. I'd love to hear any of your lessons."

At this, Sarah relaxed and began to speak. "We were told of this marriage, that the bride and bridegroom to come would carry the light hidden within the stones. That our way would be protected as we walked through the second great deluge."

"And, we were told that the sacred scrolls would be placed upon the great ship of Apollo, the second Ark of Noah, a ship fashioned like the first."

As she recited Stella thought quickly. "Let's see how well you have been taught, can you recite it word for word from memory."

Sarah closed her eyes for a moment then straightened and began to speak slowly by rote. "It shall be built exceedingly tight, even that it would hold water like unto a dish, and the bottom thereof was tight like unto a dish; and the sides thereof were tight like unto a dish; and the ends thereof were peaked, and the top thereof was tight like unto a dish; and the length thereof was the length of a city, built to hold a great multitude; and the door thereof when it was shut, was tight like unto a dish. And, the people cried to the Lord, 'we have made the barge according to how thou has directed us. Yet, there is no light to steer, and no air to breathe.' "

"And, the angel said, 'The bride and groom will lead thee, the stones shall light your way and the spirit of the Lord shall become your breath.' "

Stella stopped herself from gasping at the implications of what she was hearing. "And, this ship," Stella gestured. "Have you been given the privilege of seeing it?"

"No, well yes, I've seen a picture of it," Sarah became enthusiastic and more childlike, declaring excitedly, "It's so beautiful, all silvery and shiny, immense, with no windows. It did remind me of a dish, a big, shiny, stainless steel dish."

Stella thought of what she had said and ventured another guess. "What does the prophecy say about the barge that flies?"

Sarah smiled at her, radiant now in her excitement to give the correct answer. "That now we are scattered on the hills like sheep without a shepherd, but in that day we shall fly to the stars and the light of the chosen shall guide us."

"Sarah, you have done well. Now, I must be left alone to gather myself together before the wedding ceremony. Will you be joining us there?"

Sarah looked startled. "Of course not, Lady, only the Initiated are allowed at the hieros gamos."

Stella felt a flash of alarm.

"Yes, well, run along now and keep studying as I may test you again."

As Sarah quietly left her chamber, shutting the tall doors behind her, Stella sighed, slumping in her chair. Here it was again. Another odd prophecy set in place and coming true. What was this about a flying spaceship large enough to be a Space Station, ready to be powered by the two stones. It must be an atomically powered ship, built in the last ten years, Stella thought, remembering the text that Esrom had quoted to her. This was all bigger than she had imagined.

And, there was a problem, the same problem Esrom had had.

She didn't know the formula to start fusion with the stones. The mysterious compound would be the final key to the puzzle. She had to find out what the purpose was of this exodus from earth. What was really behind the Starseed Program? There might still be time to influence the direction of the Fellowship.

In his own chambers, Dagon was uncomfortably pulling on the tights that his servant had brought him. If men were meant to wear panty hose, we would have kept it up from the middle ages forward, he complained inwardly, embarrassed that the tights showed off the muscles in his legs under the short tunic with its gold sash.

The servant carried in a large Calvarian cross on a velvet pillow and knelt down, saying "for you, my Lord." The cross was solid white gold and embedded with red diamonds. Each of the four corners were a Fleur De Leis, the ancient symbol of the Knights Templar and the Merovingian Kings.

Oh, brother, thought Dagon. This is really making me feel sick. Outwardly he graciously accepted it, slipped it over his head and took a quick look in the mirror.

It was shocking, as if he had been thrown back in time to the age of gallant knights and damsels in distress. If his brothers could only see him now, what a laugh they would have. Today was his wedding day.

It was a real marriage to a real bride. He'd be damned if he would let her get out of it later.

Dagon wondered at his vehemence. It's not like Stella had said, "no", when he asked her to marry him. She had seemed excited. But, she had never really said, "yes", either. In fact, if he remembered correctly, she had kicked him, yes, kicked him when he told her about it.

He frowned and the poor servant went a little pale. "Is something wrong, sir?" The servant asked tremulously, peering over thick spectacles, his old, wiry body fluttering in agitation.

"No, George, you've done a good job." George turned, intent on hurrying out of his master's room, when Dagon put up a hand to stop him. "George, I must ask one more thing of you." Dagon took on a formal manner to make his point.

"Please bring me a copy of the Holy Writ so that I can prepare for the ceremony."

"But, sir, only the Initiated can have copies, and then only a small, uncompleted portion of the script. Only Esrom, himself, had the whole script."

"Yes, well, Esrom is not here now." Dagon drew himself up to his full height.

"I am taking his place and I am to receive his copy of the Holy Writ. I am sure if you simply ask this of the chancellor at the headquarters, he will hurry to do my bidding."

George looked alarmed, practically squeaking with protest, "But my Lord."

"No more dallying. The wedding is coming soon. I would have it now!" Dagon commanded.

George began to hurry out of the room, looking frightened about approaching someone so important for something so important, but with no choice, but to obey.

"And, George," Dagon threw over his shoulder as he exited, "Could you also send my companions to me?"

George bowed his way out nervously and Dagon could hear the echo of his heels on the stone floor as he hurried down the long hallway.

Dagon looked around his quarters noting the opulence of the decor. A heavy four-poster bed dominated the room, draped with thick tapestry over the canopy. In a corner overstuffed chairs in brocade were placed in front of a large fireplace. The mantel of the fireplace was carved and glowed from being polished. Long maroon velvet curtains draped an entire wall of windows, all with spectacular views of the jungle forest and valley below. He took one last look at his unusual garb in the standing antique mirror that was next to a wardrobe in one corner of the room and settled into one of the chairs to wait.

Within five minutes, Mo, Jeremy, Joe and Henry were in his room, jostling him in a friendly manner dressed in long grey robes with gold tassels tied around their waists. "So, ho, boss, you decided to bite the bullet and marry her, huh?" teased Mo, his big burly arm nearly knocking Dagon over has he hit him on the back. Jeremy laughed, "And, in tights no less!"

"Guys, guys," Dagon held up his hand in mock protest. Jeremy reached into a pocket and pulled out a little box. Handing it to Dagon awkwardly.

"For you."

"Jeremy, what, another gift?" Dagon felt quickly for the leather cord Jeremy had braided for his hummingbird.

"No, um, well, not, quite," Jeremy, stammered in a halting manner, his huge head down. "It was given to me, so to speak, to, um, give to you."

Dagon sat up a little straighter, "What?"

"Well, what I mean is, the guy said, 'Before the wedding, give him this.' " Dagon looked really puzzled now.

"What guy? When did he give you this?"

Jeremy seemed shy. "Well, it was before you went to Vulcan. This blind man walked up to my hot dog stand led by a young woman and called me by name. I was surprised. He said to me, 'Jeremy, I want you to do something for me.' I just said, 'Well, okay' as he seemed like a pretty nice guy. He told me I had a friend who was going far away, to another planet, that when that friend got back he'd be in trouble and need some help. The blind guy told me to be sure and help, that it'd all turn out all right."

"Then, he said you'd be getting married. I was to give you his gift on the day of your wedding."

Dagon opened it carefully, shocked to see a curved band with two teal green stones on it.

"He said they were diamonds, but of course I didn't believe him. Who ever heard of a blue colored diamond," Jeremy dropped his head.

Dagon reached in his pocket finding Stella's ring, the ring she had dropped when she was kidnapped, and saw that when the two rings were put together they fit perfectly. Making the symbol of a triangle, the tripurna. It was as if someone had been listening in on their conversations. My god, all this had happened before they had left on their journey. It was like they were trapped in a story that had written before they became key players. This could only be a part of the odd synchronicity that had been guiding everything all along.

Jeremy was already retreating, but Dagon grabbed his collar. "Wait a minute," he growled, "Did the guy give his name?"

"Uh, no. Just seemed real old, sort of."

"Did he have dark glasses on or did you see his eyes?"

"He had dark glasses, but well I thought he was blind, he seemed to be helped along, sort of, by the gal."

"What did the girl look like?"

"Hell, I don't remember - pretty, dark hair." Jeremy seemed a little flustered now.

Dagon insisted, "Think, Jeremy, think. It could be important."

"Okay, well," Jeremy rolled his head. Then he put his head down into his hands miserably. "I can't remember."

"Okay," Dagon let him go reluctantly. Jeremy started to retreat, then stopped.

"There was one more thing, wait, oh, yeah. She had on a gray robe and a necklace shaped like a gold V in front. Pretty thing." Now, Dagon felt alarmed.

Had someone from Vulcan been here? Who knew about Stella's other ring? How would they know about the marriage before it occurred?

Dagon felt a desperate urge to talk to Stella, but knew that he couldn't now. According to custom, the bride and groom were kept separated until they met before the altar.

The waiting was killing him. Two more anxious hours. Then, he heard a discreet knock, and George stuck his head in. "The Holy Writ, sir," he said woodenly, handing over an ornate teak box quickly as if it were scalding him and scuttling away again.

"Excuse me, guys," Dagon said, leaving his men to play some table games that were set up on a heavy oak table over by the fireplace.

"I've got some reading to do." Dagon walked out on the flagstones to the patio that opened from his bedroom chambers and settled in a chair, the exotic chorus of jungle insects reminding him of how far away from home he was.

The supposed holy document was a small book, only four inches by five inches with very small print. It was organized into chapters called Scripts with numbered verses. He looked for an index. None. Then, he started scanning through the pages, looking for anything about a marriage. When he found it, he realized they were in real in trouble.

The marriage ceremony was explained in appalling detail. "And, then the prince and princess shall stand before the altar. On it shall be a mysterious book, a celestial globe, a watch, and a tube containing blood red liquid. A white serpent crawls in and out of orbits nearby. And, the initiated shall take the bride and groom to the laboratory where plants, stones and all types of matter have been distilled into their essence and placed into glasses. And, the awakened initiated shall reduce their bodies to a liquid state, allowing the sun's rays to heat this golden liquid. After the globe is cooled it shall be cut open with a diamond to reveal the egg, that great egg which has birthed the male and the female. After this, each wedding guest will have become a 'Lady or Knight of the golden stone' and will be given a message to teach mankind and they shall leave on a great ship, each ship named for the zodiac to go to share their message." Dagon blanched.

This was the story of the Alchemical Wedding, the story of Christian the seeker from the 15th Century. It was the same story as his dream. They had been chosen to act out the part of the bride and bridegroom for the Alchemical Wedding.

Dagon wished for a moment that he had his golden stone in his pocket, wondering if it could protect him from what was about to happen to them. I must see Stella before the ceremony, somehow. He looked below him, noticing that his little patio was on a cliff face. Sharp rock faces and perilous drops surrounded the whole fortress of the headquarters. It's like a prison castle. He knew that Stella's room was in a tower that was just visible from his patio. If he climbed over the edge and inched up using the vines that grew in the crevasses of rocks as ropes, he could make it. There wasn't a whole lot of time to spare as he slipped over the edge, cursing his foolishness, before he'd even started.

I'm going to break my neck, he thought, when one of the vines snapped and he swung away from the wall. Gripping another vine he started climbing again, grateful for his soft slippers, which helped him use his feet for purchase. I must look like Romeo headed for Juliet, he laughed to himself trying not to look at the steep drop below.

A few more inches, he thought, struggling to grasp the thick rock window ledge. Dagon began to pull himself up over it. He almost fell again when he caught sight of Stella's reflection in the mirror. Her beauty was stunning, all gold, soft, and curving. Then there was her face, her hair, and her eyes.

He shook himself, whispering, "Stella, help." She turned around startled, then smiled. Playfully, she waited a moment, "Did you say, help?" she teased.

Dagon frowned and she hurried over and helped him over the ledge. "Romeo, Romeo," she began as she dragged one leg over. "Oh, be still, will you?"

He growled again and when he was on the ground, he gripped her to him and gave her a long and passionate kiss.

"What was that for?" Stella looked up at him with dreamy eyes.

"To shut you up," Dagon grinned.

"What can I do to force you to keep me quiet again?"

"Look at me wrong," said Dagon, as he gently kissed her again taking more time to explore her mouth. "Mmm," he murmured as he drew away reluctantly. "We only have a few moments. We need to talk."

"Yes," Stella cleared her throat, aware of her breathlessness and hammering heart.

She began. "I've found out that they've built a large spaceship to carry the two stones that we have."

Dagon look alarmed. "A spaceship?"

"Yeah, according to my handmaiden, it's to carry them away from the second deluge, like Noah's ark."

Dagon pulled out the little book he had stuck in his pocket. "Well, I found out that this wedding is probably the beginning of the Alchemical Wedding. It was been planned long before we went to Vulcan. Perhaps we've been groomed for it since childhood." He thought of Stella's Vulcan ring, which she had been given as a teenager.

"The Alchemical Wedding?" Stella's eyes widened. Then she slapped her forehead, "Of course!"

"Of course, what?" Dagon asked miserably. "The story doesn't sound too good for some of the guests…, liquefied."

Stella giggled. "Still the story of the alchemical wedding must hold the secret about the compound, that, when combined with the golden stone, produces the power that's in them."

"Whoa there, wait a minute," Dagon said. "Now, what?"

"Well, remember what I told you about the tarot cards. They hold a formula which describes how hydrogen, a copper plate, magnetized lead, and mercury were used to create a synchron radon field that weakens the nucleus of an atom making it subject to splitting when combined with another rarefied element. If I am right in my guess, the golden stones are rarefied, and then solidified helium, which has gone through the first distillation. By shaving off a small part of them and combining them with another mysterious 'red' compound ... walla, kaboom! Power as big as the sun."

Dagon looked alarmed, his normal poise ruffled, "Unbelievable!"

"Do you think they know the answers to these questions?"

"I'm beginning to think someone knows the answers to everything and we're just pawns." Dagon told her about the old man bringing Jeremy their wedding rings before they left for Vulcan.

Stella resisted the thought. "No, they don't know the answers to everything. They believe in the stones, but don't know where they are. Their sacred texts are ancient documents and only a select few have even been allowed to read the texts. The stones existed long before they were around. This is a prophecy. This all might be a real act of the Gods. Who did you say was at that meeting you attended? Weren't some of those women Seers?"

"An act of God?" Dagon scoffed. What is God?"

"God," Stella said, "Is Everything. God is Starseed, Earth, Vulcan and Us."

"Let's get practical. What shall we do during this wedding ceremony?"

Stella thought for a moment, and then shook her head. "Say I do and kiss. It'll be our wedding."

Dagon sighed, more confused than ever, slipping back to the windows. "I'd better get back or I'll be missed."

Before he swung over the ledge, Stella reached for him.

"Dagon, I don't think I have ever told you this... But, this wedding, it's okay with me. I just..." She stopped, shrugging her shoulders, waiting for some kind of sign from him. When it didn't come, she stamped her foot.

"You're so hard to understand," she fumed turning pink with temper.

Dagon smiled, a lazy, self-satisfied smile. "You think I'm hard to understand now," he teased. "Just wait until we're married. By the way," he threw over his shoulder as he climbed over the balustrade onto the vine, "You look beautiful, sweetheart."

Then, he was gone.

CHAPTER 30

✠

The hieros gamos

Dagon and Stella were led to the wedding separately by two different groups of Starseed. The women surrounded Stella and a group of men walked with Dagon. As they entered the large room, which had been converted into a temple, Stella could not contain her gasp of surprise and pleasure. The sanctuary had been designed in the shape of the cross, with a long isle flanked by wooden pews, each ornately carved with reliefs of saints, gods and goddesses. The altar was set with sacraments including wine and bread, seven candles, incense burners, and a gold Rosicrucian cross with a rose in the center of it. White lilies and a pale pink lotus lay across a pure white cloth near a chalice of holy water. Stained glass windows depicted mythological scenes of the gods and the rulers of the twelve planets on the zodiac with a Star of David over the altar. The incense of sweet Egyptian spices, Bulgarian rose, myrrh and frankincense filled the air. A mosaic on the ceiling captured and held Stella's attention. It depicted four living beasts, each holding back a corner of the world, the sphinx, eagle, bull, and fish/man. Around them was a seven-pointed star, and seven sealed scrolls. Off to the right, appearing to be in the distance was an image of the city of Jerusalem descending out of the clouds with 12 gates. *Revelation!*

These were the last words of Astraea as she left us in the cave on Vulcan, thought Stella, I wish I had a camera to record this.

Stella also found herself longing for her mother and father. They should be here with me, Stella thought. Of course she had contacted them as soon as they reached the Beta III station. They had met her when she had landed back on Earth. It had been so good to see their happy faces and to hug her brother again. They probably didn't even know she was missing. Things were flying along at a speed beyond her control.

The congregation stood and music filled the temple. As she stood ready to walk the aisle, a young girl brought her a bouquet of lily of the valley. An old woman slipped next to her from the back of the church. From beneath her long flowing robe she brought out a necklace. It was a thin silk cord with a walnut sized, deep indigo blue stone on it.

She placed it over Stella's neck and bowed, saying quietly, "This diamond carries with it the hope of many people. It is called by the name 'Artemis,' the wild moon goddess. You know it as Vulcan's Tear. I pass it on to you now to wear as our Mother on earth. May you know the three faces of the goddess: Daughter, Mother and Crone, and carry them united within your heart to complete the lunar essence as you unite with the solar." Then, in a motherly voice she said, "You make a lovely High Priestess, dear, you'll do just fine." She patted Stella's back then disappeared back into the crowd.

Stella's heart swelled to see the pews filled with a quiet group of men and women who had been initiated into the Mystery, all with eyes closed in meditation as they listened to the ethereal music. A blue-white light hovered over each meditator's head.

Stella had learned in the last few days that the initiation ceremony was a life/death/life sacrament. Death and resurrection were enacted in a 'Christos' ceremony after the tradition of Adonis, the Lord. The bread and wine, symbols of fertility, were ritually eaten as the worshiper sacrificed them to death for life eternal. The sacrifice of the food represented the death to darkness and rebirth to light or enlightenment. At the end of the ritual initiation the new member often experienced charismatic mystical experiences of the Holy Spirit.

To Starseed, this ceremony was dedicated to the old pagan god, Dionysius. Some of the members referred to him by his more recent name, Jesus. Charismatically, they would be filled with the Holy Spirit at the Eucharistic moment, often prophesying, creating poetry or art and sharing miraculous healings after the tradition of the Apollonian worshipers of Delphi. The members voiced a secret liturgy before partaking in this alchemical initiation ceremony.

Stella noticed that the congregation was chanting, the hum filling the temple. Stella brought her attention to the front of the church. An elderly gentleman and white haired woman in dark purple and gold robes walked to the front of the chapel.

The man's voice rang out rich and deep, "Behold, I send an angel before you, to guard you on the way and to bring you to the place which I have prepared." The woman called after him, "Behold the angel, Uriel, has appeared and brings us the bride and the bridegroom, the four directions have been gathered and the end of the vision is revealed."

Then, music began to swell from the choir loft and Dagon and his best man, Jeremy, walked out to the altar. A dark crimson runner of heavy brocade was rolled slowly down the isle. Stella was nudged to begin her journey down the velvet pathway. As she walked, she caught Dagon's gaze and held it. There was no nervousness now, only an overwhelming feeling of blessing and joy. She was the symbolic bride, he the symbolic bridegroom, just like every man and woman that had taken the sacrament before them throughout history.

As she reached the front of the church, the music seemed to swell, connecting all of the listeners in bliss. "Virtus Junxit Mors Non Separabit, What Virtue Joins, Death Cannot Separate," The ancient priestess intoned as she placed Stella's hand in Dagon's hand.

A hush fell over the temple as the people all bowed their heads for a moment of silent meditation. Then, the old woman began to speak slowly and clearly, gathering power as she swept them up in the glory of the moment. "Today we join, Stella, Sister of Sekhmet and Dagon the son of Ptah, joining their solar and lunar essence in a ceremony as old as the earth. They follow Geb and Nut, Mary and Jesus, Isis and Osiris in a union intended to produce a spirit child. May the child of their union be like Nefertem, a great healer for the people, full of creative fire and divine spirit and purpose. May their union serve the world. We thank, Adonis, the Lord who has walked in darkness for all believers acting as the ritual sacrifice to bring all believers to enlightenment."

The congregation here began to chant in unison. "Their soul's song sees into all darkness, their song sees beyond all death and awakens the world to the resurrection of the Day Star. Together they birth the World-Egg, joining the earth and sky, birthing the universe. From this egg comes the phoenix, sacred peacock, the sun, our Christ who has conquered death."

The priest then spoke, his voice resonating to every corner of the temple. "Day-spring, brightness of light everlasting, sun of righteousness: enlighten them that sit in the shadow of death. May the union of the bride and groom produce the holy egg, as this man and woman co-create with gods and goddesses. Within this egg lies the sun and moon, silver and gold, the duality, which formed the earth from the waters of chaos before time had begun. Our god, you have fashioned the World-Egg with the powers that are present to transform humanity into divinity. Place us in the vessel, the aludel, purify us with the fire of this athanor, and birth within each of us immortality through the philosopher's stone."

The congregation began to recite again from a small prayer book in front of them. "The gods and goddess spring from the returning waters, walk from death to life. May your spirit soar gracefully on the whispering breeze. May your joy run strong as the deepest sea. May your souls reach out to embrace the sky. May your hearts guide you truly, drawing you as one, always and forever."

Music swelled and the congregation began to sing a simple, but profound, song. "Primeval Waters, Queen of Heaven, Daughter of the Ra, at the dawn victorious. Walk us on the path. Show us your ideal pattern, the Word designed by the Architect of the Universe. For there is one spirit, one rhythm, one moving pulse, one true son of the deep waters, one great mystery."

As the song closed, the elderly priestess stepped forward and asked Stella to repeat after her.

"I, Stella, do take thee Dagon to be my lawfully wedded husband. To have and to hold from this day forward until death do us part." She took Dagon's hand as she gave the ancient vow, focusing on the calm sense of purpose in his eyes. Then, the elderly priest did the same with Dagon. "I, Dagon, do take thee, Stella to be my lawfully wedded wife. To have and to hold from this day forward until death do us part."

Together the priest and priestess walked to the altar. The priest gripped a small, jeweled dagger representing the masculine and the priestess held a chalice representing the feminine. As the priest dipped the sword into the cup they recited together. "What God hath joined together, let no man tear asunder."

The priest and priestess then turned to the congregation, admonishing them as they chanted together. "Now is the bride and bridegroom come, the wedding has begun. All who are here have been called to become Knights and Ladies of the Golden Stone, but first you must be examined to see if you are worthy. Study your inner motives in these last days before Vulcan's Feast as we face the Great Deluge. Place the holy sign above your door that you will be passed over by the darkness and led to everlasting light."

The priestess then turned to Stella placing her hand in Dagon's. "You may give her the ring now." Jeremy reached into his pocket and pulled out the glittering diamond ring, the blue-green stones winked and beckoned in the light of the candles, which flickered on the altar. He handed the rings to Dagon.

Dagon smiled as he saw the look of astonishment, and then pleasure in Stella's eyes at having her precious lost ring returned to her. She admired the unusual design created when the other wedding band was added to it. It formed the image of the tripurna, male, female and the channel that joins them. The priestess continued, "Ashes to ashes, light to light. May the brilliance of this jewel, bridge death to life, burning unblemished within your hearts, like the rise of the phoenix."

"May this ring act as symbol for your immortal connection as bride and bridegroom. You may kiss the bride."

Dagon pulled Stella toward him, sealing their love with a gentle kiss. A choir began to sing, their voices pure in the lofty temple.

"Rise my love and come away. For low the winter is past. The rain is over and gone today the flowers appear, the time of the singing is cast. Set me as a seal upon your heart for love is as strong as death that can keep us apart. Take the life I give and make it yours, today and tomorrow, forever, yours."

The congregation stood then, their smiles joyous as Dagon and Stella walked down the aisle, arm in arm. The wedding was followed by a reception with lots of hugging and well wishing for the pair. The tables were laden with abundant and delicious foods. There was music and dancing and general merry-making until late in the night. Then, in traditional fashion, the pair was escorted to the heavy carved doors of their master bedroom suite by the crowd who clapped and yelled encouragement as Dagon swept Stella up into his arms and carried her inside. When they were alone, Stella fell back on the huge canopy bed, the silk of her simple gown curving enticingly around her body. She gazed up at Dagon, flushed with pleasure and love. "You were great!" she laughed. "And, I love the tights."

"And, you, were better," Dagon teased. "You look much better in a dress than me." Stella laughed. "I can't believe we are actually married, and boy, you couldn't get more married then that. That was an amazing ceremony, wasn't it?" Then, very seriously she looked at Dagon and her voice changed. "Is this what you want? Are we headed for a quick annulment after this is over?" She braced herself for the answer. Wanting complete honesty and not willing to let all the beautiful words from the ceremony, keep her from seeing the truth.

Dagon put his finger on her lips. "I want this, and I want you to want it too."

Stella sighed with pleasure and relief. "You're quite handsome in your tights. What's holding them up?"

Dagon reached for her. "I'll show you." and she playfully eluded him, rolling to the other side of the bed. "Did you hear the part about creating a child from this union? They all seem to be one step ahead of us on this prophecy. Do you want that to? Because if you don't, we need to be figuring out some precautions."

"I'm never letting you go, I was ready for that when we made love on Vulcan." Dagon's voice turned serious, and then he was kissing her passionately. "I mean it, I'm never letting you go, so don't even try it." In one smooth move he had slipped her dress off and Stella was lying naked beneath him.

"Now, to get these stupid panty hose off."

Neither of them noticed that someone had opened the door, then closed it quietly it after making sure the marriage was being consummated.

CHAPTER 31

✠

The golden stones

Dagon rolled over and smiled in his sleep as he remembered the passion of the night. He reached out for Stella again, wanting to pull her close as the birds began their morning cacophony outside of the tall windows. Instead, he felt an empty bed. It startled him awake.

She was sitting in front of a window on a settee reading and writing, the morning light soft on her face as she closed her eyes in meditation. Dagon groaned inwardly. How could I have stayed away from her for so long? She is so pure, so real with her feelings. He wrapped the cover around his naked body, twisting it with a knot at his waist and walked up behind her, nudging her neck.

"Come back to bed," he whispered.

Stella smiled up at him, wanting to fall back into his warm embrace, but holding herself back. "Dagon..."

Her paleness caught his attention. "What's wrong?"

She pulled him down next to her on the couch and handed him the calendar.

"I got up to do my morning meditations and found this little planetary calendar in the desk. Look at it."

Puzzled, he studied it, "I don't see anything...oh, wait." Then, he closed his eyes and ran his hand over them. "A total eclipse of the sun!"

"Look at the date, Dagon, its happening on March 30th, Earth Day, the day that Starseed has set as Vulcan's Feast Day." A feeling of dread washed over them, raising the hair on Dagon's neck.

"That's only four days from now. We need more information." Dagon pulled on his jeans and a T-shirt, thinking out loud as he ran his fingers through his hair. "I'll use my pocket computer to patch into my computer at home, then we we'll access NASA."

"What are you thinking? Oh," she turned even paler as it suddenly dawned on her, "Vulcan!"

Dagon was already at work at the desk, his fingers flying over the keys as he logged into his home computer and networked into NASA, putting in his personal password.

"Stella, do you remember the code numbers to get into Astronomical calculations for Vulcan's orbit?" she thought for a moment, then said in a rush, "A-s-t-r- o-V-u-2-2-2-.-1-1."

"Right, we're in!" Dagon quickly typed in the their codes again.

Stella was looking over his shoulder. "Oh, my god. Vulcan is going to be eclipsed also during the exact moment of the eclipse of the sun and the moon."

"Shit," Dagon ran his hands through his hair, "What do you think the probability is of that, with the speed that Vulcan travels? Do you remember anything about this? One of the teachers on Vulcan said something about this," Dagon stood up and began pacing around the room impatiently.

Stella hit the exit on his computer, and then logged into her home terminal. "I have my journal at home. I wrote everything I could remember down in it word for word. I'm in! Here it is." She was scrolling down. "This came from Astraea when we were in the cave."

She read slowly, "Vulcan will be eclipsed and the electromagnetic radiation patterns of the earth will be completely shut down when this happens."

Dagon groaned, "This means that all communication systems will be shut down. The whole power grid will go down. There won't be any electricity worldwide and it will blow the transformers providing energy to every major city. The satellites will go down, airplanes won't be able to fly, and our banking and economic system will shut down. That means no gas, no food, riots, and disaster on a huge scale. They may not be able to get those transformers up again for years. And, we are completely dependent on the power grid for national defense. He ran his fingers through his hair with frustration. Even our cold fusion transport stations will shut down because they're still dependent on electricity. How could we have not been looking at the possibility of something like this and preparing for it? This will be a natural disaster that could destroy all of humankind."

"Crap", said Stella, "And the probability of an alignment like this happening was 1 in 5,000,000. If this happened at some other time in earth's history we weren't around for it."

"Maybe the dinosaurs were," Dagon said. "A lot of the theories about the ice age are still shrouded with mystery. We don't know if we can expect earthquakes, tsunamis, total darkness, bizarre changes in temperature, hurricanes, or even volcanic activity. Besides, the earth's atmosphere is what repels all the meteorites that can get through and we are going to have geomagnetic flux if the sun is destabilized."

"Dagon, there's more." Stella kept scrolling down reading Astraea's words out loud. "There's great danger, as well as opportunity, for this is one of the places 'in-between,' in the Void where all things are possible. It is possible for your planet to align with a totally different radiation frequency, changing the vibration of the planet."

Dagon was thinking aloud. "Who do we know that is working in the Satellite program?"

"Don Cummings, he was at the NECSA meeting."

"Call him," he commanded rapidly. Stella typed the request and was surprised to get an immediate response. "We have him on-video."

"Mr. Cummings, this is Dr. Dagon Andrew, Commander of The Golden Eagle, Captain, United States Air force. I need you to coordinate all communication satellites to the orbit of Vulcan and relay back information to me as requested during the next five days."

There was a moment's pause as Cummings pushed his thick glasses up onto his nose with a shell-shocked look. The answer came back with hesitation. "What is your authorization code for this order?"

Dagon could sense the technician's resistance to do anything out of the book. "Dragon."

There was a quick response. "I'm with you, then. I'll stay available on-line or on video. Do you need to speak to anyone else in command?"

"Not yet," Dagon responded, "I'll keep you informed."

Stella looked at Dagon, amazed. "How did you know the code? He must be a member of Starseed."

"They're everywhere and the code word for those in charge of the network is 'Dragon.' "

"Dragon," Stella said out loud, "Dragon. It is sacred to the Chinese as the beginning and ending of all things. They saw a

Dragon lying across the sky in their mythology. It connects the past to the future."

She looked dazed. Numbers from the Satellites were already appearing on the screen. They showed the coordinates of the synchron belt. Dagon was writing down the numbers and making quick calculations.

"Yes, Vulcan will be eclipsed at the exact moment of total solar eclipse. Because of the Uncertainty Principle when dealing with a wave belt, we can't pinpoint it exactly, but we should be able to find a close coordinate."

"Dagon," Stella's voice was shaking with excitement, "Astraea said this could be an opportunity for our planet to align with a totally different vibrational frequency. What could she mean?"

"Perhaps, using Vulcan's radiation to project out a message to the universe," Dagon said.

"How would that align the planet to a different frequency?"

Dagon was puzzled for a moment. "I'm not sure. But, I can see how we could do it. We would use the moon. The message would go to the moon, at the precise moment of solar eclipse it would be mirrored to Vulcan then projected out into the universe using the synchron belt." He began to mutter out loud. "Solar, lunar. Solar essence, lunar essence. Vulcan as the golden center."

Stella was taking a different tact. "Perhaps, 'vibrational' means something different. Perhaps, this is more about our evolution as a species. Our biology through our body has evolved very slowly, but we have unlimited possibilities in evolving our mind or connecting to a different energy/matter connection. Look at what happened to us on Vulcan. We could create what we visualized. You heard what the computer Rudy said the other day about this being more possible on the planet Vulcan because of the synchron belt."

"Also, humans have been looking for what all the great teachers call 'enlightenment' for thousands of years. It is the goal of every sage and teacher. If you think about it 'nirvana' sounds like getting hooked up to a higher vibration of light that is connected to God or the unified field."

Dagon was frozen next to the window as he listened. The morning light bathed him and seemed to put an exclamation to Stella's theory.

She went on with her idea. "Or perhaps this is alchemical. This is a story of transmutation, not, the transformation of humans, but the rebirth of earth. The earth is the World-Egg, the philosopher's stone."

They both stopped in stunned silence, then Dagon said for them both. "Or perhaps it is all three things. They're not mutually exclusive."

The soft knock on the door startled them both. A young girl entered carrying a tray of food. "Your breakfast, Lord and Lady," she bowed, looking surprised that they were pouring over papers instead of lying in bed together."

"Thank you," Stella took the tray, which smelled delicious. She noticed her stomach was growling. Making love was good exercise.

"Can I bring you anything else?"

"No, you can go now." Dagon began, but then stopped himself. "Wait. Bring me the book of Holy Writ from the writing desk in my room. Also, I would like to have a copy of all prophetic texts sent to our library."

The maid looked alarmed. "But, My Lord, I'm not allowed to touch sacred word."

"Then, call someone who *is* allowed, and have them bring it all into the library. Stella and I will be spending the morning there."

As the door closed, Dagon walked over to Stella, pulling her close into a comforting embrace. Through the soft material of her nightdress, she could feel his hard thighs under the blanket. "My Lord? This is going to go to your head." Stella teased. "You boss people around like you were made for it."

"Well you can be my comely maiden," Dagon reached an arm behind her running his hands down her smooth back, feeling the ache in his groin. Then he groaned lifting her up to carry her to bed.

"Breakfast is served," Stella quipped.

"I have a better idea. You taste sweeter." Dagon nibbled at her shoulder pulling her tiny strap down with his teeth.

The fire of touch enveloped them, the fever pitch of their lovemaking reflecting the intensity of the morning and the coming events. Soon, they were tangled in the sheets sighing their release and moaning their pleasure. The moment devoured them stealing all of their thoughts and worries as Dagon lifted Stella and turned her beneath him.

"This is our honeymoon," Stella mused later as she ran her hand down Dagon's arm and curled her head into his chest. She was amazed at how small she felt next to his body. Their sex was consuming and a little mind blowing. Dagon was a dominating and demanding lover, lifting her bodily into new positions and filling her so completely she cried out often, overwhelmed. He pushed her to have multiple orgasms and seemed to have incredible will power and self-control over his own release. She had never seen such focused concentration. With all of his intensity directed toward her she felt like she was flying apart into fragile pieces while he was the eye of the hurricane. It was a bit frightening.

"Are you still hungry?" Dagon got the tray and brought it to the bed.

"Starved!" Stella began to dig in.

Dagon got up and headed for the shower. "We have a lot to do today. But, I'd prefer to stay in bed."

"Well I for one would be so sore tomorrow, I couldn't walk," Stella giggled.

"Did I hurt you," Dagon scanned her body for bruises, noticing the love bites on her shoulder and the rash on the side of one breast from his morning whiskers. His body tightened again with rage again seeing the bruises on Stella's jaw, ribs and throat.

"You have a four-o'clock shadow, I think it looks sexy," teased Stella.

"Well," Dagon teased back. You have a little tattoo that I think is sexy. Save me some bacon and I'll save you some hot water," Dagon headed for the shower.

Later, when they had dressed and ready to face the day, they started to focus on their problem.

"Okay, let's think. We need to come up with a plan of action." Dagon was pacing past the rows of bookshelves, occasionally stopping to twirl the globe on the stand by the thick oak table in the library attached to their suite of rooms.

"This complex is amazing," Stella said. "This building alone must cover 25 acres, and the temple another four or five. Then, there is the laboratory and the mineshaft. How did they get the money to build something like this in a remote area of South America? Starseed must have huge donors or their hand in lucrative investments."

Stella ran her hand over the thick leather cover of the priceless book that she was holding. "These are first edition copies of rare books and I know that Lawrence's library is full of them."

Stella felt a moment of discomfort as she remembered that Lawrence was dead. She had seen it happen, just before she had walked out of the woods. The memory was so tied in with her panic that Dagon might be killed that it was hard for her to think about it. It still amazed her that she had had the strength to die, rather then give up information about the golden stones. This was something she would need to spend more time reflecting on later.

Stella had explained her whole chemistry theory about the tarot cards to Dagon, but he hadn't been as convinced as she was. It would be somewhere here, in one of these alchemical books, opened, and strewn around her on the table. Then, she had an idea.

"Dagon, do you still have your dad's diary?"

"Yeah, I have it with me."

"Would you mind if I studied it for a bit?"

"Go ahead," he said, "It is in my backpack." He kept working on his computer.

Stella thumbed quickly through, just glancing at page after page of fascinating ideas and formulas until she saw it, almost toward the end of the diary, a diagram of the alchemical wedding.

Stella caught Dagon's attention and showed him the diagram. "Astraea's last words were this," she looked over at her computer at her Vulcan journals and began reading: "*The miracle that would save the earth is encoded in records from the past, records, even now, which are being misused and misconstrued. Revelation... the seven seals... the power within the four royal fixed stars and the living beasts... twelve to come... fusion of spirit and matter... ten thousand times ten thousand times brighter... Gold.*"

Now, look at this. She showed Dagon the drawing that his father had put in his diary.

"He figured out most of the formula, like I did. He has the same elements listed, describes the need to wait, and then continue the experiment with rarified elements. Look at these little squiggles over here. It is a seven-pointed star, and a twelve pointed star. Now, think about the prophecies of the Starseed sect. Did you see the painted mosaic in their temple yesterday at the wedding? It showed all of the images that Astraea mentioned, it was a representation of *Revelation*, depicted in apocalyptic detail."

"Now, listen to these lines from the prophetic texts of Starseed," she opened their book of prophecy and read:

"There shall be earthquakes and pestilence, then shall come the Bride and Groom, carrying the World-Egg, two stones to light the way through the Great Deluge. A ship, like unto a great dish, shall be built. And, it shall master the four living beasts, harnessing the power of the four royal fixed stars. And, the seven seals shall be broken. What God has sealed shall be opened."

"Then, shall darkness be upon the face of the earth and over the face of the waters and the people shall be afraid. But, the people of God will open their arms to the Judgment day and welcome the new city, the city of Jerusalem, a city of gold with 12 gates. And, the light of the firmament shall be ten thousand times ten thousand times brighter in that last day, the Day of our Lord."

"Wow, it was what Astraea was saying." Dagon looked amazed. "Let's try to decipher the code."

"Your dad already started that. Look he has a list here. '*Seven seals*' and he jots after it, '*the seven planets of our solar system visible with the naked eye, the seven chakra. Seven is a sacred number that also means awareness of truth and scholarly research.*"

"Great," said Dagon holding his finger on the sects prophesy book. Now, 'The power in the four royal fixed stars.' "

"Antares, Aldebaran, Regulus and Fomalhaut," Stella said. "The alpha stars of the four fixed constellations that Egyptians felt were the four faces of god, representing earth, air, water and fire. They were also the living beasts: Leo, the sphinx, Taurus, the bull, Scorpio, the eagle, and Aquarius, the man. To the Christians they were Matthew, Mark, Luke and John."

"Twelve to come," said Dagon amazed that Stella seemed to know these answers. Your dad has that one written here, '*Twelve disciples, twelve signs in the zodiac, 12 Helix DNA, twelve tribes of Israel. The number twelve means completion. Twelve nations.*" Stella was having fun.

"Ten thousand times ten thousand times brighter," said Dagon.

"A nuclear explosion, a super nova explosion, enlightenment? Who knows?"

"So," Dagon said, "Read the text again, adding possible meanings."

Stella did that pausing after each line of prophetic text to put in the possible interpretation. "There shall be earthquakes and pestilence, *(the eclipse).* Then, shall the come the Bride and Groom, carrying the World-Egg, two stones to light the way through the great deluge. (*You and I coming with two stones from Vulcan that may be rarefied chemicals with atomic fueling possibilities.*) A ship, like unto a great dish shall be built. (*'Like a dish' makes it sound like a communications satellite station.*) And, it shall master the four living beasts, harnessing the power of the four royal fixed stars.

(*Harnessing Air, Earth, Fire and Water is the Alchemical Elixir and the power that it creates.*) And, the seven seals shall be broken. (*All of the evolutionary steps will be taken, the seven days of the alchemical wedding will be complete*) What god has sealed shall be opened. Then, shall darkness be upon the face of the earth and over the face of the waters and the people shall be afraid. (*The eclipse of the sun, moon and Vulcan*) But, the people of god will open their arms to the Judgment day and welcome the new city, the city of Jerusalem, and a city of Gold with twelve gates. (*The 12 nations will join forces.*) And, the light of the firmament shall be ten thousand times then thousand times brighter in that last day, the day of our Lord. (*Enlightenment, some kind of spectacular light display, an explosion*)."

Stella took a sip of hot tea and rubbed her hand across her forehead. "Starseed has interpreted these texts to mean they need to build a ship to leave the planet which will be destroyed on the Judgment Day. They plan to colonize other planets using atomic fusion to create their own star. However, they have been waiting for us, the Bride and Groom to provide the prophesied stones. They are expecting the deluge, the Judgment Day, to come on March 30th, 2033," Stella said.

Dagon joined in. "Then, they must have known about the eclipse and what it might mean for the earth."

"Yes", then Stella thought of something. "Dagon, thumb through your dad's diary again and see if you find anything about an eclipse."

Dagon put his head down flipping through pages and quickly found it. "It is near the end. He has drawn Vulcan aligning with our sun and moon and noted the day of the event. He has written *catastrophe* and it says here, *relayed this to the Elders.* My dad was one of the Elders of Starseed?"

This was blowing Dagon away.

"You said when you were young you remember men in suits coming, feeling like you were in hiding. Maybe instead of Starseed, your dad was part of the global Secret Circle. He was a genius after all. He is the one that came up with cold fusion, not the Russians. Why was he spirited away to live on a farm in the middle of nowhere? He must have been in some kind of danger. There have been factions all along of people wanting knowledge so they could have power. Most likely these faction originated in Starseed with Statton's family. They could have found and killed your dad."

Dagon was looking grim, glad now that Statton was dead. "We may never know, but if that is the case the Circle has known about me since I was a little boy and may have had something to do with me ending up on Vulcan."

"Me, too," Stella said, "My grandmother was a well known Seer. I wouldn't have been surprised at all if she had some connection to the Circle in her day."

"That still doesn't explain our wedding ring," Dagon said, "Or anything that happened on Vulcan."

Stella continued, "If we're right, Starseed has misconstrued what to do about it the eclipse. They were planning to abandon the earth with only a small select group of people who can survive the disaster to populate another colony. They didn't consider realigning the earth's existing energy field and vibrational pattern."

Dagon and Stella both sighed, overwhelmed by the enormity of the situation, contemplating possible solutions in silence for a moment before Dagon nodded his head with conviction.

"We need to call an emergency meeting of the Secret Circle, Stella. There are representatives there from all of the nations, powerful heads of the government and science. There are five scientific geniuses sitting on that counsel. They are currently the only force in the world trying to unite religion and science in governmental policy. The heads of Starseed are there. We need to tell them our whole story and work out a plan of action."

"But, Lawrence Statton was in that Circle. Maybe the person who killed your dad was in that Circle," Stella said.

"Yes, and there might be other traitors to the cause, too. We'll just have to be on our guard and take our chances," Dagon replied.

Stella thought about it. "Fate is an odd thing. If it hadn't been for Lawrence kidnapping me, we'd never have ended up here."

She continued, "You're right, this is much bigger than us. It will require mobilizing a global network within days. How do we do it, call a meeting?"

"We call Lucian Westfield."

Lucian seemed to be expecting their call, because he calmly announced that an emergency meeting of the Circle had been set for tomorrow at Mount Padung, a volcanic peak located in Indonesia on the Island of Java. A Concord was picking them up, early in the morning, to whisk them there.

Lucian had sounded matter-of-fact as he made the arrangements, but Dagon still remembered his first mysterious response as he had heard their voice on the phone, "So, it has begun."

Now, all they could do was wait. They sat at the window of their bedroom watching a passing afternoon lightening and thunderstorm. The spectacular view encompassed the jagged spires of the Draesbran Mountains as well as the Rio Cochomo valley and jungle. Each rumbling crash warned about mortal weakness in the face of vast power.

After holding each other quietly they began to remember other messages they had received on Vulcan, trying to plan how they would tell their story to the Circle in the morning.

Stella recounted, "Astraea, mentioned the earth changes and said our only hope was a meeting of religion and science. She warned against the dangers of religious extremism."

"And, do you remember the very last moments when she faded out of sight? She said, 'Are you willing to walk within the bowels of the earth, to crawl on your hands and knees in the darkest pit to see the master forger at work?' Then, we saw the body of a dwarf instead who asked if we had ever seen a Dragon? He didn't seem very pleasant. I wonder what all of that meant."

"I have a feeling we are going to find out soon, Stella," Dagon reached for her hand, rubbing his fingers over the soft skin of her palm, gently fingering her wedding ring.

A look of resignation passed over his face. "We only had one day for a honeymoon. Now, we have to go save the world." He laughed at the incongruity of the thought.

Dagon reached out and pulled her in front of him so they could both see the view. Then, he leaned forward to nip her ear lobe and whispered, "We'll still have the nights."

They ordered a mid-afternoon lunch and reluctantly went back to work, recognizing they needed some answers pronto.

"Okay, here is our list of unanswered questions." Dagon started. Stella's eyes brightened, but she shook her head.

"No, first we need to figure out how the stones work. We're going to need them in the near future."

"Where's yours?"

"I hid it in a vase in my living room under some dried flowers."

Dagon shook his head with wonder, "I did the same thing, a vase in my living room,… dried flowers."

"Now, why do you suppose *this* coincidence happened?"

"Perhaps, subconsciously we were reading each other minds," Dagon offered.

He had been learning to trust his inner intuition, which seemed to be on track right now. Facing his skepticism had been his hardest and most difficult lesson.

They moved back over to the table and Dagon pulled out the Order's texts on alchemy, studying the Mutus Liber, and the reprinting of the Ripley Scroll for the first time. Then, he looked up at Stella.

"You started to tell me about all this yesterday before the wedding. How is this explained chemically?"

"Okay," Stella spoke with excitement, "We need mercury, copper, H^2O and lead. We place the H^2O in a special vessel that has a copper conduit running through it. It has a lead bottom and mercury is added from the top. The mixture is excited with heat to start an electro-magnetic field. The mercury chemically cools the helium molecules causing a warm/cool separation in the container. Electrons and photons then refract between these two layers, becoming supercharged as they begin to move at high speeds in a synchron belt around the conduit. Eventually they will emit radiation. We need to be in a quiet, safe place then we wait. Particles should spin out, bonding with other particles to form new arrays, creating a super-concentrated, unstable form of helium."

"Then, it gets dangerous. There is a second distillation of this rarefied element. Crystals of it are heated again and another chemical is added that will create an immense atomic explosion, more along the line of a super nova."

She remembered again the words of the mysterious stranger to scientist Bergier, quoting this to Dagon, "Certain geometrical arrangements of highly purified substances are sufficient to release atomic forces."

Dagon looked at her amazed and Stella tried to tell him how she had just followed the sequence within the tarot cards that had been left on her doorstep to figure out the formula.

Stella continued, "My guess is that the stones themselves are a form of rarefied helium that has already gone through the first distillation described above."

"Then, how did the stones get to Vulcan? And, who left the tarot cards on your doorstep?"

"Well, I think that Lawrence left the cards. He had been searching for the answer to this and had gotten part of the way to a solution. We know that he had been using Rudy and NECSA to run computer data. The stones on Vulcan? That is a great mystery. My first guess would be Lucian, but even he seems somewhat in the dark, as if only he gets information just prior to events."

"Now, our task is to discover the solution required to split already unstable atoms," Dagon concluded.

"I think the formula is hidden in the story of the alchemical wedding," Stella said.

Dagon opened to the chapter on the Alchemical Wedding, "It says here there are a globe, a watch and a tube containing a red compound, also a white serpent crawling in and out of orbits nearby, then some kind of plant essence." Stella read out loud.

Dagon thought about it for a while. I think that there is some sort of incubation or exact timing required for this. The globe is where the chemist combines elements, the watch times the process. The red compound is the missing element we're searching for. The serpent sounds like an electric current, as the serpent was always the symbol for electrical kundalini. The plant extract may be the way for making the red compound."

Stella started guessing. "Red, perhaps arsenic or Laurel, the red bark of tree or the juice of some berry. Some form of sulfur, possibly. Those were materials the alchemists of old used."

Dagon jumped in. "Or perhaps red light, a photon vibrating at a specific harmonic or frequency to split apart the already weakened nucleus. Or, if not a photon perhaps we are actually working on the level of the quantum chromo dynamics, quarks, antiquarks and gluons. Gluons could be exchanging gluons according to the Color Theory. It is the 'color' force or charge that holds the nucleus together. It is the strong force. In high-energy collisions, like cosmic ray experiments, these forces are weakened. A synchron belt would create this kind of environment."

Stella looked alarmed. "What compound would already be unbalanced or weighted quantum chromo dynamically toward that type of volatile instability?"

Dagon looked up, his eyes shining. "Red acid and we are sitting on a field of tailing ponds, waste products from gold mines."

Suddenly, Stella remembered the Ripley Scroll from Lawrence's library.

"Of course, the Dragon, the Red Dragon. The Latin inscription read, 'the stone can only be dissolved with the blood of the dragon.' 'Dragon' is the common alchemical symbol for 'aqua fortis,' or 'nitric acid.' "

Stella looked at Dagon with alarm. "I hope you're not thinking what I'm thinking."

He nodded his head. "Something's up. Why is this Order located over a gold mine, and what was Lawrence alluding to about the mine when he kidnapped you? We need to go down into the mine shaft and explore."

"I can't do it, Dagon," her fear rose up threatening to overwhelm her. "You know I have claustrophobia. I was blindfolded, drugged and dragged into that mine. I can't face that elevator again. Besides, I didn't tell you, but I'm sure that Lawrence was the Judge that accused me and had me drowned for witchcraft in a past life."

"You don't need to go down. I can do it myself."

Stella seemed to straighten up with resolve. "Astraea said, we needed to go into the bowels of the earth to see the master forger at work. Vulcan was the Master Alchemist. There is no way you're going without me!"

Stella gulped, her determination fading for a moment, noticing that her knees were shaking. "Still, this feels like the ultimate test."

Her words brought a smile to Dagon who suddenly brightened. "You're tested so that you'll receive the Golden Fleece, symbolic of Kundalini, the Dragon."

Stella looked up, "What?" Dagon began to recite. "Day one the guests of the wedding went through turbulence, that was your kidnapping and our fight to save you. Day two was the invitation to the wedding, the ceremony that we experienced yesterday. Day three the participants were tested and when they passed the test they received the Golden Fleece."

He continued, "We're on day three with only four more days to go, literally, to the eclipse. The seven days are playing themselves out again! We are living out the story of the Alchemical Wedding, just like we did in those seven days that we were on the planet Vulcan."

"Oh, my god" Stella said. "It's like something else is directing the whole show. You know, I've been thinking about more of the symbolism in this story."

Dagon turned to listen.

"For instance the golden fleece. The story of the golden fleece tells of how two small children seek safety by getting on the back of a ram which carries one of the children to a distant shore. The ram, a symbol of Mars, the Vulcan planetary ruler, is sacrificed in a sacred grove of Aries. Its fleece becomes the Golden Fleece, symbol of immortality. A Dragon guards the fleece because it is the secret to the mysteries of the unseen world. The eclipse will be happening when the sun and moon are in Aires, the sign of the Ram."

Stella continued, "Then, there is the cosmic egg. The death of the King and Queen who allowed their bodies to be liquefied and transmuted by the fire of the sun is what gives birth to the cosmic egg."

Dagon joined in, "That means some ascended master must sacrifice him or herself for the safety of the earth, the World Egg."

"There's more," continued Stella. "The great cosmic egg is the earth herself. In the story it says she will give birth to an ugly bird that is fed on blood. After each feeding its feathers change color until it's varicolored and very beautiful. Perhaps, this is the process of our evolution should we survive this eclipse. The earth will be vulcanized. Vulcanization is a process where sulfur and intense heat are applied to a substance to increase its elasticity and durability. The Eagle is the hermetic symbol of sulfur and signifies the mysterious fire of Scorpio or Pluto. In the east, fire was regarded as an all-powerful purifying agent which could destroy material, release the bonds of matter and create a purity of nature that could liken us to gods. Thus the eagle became the firebird or phoenix, undergoing a baptism of fire only to rise from the ashes. It is as if we are entering the crematorium to go back to spirit so that we can be born again."

"What do you think is meant by 'feeding on blood, in order to become beautiful?' asked Dagon with humor. He knew Stella would have the answer. She was like a walking encyclopedia.

"A close relative to the eagle, the vulture, symbolizes that form of divine power which by feeding on blood, disposes of refuse and other matter dangerous to life and health of humanity, cleansing and purifying the lower spheres. The Greeks and Romans believed all vultures to be female embodiments of the Mother's spirit. The vulture-headed mother of all things was Isis and the word 'mother' was written in hieroglyphics with the sign of the vulture.[77] Vulture and Vulcan contain the same essence. Both the eagle and vulture, Ptah and Sekhmet, Order and Chaos are totems of Vulcan."

"Well," continued Stella with a shudder, "I'm going to have to draw on the power of vulture to face death and transform. I can't believe that I have to go back down into the mine of all places to get the red compound that we need. I died down there!" Stella wailed.

"Can you do this? You don't really need to." Dagon looked concerned as he took in Stella's pale face and trembling lips.

"I need to. I'm sure of this somehow. It will take both of us to figure this out and put all the pieces together, each step of the way. I don't want to be afraid of death again. I've already died, seen the white light, and been told I have to go back."

Dagon shuddered. He had come so close to losing her down in that mine. But, there didn't seem any other way. It was the act of being together, that was bringing them all the answers, and literally everything stood in the balance.

Stella spent the next hour resting with Dagon. When he left to prepare for their descent, she began yoga and to practice meditation. First, she did a series of steps she had learned from Ramana Maharshi. Inhale and let go of the I or the ego, asking 'Who am I?' Exhale and remember you are not your mind, emotions or body. You are Existence, Consciousness, and Bliss

She was focusing on deep breathing when Dagon came back into the room. "It's set. Jeremy will go with us. We're leaving in one-half hour and will be carrying lights and ropes in case we need them. Mo and Joe will be at the top of the shaft, making sure that nobody disturbs us. It'll be perfectly safe."

Stella gulped again. She was in her most relaxed state and she could still feel the panic starting to surface.

"Okey, dokey." She dressed in warm, light-colored clothes and a pair of rugged shoes. Her hair was tied back in a tight ponytail to keep it out of her eyes. She knew that she looked like a child, so she shook it out and threw the wild mane down her back again, thinking, 'I might as well look great if I'm going to die.' Dagon just raised his eyebrows, pulling her closer to him as they made their way to the outer buildings that housed the elevator shaft.

Stella stepped in, then panicked and stepped out quickly again. "I don't think I can do it." Tears were trembling on her lids and her hands were shaking uncontrollably.

"It was terrible what happened to you, Stella, and a good thing that karma wiped that scum, Lawrence, off the face of the earth. When it came down to the wire you had the courage to die for what you believe. You can go down into this underworld and face this too. But, if you decide not to, that's fine with me. You can stay here."

Knowing the choice was completely hers seemed to help. A determined intent took hold of her; Stella set her inner will under firm control.

Of course, I can. The ride down the antiquated, creaking elevator took over forty-five minutes to drop the 29,000 feet. Stella prayed the whole time and gradually found that she was able to stay more in the moment with her breath. Her body was relaxing, bit-by-bit.

Dagon's arm stayed warm and solid around her shoulder. The door opened up to a large room with two doors. One door led to the room where Stella had been kept prisoner.

"We will need to follow one of the tunnels in order to reach the underground tailing ponds. Can you handle this Stella?"

Her head was nodding. In fact she was looking rather excited. "Sure." The tunnel was much smaller. Dagon found himself bending down slightly, uncomfortable from the beginning.

It was almost impossible for Jeremy to fit his huge, burly frame around some of the tighter corners. Dagon reluctantly told him to go back to the entrance of the tunnel and wait for them there. He and Stella proceeded on alone. They had turned on the lights from above, but found that they were often just small bulbs hanging from the ceiling. Half of them were burned out. Dagon looked at his map of the mine again and motioned Stella to turn right at the next junction, and to turn on her head lamp. Part of the wall of the tunnel seemed to have caved in there.

"Stella, according to the map there is a room only a few feet beyond this cave-in. I can see a way through, if we crawl. Can you do it?"

"There is no way, I'm going to miss it this time." She was thinking about that pool on Vulcan. The assertive reply came off the top of her head.

My god, thought Stella, What kind of test is this? Astraea asked if we were willing to crawl on our bellies.

Stella lay down on the cold dirt floor and began to crawl on her belly through the small opening, pushing her pack ahead of her so that she could pull her trunk through. One arm felt pinned at her side. She struggled to reach it forward, and then wiggled forward with both arms over her head. I can't breath, she panicked. I can't breath, she thought. How can Dagon possibly make it through, if I barely fit?

Yes, you can, another inner voice fought the dark, and the feeling of terror. *You can.*

Stella wiggled through carefully taking special precautions to keep her oxygen mask firmly fixed in place. What she saw on the other side made her want to laugh hysterically. There was a pond in front of them, bubbling and registering the strong stench of poison. The color of the water was a dark maroon red. Behind the pond a wide vein of gold could be seen trailing across the tall rock wall looking like a Dragon hovering above the pond.

Dagon was struggling to get through the opening. After a series of curses, he finally let out an exclamation.

"I can't get through this. My guess is that nobody can right now because of this rockslide. You might be the only one who would have made it."

"I'll photograph this for you," Stella said, "You'll never believe what I'm seeing."

"How could they leave this mine unworked?" Stella voiced her thoughts out loud into her microphone in her oxygen mask.

"They didn't," Dagon voice sounded muffled through the wall of rock. "This work is fresh. Someone has been working here in the mine and uncovered this gold vein recently. This must be how their funding this space colony."

"Lawrence?" Stella said putting on gloves, carefully taking a test tube flask out of her pack.

"Lawrence and a whole lot of other people," Dagon sounded pissed off and unhappy. "Are you okay in there?"

"You should see the size of this room. There is an amazing vein of gold on the rock wall that looks just like a dragon hovering over a red pond. The pool registers extremely poisonous on my equipment. This *must* be the work of Interspace Research, they don't care anything about the environment. They should have cleaned these tailings up!"

"Be careful, Stella."

"Hey, Dagon, I'm a scientist, remember. I take samples all the time. Just a second." She gingerly squatted down, being careful not to let any part of her clothing touch the residue around the pond, and checked the ground for stability. Then, carefully filled the flask and sealed its top, stowing it in a padded case she was carrying in her small pack.

She turned her head, adjusting her oxygen mask again, and checked the floor carefully with her headlamp before standing up and stepping back.

"Interspace," she heard Dagon mutter. "They're the most likely candidates. I never liked Emilio Fauntis, the head of it. They've probably been using Starseed members or natives as workers."

Stella looked back at the tiny opening they had wiggled through. "Do you suppose Jeremy and Mo are okay? What if someone finds out we're down here?"

"I didn't tell anyone. I think we're safe. Come on hurry now. I'm not going to feel better until you're out of there."

Stella looked around her again, noticing how her voice echoed on the cave walls.

"Dagon, I know we're miles below the Draesbran, but this looks like the pond in the picture that we took on Vulcan. We're being given a message!"

"How could that be possible?" Dagon voiced the question on both of their minds.

"Prophecy! Someone who knew the future came to warn us, to warn everyone on earth. They, whoever they are, have the ability to translocate and send messages in dreams."

"Is this where we come to do the final experiment?" Dagon asked with doubt in his voice. "I can't even get into the room!"

Stella giggled at the oddity of hearing Dagon's disembodied voice coming out of her headset. She turned her head so her light would catch the huge body and coiling tail of the thick vein of gold in the rock that appeared like a dragon. She snapped some photos setting her camera on panoramic view and then started a video, turning slowly to catch everything.

"Not the final experiment. Remember my dream poem of the Dragon. A lady in gray rescued me and brought me out of the darkness of the underground gave. No, this is where we descend to pit of death, then rise to the surface like the phoenix."

CHAPTER 32

✠

Gathering forces

The next morning they rose while it was still dark to go to the airfield where a Concord was waiting to jet them to Indonesia. Dagon had been amazed at her photos and video. They were hyper aware of the flask of red acid in their bags.

Mo, Joe, and Henry were looking forlorn at being left behind. They stood huddled together, their skin covered with a fine layer of sweat from the morning's humidity.

Dagon comforted them. "You guys will be joining us on the day after tomorrow. It's important that you go back to Washington on the next transport and retrieve the stones from our apartments. These stones are Top Secret. Nobody must know anything about them. You'll have to be careful. Stella and I have probably both been reported as missing persons by now. The police may be watching our apartments or realize there has been foul play, since Statton's place was broken into."

"There are also others who would like to get ahold of those stones. You must guard them with your lives. They are very important. Can we depend on you?"

At this the three guys seemed to brighten. "Sure boss, no problem." Mo threw out his chest, limping painfully toward Dagon.

Dagon said a silent prayer and shook his hand warmly before turning to walk up the steps into the plane. I hope nothing happens to these good fellows.

Jeremy was coming with them and was struggling to fit his large frame into one of the seats. Dagon stowed their overhead luggage, settling to wait for the last call before take off.

The pilot came onto the speakerphone, his voice crisp and efficient saying they were waiting for another passenger who would be traveling to the meeting with them. Curiosity was satisfied when they saw the old 'mother' who had given Stella her necklace during the wedding ceremony being helped aboard. Stella reached beneath her jacket and fingered the large indigo blue stone that was hanging there.

Stella smiled, encouraging her to sit in the seat beside her. "What's your name?" was her first question when they were airborne. "Nadria," the old woman said simply. She wasn't volunteering any information.

Stella pressed on, "How is it that you joined Starseed?" The old woman looked surprised by the question. "I am not a member of this Order, however, I have been watching over them for years. They are like children without a mother."

Stella lifted her eyebrows. "What, aren't you their priestess?"

"No, I have been simply an old crone among them."

"Then, how did you get a stone like this? This is obviously priceless."

"I've had it for a long time," Nadria said guardedly, not volunteering any extra information. Then she smiled slightly. "I see you recognize the power of diamond for the crown chakra and indigo to open the third eye. Let's just say that 'What is lost is found.' You will find out soon enough, relax and enjoy the flight."

Stella felt a little startled by that response, but she held her peace and let the old woman sleep. They arrived at a Javanese airfield 47 minutes later and stepped out to warm balmy weather.

Stella shrugged off her white jacket, putting it over her arm. She reached for Dagon's arm and walked with him down the dirt airfield noticing that Jeremy was practically carrying Nadria, a loving look on his face as he helped her get into a waiting car.

"Dagon, this old woman is very mysterious. She would only tell me that her name is Nadria."

Dagon was muttering to himself, his mind on other things. The plane had circled over a beautiful string of tropical islands, coral reefs painting the sea jade. It was like stepping back in time. Nothing had changed here for thirty years. The airfield was next to a rutted road, which ran through a row of village homes, built on shaky wooden stilts. Large colorful flowers and tall exotic weeds flanked the sides of the road. A beat up jeep picked them up and began bumping up the road along the curving bay, and then through green hills, which encircled a volcano, veiled by clouds. The driver indicated that the volcanic mountain was named Pele. The primitive road passed through villages, each with a straggle of stalls and colorful markets. Native women unloaded their bamboo packs spreading out green and red-skinned bananas, wild honey, brown 'hill rice,' and pineapples. As the road continued to wind up through the lowland they could see orchids and magnificent iridescent green and purple butterflies. The noisy laughing of birds sounded through rhododendron forests, where festoons of moss dripped from trees.

An hour later they were welcomed by a group of people at the home of Lucian, midway up the mountain. The rock and wood home was a wonderful hodgepodge of oddly shaped rooms, organized at different levels up the slope. Lucian gave them each a warm greeting and immediately they ascended a winding staircase to a large room on an upper level with a huge oval table in it. The windows looked out over forest-clad ridges revealing a lovely waterfall and natural hot spring that would have otherwise been hidden by the thick undergrowth.

Stella looked at the group of people gathered for this meeting. There were forty-four people in the large room. Some of them looked very wise and aged, like Nadria, others were brilliant young scientists and thinkers. Lucian stood.

"I call a meeting of the Secret Circle of the Twelve United Nations. Represented in this room are the heads of all of the nations. We have met to respond to a universal global emergency."

Then, he introduced 'Dr. Stella and Dagon Andrew,' acknowledging their marriage in that simple statement and giving them the floor. Stella and Dagon took their time to tell the whole story. They recounted their experiences on Vulcan and the messages they had been given. The room was tense with expectation as the story unfolded. They recounted their experiences on earth starting, with NECSA, the betrayal of Lawrence, the prophecies of Starseed, the impending disaster awaiting earth through this eclipse and finally their plan for completing the alchemical transmutation by attempting to alter the effect of the eclipse by replacing the sun with a huge explosion set off in space. This explosion would coincide with a radio frequency sent out from earth into the galaxy. All of this was a plan to avert a disaster of immense proportion. They stated that they hoped that this would be a step in the evolution of man's consciousness as well as a way to save the earth from annihilation.

Stunned silence greeted them, and then the room seemed to erupt in confusion.

Lucian held up his hand, calling for order. "We will start with open discussion from one speaker at a time." Dagon asked the first question.

"I would be interested in hearing any thoughts on why it might be important to use Vulcan's synchron radio power to change earth frequencies."

A famous physicist, Bernard VanHauser stood up. "The question to me is really about stepping up evolution. Evolution of the species has been occurring more rapidly than can be explained by Darwin's theories of evolution. My hypothesis is that the connecting fields between organisms are real structures, which holographically encode information that can be passed from organism to organism. This field functions as an encoder of order, but can also cut across space and time, allowing connections to ancestral organisms, current species or extra-terrestrial organisms within the universe.[79] One way to make these connections in that field is through the use of sonics or sounds. In my work with sound, I have discovered that the earth and each planet in our solar system resonates at a specific pitch, but that some tones, specifically those that vibrate at 1,111 megahertz per second and 1,212 megahertz per second push forward evolutionary timing. Experiments with crystals and crystal growing showed that the 1,111 frequencies doubled the speed of growth."

Stella asked, "But, why this day, March 30, 2033? What do we know about eclipses? Has an eclipse of Vulcan ever happened before? What happened then?"

A South American political leader took the floor. "The year 2012 in Mayan prophecy was the end of a great age and the beginning of a new age. The Mayans had information that our earth would align with the galactic center, a cycle completed every 26,000 years. They feared then that great solar storms would interrupt the sun's electromagnetics to earth. This, of course, did happen, creating earthquakes and climate change. It was minor, compared to what you are describing regarding Vulcan and the sun, but it ushered in The Golden Age that we live in. This is also called the Age of the Hummingbird. It is of a higher resonance of energy then we experienced in the past. According to prophecy the earth must either align to this new frequency or be destroyed."

A regal looking woman stood up to support this idea. "As an astrologer I can confirm that these realignments have been occurring periodically in earth's history. For example at Harmonic Convergence in 1987, during the 11:11 Doorway Opening in 1992 and finally at the Final Awakening of the goddess from 8/26/97- 9/29/99. At each event it has required that mass global consciousness be mobilized. In the year 2012 this required the Oneness Movement, which brought the awakening of 70,000 people to higher consciousness so that the remaining population would automatically be elevated. If enough people are thinking the same thoughts it changes the vibration of the earth and accelerates evolution."

Lucian answered the last part of the question. Speaking carefully and slowly. "I was present at the last partial eclipse of Vulcan by its moon Apollex. It occurred on May 19, 1780. At mid-day there was near total darkness throughout much of New England. Candles were lit, fowls went to roost and many-feared 'Doomsday' had arrived. At New Haven, Connecticut, it was recorded in the minutes of a town council meeting. There was no scientifically verifiable reason found for this widespread phenomenon. Another partial eclipse of Vulcan coincided in 1942 with the beginning of World War II. Within days troops had been mobilized and the world experienced the Holocaust. The atomic bomb was used in warfare against Japan and threatened global destruction. My response to the crisis was to form this Secret Circle, a private United Nations to bring spiritual reasoning into our global decision-making. So, you see, the seed reason for all of us being here today was a minor, partial eclipse of Vulcan."

A well-known social psychologist, Henrietta Harmon, took the floor. "It is known that during an eclipse the electromagnetic frequencies to the earth are shut down. Because we are composed mainly of water, human's experience emotional trauma and are likely to resort to childlike, uncontrolled behaviors. I predict chaos and war, or worse, genocide, if the human consciousness is not rechanneled into the Higher Self." A couple of other psychologists in the room nodded their heads in agreement.

Someone addressed a question to the scientists in the room. "How could this communication from earth to Vulcan, then out to the solar system be possible? I don't understand the mechanics of what Dagon is proposing?"

Dr. Thomas, the world's greatest nuclear physicist stood up his face alight with excitement. "Atoms around us both absorb and emit radiation. Under ordinary conditions, most materials absorb much of the energy falling upon them since most of their atoms operate at lower energy levels than the incoming radiation. Vibrating atoms and molecules interact with one another in complex energy transformations. In this instance we will be increasing radiation as well as projecting those atoms in a laser stream. On a small scale the technology of a laser is simply to make light energy work together. This is first done by bringing all of the atoms to the same low energy state and the 'pumping' them up by introducing electromagnetic energy into the system. The wave is in a container that bounces the energy back and forth to excite it to further growth. By the time the beam is emitted from the laser, it has grown into a light intense enough cut through steel.[81] In this case, you have to imagine the amplification of the laser growing. We send a message from earth on a small wave, but Vulcan itself because of its position within the synchron belt, is already functioning as a huge laser. It is emitting radiation out into the farthest reaches of the Universe, functioning like antennae on a radio station. As that this stepped up, the frequency vibrates in all directions, the whole universe is affected."[80]

Another older East Indian man, dressed in the traditional garb of a Yogi, stood up to speak. "Based on what we have learned about the human energy field, humans also act as a type of laser emitter. We have the same ability to harness Chi to create more light or power in the physical body. The energy is 'pumped up' during meditation, and then can be projected out. This is a form of physical alchemy, which requires the uniting of masculine and feminine energies to transmute it to light. Enlightened Yogi's learn to increase their etheric power by becoming superconductors for high voltage electrical currents called Kundalini. As we learn to raise Kundalini we also stimulate the cerebral cortex, creating over twice the brainpower for new cognitions, inventions, and discovery. It is through Kundalini rising through all of the chakras, and then going down again that enlightenment occurs. In a state of enlightenment the seeker has transcended death. He or she has full mastery over physical matter. We are in fact connected to God. Everything is One. In that connection we change the world."[81]

"In this instance when we focus through mass human consciousness, we will be using our bodies as a laser." Dr. Dennis Brach broke in looking grave. "However, We have some problems. There is more to it. Vulcan acts to maintain galactic polarization between the earth and sun. During the eclipse we are facing danger when this function is interrupted."

"What is Galactic polarization?" someone asked. Dr. Brach looked around and cleared his throat, "I'll try to keep it simple."

"In theory, Vulcan is a magnet that stabilizes the life force of our sun and keeps our earth in orbit. It is electromagnetic." A few of the people in the room were looking puzzled so he began to expound on his simple explanation. "First, magnetism is a science which studies the attraction principle between two objects. Magnets create energy through the bi-polar pull of positive and negative charges.[82] Second, electromagnetism means harnessing the power within the magnetic field within a closed loop which harnesses the 'driving force' of the magnet in its bi-polar pull.[58a] The principle of magnetism is that duality or opposites form energy forces fields. These fields exist within a unified field where movement, attraction, and repulsion become the building blocks of creative initiating energy."

"The electromagnetic pull of Vulcan is key to the life of our sun and in turn the earth. In our solar system this planet fulfills the role of galactic polarization. It effectively acts as a magnetic handle to keep our sun in its position in the universe." Everyone looked up expectantly, waiting for his conclusion. "I would hypothesis that without this magnetic pull, the sun would shift on the polar axis, changing its current alignment with the earth. It could be the death of life as we know it."

The other scientists were nodding their heads in agreement and an oppressive silence had settled over the room.

Someone piped up, "What do you propose to counteract this?" Dr. Brach looked down at his hands, "An atomic explosion in space big enough to replace Vulcan during the critical moment of the total eclipse. I think that Dagon and Stella may have been led to the answer."

Suddenly, everyone was talking at once and Lucian put up his hand to stop the uproar. "I propose that the scientists and defense strategists among us confer with each other for two hours and come back to this room with their joint theories and proposals. All spiritual teachers, psychologists and world leaders will meet in the round room next door. Please assign someone in each of your groups to present a summary of your conclusions to the whole group. We will want a meeting of the religious and the scientific groups when we are through. I will meet with Dagon and Stella alone."

After the room had cleared, Lucian sat down with a sigh and motioned for Dagon and Stella to join him. "Would you like some tea?" he offered. They gladly accepted, exhausted from their trip and their part in the meeting. They sat in companionable silence for a moment before Lucian addressed them.

"So, what have you decided you know about the philosopher's stone?" Lucian asked. Stella recounted their theory that the stone was actually rarefied helium, which would split when put in contact with the right compounds.

Lucian nodded his head. "You have part of it, but not, the timing and how the actual experiment works."

Stella looked up excited, "Do you know?"

"Yes, I do. Remember, my name is actually Compte de Saint-Germaine. I have had many names throughout history and am very familiar with the stones as I have had one in my possession for thousands of years."

Dagon felt his skepticism rising, but pushed it back. Now, wasn't the time to give in to doubt, not, after everything that had happened to him. Lucian smiled at him as if he understood what he was thinking, but went on.

"I would like to call in Nadria to meet with us about this subject," she went out of the room and came back in with her. As Nadria graciously took her seat, Dagon and Stella both found themselves looking from one to the other. They seemed like a matched pair, a King and Queen, both about the same age and both radiating incredible wisdom.

Lucian went to a safe nearby and opened it, bringing out an ancient handwritten manuscript. "We are the only two people on earth who know of this journal. In it you will find the exact requirements needed to perform the alchemical experiment. It requires careful timing, the use of the proper vessel or container, the essence of certain plants, which I will teach you about tomorrow, and an electrical current. The experiment can only be done by a man and a woman together, for certain reasons that are specified in the text. I suggest you both read it carefully this evening. I would recommend that you keep these stones a secret. Through out history there has always been someone trying to misuse their power."

He reached for Nadria's hand. "We started our journey thousands of years ago with our first experiment. Through the centuries we have learned many secrets about how to transmute matter to create spirit and how to use spirit to create matter." Stella found herself gripping her necklace.

"We have learned all that life can offer. However, we are now ready to go on an extended vacation. We would like to turn our jobs over to both of you."

Nadria smiled at Lucian, and he patted her hand. Stella could see the love shine between them.

"Are up to the task?"

Dagon was looking doubtful. "Exactly what is the 'task'?"

"If the earth survives this possible apocalypse, mankind will have entered fully into the Golden Age of Magic. There are already many enlightened beings on the planet. They will be able to manifest the new earth paradigm. Soon, there will be no need for this Secret Circle. Your jobs will be easy. In the interim someone must call meetings of the Circle as needed to work out global issues as they arise."

"You will be able to live your own lives and can choose whether or not you will use the stones to create immortality for yourselves. It is your choice."

Lucian went on, "If you are willing, we will show you how to distill the plant essences to create the necessary elixirs and explain what you must do from there."

"Let me stress that using the stone is the only way to produce enough atomic power to keep the sun from shifting on her axis during the eclipse of Vulcan. You are the only people who have stones in your possession at this time. I must also warn you that they cannot be used by anybody, but you. The stones will not respond to will directed from anyone, but their Spiritual Masters."

Dagon and Stella looked stunned. "Why did you choose us?"

Nadria spoke up for the first time. "We didn't. You chose us, ages ago. You are both from Vulcan originally and it was your fate to return. Nothing could have stopped that journey, but your own choices. I have never been to Vulcan. What you saw there must have come from your own ancestral memories or from some other Source. Time is circular, not, linear. You had to have known long ago that this day was coming."

An hour later, the meeting reconvened with everybody looking much more calm. It was obvious each group had reached some decisions.

The scientists and strategists went first, with General Chapman as their spokesperson. "First, we all concur, after looking at the calculations for the orbits and our studies on the synchron belt and galactic polarization that there will be an eclipse of Vulcan at exactly 1:01.11 am, USZ6, Javanese time, two days from now, March 31, 2033, and at 1:01.11 pm EST on March 30, 3033 in Washington D.C., their time zones being 12 hours apart. The result of this eclipse could mean possible death for planet earth."

"We are suggesting use of atomic power to rectify this situation. We also agree that Vulcan can act as a radio center to sonically realign the frequencies of earth, speeding up evolution on earth as well as sending a strong signal out into the universe. A search was done to examine how a laser could be bounced off of the moon to Vulcan. We have identified the procedures necessary to accomplish this task and assigned technicians and a satellite system for this purpose."

"To date, we do not see that there are enough atomic reserves on earth to create an explosion of the magnitude necessary to keep the sun on track or even see how we can calculate the intensity of the blast needed to achieve this stabilization. Even with our cold fusion supplies, we are short on needed fuel and time to develop it. However, we are still searching for an answer to this problem and have put a team of nuclear physicists on it."

"We have reserved the ship, 'Red Dragonfly,' from Starseed which is nearby on Thuban Island, and its launch site, to carry the explosives into space. This ship can serve two purposes. First it was built to carry explosives. Secondly, it is built in a 'dish-like' shape, perfect for functioning as a satellite to reflect the laser as it bounces off the moon to Vulcan."

"It can be manned from flight computers on earth and we have designated that Captain Dagon Andrew shall be Mission Coordinator of the operation with myself as Site Commander. We have titled the mission, Operation Dragon."

"The command center shall be Thuban Island, however, everything will also be monitored from the NASA Center in Washington, D.C. We have been given the funds from NASA and Interspace Research/Starseed to complete the project." General Chapman sat down and looked around him to see the reaction in the group. Everyone was calmly accepting his propositions.

Then, a spokesperson for the spiritual group stood up. "We concur that through this event earth is stepping up vibrations because of our full entrance into the Golden Age predicted by the Mayans and the Vedas. We concur that Vulcan was also the god, Ptah, the master masonic or builder. As in ancient Egypt, matter was created through the sacred 'Word' originally or through 'sound' or sonics. Because of this we support using sonic frequencies during the eclipse. We feel, however, stepped up evolution must occur through humankind as well. To successfully complete this we are activating the entire Golden Network to create a rise a group mass consciousness."

"On the exact moment of the eclipse, we are requesting worldwide prayer and meditation. Each head of the twelve nations has agreed to activate the Golden Network in his country. We have also noted that March 30th is Earth Day, and that it falls on a Saturday. It will be a day of picnics, environmental programs, concerts, Global Feast Day, and celebration of cultural and biological diversity. This year it is also 'Just Pray' day, a worldwide weekend which calls churches throughout the world to prayer. Those who are not on the network will still be creating good intention during the eclipse."

"After studying the prophecies of both the Christian Church and the Starseed Order, we believe that the seven seals are a reference to the seven chakra centers or vortexes of energy on the earth's surface. To that end, we have sent spiritual adepts to pray, chant, and tone at each of those sacred sites on earth. They will be arriving there tomorrow for a 33 hour vigil. This will also amplify the harmonic or frequency during the eclipse."

"Finally, we have run the astrology charts for the event and found them significant. During this moment five points of the chart are 00, zero degrees, the earth is balanced between the Four Royal Fixed Signs, and the exact moment of the Winter and Summer Solstice. This creates a doorway opening to other dimensions and a channel for spirit to manifest into matter. Further, there is a grand square, and Chiron squares Pluto indicating a time of powerful transmutation and healing." The chart for Thuban Island, shows a grand trine is present with Uranus/Saturn, the north node of the moon and Pluto/Jupiter at the exact moment of the eclipse. We are very optimistic that the operation will be successful. It is also significant that the solar eclipse will be conjunct the Andromeda M31 Galaxy. We feel that the event will connect our planet eventually with other beings from this Galaxy. Because of that we would recommend that the message sent out during those four seconds be. 'We come in peace, looking for friendship and cooperation for the good of all beings.' "

"Finally, we believe that the healing will occur because of global recognition of the right use of will. For centuries before its discovery, Vulcan was associated by astrologers with will or power.

During this eclipse the sun and moon are 10 degrees in the sign of Aries, indicating that the lessons of the '1st Ray' have been learned. It is through uniting the will of the 12 nations that the project can be completed."

"Finally, the psychologists and sociologists in our group are asking to balance male and female energies in the transmutation. We are asking that the Alchemical Wedding be continued to its completion, remembering that Vulcan was a male god searching for balance in the feminine.   So, we honor the goddess in this transaction, recognizing her strong presence in our lives through the mew moon, a new beginning."

Dagon and Stella spoke after getting a nod from Lucian and Nadria, breaking the news that had been withheld until now. "We have in our possession a means to create the necessary atomic power to create the explosion.   The four of us will be responsible for that part of the Operation." A buzz of excited speculation and joy filled the air.

Lucian and Nadria stood up holding hands. "In closing, we ask that everyone here pray with us this alchemical prayer."

The group stood, joining hands in a circle and bowed their heads repeating out loud a prayer they all knew by heart. The 44 people gathered in the room seemed to seal and empower their purpose as they solemnly intoned.

> 0 hallowed Unity, ... sink me into limitless eternal Fire, ... transmute me so that rising I may be changed into a pure spiritual body of rainbow colors like unto the transparent, crystal-like, paradisiacal gold, that my own nature may be purified like the elements before me in these glasses and bottles. Diffuse me in the water of life, so that with the aid of this Fire, I may also attain unto immortality and glory.[19]

CHAPTER 33

✠

Awakening

The next day, Stella and Dagon woke up early to the sounds of insects and tropical birds and decided to walk down to the hot spring for a swim. The walkway to it was a rainforest canopy. A small stream led to a waterfall surrounded by vivid blooms of exotic, sweet-smelling flowers. The mineral-rich water attracted hundreds of beautiful, rare butterflies and hummingbirds.

Stella smiled when a large blue butterfly landed on her shoulder, tickling her before it fluttered away. They made love slowly and softly in the warm water.

Later Lucian and Nadria joined them on an enclosed patio for a light breakfast of very sweet coffee, fruit and salted fish.

"Today will be a day of rest," Lucian commented. "We will take you to our laboratory and show you how we have distilled the essence of a wide variety of rainforest plants to be used for various healing purposes. Then, we will show you how we distilled the Red Compound which you will need for your alchemical experiment."

Nadria and Lucian led, walking slowly, hand in hand before them. The walk to the laboratory was pleasant as they followed stones that had been set among tangled wild orchids climbing out on the branches of trees. The sounds of monkeys calling could be heard off in the distance. The temperature was balmy, the air caressing their skin. The laboratory was a bamboo greenhouse containing thousands of specimens, each being grown in separate containers marked with simple labels. A sprinkling system in the roof watered everything, and large butterflies batted against the panes.

Lucian motioned to a small desk in front of the greenhouse, pushing aside the clutter of old potting jars, trowels, and his gardening gloves.

"This is my favorite place on earth," he said. "It is the only place that I will miss. When we leave, you are welcome to have this house and this laboratory. It would be a shame for all of these specimens to die. Our gardener is a friend who I'm sure would be very happy to continue working here, taking care of things, as you will be away most of the time."

Dagon and Stella felt sadness at his words, wondering why he looked so tired today. They had discussed it last night. Every time they had seen Lucian, he looked older. Stella remembered that about Nadria, too.

"I don't understand it." Stella had said to Dagon before bed. "It's as if he has aged twenty years in four days."

Now, gazing at his transparent skin and white, wrinkled hands, Lucian seemed even frailer. Lucian sat quietly for a moment enjoying the sun, and then seemed to rouse himself, going over to an antiquated filing system and pulling out a messy file full of notes. "I know that computers have ruled the world for a century, but I still like to see my own handwriting."

"Most of the near-extinct species of plants alive today are on continental islands. Being once bridged to land most species occur on these islands. Yet, they have been able to maintain their fragile ecosystems because of isolation. Unfortunately, this is no longer the case. Human overpopulation has been gradually destroying these island rainforests."

"This 12,000 acre tract of land is privately owned and has never been harvested. There are plants here, which are now considered extinct by the outside world."

"I have done experiments which show we have a cure here for all forms of cancer. I have not been willing to release it to the public, however, because the species would not survive being mass-produced."

"You must use your own judgment about what to do about these issues."

He indicated some old iron chairs over by one of the rickety wooden benches.

"Let's sit there and I'll show you my file on the 'Red Compound.'"

"It's very simple, really. It requires that you use two flowers indigenous to this area, and three red berries that grow only in rainforests, this is mixed with the acid you found in the tailing ponds under the mine. The final solution is extremely dangerous. Under no condition should you let a drop of it touch your skin."

"The plant formula has already been mixed for you and is in this vial and needs only the acid to be added to it to begin the distillation." He held up a glass vial filled with a blood red liquid.

"It should be treated with extreme care." With that, he carefully placed the vial in a padded, ornately carved metal box.

"It is important, here, that I tell you the story of Pele, the Volcano goddess of the Hawaiians for which this mountain was named."

"Pele fell in love with a handsome chief, Lohiau. However, he fell in love with her sister. Filled with jealous rage, Pele transformed her sister into one-half of a starflower that she put on a Volcano. She changed Lohiau into the other half of the starflower, which she put near the ocean. Her plan was to separate the to lovers by fire and water. The Lovers, however, were determined to be reunited. They chose to become one starflower, giving up their separate identities forever."[84]

Stella was intrigued. "This is a similar to the story of the betrayal of Mars and Venus in the Roman story. In the end, it is the net of Vulcan which binds them together, as lovers, forever."

Lucian patted her hand benevolently. "The two flowers actually exist, they are real. In rare instances they grow on volcanic islands, here on Pele and also on the Hawaiian Islands. I have them on my private reserve here, a tract of land, which includes volcanic soil as well as a narrow stretch of beach. These two plants chemically mixed are the main ingredients of the red compound."

"Symbolically the male, solar essence, and female, lunar essence must be joined in spiritual alchemy. Thus this compound can only be mixed by a man and woman together."

"If the starflowers which produced this distillation become extinct, the formula can not be produced in any other way. They are being privately nurtured in this little nature conservatory to guard against that possibility."

"That is one reason to maintain this reserve. I would also suggest that you maintain the servants of this household. I would like to let you in on a secret, which will delight you."

"Our head caretaker and gardener is your friend, Jeremy. He has been loyal to us, like the son we never had. I confess that we asked him to make friends with you, knowing that you would be in danger after your trip to Vulcan."

Dagon and Stella both gasped. Then, Dagon asked, "Did you give him the blue-green diamond to pass on to us for our wedding ring?"

Lucian looked puzzled. "No. You were given a blue-green diamond? Nadria and I have one also, it was presented to us before our wedding thousands of years ago."

Dagon was gawking in amazement. "Jeremy! What about the hummingbird he wears."

"Oh, that little hummingbird is from me, it is a symbol of the New Age that the Mayans predicted. There are many beautiful and rare hummingbirds on this island." Lucian waved his hand to take in the solarium and the main house.

"Do not worry about expenses, the stones can be used to transmute lead into gold or to create other gems depending on the compounds that you use."

He pulled out some messy notes, scrawled on wrinkled sheets of paper. "This is the formula for a diamond for instance. Certain colors, of course, are easier than others."

Dagon was catching Stella's eyes with a look of amazement. Could all of this be true? He looked over at Nadria. She was as quiet as ever, seeming to soak up silence, totally at peace with her surroundings, with no need to express. Lucian and she seemed to understand each other perfectly and would occasionally share a loving glance.

I hope that one day, thought Dagon, Stella and I have that kind of love. It must be the kind of friendship that develops for centuries.

"Lucian, how old are you?" Dagon asked.

"Like you, I have no beginning. I have been here since the beginning of time. Soul does not die, it is always reborn in some form."

"How long have you been in this physical body?"

Lucian reflected. "2,512 years. I was born in 479 B.C. as an Egyptian metalworker. Nadria was my wife. It was in that lifetime that we discovered the stones and did our first experiments. After that I lived under many guises. In each case, I would pretend to die and come home to my hideaway until it was time to come out in another disguise."

"Nadria probably had more fun than I in her day, as she broke all the rules for women and lived through many hair-raising adventures. We have both decided it is time to retire from this parade of masks to find a more peaceful home."

"Before we leave you to study these notes, I would like to explain one very important principle to you," Lucian continued.

"Your work with distilling the essence of plants or the properties of stones requires that you infuse yourself always with spirit, pledging yourself to the greatest good of both the essence of life, which has been gifted you, and the greater plan for all of us. There is a God. After thousands of years on this earth, I can tell you this without any doubt. The god and goddess are real and must be served faithfully."

Lucian began to speak. "Stella, by studying the Tarot you learned a formula that could create fusion. The Greater Arcana of the Tarot in numerical sequence also holds a formula for the way to create the unlimited energy and fusion of personal Awakening. It shows you the stages of this growth as well as how to raise kundalini. The zero card says the key is trust in unbounded universal consciousness. The Magician is setting an intent or Sankalpa for awakening. You must want this and ask for it. You call on the High Priestess, the goddess, Kundalini, to receive this gift. Then you give yourself to the Goddess, the love of Empress and mother, and to the God, the father and Emporer, calling on his ability for manifestation on the Earth plane. Having now called on fire, air, water and earth you make your body the Athanor, the container for light, the Heirophant, the fifth element. In the sixth stage, the male and female current, the root and crown chakra, unite in the Lover Card, and create balance between them, the Chariot. This first stage of awakening allows you to feel this growth of light as Strength. Now you are at the 9th card, nine being the transition to another stage of enlightenment. Here you submit your will to silence and the divine will, the Hermit, with a recognition that only God can create the timing in your life to give you permanent awakening. This is the Wheel or Fortune or Fate. The energies amplify and come into balance through divine intervention. It is important here to release charges and emotional conditioning of karma or Justice. Through complete surrender, The Hanged Man, the powers of masculine and feminine mix and you are permanently transmuted, this is the Death of the ego. A great power is building which can be amplified by mixing the elements in your life with awareness and spiritual alchemy, Temperance. This is often where people fly apart. The energy has built so that it permeates every area of life, becoming sexual as well as deeply pleasurable. Beware of any grandiose thinking or rationalizing acts which have karmic consequences here. Passing through that danger zone, you resubmit your ego and let Kundalini rise and build to the next stage of transmutation, The Tower. From there it explodes into the STAR, light, bliss, and God awakening. It his here that the fusion can take you to Stage three of awakening, full awareness of the Moon, Shakti the lunar Essence, and the Sun, Shiva the solar essence. The Sun and Moon join together in Aeon, the final union that happens within God and you become the Universe, universal consciousness. Here you sense no difference between yourself and what is outside of you. All is One. Should you choose at this point to leave your body and unite with God, you can do so. My advice to you is to study these stages of initiation, live this spiritual path, become the alchemists who mix the ingredients in your life to create Awakening.

Nadria simply reached out her hand and touched Stella.

"Desire awakening and call on the Goddess. She is first step."

"Those are my only words of advice," she said to Lucian, and stood up slowly, taking his arm to go.

Together they walked in a leisurely stroll, arm-in-arm up the path, stopping occasionally to touch one of the orchids hanging in front of them.

Stella was filled with sadness that she couldn't put into words. She blinked back tears, and then looked over at Dagon who was studying the scribbled notes in front of him. Stella looked over his shoulder, and then shuddered. "Oh, my god. They are geniuses, these files are priceless."

That evening Lucian and Nadria did not come down for dinner. Even the servants seemed to be honoring the hushed atmosphere about the place.

Dagon and Stella went to sleep early, huddled together for comfort. However, just after midnight, Stella heard the beating of an owl's wings against the window and looked up to see a white owl gazing in at them through the window as they slept.

She woke Dagon. Then, they heard the hooting of another owl, and watched their friend spread silent wings, to join its mate.

"Dagon, something has happened. We need to go check on Lucian." She got up quickly and pulled on her long dressing gown, picking up a candle off of the nightstand to light her way. Dagon followed her as they quietly tiptoed down the hall to Lucian and Nadria's room.

The light was on, so they knocked softly. No answer. Calling out, they gently opened the door to find the beds empty, except for two small vials of clear golden liquid and a single white feather. There was a note and a few handwritten sheaves of parchment paper. The note read.

"Dear Dagon and Stella, Goodbye, children. We have left this material form to go back to spirit, to take our souls to a quieter place in the universe."

"Do not grieve our death, for the spirit never dies. We stopped taking the elixir for the last four days and you may have noticed we were aging quickly."

"We prayed that at one stroke after midnight the gods would reduce our bodies to a liquid state. This essence is our gift to you to be used for the formula in the Alchemical Wedding. It is our gift to the earth, also, which we have loved as a daughter. Take good care of our gardens. We leave them and the house to you."

A Will distributing the rest of our fortune to various charities and our staff is located in the desk beside the bed. P.S. I think the formula for the immortality elixir is in the bottom of the filing cabinet filed under Miscellaneous. P.S.S. The enclosed letter was written by Nadria. We hope it will comfort you, please pass it on to Jeremy for whom it is intended. Love, Lucian."

Stella sat down on the old Victorian chair beside their bed and started to sob. "Oh, Dagon. They're gone, they're really gone. We're alone now, alone."

Dagon wiped tears from his own eyes and looked at the sheaves of paper in Nadria's handwriting. Sadness seemed to overwhelm him as he remembered the loss of his mother whom he loved. He began to read out loud, hearing Nadria's voice speaking to them with wisdom and love.

My dearest Jeremy, Please don't grieve our passage. You have been like a son to us, and we love you dearly.

You could not have stopped our deaths, for we go willingly. In fact after all of this time we have learned how to step into the next dimension with a certain degree of ease. We only stayed in our bodies to play our part in helping out the earth on her path of growth. And, of course, we stayed because of you!

Live your life passionately. It is okay to feel deep sorrow and anger. For in allowing a full array of emotions, you also open your life to deep love and profound joy.

Jeremy, as I write I can feel my life force shifting away from me and in that state I can see that the changes which seem random in nature, the constantly shifting wind, the tangled growth of roots, the frost on a window pane are part of a larger implicit order. The wind erodes graceful patterns in the rocks. The roots spiral out with fractalizing energy, and each flake of frost is a masterpiece in beauty and design. Nature is a wonderful landscape artist. Beauty and order abound even in what seem like random occurrences.

The last beats of my heart seem to me to be the fluctuating rhythm of unfolding and enfolding of the universe.

Jeremy, you are a part of that rhythm. That is why we will never be apart. We are all part of one aspect, one dimension of the whole picture.

I am letting go now to float above this body. Letting go until my body feels light, until every cell is flooded with a different kind of breath.

There are no boundaries. Follow the light of the Goddess. We are *awakened*!

Jeremy, these must be my last words to you, as I can no longer hold this pen and paper. Believe me when I tell you it is possible to walk in your garden and love both the Order and the Chaos.

Your mother in Spirit, Nadria

Dagon gulped back his tears, but stopped and let them go. It felt good to cry. Lucian had said it was okay to trust your heart.

Stella was remembering one of her dreams that she had when she was on the planet Vulcan.

The woman wore a grey robe and a necklace with a golden V on it. She motioned Stella through a stone archway into the inside of the pyramid. The room glowed from refracted light coming from narrow rectangular openings in the walls. Huge amethyst and tanzanite panels rising 10 feet high in triangles hung on white walls. A gold citrine sphere sent prisms of light into all of the corners.

She led Stella past a pillar to an intricate Sri Yantra mosaic. A number of Initiates sat in a circle inside it chanting mantras. Each was sitting cross legged in Lotus eyes closed and their thumb and index finger touching.

"Here is the lesson you seek," said the woman in grey. "These initiates are learning to increase the flow of energy or Kundalini in their bodies. Kundalini flows through us as a gift from the great life force, Shakti. It cannot be earned and is not the result of years of study and practice. It comes as a bequest. This rising of the golden light of the goddess, Kundalini, is necessary to experience Awakening. When you honor her, call to her, pray to her, she hears you. But ultimately it is a offering of love, given to you by her so that you can 'Know' her."

"Shakti has thousands, millions, uncountable numbers of faces. She is pure energy, pure life. She is all sound, color and form working in patterns of genius. She is the beating of your own heart. She is the moon and the sun within you that constantly yearns for her. She is your breath."

Stella dropped her head and prayed. "Nadria, please take me to the Goddess. Let me experience this Golden Light of Awakening."

CHAPTER 34

✠

Operation Dragon

It was an emotional parting early the next morning.

Jeremy had decided to stay at Lucian and Nadria's home to conduct a memorial with close friends and staff members, the only ones other then Dagon and Stella that knew that Lucian and Nadria were gone. Dagon hugged Jeremy to him, fiercely, before leaving.

"Remember what Nadria wrote for you, Jeremy," he murmured as he comforted him.

He felt under his arm for the metal box, which now contained not only the red compound, and the notes for their experiment, but also the two precious vials containing the corporeal essence of Lucian and Nadria.

Jeremy gripped Dagon's arm as Stella and he listened to the pounding of the surf, ready to board the ship that would ferry them out to Thuban Island.

Dagon was touched to see Jeremy put up his hand, fist to heart. Then he said, "What Virtue Has Joined Death, Cannot Separate. *Vitus Junxit Mors Non Separabit.* We will be with you during Operation Dragon from here. I will stay and take care of things on Mount Pele until you and Stella can return."

Dagon nodded, suddenly choked up and the grabbed Stella's arm to hurry her toward the beach to dockside. It was a red, foggy dawn. The wind was fresh and the seas were running high. The deck of the large ship flashed pink, then violet, as it dipped and caught the morning light.

They boarded quickly. With a groan, the creaking vessel pulled seaward out into choppy waters. Dagon and Stella stood on deck, and braced against the wind as they pulled away from Java.

"I wish this were a honeymoon vacation. This island is like paradise, so majestic and verdant."

"Perhaps, it *is* paradise, archeological finds have discovered some of the oldest human remains here on this island. Some people believe that before transcontinental migration occurred, in Gondwanaland, that this was the location of the Garden of Eden spoken of in the Bible."

"You mean Eden as in Adam and Eve?" Stella questioned playfully.

Dagon smiled and drew her into a reassuring embrace. "No, Eden as in Dagon and Stella," he smiled.

As they pulled out into the ocean, the land began to fade farther and farther from sight until they were left with a blue and gray world, and the sharp, salty breezes of the ocean.

"How long will it take for us to get there?"

"Only forty-five minutes. It will be our only time to relax today. There's a lot to accomplish when we arrive." Dagon said.

Once Thuban Island had been sighted, Dagon pulled out the checklist he had made for Operation Dragon, feeling the responsibility of being Commander weighing heavily on his shoulders.

As the ship pulled into the harbor, he realized that the members of the Circle had rallied all forces to accomplish the Operation. A transport vehicle was there to pick them up and people in Navy uniforms were scurrying around the dock unloading large boxes from another cargo ship.

There was a sense of order in the busy activity of the group. The Transport sped away floating over bumpy roads that were paved with crushed lava rock. After the lushness of the main island, this semi-barren landscape seemed like a desolate outpost.

Thuban Island had been born from the Ring of Fire, the Volcanic Island Arc of deep-focus earthquakes and oceanic trenches off the coast of Indonesia. The small island was fairly new, having risen up out of the sea in the year 2019 as a result of volcanic activity beneath the surface of the ocean. It was one of the few places in the world where the Dolphin or Atlantis stone, Larimar, was found dotting the beaches. The lovely light blue stone had become a symbol of enlightenment worldwide.

The Transport hovered over the deep ruts in the road making the ride comfortable. They quickly arrived at a large lava dome in a clearing flanked by an airfield. There were bunker buildings there, as well as a group of smaller native bungalows. In the center of the small village was a Hindu temple. As the Transport ground to a halt, they were greeted by General Chapman. Dagon saluted him then stepped toward forward. The General's crisp white uniform caught the full light of the, now bright, morning sunshine. Chapman worked for NASA and had been at the Secret Circle meeting. A large man with red checks, and long sideburn, he spoke in a crisp, formal voice, giving Dagon a briefing on the status of the Operation.

"The ship, the Red Dragonfly, is waiting on the launch pad at Thuban North, the other side of the Island. According to the

Starseed technicians who designed her, she has already had three successful test flights."

"Don Cummings, the head of Satellite Command Post is a member of the Starseed Sect. We explained to him what was happening and he had a meeting with the members of the Order who live in this village. These members have been very cooperative, providing food and housing for the troops."

"Cargo landed on the airfield yesterday to deliver and set up the satellite disk which will be beaming a laser to the moon. Lieutenant Bonnie Casey is in charge of this phase of the operation. A computer terminal has been set up in one of bunker buildings and is linking into the satellite post, as well as the remote control equipment for the spaceship, Red Dragonfly."

"We are in communication with Washington, synchronizing the events with them."

"As you can see before you," he motioned to the computer equipment and video screens that were in place, "the calculations for trajectories, as well as the refraction amplitudes are being generated."

"We are targeting the moon and projecting a refraction of the beam to 4.5124 astronomical units above the earth."

"Red Dragonfly will be there as a satellite to direct that beam to Vulcan. The Laser will have radio frequency to dispatch a sonic vibration which has been programmed 1,111 megahertz per second, this slightly above D# on the music scale. The communications equipment for this has been set up in the remote control tower at Thuban North."

The General walked forward and they followed him into another large room and saw that a cold fusion power generator had been set up to ensure a constant power source for the equipment in case of blackouts.

Dagon was happy to see everything in such good order.

"It seems your men, General, have accomplished a lot in a short time."

The General shrugged his large shoulders, deflecting the praise.

"We've been working around the clock for 24 hours and have had access to the NASA Strategic Swat Team. Our location for this command is ideal. We have a well maintained airfield, large buildings to place our equipment in, and the bulk of the equipment, the remote control and launching tower at Thuban North is already in operation here because of Starseed."

"Besides, the men and women are motivated. They know how important this mission is. It's gone like clockwork."

Clockwork. Stella thought looking at her watch. It was 7:00 am. The exact moment of eclipse would be occurring late tonight, Javanese time 1:01:11 pm on March 31th 2033. The total solar eclipse would also be monitored by the NASA Operation Dragon team in Washington D.C. at 1.01.11 p.m., March 30th, Earth Day, 3/30/33 their time zone being exactly 12 hours earlier then Thuban Island. When she had seen the master numbers in the exact timing for the eclipse, shivers had gone up her spine.

The resonance of the number 11 was magnetic and astrologically represented Uranus or Aquarius, meaning a radical change or shift. The number 33 meant God Consciousness. However, Stella realized there was more to this sequence of numbers. To the Mayans every number had a resonance. This specific number, eleven, meant 'spectralized' energy. This vibration described a time when the veil between spirit and matter would become thinner. Matter would be able to shift into spirit, spirit to matter in the blink of an eye. Belief could change the world in an instant. God consciousness would make this possible, 3333.

Stella thought of the synchronistic events that had told her that eleven number was her personal vibration number. The Mayans believed that each person belonged to a tribe and had a numerical vibration that could be derived from your birthdate. Stella's Mayan birth name was, 11 Spectral Mirror. Because of this the number 11:11 had seemed to follow her everywhere. In the last year awareness had been rising in human consciousness about the importance of the date 3/30/33 for raising God Consciousness. There was no doubt in her mind now. This operation would be a success. It had to be. It was completely ordained by the gods.

Dagon had moved into another room with General Chapman and, as Stella looked up from her reverie, she realized she was standing alone gazing at the spinning numbers on the countdown module. A voice behind her startled her, and she looked around in time to see a man walking toward her who had a slight limp.

His red hair was cut in military style and freckles stood out against his pale skin. His handshake was cold, his palms moist, and Stella quickly drew her hand away.

"Hello, I'm Don Cummings. Maybe you don't remember me." He reached in his pocket on put on his thick glasses.

"Oh, yes, of course, I do," Stella said. "You were at the NECSA meeting arranged by Lawrence Statton."

"Yes, sad thing about Statton. I hear that he died. He was a good man."

Stella nodded, trying to cover her discomfort. She examined Don unobtrusively, noticing that he was wearing army fatigue pants and old army boots.

"What will be your role for the next 17 hours?" she asked.

"I have been supervising the set up of the laser satellite. My job is almost finished, but I'll be sticking around to watch the fireworks."

Stella felt uncomfortable with his flippancy, and faintly repulsed by his aura. "I'm sure I will be seeing you around then," she said as she started to leave, unconsciously wanting to escape the interview. He touched her arm as she turned to go and she shuddered.

"Yeah, I'm sure you will," he said.

As Stella walked out of the room, her mind was reeling. What was it about this man that was so unpleasantly familiar? She didn't remember actually ever having met him, yet she knew that somewhere, somehow she had. It alarmed her that Cummings might have been a friend of Statton. He was a member of the Order and his involvement with NECSA linked him to Interspace Research and it's head, Emilio Fauntis, who was evil personified.

I'm going to find out about this guy, she decided remembering the rich vein of Gold that Dagon and she had discovered under Draesbran.

After greeting her servants and the Starseed sect members, Stella decided to do a bit of sleuthing.

She started by talking to the maid that was cleaning Cummings's room, asking her general questions, first about how busy she was with all the new guests, and then focusing in on Cummings.

"I suppose it must be difficult for you, cleaning, with people in and out at all hours of the night. I know Cummings, for instance, has had to work all night setting up the satellites."

"Yes, Ma'am, it has. And, his room has been a mess, it takes me a while to clean it, let me tell you."

"When were you finally able to get in?"

"He was gone most of the night and then left again about 6:00 this morning. I got to it first thing this morning, that way the extra time didn't mess up my whole schedule." The woman said in a complaining voice.

"What was he doing all night?"

"I suppose working on the satellite system, Lord knows, there's enough people around here at all hours of the day and night, right now."

Next, Stella saddled up to one of the satellite technicians, a strapping dark-haired young man with a long shank of hair that fell over one eye.

"You must be exhausted after working all night." The young man just looked at her surprised.

"Aren't you Stella Miren, the Astronaut?" "Yes," she smiled, "Only, I'm Stella Andrew, now. Captain Andrew and I were married recently."

The young man wiped some grease off his palm and pumped her had effusively.

"Congratulations! Jimmy Kerr, Ma'am, It's really nice to meet ya'll," he said with a slight southern accent.

"As I was saying, you must be exhausted after working all night. You guys are doing a great job," Stella said brightly.

"Ah, it's been easy," the young technician grinned. "We had it all moved in and up yesterday. This is a mobile system; it's pretty much self-contained. The disk folds up so that it can be transported in a Jumbo Mach III cargo plane. The Red Dragonfly can easily carry it. Unloading it is mind-boggling. The plane is built so it can hover. Each of the four outer rings is then cabled into helicopters to slowly lower it in place while opening up the umbrella. It was pretty impressive to watch it happen, I can tell you that. I've seen it two other times when we've relocated. I never get over it."

Stella looked out over the disk, which was two football fields long, amazed by the size of it and its potential power.

"What time were you done by, Jim?"

"Well, I'd say we were finished by 8:00 pm, got a late meal and I was countin' sheep by 10:30."

"Do you work for Don Cummings?"

Jim shrugged his shoulders. "As far as I can see, he doesn't work. My head is Bonnie Casey over there. She could tell you where Don's been hangin' out."

Stella sensed that Jim disliked Don. She said easily. "It's hard working for someone who doesn't chip in and become part of a team."

"Yeah," Jim shook his head with disgust.

"That guy's got something up his sleeve. He's always either gone, or on the phone. He's supposed to be in charge here, but it's usually all stuck with Bonnie. Good thing we have her. Well, hell, you don't need ta' know all this."

Jim turned back toward the cables he was checking, and then waved her off. "I'll be seein' ya."

Stella walked away even more disturbed. Her next stop would be Bonnie Casey. She walked up and shook Bonnie's hand warmly.

"Hello Lieutenant Casey, I hear you're the person responsible for getting all of this equipment mobilized and in operation. Good job!"

Bonnie was an attractive middle-aged woman, with a wide smile and two charming dimples. "Please call me Bonnie," she said.

Stella felt immediately drawn to her open attitude.

Bonnie pushed her hat back tucking her shoulder-length nut-brown hair back into her barrette. "Nice to meet you. I've always admired your work," she said. They both turned and looked out over the disk.

"Will you be testing it before we send a laser from it to the spaceship and the moon?" asked Stella.

"It's already been tested and everything seems to be working fine."

"How much do you know about what's going on here?"

"Enough," Bonnie said. I'm behind this mission all the way. An eclipse of Vulcan is life threatening to the planet, but I also know a little about the spiritual side of the mission. I'll be saying my own prayer with the rest of the world."

Stella decided to trust her. "Lieutenant, I'm worried about Don Cummings and his loyalties to the mission. I don't have anything to base this on, just a feeling. Is there anything you can tell me to help me out on this question?"

Bonnie looked grim for a moment. "Cummings is a bad one. He is only a figurehead here as far as fulfilling his responsibilities. I'm sure he has some other kind of operation going behind the scenes. I don't trust him myself."

"Can you get me into to his office to see the files on his computer?"

"He keeps his office at home locked all the time. But, here in the mobile unit he has to operate out of our general system."

Bonnie motioned to the trailer. "His computer is in there, but he keeps the cabinet locked all the time, too."

"Where do you think he keeps the key?"

"I've seen it on a chain around his neck."

"He's got to take it off sometime. Perhaps, when he sleeps or showers. Where is he now?" Stella looked around the busy site.

"I expect at noon he'll be in the mess tent for lunch."

"Thank you, Lieutenant."

Bonnie said quickly. "If you need any help, I'm in the first bungalow south of the Temple."

Stella's next stop was to go see the leader of the Starseed Order on the Island, Miri Bintulu. The dark skinned Malaysian bowed to her then looked at her as if he was seeing through her, his attitude reflective.

Stella could see from his light aura that he was a Spiritual Adept. "Master," she addressed him with reverence, "are you satisfied with the explanation you have received from Don Cummings regarding the events which are occurring here today?"

The old man just looked at her for a moment. Then, he said, "I see good intentions in you, so I will reveal to you my true heart.

"There is unrest among the people. Some were close followers of priest, Esrom, Lawrence Statton, and heard about his death. They are very superstitious about Dragon Mountain and feel his death is a bad omen. They are afraid of evil spirits. They blame you, but they do not know the whole story. These people trust Cummings and are satisfied. I, however, am among those who would like a better answer to my inner questioning. Our prophecies are very old. It seems they are being fulfilled today, but not, in the way that we have been taught. I do not want there to be error."

"Let's go into your temple. I will tell you the whole story, then you can decide for yourself," Stella said.

They walked into the square, thatched roof pagoda building and sat down.

An hour later, the old man was nodding. "Yes, yes, I see. We have misinterpreted the prophecy. You are truly the bride that we have waited for."

Stella confided her fears then about Cummings and what had happened with Lawrence Statton.

"Someone had been carrying on a mining operation down in the bottom of the shaft. I believe that Lawrence was involved in this when he kidnapped me. He wanted gold for some plan of his own. If Cummings was working with Lawrence, he may have other friends here, other members of the South American branch of the Starseed Sect that were working in the mines secretly."

"Just after dark this evening, Dagon and I need to complete the final steps of the Alchemical Marriage to provide the atomic power needed for Operation Dragon. This is a very delicate and dangerous procedure. We will be working with highly explosive compounds."

"I do not feel safe with Cummings here. I am asking that you talk to those people that you trust to help guard us. We will be working at Thuban North, in the Polestar bunker building on the other side of the island. If the experiment is successful we will be installing the atomic devises in the Red Dragonfly."

Stella looked in Miri's eyes and said with conviction.

"Nothing must stop Operation Dragon."

The sage nodded and Stella continued "It would help if I could get the key to Cummings's computer. He keeps it on a chain around his neck."

Miri smiled and bowed. As Stella stood up, he made a sign to bless her. "Go with God, daughter."

Stella hurried out to find Dagon. He was immersed in meetings with all of the command leaders. She turned back and went to the makeshift kitchen for a quick bite of lunch. As she was handed her plate, she was also slipped a small key on a chain with a folded note. She turned her back to the chattering officers and read the note quickly. In scrawled block letters were the words, "Hurry,

Cummings is being massaged. Need key back by 12:15 p.m. Master Fu, Bungalow 304."

She sat down her plate and rushed out the rear entrance of the bungalow, running across the dirt lot toward the satellite station.

The satellite dish had been set up a quarter of a mile away from the bungalows and soon her side was aching. She tripped over a sharp rock, *"Oh, double damn!"* Her shoe had caught, pulling the heel loose. She moved with a fast limp the rest of the way, pulling on the trailer door frantically.

It's locked. I need Bonnie. Without stopping to think, she pulled off her shoes and raced back in her socks. By the time she hit Bonnie's room she could hardly breath.

Please be here, she panted. Bonnie answered immediately, and seeing her state, reached for her pack, shutting the door behind her as Stella gasped out the words. "I need into the computer at the mobile trailer, now!"

Bonnie grabbed the key and took off on a run ahead of Stella. She had opened the door, and had the mainframe computer and printer on by the time Stella got there.

Bonnie had unlocked Cumming's terminal and had her hands on the keyboard. Stella doubled over as she tried to catch her breath. "Geez, were you a runner or something? You're not even winded."

Bonnie just smiled, concentrating on logging on the codes that they used for satellite command. Then she started scrolling through the files.

"Here it is, his personal file."

"Hurry," Stella said anxiously, "We only have 12 minutes to get the key back."

"Bingo," Bonnie yelled gleefully. "Oh, my god."

Stella looked over her shoulder reading. "Starseed. SSR-strategic defense package. Nuclear warhead target: Jupiter: Colony 1 planning procedure."

Bonnie said, "There is another file marked 'Resources.' Under it is the heading 'Draesbran Mine.' " Bonnie clicked it and said, "They've already taken out billions and are funneling it to a special branch of Interspace Research called Operation Star Burst."

"Copy the files, quick," Stella said anxiously.

Bonnie put a flash drive in and seconds later they were locking the terminal again.

"Okay," Bonnie handed her the key as she stayed to lock up the trailer. "Run!"

Stella sprinted back to the bungalows, found room 304 and knocked softly with only 30 seconds to spare. A small Chinese gentleman opened the door with a smile. He took the key without saying anything and shut the door gently.

Stella slipped off her broken shoe and panting limped back towards the Bunker building, the flash drive clutched in her hand.

I have to get hold of Dagon. He needs to know what's going on. She found him just finishing up another meeting. The earnest faces of the men and women in the room touched Stella. They all stood in a tight circle as they concluded their meeting joining hands in the center. Dagon smiled. "To the success of Operation Dragon. I will meet next with the mobile command officers at 1:15. Remember all personnel must be on board at their stations at 10:00 pm this evening. Thank you."

A few people stayed to talk briefly, but soon only Dagon and Stella were left.

"Dagon, I know you must be overwhelmed with details, but I've some important news."

"I'm starved," said Dagon.

"So am I, let's eat lunch in our room and talk there."

Dagon noticed then, for the first time that Stella was carrying her shoes, one heel dangling down and that her face was dust streaked with a line of sweat soaking through her shirt. A scratch on her ankle was bleeding.

His immediate response was anger. "Okay, what have you been up to? And, if it was dangerous, so help me Stella, I'll ring your neck."

Stella pretended meekness, following him as he stalked back to the main hall to grab a plate, and then to their bungalow.

Dagon's arms were crossed tightly over his chest. When they had closed the door, he turned to her expectantly, the angry glint still there. "Okay, spill the beans."

"Perhaps, it would be better, if I just showed you."

Stella brought the drive out from behind her back. Dagon loomed over her as she put it in her pocket computer. As soon as she had pulled up the file, she heard Dagon's sharp intake of breath.

"Who?"

"Don Cummings."

"Does he know you have this?"

"No." She explained how she had found her information and gotten the key.

"Stella," Dagon scolded, "That was foolhardy. This man is obviously dangerous. He would have killed you if you had been discovered. He might still be planning to kill us tonight."

"We'll have help," Stella explained, telling Dagon how she had enlisted the aid of Miri Bintulu.

"How did you know you could trust him?"

"Intuition, I could read it in his aura."

Dagon just nodded his head. He had found that this was becoming easier for him to do also.

"Could we have him arrested?" Stella brainstormed.

"He hasn't done anything illegal that we know of. We need to wait. If he tries something tonight, we'll be ready for him. In the meantime, eat and try to get some sleep. We have a long night ahead of us and we didn't get much sleep last night."

Stella noticed, though, that he hadn't touched his plate. He was on his Link. When he got off his face was grim.

"Stella, more news. Mo, Joe and Henry just arrived. It seems they have retrieved both stones, but not, without problems.

Our apartments have been ransacked. When Joe was in your apartment, he was hit over the head and knocked out by an intruder. Fortunately, Mo was right behind him and managed to wrestle the burglar to the ground with Henry's help. It turned out to be Emilio Fauntis. They tied him up, left a note for the police and have personally escorted the stones to the Thuban Island launch site. Since arriving, they have been guarding the stones in a private Bungalow on the North side of the island. I made arrangements for them to meet us in the Polestar building at 6:00 this evening and warned them that we are in danger."

Dagon gave Stella a hug, seeing the bruised look under her eyes. "Are you okay? We have a long night ahead of us."

"Yes, I'm fine. Just let me eat my lunch and shower."

"You should take a nap, I have other meetings this afternoon but I'll come back and get you at 5:30. Then we'll go to the bunker and mix the formula."

Stella set her alarm and immediately passed out under the slow overhead fan. When Dagon woke her she struggled up out of a deep pool of exhaustion. "Did you eat?" Stella asked Dagon as she slipped on a thin black sweater, tights, and tied her hair back with a black ribbon. "I'll eat tomorrow," Dagon replied. "Ready?"

"I'm ready," she said throwing her backpack over her shoulder.

It contained the manuscripts and notes that Nadria and Lucian had left for them along with a flashlight. Dagon carried the precious compounds and essences and they quickly loaded themselves into a waiting Transport. Stella grabbed a banana and some nuts for Dagon on the way out the door.

The trip there took only 5 minutes, as the island was only 5 miles wide. The lights of the Transport wavered in the afterglow as the sun began to sink into the horizon.

Dagon turned to Stella. "Do you know why this is called the Polestar bunker?" asked Dagon as gratefully ate his banana.

"Because Thuban is the Alpha star in the constellation Draco, the Dragon. Because of the Precision of the Equinox, Thuban was once the North Star thousands of years ago. The Egyptian's worshipped the star as Isis and oriented their pyramids and temples toward her. This island must have been named by someone with that in mind."

Dagon laughed. "I should have known you'd have the answer."

They both thought of Lucian. How could he have seen this far into the future? Did he know of Operation Dragon that long ago?

The Polestar bunker was completely silent, the eeriness of it somewhat disturbing. They swung the wide doors open and stepped inside closing the large doors after them. Just then, a hand reached out and touched Stella's shoulder in the dark. She started to scream, turning to fight against her assailant, when a hand covered her mouth.

"Shhh, It's only me, Joe." A voice whispered close to her ear. "Mo and Henry are in the back, but we've been hearing sounds and decided not to turn on the light. Someone is coming through the back entrance right now."

Dagon had been alerted, too, and the three crouched down in the darkness. The back door opened. They could see the body of a man silhouetted against the door, the setting sun blood red behind him. He was carrying an automatic weapon. After a moment, he started walking toward them.

Night Sensors. Dagon thought quickly. He had on night glasses. That meant he could see them crouched there on the floor in the dark. Dagon whispered, "Roll to the left ... Now!"

At that exact moment Dagon slid his box of precious elixirs into a corner and sprang up, rushing toward the man.

Cummings was spraying the spot where they had been only moments before with bullets from his automatic weapon. There was a struggle, and then the lights came on.

Mo and Henry were jumping on the guy, holding him down, as they wrestled the gun away. The look of venom on Cummings's face was not pretty.

Just then, Bintulu, with a group of villagers, came racing through the back door.

"We will put him in jail. You will have no more trouble. I have met with all of our people. They ask forgiveness for their bad thoughts of you."

Stella smiled warmly and watched them drag Cummings away, while he struggled, cursing.

She wiped her hands on her thighs, patting her unruly hair back in place. "Well, that was easy. Now it's free sailing."

Dagon playfully swatted her. "Easy?" He rubbed the lump on his forehead. Then, she hugged Mo, Joe, and Henry telling them how glad she was to see them as they led her and Dagon to a back room.

The stones lay on two purple velvet cushions, their golden glow and luminescence lighting the semi-darkened room. Joe approached them reverently. "Thanks for trusting us with 'em."

"Honored," Mo said humbly.

"Well done," Dagon praised them. "If we still decorated people, you three would all receive knighthood. Remember, you must never say anything about these stones again. This is a secret you must carry to your grave. Now, please go out and guard the doors to the bunker. The next part of this must be done by Stella and I alone."

As the men left, Stella and Dagon looked at each other, each feeling a little shaky about the task that lay before them. Through the window they could see the running lights of the launch pad and the ship, Red Dragonfly, gleaming in the dusky light.

"We're a long way from the Golden Eagle," Stella said, suddenly feeling nostalgic for their ratty old ship.

"Yes, but what we did together on Vulcan is similar to what we are going to do here tonight."

Stella looked around the small room. "Lucian said that everything we need would be here." They pulled open a cabinet. Sitting in a padded box were two unusual looking glass vessels, gloves, an electric filament running through a glass tube, a scale and a timing clock. There was a little note. "Have fun, L."

Stella began to laugh with the absurdity of it all. "It's as if the guy is the master trickster. He set all of this up before he died."

"Well, let's get busy," Dagon rolled up his sleeves.

"No, first we must say my prayer together." She bowed her head with devotion and Dagon joined in slowly, realizing he knew the words to the prayer by heart.

0 hallowed Unity, ... sink me into limitless eternal Fire, ... transmute me so that rising I may be changed into a pure spiritual body of rainbow colors like unto the transparent, crystal-like, paradisiacal gold, that my own nature may be purified like the elements before me in these glasses and bottles. Diffuse me in the water of life, so that with the aid of this fire, I may also attain unto immortality and glory.[19]

When they began working, their actions seemed to originate from some inner memory as they followed the notes, making sure that they were following the instructions to the letter. Stella carefully combined 7 drops of the red compound with Nadria's golden elixir in a vessel marked with a symbol of the moon. Then, she shaved off a small piece of her rarefied helium weighing it. Dagon combined the same mixture in Lucian's elixir in a vessel mark with a symbol of the sun. An electrical conduit would connect the two vessels activating the chemical reaction when a switch was thrown. Very carefully Stella carried the lunar vessel and Dagon the solar vessel, walking gingerly together toward the spaceship. Four night guards stood on duty at the ship. They saluted, "Captain, Sir," and stood at attention as Dagon walked up.

"At ease men," Dagon said.

Dagon pushed a button so that the entrance ramp opened with a 'whoosh. ' Once inside it was clear that the ship had been built to carry this specific nuclear devise safely. A glass encased shelf showed two saucer shaped indentations that were built to cushion each vessel to keep them from vibrating during flight. The essences were carefully placed in the holder and the conduit carefully connected between the two vessels and the glass door in front of them closed.

Stella noticed that the shavings of the golden stone were glowing like hot coals. As the cover slid back in place, a note fluttered down from the top of the sliding door. "Good Job! L"

Dagon chuckled. They sat down together on the outside ramp, Stella's head on Dagon's shoulder.

Dagon said. "You might want to rest. I'm going to stand guard with these soldiers for the next three hours until the rest of the command arrives to begin the operation."

"We've almost completed it," she said.

"What?" Dagon asked.

"The seven days of the Alchemical wedding."

Dagon thought, Just after midnight our task will be complete. Hopefully, that will result in a flash of light ten thousand times ten thousand times brighter than anything humankind has ever witnessed. Dagon's prayer was that this light would be also be occurring as an explosion of awakened consciousness on earth and in the universe. For now, though, he needed to calmly wait as the sun sank beneath the ocean's horizon.

It was a flaming sunset, the sky a brilliant red above the rolling blue of the ocean, shooting a golden arc over the Island as the sun sank into the Java sea, a signature sunset. Dagon pulled Stella closer to support her, buzzed from the day of meetings and decisions. Everything had gone better then he had thought possible. He watched Stella drift into a restless sleep as she leaned against him, glad for the deep darkness of the new moon.

Before he knew it, it was 10:00 pm and the troops were arriving.

The operation mobilization went without a hitch. Everyone had rehearsed their roles beforehand. Dagon and Stella sat with General Chapman as the countdown began. It was midnight.

"Sixty minutes and one second to go," called Lieutenant Wayne Schwartz who was manning the videos. A reporter's voice came over a loud speaker.

"The twelve tribes and nations have each reported in. Millions of people around the earth are now meditating in preparation for this moment. Spiritual Adepts are opening the Seven Seals at the earth's chakra or sacred vortex sites. We have had reports of miraculous healings and channeled powers."

"An awareness of the eclipse and its possible consequences, has hit the media. Millions of viewers are watching the sun in North America, enthralled."

Another video screen showed thousands of people standing in front of the Canterbury Cathedral and waiting in front on the temples in India, Egypt and Asia.

"The Global Prayer of the Churches began at Saturday at noon EST. They are praying for a new age of peace and love to descend upon earth." As the minutes ticked by, another report was called out.

"North Americans have been gathering on the streets to watch the eclipse in the overhead sky. They have heard rumors of an event of monumental proportions. They believe the darkened sky will be filled with a blinding light, and that it will be a sign from God. They know that the time for this will be 1:01.01 EST, 11:01.11 MST on 3/30/33. The gatherings are peaceful, many taking place at concerts or parks where Earth Day is being celebrated. There have been no riots. Millions have agreed to join in silent prayer at the exact moment of the eclipse."

The minutes ticked by with more reports of global unification.

"The United Nations set a meeting of all nations to honor Earth Day at the moment of the Global Prayer of the Churches. This has been broadcast around the world, to the third world countries. News of a coming Sign from God has spread to third world countries." The TV screen flashed on a woman in Africa clutching her children as she looked up into the night sky. She was weeping. Stella found tears streaming down her face and began to pray herself.

"Oh, god and goddess, solar and lunar essence united," she prayed, "Transmute this world to a pure spiritual body of rainbow colors, like unto a pure spiritual body of crystal-like gold. Take our earth and purify it that we may unify the water of life with the heavenly fire. That we may pass through this death to a Golden Age, and having learned the Golden Teachings attain to immortality and glory. Take us each on an individual path of Awakening."

She reached over to hold Dagon's hand as they watched the clock go to 12:44 pm. "Launch sequence ready," an Officer called out.

Dagon nodded. "Ready, 4,3,2,1, Launch #1!" The Red Dragonfly roared to life, hovering above the launch pad. The Dragonfly shot up, moving out of site quickly as it rose above the Java Sea. A loud cheer went up from the islanders and crew. "We're up," called an excited officer, "Everything seems to be working perfectly."

There was a small moment of concern as the ship pushed through earth's atmosphere out into space, then another voice called, "On schedule, out in space, approaching 1.5 astronomical units."

The countdown began. "2 units, 2.5, 3 units we're at 3.5142 and holding." Dagon looked at the countdown. It was 0:50 pm. Already the sun was almost totally covered by the eclipse. In the America's a ring of fire surrounded the darkened sphere.

Another officer called out. "We have a fix on Vulcan now. Its synchron belt is just starting to move into the path of the eclipse."

The communication satellite station called in. "We're are ready to send the radio beam."

"Connect the satellite to other stations world wide that are covering the millions of people and their prayers at this moment and send sonics for 1111 vibrations and 1212 vibrations per second." We will go on 0:55 and 05 seconds."

Dagon made an announcement on the island loudspeaker system.

"I'm asking that every man and woman stop what you are doing and pray with the world at this moment." The message was being picked up clearly worldwide. Along with the 1111 sonic was the message, *We ask that the earth pass into the Golden Age of Enlightenment, an age of peace and love.*

They began to feel a tremor beneath them, a subtle steady vibration. It was 0:59, just minutes from count down. Dagon looked at the remote and gave the command.

"Send the laser frequency...to bounce off of the moon to Vulcan now with a message for the universe!" The button was pushed. A brilliant white light shot up from the Satellite dish on the Island, arching over the ocean and up into the sky. It's trajectory headed for the Red Dragonfly space ship to be bounced to the moon, Vulcan and then the universe. The slight shaking of the control tower had increased.

"We come in peace, looking for friendship and cooperation for the good of all beings."

The satellite station reported, "There is fear out on the streets today. It seems all nations are reporting a slight tremor of the earth's surface. However, if anything people are praying more fiercely, determined to show absolute faith in this crisis."

The tremor was getting worse. 0:60 46 seconds, the countdown began Everyone held his or her breath. The tremor was almost violent now. The countdown began

10,9,8,7,6,5,4,3,2.1…… 1:01:11!

Dagon pushed the button to connect the Lunar and Solar Essence in the elixirs on the spaceship. As the current arched between them it created a huge explosion that filled the entire night sky with a blinding white light that was brighter then daylight. There was a last violent tremor, and then, all was still.

"We're alive," came the cry, worldwide. "We've been saved." The people in Washington, who had viewed this from the eclipse darkened sky, were on their knees in the streets.

"The Kingdom has Come," cried the Preachers. "The Kingdom of God has arrived on earth."

"The meek shall inherit the earth."

Everyone at the control tower was cheering or in tears. Dagon grabbed Stella, swinging her feet off the ground and kissing her passionately.

Stella noticed that her wedding ring was glowing. They both had the same thought at the same time.

A small note fluttered beneath the switch that would shut down Operation Dragon at the end of the Mission.

It simply said. ***"Love, God."***

ABOUT THE AUTHOR ✠

Diana Yvonne Walter is a Licensed Professional Counselor and Marriage and Family Therapist who works out of her yoga studio, Padma Mountain Studio in Jackson Hole, Wyoming. She has been practicing as a counselor, astrologer and yoga instructor for the past thirty years, healing the mind, body, emotions, and spirit. When not at her studio, she spends her time riding horses and enjoying the Tetons and Yellowstone Park.

Comments can be mailed to:

Opensky One Eleven Press
PO Box 3551
Jackson, WY 83001

www.opensky111.com
opensky111@me.com

REFERENCES ✠

Adams, Douglas, and *The Hitchhikers Guide to the Galaxy: Life the Universe and Everything*, Pan Books, United Kingdom, 1982.

Allay, Michael, *Fire: The Vital Source of Energy, Facts on File*, New York, 1993.

Amos, William H., *"Hawaii's Volcanic Cradle of Life"*, National Geographic, National Geographic Society, Washington, D.C., July 1990.

Arguelles, Jose, *The Mayan Factor: Path Beyond Technology*, Bear & Co. Santa Fe, New Mexico, 1987.

Arguelles, Jose, *Earth Ascending*, Bear & Co., Santa Fe, NM.

Arvigo, Rosita: *Sastun: Mv Apprenticeship with a Maya Healer*, HarperSan Francisco, HarperCollins Publishers, News York, NY 1994.

Bailey, Alice, *Ponder on This*, Lucis Publishing Company, New York, NY, 1971.

Beckwith, Martha, *Hawaiian Mythology*. University of Hawaii Press, Honolulu, 1976.

Behari, Bepin, *Myths and Symbols of Vedic Astrology*, Passage Press, SLC, Utah, 1990.

Benchley, Peter, *"A Strange Ride in the Deep"*, National Geographic, National Geographic Society, Washington, D.C., February, 1981.

Bitter, Francis, *Magnets: The Education of a Physicist*, Doubleday & Company, Garden City, New York, 1959.

Bly, Robert, *Iron John:A Book About Men*, Addison Wesley, 1990.

Bulfinch, Thomas, *Bullfinch's Mythology*, Avenel Books, New York, 1979.

Capra, Fritjof, *The Tao of Physics*, New Science Library, Boston, 1985.

Castillejo, Irene, *Knowing Woman*, Harper Colophon Books, New York, NY, 1973.

Chases Calendar of Events, *Contemporary Events*, Chicago, 1993.

Clow, Barbara Hand, *Chiron: Rainbow Bridge Between the Inner and Outer Planets*, Lewellyn Publishing, St. Paul, MN, 1987.

Davies, Paul and Gribbin, John, *The Matter Myth*, Simon & Schuster, New York, 1992.

Davies, Brown, *Superstrings: A Theory of Everything*, Cambridge University Press, Australia, 1988.

Dinnerstein, Dorothy, *Mermaid and the Minotaur*, Harper & Row, Publishers, New York, 1963.

Editors, Time Life Books, *"Frontiers of Time,"* Alexandria, Virginia, 1991.

Editors of Story of Life Magazine, Story of Life, *"Take Two Living Cells"*, Marshall Cavendish Ltd., London, England, 1969 and 1971.

Editors of the *Book of Knowledge*, The Book of Knowledge Annual 1964, Grolier, Inc., New York, 1964.

Editors of Time-Life Books, *Computers and the Cosmos*, Time Life Books, Alexandria, Virginia, 1988.

Editors of Webster's Ideal Dictionary, *Webster's Ideal Dictionary*, Marriam Webster, Inc., Springfield, MA, 1984.

Epstein, *Thinking Physic: Practical Lessons in Critical Thinking.* Insight Press, San Francisco, 1993

Estes, Clarissa Pinkola, *Women Who Run with the Wolves*, Ballantine Books, New York, New York, 1972.

Feynman, Richard P. *Six Easy Pieces: Essentials Physics* Addison and Weston.

Franz, Marie-Louise, *Creation Myths*, Spring Publications, Dallas, TX, 1972.

Franz, M.L., *The Feminine in Fairy Tales*, Spring Public Inc, Dallas, TX, 1972.

Gettings, Fred, *The Arcana Dictionary of Astrology*, The Penguin Group, London, England, 1985.

Gore, Rick, National Geographic: *"Our Restless Planet Earth"* National Geographic Society, Washington, D.C., August, 1985.

Grant, Michael and Hazel, John, *God and Mortals in Classical Mythology*, G & C Merriam Co., Publishing, Springfield, MA, 1973.

Graves, Robert, *The White Goddess*, Farrar, Straus and Giroux, New York, 1948.

Graves, Robert and Editors, *A Year and A Day Engagement Calendar 1993*, The Overlook Press, Woodstock, New York, 1993.

Hall, Manly, *The Secret Teachings of All Ages*, The Philosophical Research Society, Inc., Los Angeles, CA,1988.

Heindel, Max, *Occult Principles of Health and Healing*. The Rosicrucian Fellowship, Oceanside, California, 1938.

Herbert, Frank, *Dune*, Berkley Books, New York, 1965.

Herman, Robin, *Fusion: The Search for Endless Energy*, Cambridge University Press, New York, 1990.

Hope, Murray, *The Sirius Connection*, Element Books, Inc. Rockport, MA, 1990.

Hughes, Donald J. *The Neutron Story: Exploring the Nature of Matter*, Doubleday & Company, Inc. New York, 1959.

Hurtak, J.J., *The Book of Knowledge: The Keys of Enoch*, The Academy for Future Science, Los Gatos, CA 1977.

Jackson Hole Daily, "*Scientists Discover Two More Large Planets*", San Antonio (AP) 1118/1996.

Jansky, Robert Carl, *Interpreting the Eclipses*, ACS Publications, Inc., San Diego, CA 1977.

Johns, June, *King of the Witches*, Coward-McCann, Inc., New York, 1969.

Jung, Carl, *Man and His Symbols*, Dell Publishing Co., New York, NY, 1964.

Karagulla, Shafica and Gelder, Dora Van, *The Chakras and the Human Energy Fields* The Theosophical Publishing House, Wheaton, IL, 1989.

Kinstler, Clysta, *The Moon Under Her Feet*, HarperSanFrancisco, New York, NY, 1991.

Kryon, *Alchemy of the Human Spirit*, The Kryon Writing, Del Mar, CA, 1995.

Kryon, *The End Times, The Kryon Writings*, Del Mar, California, 1993.

LaChapelle, Dolores, *Earth Wisdom*, La Chapelle, Silverton, CO, 1978.

Larousse, *World Mythology*. G.P. Putnam's Sons, New York, 1963.

LeDoux, Joseph E. Scientific American: "*Emotion, Memory and the Brain*" New York NY, June, 1994.

Leslie, Robert Franklin, *Miracle at Square Top Mountain* E.P. Dutton, New York, 1979.

Llywelyn, Morgan, *Druids*, Ivy Books, New York, 1991.

Lundin, Robert, *Theories and Systems of Psychology*, DC Heath & Co., Lexington, MN, 1979.

MacCana, Proinsias, *Celtic Mythology*, Peter Bedrick Books, New York, 1968.

Maharshi, Ramana, *The Spiritual Teaching of Ramana Maharshi*, Shambhala Publications, Boston, MA, 1972.

Marciniak, Barbara, *Bringers of the Dawn*: Teachings from the Pleidians, Bear & Co., Santa Fe, NM, 1992.

Mary of Agreda, *The Mystical City of God*, Tan Books and Publishers, Inc. Rockford, Illinois, 1912.

Marziniak, Barbara, *Bringers of the Dawn*, Bear and Co.) Santa Fe, New Mexico.

McDowell, Bart, *"Eruption in Colombia"*: National Geographic, National Geographic Society, Washington, D.C., May, 1986.

Menzel,Donald, *Our Sun*, Hartford University Press, Campridge, Massachusetts, 1959.

Mollenkott, Virginia Ramy, *Women, Men & the Bible*, Apingdon, Nashville, 1977.

Muck, Otto, *The Secret of Atlantis,* Time Books, 1976.

Mukheljee, Bharati, *The Holder of the World,* Alfred A. Knopf, New York, 1993.

Nader, Ralph and Abbots, John, *The Menace of Atomic Energy*, W.W. Norton & Company, Inc., New York, 1977.

National Geographic, Timothy Ferris, Sun Struck, Vol. 221, No 6, pg 36, 2012.

Noble, Vicki, *Motherpeace: A Way to the Goddess through Myth. Art and Tarot*, Harper & Row Publishers, San Francisco, 1983.

Norelli-Bachelet, Patricia, *Symbols and the Question of Unity*, Service Publishers, Wassenaar, Holland, 1974.

Nourse, Alan, *Nine Planets*, Harper & Brothers Publishing, New York, 1960.

O'Conner, James T. *The Hidden Manna: A Theology on the Eucharist,* Ignatius Press, San Francisco, 1988

Pagels, Heinze R., *The Cosmic Code: Quantum Physic as the Language of Nature,* Simon and Schuster, New York, 1982.

Parrinder, Geoffrey, *The World's Living Religions,* Cox& Wyman Ltd., London, 1965.

Peat, David F., *Cold Fusion: The Making of a Scientific Controversy,* Contemporary Books, Chicago, 1989.

Perowne, Stewart, *Roman Mythology,* Hamlyn Publishing Group, London, 1969.

Pike, Albert, Supreme Council of the Southern Jurisdiction, *Morals and Dogma of Ancient and Accepted Scottish Rite of Freemasonry,* Published by it Authority, Charleston, 1871.

Raymo, Chet, 365 *Starry Nights,* Prentice Hall Press, New York, NY, 1982.

Reik, Theodor, *The Creation of Woman,* George Brazier, Inc., New York, NY, 1960

Rinpoche, Sogyal, *The Tibetan Book of Living and Dying,* HarperSan Francisco, 1992.

Royal, Lyssa, *The Prism of Lyrae,* Royal Priest Research, Phoenix, Arizona.

Silver, Warren, The Green Rose, Warren Silver, 1977.

Sakellarakis, Yannis and Sakellaraki, Efi Sapouna, *"Drama of Death in a Minoan Temple"* National Geographic,National Geographic Society, Washington, D.C., February 1981.

Schechter, Bruce, *The Path of No Resistance: The Story of the Revolution in Superconductivity.* Simon and Schuster, New York, 1989.

Schonberger, Dr. Martin. *The I Ching and the Genetic Code: The Hidden Key to Life*, Aurora Press, Santa Fe, NM 87504

Schreck, Alan, *Catholic and Christian: An explanation of commonly misunderstood catholic beliefs,* Servant Book, Ann Arbor, Michigan, 1984

Seymour, Percy, *The Scientific Basis of Astrology*, St. Martins Press, New York 1992.

Simak, Clifford D., *Ring Around the Sun*, Simon and Shuster, New York, 1953.

Smith, Joseph, *The Book of Mormon*, Henry C. Etton Co., Chicago.

STAR TREK The Search for Spock, Paramount Home Video, Paramount Pictures Corporation, 1984.

Starhawk, *Dreaming the Dark: Magic, Sex & Politics*, Beacon Press, Boston, 1982.

Stevens, Jose, *Tao to Earth*, Affinity Press, Orinda, CA, 1988

Stone, Merlin, *When God Was a Woman*, HBJ Books, San Diego, CA 1976

Talbot, Michael *Beyond the Quantum*, MacMillan Publishing Co., New York, NY, 1986.

Talbot, Michael, *The Holographic Universe*, HarperCollins Publishers, New York, NY, 1992.

Time Life Books, *Frontiers of Time*, Time Life Books, Inc., Alexandria, Virginia, 1991.

Time-Life Books, *Secrets of the Alchemists*, Alexandria, Virginia.

Trefil, From *Atoms to Quarks*, Charles Scribners and Sons, New York, 1980.

Vlliers, Margot, *The Serpent of Lilith*, Pocket Books, New York, 1976.

Walker, Barbara, *The Women's Encyclopedia of Myths and Secrets*, Harper, San Francisco, San Francisco, CA, 1983.

Walker, Barbara p., *The Book of Sacred Stones*, Harper & Row, Publishers, San Francisco, 1989.

Wang, Robert, *Qabalistic Tarot*, Samuel Weiser, Inc., York Beach Main, 1983.

Wanless, James, *New Age Tarot: Guide to the Thoth Deck*, Merrill-West Publishing, Carmel, CA 1987.

Ward, Fred, *The Timeless Mystique of Emeralds*: National Geographic, National Geographic Society, Washington, D.C., July 1990.

Watson, James, *Molecular Biology of the Gene*, W.A. Benjamin, Inc., Menlo Park, CA 1970.

Watts, Alan W., *Easter: Its story and Meaning*, Henry Shuman, New York, 1950.

Weiner, Errol, *Transpersonal Astrology: Finding the Soul's Purpose, Element*, Shaftesbury, Corset, 1991.

Wescot, W. Wynn, M.B., *The Isiac Tablet of the Bembine Table of Isis, The philogophical Research Society,* Los Angeles, CA 90027.

Westervelt, William, *Hawaiian Legends of Volcanoes*, Charles & Tuttle, Co., 1963.

Welhelm, Helmut, *The I Ching,* Princeton University Press, NY, NY 1950.

Winberg, The Discovery of Subatomic Particles, Scientific American Library, 1983.

Wolf, Fred Alan, *The Eagles Quest: A physicist's search for truth in the heart of the shamanic world*, Summit Books, New York NY 1991.

Woodman, Marion and Dickson, Elinor, *Dancing in the Flames; The Dark Goddess in the Transformation of Consciousness*, Shambhala Publications Inc., Boston, 1996.

FOOTNOTES ✠

1Grant, Michael and Hazel, John, *God and Mortals in Classical Mythology* G & C Merriam Co., Publishing, Springfield, MA, 1973. Larousse, *World Mythology*, G.P. Putnam's, New York, 1963. Perowne, Stewart, *Roman Mythology.* Hamlyn Publishing Group, London, 1969.
3Perowne, op. cit.

4 Bulfinch, Thomas, *Bullfinch's Mythology*, Avenel Books, New York, 1979, p. 4.

5*STAR TREK III. The Search for Spock*, Paramount Home Video, Paramount Pictures Corporation, 1984.

6 Walker, Barbara, *The Women's Encyclopedia of Myths and Secrets*, Harper, San Francisco, San Francisco, CA, 1983.

7 Hall, Manly, *The Secret Teachings of All Ages.* The Philosophical Research Society, Inc., Los Angeles, CA, 1988, p. LI.

8 Peat, David F., *Cold Fusion: The Making of a Scientific Controversy.* Contemporary Books, Chicago, 1989.

9Ibid.

10Ibid.

11Editors of Webster's Ideal Dictionary, *Websters Ideal Dictionary*, Marriam Webster, Inc., Springfield, MA, 1984.

12MacCana, Proinsias, *Celtic Mythology*, Peter Bedrick Books, New York, 1968.

13Hall, op. cit., p. CLIII.

14Hall, op. cit., p. CXLIX

15Pagels, Heinz R., *The Cosmic Code: Quantum Physics as the Language of Nature.* Simon and Schuster, New York, 1982.

16Hall, op. cit., p. CLIV.

17Hall, *The Theory and Practice of Alchemy*, p. CLVIII (158).

18Peat, op. cit.

19Hall, op. cit., Unknown Author, p. CLIV (154).

20Jansky, Robert Carl, *Interpreting the Eclipses*, ACS Publications, Inc., San Diego, CA, 1977.

21Seymour, Percy, *The Scientific Basis of Astrology*, St. Martin's Press, New York, 1992.

22Pike, Albert, Supreme Council of the Southern Jurisdiction, *Morals and Dogma of Ancient and Accepted Scottish Rite of Freemasonry*, Published by its Authority, Charleston, 1871.

23Cantor Matt, *"Tribes Challenge Mojave Solar Plants,"* Newser.com, 3/2012.

24Finney, Dee *The End of the World* American Prophecy, www:.bibliotecapleyades.net, reference: Waters, Frank: The Book of the Hopi, Penguin Books, NY, 1877.

25 Olcott, William Tyler (1914/2003) *Sun Lore of All Ages: A Collection of Myths and Legends Concerning the Sun and Its Worship* Adamant Media Corporation.

26*The Complete Dictionary of Symbols* by Jack Tresidder, Chronicle Books, 2005, page 241

27Menzel,Donald, *Our Sun*, Harvard University Press, Cambridge, Massachusetts, 1959, p. 1-21.

28Hall, Manly, *The Secret Teachings of All Ages*. The Philosophical Research Society, Inc., Los Angeles, California 90027, p.181-184.

29Hall, op. cit., p. LII

30Benchley, Peter, National Geographic, "*A Strange Ride in the Deep*", National Geographic Society, Washington, D.C., February, 1981.

31LeDoux, Joseph E. Scientific American, "*Emotion, Memory and the Brain*", New York, NY, June, 1994, p.50.

32Editors of Story of Life Magazine, Story of Life, "*Take Two Living Cells*", Marshall Cavendish Ltd., London, England, 1969 and 1971, p. 154.

33Watson, James, *Molecular Biology of the Gene.* WA. Benjamin, Inc., Menlo Park, CA, 1970.

34Hughes, Donald J. *The Neutron Story: Exploring the Nature of Power.* Doubleday & Company, Inc., New York, 1959.

35Larousse, op. cit.

36Lowenthal, Anne, W. *Mars and Venus Surprised by Vulcan*, The J. Paul Getty Museum, 1995,p. 1.

37Ibid., p. 50.

38During the 15th and 16th Century the story of how Vulcan surprised Mars and Venus inspired oil painting sculptures, writing and murals by artists such as Wtewael, Goltzuius, Giacomo, Heemskerck, Contin and Tentoretto.

39Lowenthal, op. cit, p. 50

40*Ovid's Metamorphoses*, Book IV, Translated by More, Cornhill Publishing Co, Brookes, Boston, MA, 1922., Verse, 167.

41Wescot, W., Wynn, M.B., *The Isiac Tablet or the Bembine Table of Isis*, The Philosophical Research Society, Los Angeles, CA 90027.

42Hall, Manly, op. cit., p. CXXVII.

43Woodman, Marion and Dickson, Elinott *Dancing in the Flames: The Dark Goddess in the Transformation of Consciousness*, Shambala Pubications Inc., Boston, 1996, p.36.

44Arvigfo, Rosita: *Sastun: My apprenticeship with a Maya Healer*, HarperSan Francisco, Harper Collins Publishers, New York, N.Y. 1994.

45Herbert, Frank, *Dune*, Berkley Books, New York, 1965.

46 Rinpoche, Sogyal, *The Tibetan Book of Living and Dying*, HarperSan Francisco, 1992.

47 Claremont de Castillejo, Irene, *Knowing Woman*, Harper Colophon Books, New York, NY, 1973, p. 11-26.

48 Walker, Barbara p., *The Book of Sacred Stones*, Harper & Row, Publishers, San Francisco, 1989.

49Ward, Fred, *"The Timeless Mystique of Emeralds"* National Geographic. National Geographic Society, Washington, D.C., July, 1990.

50Mukherjee, Bharati, *The Holder of the World*, Alfred A. Knopf, New York, 1993, p. 5,19,70.

51Ibid.

52Bailey, Alice *Ponder on This*. Lucis Publishing Company. New York. NY. 1971. p. 405-415.

53Heindel. Max. *Occult Principles of Health and Healing*. The Rosicrucian Fellowship. Oceanside. California. 1938.

54 Estes, Clarissa Pinkola, *Women Who Run with the Wolves*, Ballantine Books, New York, New York, 1972, p. 258-297.

55Bly, Robert, *Iron John:A Book About Men*, Addison Wesley, 1990.

56Wang. Robert. *Qabalistic Tarot*, Samuel Weiser. Inc., York Beach. Maine. 1983Wang. Op. Cit., p. 6.

57Wang .. op. cit . p. 246.

58Russell, Colin, *Michael Farady: Physics and Faith*: Oxford Univeristy Press.

58a National Geographic, Timothy Ferris, *Sun Struck*, Vol. 221, No 6,p 38 2012.

59Bailey. Alice. op. cit.

60Talbot. *Beyond the Ouantum*, MacMillan Publishing Co .New York. NY, 1986.

61Lerner & Lerner, *Inner Child Cards*. Bear & Co., Santa Fe, New Mexico, 1992, p. 73-75.

62Holy Bible, New International Version, Zondervan, Grand Rapids, Michigan, I Corinthians, 13:12.

63 Adams, Douglas, and *The Hitchhikers Guide to the Galaxy: Life the Universe and Everything*, Pan Books, United Kingdom, 1982, Ch 9.

64Rinpoche, Sogyal, *The Tibetan Book of Living and Dying*, Harper San Francisco, New York. NY 1992, p. 49, 180.

65Royal. Lyssa. *The Prism of Lyrae*. Royal Priest Research. Phoenix. Arizona.

66Hurtak, J.J *The Book of Knowledge: The Keys of Enoch*. The Academy for Future Science. Los Gatos, CA 1977.

67Graves, Robert and Editors, *A Year and A Day Engagement Calendar 1993*, The Overlook Press, Woodstock, New York, 1993.,p. 111.

68 Hall, Manly, op. cit., p. 161-164.

69Helveticus, "*A Little More Alchemy*", www.tyler-adam.com.

70 Wikipedia, Franz Tausend. Reference: German Alchemy called Huge Hoax, new York Times, 10/1929.

71Socyberty.com,"*An essay outlining similarities in thought between Roman Catholic transubstantiation and alchemical transmutation*" Reference: Roob, Alexander, *The Hermetic-Museum, Alchemy & Mysticism*, Taschen, Los Angeles, CA, 2006.

72Brueghal, Jan, Artwork: The Four Elements,
www.nationaltrustcollections.org.

73 Scientific American Journals, Oct, Nov, Dec, 1994
Epstein, *Thinking Physics: Practical Lessons in Critical Thinking.*
Insight Press, San Francisco, 1993
Feynman, Richard P. *Six Easy Pieces: Essentials Physics* Addison and
Weston.

74Wikipedia, en.widipedia.org, *Fulcanelli*, The French alchemists name is
a play on the words for Vulcan and El, fire. Quote by Bergier from
meeting in 1937: Hauck, Dennis W., *Sorcerer's Stone*, Citadel Press,
2004, p. 174.

Time-Life Books, *Secrets of the Alchemists*, Alexandria, Virginia, p.
123

75Ibid., p. 25.

76Smith, Joseph, *The Book of Mormon*, Henry C. Etton and Co., Chicago,
Book of Ether, Chapter III Verses 3-28.

77 Walker, Barbara, *The Women's Encyclopedia of Myths and Secrets*,
Harper, San Francisco, San Francisco, CA, 1983, P. 262, 1053

78 Maharshi, Ramana, *The Spiritual Teaching of Ramana Maharshi*,
Shambhala Publications, Boston, MA, 1972 p. 3-34.

79 Pagels, Heinze R., *The Cosmic Code: Quantum Physic as the Language
of Nature.* Simon and Schuster, New York, 1982.

80 Scientific American Journal, Oct, Nov, Dec, 1994.

81 Woodroff, Sr John, *The Serpent Power*, Ganesh and Co., Madras, India
1972

82Bitter, Francis, *Magnets: The Education of a Physicist*, Doubleday &
Company, Garden City, New York, 1959.

83Ibid.

84Walker, Barbara, *The Women's Encyclopedia of Myths and Secrets*, Harper, San Francisco, San Francisco, CA, 1983, p. 262. 1053

85 Beckwith, Martha, *Hawaiian Mythology.* University of Hawaii Press, Honolulu, 1976.

86Karagulla, Shafica and Gelder, Doran Va. *The Chakra's and the Human Energy Fields*, The Theosophical Publishing House, Wheaton, IL, 1989.

Made in the USA
Charleston, SC
08 August 2012